For my amazing and courageous family,
who remind me every day that love is the thread that
survives the unravelling.

This book is for your strength, your laughter, your patience,
and your willingness to remember
when the world tries to make us forget.

May we always hear the song beneath the noise
and find our way back to each other,
in every new dawn we share.

THE SONG OF THE BLACKBIRD

Sam Gold

They built a world on lies so perfect, no one
remembered the truth... until the Blackbirds sang

The Song Beneath the Noise

You were never meant to read this book.

Not because it is forbidden, but because it was never supposed to survive.

Not because it is fiction, but because fiction is the only way truth can sometimes speak.

Not because you are unready, but because the world has done everything it can to keep you asleep.

And yet, here you are.

This is a story... a vivid, gripping, evocative, soul-stirring thriller.

Of lives entwined across timelines.
Of love, of loss, of memory.
Of brothers. Of questions no one dares ask.
Of a truth buried in plain sight.

But there's something else beneath the surface, a current you might not notice at first.

It hums quietly... pulling you in, asking you to remember what you didn't know you forgot.

You came for the story.

And it is a story... but stories, sometimes, are how truth slips through the cracks.
There are things in this world you were never meant to question. The sky... the structure... the sequence of time... the maps... the stories... the reasons for your pain... the voice in your head that tells you to behave... the screen that tells you what is real.
This book is not gentle with the lie. It exposes it, layer by layer, tone by tone.

It will not apologise, it will not flinch. Because the time for soft truths has passed.

But this is not a call to rage. It is a call to remembrance.
To the knowing buried in your bones.

To the pulse of a truth that cannot be taught - only remembered.

To a return to loving - not sentiment, but embodied alignment.

To a return to Source - not a deity, but the living intelligence that sings beneath all things.

Whatever your path - whether you call it faith, God, spirit, or simply truth - this book is not here to redirect you, it is here to help you feel that connection more clearly, live it more fully, and remember what called you to it in the first place. It is here to remove the distortions that stand in your way. Not to challenge your devotion, but to clear the static so you can feel it more clearly than ever before.

This is not about belief. It is about the truth that lives inside you... the part of you that never forgot, even when the world told you to. You were born into a game disguised as life... a theatre of light and shadow.

But beneath it all, a current has always flowed.
The Blackbird carries it still... the signal no frequency can silence.
You won't walk this path alone.

There are lives inside these pages... quiet lives, broken lives, brave lives, pulled into something far greater than they ever imagined. They search through shadow, through cities and ruins, chased by forces that do not want the truth remembered.

Beneath city streets, through ancient corridors, inside forgotten chambers, a trail unfolds. Not all will survive it. But each step taken restores something sacred, something long buried.

Something that lives in you, too.
If you feel strange reading this, if something in you stirs, resists, leans forward... trust it.

This book does not offer easy answers, but it does offer true ones, the kind that rise from beneath the noise, the kind that were hidden in plain sight. It is here to illuminate the shadows - the ones cast across your memory, your perception, and the world you were taught to trust.

It does not ask for your obedience, but it invites your awareness so that you may discover for yourself.

It is here to help you see, so that you may finally remember what you've always known.

Let the song rise.
Let the veil tear.
Let memory return.
Let love return.

The Question You Were Never Meant to Ask

You hear them sometimes.
At night, when the world has stilled, when even thought loosens its grip.

Not song... not cry. Wings.

The soft thunder of them, brushing the air overhead like a warning you can't quite place.

You rarely see them, you only feel them... a flicker against the silence.

A tremor in the field.
And still, the birds are everywhere.
On rooftops, on wires.
In every forgotten photograph of the sky.
But where do they go to die?

It's a simple question, one you were never meant to ask.
One you can't stop thinking about once it lands.
They live in swarms... in clouds... in murmurs of instinct.
You see them every day, but except for the odd few, almost never at the end.

Do they fall in secret? Return to some hidden place? Or are you simply not allowed to witness it?

There are other questions like that, not the loud ones, not the ones with answers... the kind that live in the bones:

Why do certain dreams feel more real than waking, and hurt when they fade?

Why do we wake just before someone we love calls, even from miles away?

When did we stop trusting the feeling that told us the world was meant to be more than this?

And what if the thing you've spent your life searching for… is the very thing they taught you to ignore?

This is where it begins… not in fire, not in prophecy.

In a city that doesn't blink when strange things go missing.

And a man already too close to the edge to keep pretending he doesn't hear the wings. He doesn't know it yet but the first note has already been struck.

And the Blackbird is moving.
Unseen.
Unspoken.

But not for much longer.

The song is rising.
The veil is thinning.
The Blackbird has begun to sing.

Part one:
THE SIGNAL

Some truths carry a frequency that cannot be touched.
This is one of them.
It has been written in clarity, sealed in sovereignty, and protected by the field.
Mimicry cannot enter where the signal runs true.
What is read here, is remembered.
What is remembered, is free.

Chapter 1:
The Blackbird's Call

Morning, Manchester.

The fallen pigeon lay lifeless on the pavement, its wings crumpled like abandoned ideas.

Pip paused.

He felt a twist of sadness at the sight. He loved all creatures, even the ones others ignored.

Nature, to him, was sacred in its quiet resilience, and this still form on the concrete felt like a signal.

He wondered, briefly, where its soul would go. Not in a religious sense, he hadn't made his mind up about whether a soul reincarnates. He'd heard the stories, of course, endless cycles, second chances, returning again and again until something was learned or forgotten.

But deep down, he wasn't sure. Maybe birds were different.

Maybe they didn't get caught in the same traps humans did, the endless spirals of memory and regret.

Maybe when a bird died, it simply... flew on.

Somewhere older. Somewhere freer. Somewhere beyond all of this.

Pip Wilder never liked mornings. They arrived without ceremony. No warning, no grace. Just truth.

There was something about the early light in Manchester, diluted, metallic, always slightly damp - that left no room for illusion.

It peeled the world bare before the coffee had a chance to work. The city hadn't yet slipped into its usual mask of motion; instead, it held a breath, cold, rain-streaked, and quietly aching.

The tram hissed to a stop at St. Peter's Square, opening its doors with a reluctant sigh. Pip stepped down into a shallow puddle, the water rippling outward like a clock resetting itself. His boots, well-worn and expensive, were already beginning to fray at the seams, much like him.

He glanced up at the pale grey sky, then let his eyes fall to the hulking rotunda of the Central Library. Manchester's great stone eye. Blind and all-seeing at once. The building wasn't just a library, it was a monument to knowledge carved in the heart of a city that once fuelled the world. The air here still buzzed with the electricity of invention, with the ghosts of industry and revolution. This was Manchester, cradle of the Industrial Revolution, birthplace of radical thought, and the site of the Peterloo Massacre where voices demanding change were silenced by force.

And here, surrounded by the ghosts of thinkers who once whispered revolutions into cracked spines and dust jackets. Something about that place had always spoken to him. Knowledge too big for its shelves. Silence that wasn't empty.
Pip pulled up the collar of his coat and made his way down Peter's Street, weaving through scaffolding and forgotten chewing gum, past cracked pavement and the faint, earthy stench of last night's storm. The streets smelled dank. Like moss and wet brick, like concrete mourning something long buried beneath it. A city still grieving its past.
The occasional bus rattled by, breathy and impatient. Office lights flickered to life overhead. Manchester was waking, reluctantly.

So was he.

He stopped briefly outside a shopfront, his eyes catching on a pigeon strutting through the puddles. Not lifeless like the one he'd seen earlier, but purposeful, alive, determined. It moved with a kind of streetwise grace, weaving through the city's wet scars as though nothing could touch it. Pip felt something stir. A small, silent affirmation. Not everything had given up. Not yet. He watched it a moment longer, a strange comfort anchoring him to the present. He'd thought about stopping for a coffee, but the idea of sitting still felt heavier than motion.

He turned onto Deansgate, where glass met stone and ambition met rot. There, nestled between steel cranes and mirrored façades, stood the office of Halo & Easton, a name he had invented during a drunken branding session in Shoreditch, meant to sound aspirational, transcendent, and trustworthy.

Now it was engraved into brushed aluminium.
He stared at the name as if seeing it for the first time. It felt foreign. Too slick. Too empty.

A square peg in a high-gloss hole.

Inside, the studio pulsed with curated energy. Exposed beams. Edison bulbs. Polished concrete. Biophilic wallpaper and branded oat milk in the fridge. His agency was a temple to aesthetic anxiety, every detail mattered, so long as it photographed well.

Pip moved through it like a spirit. The younger staff adored him. The partners relied on him. Clients trusted him. But none of them really saw *him*.

His official title was Creative Director, Partner, Vision Architect, though he always laughed at that last one. Vision Architect. As if he was still building anything other than versions of himself.

He'd once loved the chase, the pitch, the pivot, the creative rush. He'd loved the late nights and the liminal mornings when your brain fizzed with caffeine and you believed you might actually change the world through a campaign about vegan yoghurt.

Now it all felt... distant. Like watching a highlight reel of someone else's life.

That someone was younger. Hungrier. Funnier.
Someone who still believed in meaning.
He watched the team through the glass of a small side room, coffee cups steaming beside laptops, Canva boards glowing, a Spotify playlist offering lo-fi salvation to the overworked.
He wasn't bitter.
He just wasn't in it anymore. Not like they were.
Not since... well. Everything.
He stepped back from the glass and wandered down the hall, past the pitch room, the brand theatre, the nap pod no one used. Each space designed for creativity, but rarely quiet enough to let any truth grow.
At his desk, a minimalist slab of oak too perfect to touch, he stared at an open deck titled:
"Redefining the Human Experience Through Interconnected Tech."
A line he'd written. A promise he didn't believe. Not anymore.
He closed the laptop. Picked up his coat. Left without a word.
He wandered. No plan. Just motion.
Through the tight veins of the city, past shuttered shops and limping taxis. Past the bar where he first kissed his now ex-wife, her name largely unspoken, but once held like light, and the steps where they'd stood, watching fireworks rise above a frozen canal.
He had loved her immeasurably.
The kind of love that makes you try.
Try to be better. Try to stay.
And when trying wasn't enough, they let each other go without fire. Just a fading sun and the promise not to ruin what was already drifting.
Now, the flat was just his. The city, just noise.

Until tonight.

He turned down a side street he hadn't taken in years. The kind that still felt unclaimed. The air was thick with damp and secrets. The tang of old stone and engine oil lingered, mixing with the earthy scent of moss that clung to the walls. His boots echoed on the slick ground, scattering grit beneath each step. A soft wind carried the faint hiss of distant traffic and the distant warmth of someone's morning toast, oddly out of place here. Faint graffiti crawled along the walls like secret prayers, their colours softened by time. The alley hummed with memory, every surface whispering something half-heard, half-felt.

And then, the man.

Sitting on a low wall by a partially demolished building. Wrapped in navy. Hood up. Hands folded.

He didn't reach out. There was no cup. No dog. No cardboard sign. He radiated something else, a quiet gravity, as if he knew things no one else dared to say aloud.

Just... there.

Or had he been? Pip blinked. The man seemed both present and unreal, as if stitched from the fabric of the alley itself, shadows wrapped in human shape. He felt more than saw him at first, like an afterimage or a held breath. Was he even real? Or just a projection of something Pip wasn't ready to face?

Pip walked past without a word.

But something in him bristled, a quiet static, like the air before lightning. He didn't understand it, not yet, but his body knew. Something sacred had just been crossed.

Then the man spoke.

"Your life was never meant to go this way."

The words stopped him mid-step.

Not the sentence, the voice.

Not loud, not dramatic. But weighted. As if it had been waiting.

He turned. Slowly.

Met the man's eyes. Calm. Unflinching.

"Do you hear it yet?"

"Hear what?"

"The blackbird."

Pip stared, unsure whether to laugh or run.

"What are you talking about?"

But the man only smiled.

And stood.

And walked away, not with footsteps, but with the hush of drifting smoke, his figure seeming to dissolve into the shadows that curled at the edges of the alleyway, as though he'd never truly been there at all.

Down the alley. Into the dark.

Gone.

Pip stood, heart rattling like loose glass in a frame.

Above him, a single blackbird sang, a sound so sharp and clear it felt like it split the sky. It wasn't just birdsong; it was a signal, a blade of memory, a note pulled from the lungs of something older than the city itself.

He didn't know why it hit him like that, why one call could slice through everything he thought was solid.

But something in him broke open. Clean. Deep. Like the first crack in a wall that had held too much for too long.

Back at the agency, the scent of roasted coffee and the faint warmth of sunlit concrete greeted him like a memory rehearsed too many times. The morning hum had risen, keyboards clicking in controlled chaos, muted laughter behind glass walls, a brass bell by the door someone had decided was ironic.

"Morning, Pip," said Jodie from accounts, clutching her oversized mug like armour. Her smile was genuine, always was. She reminded him of who he'd been when this all began, eager, inventive, a believer in the beauty of a well-timed idea.

He nodded, offered her a warm smile in return. "Morning, Jodes."

In the open studio, he passed Sam and Riley, heads bowed together over a storyboard. They were good, better than they knew, and he resisted the urge to interrupt. Not with critique, but with encouragement. He'd started doing that more lately. Less control, more care. Something about the encounter in the alley had shifted him, cracked his shell just enough to let light in.

Back in his glass office, he stood for a moment, watching his team work through the morning. The city beyond pressed its greyness against the windows, but inside, there was colour. Life. And despite everything, he felt something stir. A flicker of connection. Of meaning. Like maybe, just maybe, there was still something here worth nurturing.

A pulse beneath the routine.

A quiet beauty in what they were creating together, even if they didn't fully see it yet, even if he did. Even if he now saw the cracks in it all, the half-truths, the packaging of hope, the selling of dreams in sleek decks and crafted slogans. Marketing had always been a kind of magic. But now, he saw the illusion too clearly to believe in it completely.

Then he turned, and everything fell quiet again. It felt too quiet. It always did now.

The walk home was uneventful, but Pip noticed everything. The rhythm of his footsteps against wet pavement. The scatter of fallen leaves curling like paper secrets. A low mist had rolled in, softening the city's edges, muting headlights and neon signs. The world felt quieter somehow, not in sound, but in meaning.

He passed familiar corners that felt unfamiliar tonight. Windows aglow with quiet lives, bikes chained to lampposts like forgotten promises. Somewhere, a dog barked. Somewhere else, laughter echoed from an open upstairs window. Normal things. But tonight, they carried weight.

By the time he reached his flat, his shoulders were damp, and something inside him was buzzing, not panic, not clarity, but something just on the edge of remembering.

No music. No movement. Just the faint whir of the boiler and the clink of a glass as Pip poured himself a whisky and let it breathe. He wasn't a big drinker, never had been, but lately, he'd started enjoying one or two to wind down. He recalled a book he once read, something obscure, that spoke of the liver as the seat of unprocessed emotion, even of spiritual transformation. The hypocrisy wasn't lost on him, that alcohol, so often glorified, even marketed as liberation, was quietly destroying the very organ ancient wisdom regarded as sacred. A cultural contradiction, normalised and numbed. He stared at the glass, golden and still, and wondered what else they had all agreed to forget. He leaned against the counter, the city lights crawling across his floor through high windows. The glass, golden and still, caught his reflection, older, alone, but not quite defeated.

He sat down with the drink, opened his laptop without looking, and stared into nothing. The encounter with the man in the alley spun through his mind like a looping reel, jarring, vivid. It clogged his thoughts, like static in his neural pathways. There was something about the words, the presence, the knowing, it disturbed him more than he wanted to admit. It clung to him. Refused to dissolve. He felt as if a code had been spoken into him, and now every part of him was trying to interpret it.

Until a memory surfaced.

Oxford Road. A lecture theatre. Rain on the windows. And her, walking in late with no apology, eyes scanning for a seat, hair slightly damp, copper-brown and curling at the ends like it couldn't quite be tamed. She had a heart-shaped face, high cheekbones that flushed when she laughed, and eyes, deep green, restless, that held stories even when her lips were still. There was a quiet fire to her, an elegance that wasn't rehearsed but instinctive. And when she smiled, it was like a room remembering its purpose.

Anna McCrae.

They met by accident. A tutorial on cultural theory. He said something dry; she laughed, not because she had to, but because she meant it. That laugh had stuck with him. Clean. Kind. Alive. They hadn't just shared a few afternoons.

They had shared a year.
A whole year stitched together by small moments - and in the end, it was the small moments that mattered most. Not grand declarations, but the slow entangling of two lives that never quite untangled, no matter how far they drifted.

It began simply.

Coffee shops and second-hand bookshops, arguing about Rilke and Bowie and whether you could ever really live without becoming your job. Walks along the canal where Pip tried, and often failed, to make her laugh, but she laughed anyway, and it sounded like sunlight catching glass.
Dinners cooked badly but eaten anyway.
Vinyl records spun while they danced barefoot in cramped living rooms.
Notes tucked into coat pockets.
A glance across a crowded room that said: I see you.

She had a mind like a kaleidoscope: sharp in its perception, restless in its movement, and brilliant in the way it cast colour onto even the greyest moments.

He had a soul that ached for belonging, a place where he wouldn't be punished for dreaming too much or for feeling things too deeply.

For a time, they created something fragile and fierce between them, a hidden world tucked inside the cracks of the larger one. It was a place built from jazz records, cheap wine, and the kind of wild hope that only ever burns bright in the young or the brave.

He loved her with an honesty that never asked to be returned. Not because she rescued him, but because she reminded him he was already worth saving.

And Anna? She loved him for none of the reasons others might have: not for his ambition, not for his wit. She loved him for the raw sincerity he tried to hide from the world, the parts of himself he thought no one would see. She loved the way he listened when she spoke and the way he stayed when she fell silent.

They never meant to end.

There was no betrayal, no dramatic split, no shouting to mark the final blow.

Only a slow drifting apart, like a seam splitting under quiet strain, pressure neither of them acknowledged aloud.

Pip had been offered a job abroad. A big one. A move to New York. A role that promised to make everything he'd worked for feel legitimate.

He hesitated. Truly, he had.

But Anna, proud and quietly breaking, told him he had to go. That he couldn't stay just for her. That if he turned the opportunity down, he would one day resent her.

She smiled when she said it.

And Pip, unsure and afraid, believed her.

So he left. And she let him.

Neither of them spoke the words they were choking on.

Don't go.

Because pride wrapped itself around their voices like armour, and neither could lower their guard long enough to let love win.

He thought he was doing the right thing.

She believed she was setting him free.

Both were mistaken.

The letters they promised to write came less frequently.

The phone calls faded.

And eventually, life crept into the space between them, taking root.

But time never erased the shape of one another from their hearts.

No amount of distance, distraction, or new beginnings could undo the way they had loved - like roots growing underground, stubborn, hidden, and irrevocably tangled.

Life moved forward.

He met someone new.

The years gathered momentum: London, success, fleeting romances, then a marriage that began with laughter and ended with rooms full of unspoken words. There was no single moment of betrayal, just the slow ache of two people slipping past each other, watching the light go out.

But Anna had never truly gone.

She remained as a sketch in the back of his mind, an unfinished drawing that hummed in the quiet moments of his life.

He didn't know why she had surfaced in his thoughts tonight.

Not until the screen blinked.

A notification.

The sound was so small, yet it struck like a stone in still water.

There was something about the air tonight. Something thin, as if reality itself was worn at the edges.

Pip stared at the message glowing on his phone, unsettled. It wasn't just memory, or unease about the man he had seen earlier, or even the strange words that had lodged in his mind.

It was the blackbird.

And the feeling that something in the unseen world had shifted.

He rubbed his eyes, trying to centre himself. The room was still, but he wasn't.

He felt dislodged, as though the stage he had lived on all his life had just revealed a hidden backdrop.

And now, nothing felt certain anymore.

Anna McCrae sent you a connection request.

When her name appeared on his screen, there was no soft wave of nostalgia.

Only recognition.

The kind that reaches into your chest and presses on something tender.

"Hey Pip. I wasn't sure if this was you. If it is, I'd love to catch up sometime."

He clicked without thinking. His pulse had quickened and his hands were slightly trembling.

It was her.

The eyes that once lingered over poetry, the spark he had tried to forget but never could.

She was the kind of woman whose presence etched itself onto your thoughts, whose absence never truly arrived.

The screen no longer felt like glass. It felt like memory breathing.

He stared, hardly believing.

She looked a little older, yes, but still unmistakably Anna.

Emotion surged. A wave of disbelief, warmth, regret, and something that almost felt like hope.

His throat tightened.

And for a moment, he could do nothing but sit there, staring.

The years folded in on themselves.

She was the lighthouse in the fog.

And somehow, impossibly, she was here.

Those eyes that saw more than anyone ever said.

That calm exterior, always protecting a rare warmth.

The kind of face that made you feel remembered, even after a lifetime.

The Message Wasn't Just for Him

After she hit send, she didn't move.

The room stayed silent, holding its breath the way she was.

The cursor blinked beneath the last word of her message, not expectant, not accusing. Just waiting.

It had taken her hours to press those few words into being. And now they were gone. Out there. Travelling invisible cables, surfacing somewhere to be read by someone she hadn't seen in over a decade.

She imagined him reading it.

She didn't know if he would reply.

But something in her did.

And in that moment, something eased, not released, exactly, but recognised.

Like memory pressing lightly on a scar.

She placed her phone face down and stepped away.

But the ache in her chest, old and golden and dangerous, pulsed softly behind her ribs.

He read her message twice before replying. His hand hovered over the keys, shaking, just enough to make him hesitate. He was scared that a wrong press might make the message vanish, might lose her forever in the ether.

One accidental keystroke, and she could disappear again, like she had before. His heart pounded in his ears.

All that he hadn't said, all that he didn't know he still carried, suddenly right there, fragile and flickering on the screen. His fingers hovered, unsure, then, with a breath held and released, he began to type. The words came slow, then all at once, like something long dammed now breaking free.

"It's me. And I'd really like that."

His hand lingered above the return key. What if he lost her again? What if this tiny moment vanished like so many before it? He pressed send.

Then sat back.

The moment felt surreal. Sacred. As though replying had activated something else entirely, something ancient and waiting, like a mechanism deep within him had turned over for the first time in years.

She made her way to the garden and stood barefoot.

It had rained earlier, and the moss was still cool beneath her soles. Her phone buzzed once inside the house, and she didn't run to it. She already knew.

He had replied.

She closed her eyes and tilted her head to the sky.

Somewhere above her, clouds passed like secrets. But beneath them, the sky was clear.

Later that night, Pip moved through his flat like it had rearranged itself. Books on the shelf seemed to lean toward him.

Old playlists queued songs they hadn't played in years.

He caught his reflection, not haunted, but hollowed.

Prepared.

He poured himself a glass of water, but forgot to drink it. The room felt like it was listening.

She pulled out her old dream journal.

The one with the name written in the margin.

Pip.

She didn't remember why she wrote it.
Only that she never crossed it out.
Now it was glowing in her hands, a quiet pulse between the pages.

They stood in different rooms. Miles apart. Holding different objects. Breathing different air.
But the same knowing wrapped around them now.
Not fear.
Not longing.
Readiness.
The message hadn't been just for him. Or for her.
It was for both of them.
And neither of them would ever be the same again.

Somewhere far off, a blackbird sang again, feebly at first, but with a boldness that shot through his mind like light cracking stone.
Something stirred.
Not memory. Not grief.
Something older than both.
He moved to the window, driven by a tremor he couldn't name. The city was quiet, the street empty. But in the dim wash of sodium light, at the far end of the road, was that a figure? A hooded shape, too still, too placed. Pip blinked, pressed his forehead to the glass. No one there.

But he was sure. Certain. For a heartbeat, he'd seen the man again. Or had he?

The Girl in the Field

Before everything fell away, before the silence, before the ache she learned to wear like a second skin, there was a field.

A summer field, wild and wide, stretched out at the back of the house where the garden ended and the world felt endless. Tangled with poppies and cornflowers, the field shimmered in the heat, alive with the lazy hum of bees and the scent of warm earth. Nine-year-old Anna lay in its centre, an only child with no one to compete for space or stories, her bare feet browned by the sun, a daisy chain wrapped twice around her wrist. Out there, in that sunlit stillness, she never felt lonely, but looking back, she must have been. She spoke to the birds as if they understood, gave names to caterpillars and ladybirds, and once built a palace from twigs for a beetle she called Sir Cedric. Her dolls became dinner guests at imaginary feasts, her laughter echoing across the wildness as if a whole invisible world had gathered to join her. Somewhere in her mind, a friend named Elowen lived, a shadow girl with silver hair and kind eyes who always knew what to say. Anna didn't need real people. She had wonder, and wonder kept her company. The sky above her pulsed blue, impossibly blue, like a colour only children remember, the kind you never quite find again once you grow up.

Her mother laughed nearby, tossing a straw hat into the breeze and chasing after it with theatrical clumsiness, half-falling into the long grass, her skirt catching in the wind like a sail. Anna's father was painting the old bench under the birch tree at the far end of the field, the air rich with the sharp, sweet scent of fresh white gloss and turpentine. He hummed a tune that didn't belong to any song she knew but felt familiar just the same. It was the sound of peace. Of home. They were each absorbed in their own quiet joy, yet somehow still connected, threads in the same tapestry, weaving and overlapping, none of them needing to speak to feel together. It was a kind of harmony Anna would later struggle to describe, not perfect, but alive, unbroken, effortless.

The blackbird watched from the fencepost. Always the same one, she believed. Her mum had even named it Short Shanks due to its shorter-than-average legs, a name that stuck like an inside joke only they shared. There was something knowing in its eyes. Anna had whispered secrets to it once, and it hadn't flown away.

Later, they would drink lemonade that her mother made with honey instead of sugar. Her father would lift her onto his shoulders and pretend she weighed nothing at all. She would fall asleep with grass in her hair and the echo of his voice in her dreams.

This was before the forgetting. Before the slow erosion of light from the edges of her days. Before the words that didn't land and the laughter that stopped coming, slipping away like a melody half-remembered. Before her mother's voice began to fray with tiredness and her father's humming fell silent. Before the colour of things dulled and the weight of unspoken things grew heavier.

Before the grey.

Before she became someone who walked quietly through rooms, not wanting to disturb anything that still worked, tiptoeing around other people's sorrow like broken glass. The girl who had once sung to caterpillars now counted her footsteps and spoke only when spoken to. Wonder didn't vanish, it just went into hiding.

She didn't know it then, but this field would become her chapel. Her anchor. Her proof. In the years to come, when the world bent out of shape and people spoke in empty phrases, Anna would return here in her mind. When guided to find a 'safe place' during therapy or meditation, while others imagined walled gardens or quiet beaches, she always came back here. The grass, the birdsong, the paint in the air. She would close her eyes and feel the sun again. Hear her father's humming. See her mother's smile caught mid-laugh. It wasn't just memory, it was sanctuary.

And the blackbird. Still watching. Still listening.

The Boy Who Forgot

The flat was quiet in a way that didn't feel restful. It had the kind of silence that collected in corners, thick and undisturbed, like dust no one had dared to move. Pip stood in the doorway of the living room, holding his phone as if it were something delicate, breakable. The message was still there... Anna.

He hadn't seen her name in years.
Not properly. Not without it carrying the ghost of something unfinished.
Light from the streetlamp outside filtered through half-drawn blinds, striping the walls with gold and grey. The room smelled faintly of old books, cold coffee, and that vague tang of electronics left on too long. Everything had a low hum. The fridge. The screen.
His own heartbeat.

He should sit down. He should delete the message. He should pour another whisky.
But he didn't. Instead, he drifted to the edge of the sofa and sat, slowly, like someone much older than he was. The cushion sighed beneath him.
His eyes never left the screen.
He used to be someone else. Before the job consumed him. Before the marriage crumbled. Before the thing in Rome. He used to laugh louder. Run harder. Believe in impossible things. Now he

just managed. Replied to emails. Paid bills. Nodded in meetings.
He couldn't even remember the last time he cried.

There had been a photo, once, of Anna in the corner of the mirror. They weren't even posing, just brushing teeth in some B&B outside Lancaster, half-asleep and smiling. It was still in a drawer somewhere. Along with the others. Moments that meant everything and nothing at the same time.

He stared at the phone. Her name didn't blink. It just sat there. Waiting.

Maybe he'd imagined her. Maybe it wasn't even real.
But it felt real. It felt like something had stirred that had no business waking up again. Something he'd buried. Not just her. Not just them.

Himself.

The boy who used to write poetry and hide it in library books. The boy who sketched maps of places that didn't exist. The boy who once stood in a university courtyard and saw a girl with wild hair and a storm behind her eyes, and thought, I know you.
He had forgotten all of that.

But now, somehow, it was remembering him.

When the Birds Stopped Singing

Anna and her dad. Partners in silliness, rulers of imaginary kingdoms. He was her world, her sun, her safe place. They played dollhouse together on rainy days, building elaborate stories with voices and accents that made her giggle until her sides ached. He danced badly in the kitchen, flinging tea towels over his shoulder like capes, declaring breakfast a royal banquet. They sang into wooden spoons, made shadow puppets on the walls, and invented words that only they understood. He never talked down to her. He listened like what she said mattered, and in doing so, made her feel like she could be anything.

She adored him. Not in the blind way children sometimes do, but with wide-eyed reverence. He was gentle, but full of mischief. And the more ridiculous he was, the more she loved him for it. She didn't just feel close to him, she felt known.

And then that sound came... that alarm bell in the quiet, the cough. So small at first, it barely registered. But it was out of place. That's what made the cough so strange. Out of place. Like something from another story that didn't belong in theirs.

At first, it was just a tickle, a dry, shallow cough that surfaced after laughter or in the evening chill. Her father would wave it off with a smile, blaming the paint fumes or the shift in the seasons. He still laughed, still lifted Anna onto his shoulders, still made up silly songs at the breakfast table. But the cough didn't leave. It began to show up more often, usually in the morning, or after long conversations. The cigarettes had always been there, always present, always burning in some ashtray or between two fingers. The scourge of a few generations, her mother once said, as if they were old ghosts no one had quite banished.

The tickle became a bark. Uninvited, rasping, and persistent. It echoed in the hallway, sharp against the soft quiet of home. At first it was just a sound. Then it became a presence. And then it stayed.

The field at the back of the house still stood wild and sun-drenched, but the colour had drained from the days. Her mother stopped laughing quite so freely. Her father sat more than he moved. And Anna, Anna learned how to listen to silence. A silence that was never quite whole, always interrupted by that same sharp sound, the cough, like an alarm bell echoing through rooms that used to be filled with laughter.

She was eleven when the diagnosis came. Old enough to read between the lines, but young enough to hope they were wrong. Her father had just started needing more naps, and the cough was harder to hide. There were appointments, scans, hushed conversations behind half-closed doors. When the word "cancer" was finally spoken aloud, it didn't arrive like a thunderclap, it arrived like dust settling. Quiet, slow, undeniable.

It was her mother who told her. Eyes red, voice steadied only by will. She explained as gently as she could, using words like "treatment," "specialists," and "we'll try everything." But the hollowness behind her eyes betrayed the truth. Anna didn't cry. Not then. She just nodded and asked what it meant. Nobody really answered.

Like so many families, they stepped into that in-between world, of hopeful denial and creeping dread. Some days he seemed better. Other days, he didn't get out of bed. They stopped making plans. They learned to live between appointments, to measure time in test results and quiet sighs. And Anna watched it all, feeling older than her age, waiting for the moment when someone would say it was over, or it had begun.

She marked time not by calendars, but by the shape of his silhouette, how upright he stood, how much he leaned, how his voice grew quieter even as his love remained loud in its own way. Their bedtime stories became whispers. Their kitchen dances stopped. But his hand still reached for hers, every single day. That never changed.

He lasted another three months. Long enough to show her how to bear it, not by denying the pain, but by meeting it with grace. Long enough for her to see what courage looked like up close: not loud or defiant, but quiet and steady. In those final weeks, he showed her that love could stretch beyond fear that presence mattered more than strength. Long enough for the treatments to begin, and then to fail. The early optimism of tablets and appointments turned quickly into chemotherapy sessions, coughing fits, and the cold sterility of hospital rooms. At first, he tried to shield her, cracking jokes in the waiting room, winking at her when the nurse missed a vein. But the sparkle in his eye faded week by week, replaced by a kind of distant peace that Anna didn't yet know how to fear.

And then his hair began to thin. That familiar mess of sun-warmed curls, the hair she'd clung to when riding on his shoulders, that smelled of paint and air-dried linen, started to fall away, slowly at first, then in clumps. She missed the softness of it against her cheek when he hugged her, missed how safe it had felt to bury her face in it and pretend the world didn't exist. The loss wasn't just visual, it was scent, memory, texture. A piece of him, and a piece of their life together, unravelling one quiet strand at a time.

He used to wrap her in his jumper and whisper that she was made of stars. That whenever she needed him, she should look to the heavens, find the brightest star, and that would be him, watching, guiding, loving from beyond. In his remaining time, he would write her notes, little folded truths scribbled in pencil on scraps of lined paper. Messages tucked in the most ordinary places, waiting for the perfect moment to be found, inside the piano stool, under the teabags, behind her favourite book.

"You were always more than the world will understand," one of them read. "That's your power. Don't let them take it."

He died in the early morning. No drama. Just stillness. She had gone to bed with the sense that something was waiting. When she woke, the house had changed. It felt hollow. The air, though still, somehow seemed to echo, too wide, too thin. Her mother wasn't beside her. She wasn't in the kitchen. Anna wandered through the rooms that morning with growing unease, not fully understanding what had shifted, only that it had. The silence wasn't just absence; it was something new. Something missing. A shape no longer filled. Her mother was in the garden, sitting on the old bench beneath the birch tree, the same one Anna's father had painted during one of those long, golden summers before, back when life felt idyllic and days stretched out like stories with no end. Anna's Mum was perfectly still, hands curled in her lap, her shoulders trembling. From the window, Anna could just make out her face, turned slightly toward the house, eyes puffy and red. She was sobbing quietly, not in waves, but in a soft, continuous way, as though she'd been crying for hours without pause. And when she finally turned and saw Anna standing there, her expression shifted into something fragile and devastating. A silent apology. A look that said, I'm so sorry.

Her mother became quiet in a different way. Like all the sound inside her had been folded up and locked away. She moved, she functioned, but her light had dimmed. Sometimes she would stare out the window for hours, as if waiting for something to come back.

Anna started walking alone in the field. But the flowers didn't feel the same. The bees still hummed, but it felt like a different song.

And the blackbird, Short Shanks - didn't come anymore.

One morning, standing barefoot in the dew, she whispered to the empty fencepost, "You could've stayed."

The tears didn't come all at once. They arrived like rain through a broken roof, unexpectedly, in the quiet, when no one else was around. They soaked into her pillow, her sleeves, her drawings.

And from that point on, something in her began to close. Just a little. Just enough to keep the wind out.

Wonder went deeper underground. But it never left.

It waited.

And the girl who once ruled a kingdom of insects and invisible friends… began to walk with her eyes down.

But somewhere, in the marrow of her memory, the birds still sang. They always would.

The Boy with the Paper Worlds

Before he buried his dreams beneath deadlines and distractions, Pip had a world made of paper. He was eight when he began folding maps of places no one had ever heard of, islands shaped like dragons, continents where clouds grew on trees, cities that vanished if you turned the map upside down. He kept them in a shoebox under his bed. Not to hide them, but to protect them, as though some part of him knew that real magic didn't survive long in plain sight.

His room had always been his refuge. Not because it was quiet, but because it was his. Shelves lined with second-hand books from his mum's stall at the market. A troupe of action figures, some with missing limbs, stood at the ready in their uniforms, guardians of the shoebox realms, veterans of battles only Pip could narrate. A lamp shaped like a moon. And everywhere, notebooks. Stacked, scattered, half-filled with adventures that never quite found their endings.

He didn't know his dad. The man had vanished when Pip was still learning to speak, a ghost with a name and not much else, a shape that never quite filled. But his mum, his mum was everything. She was the warmth in the morning and the light left on at night. She worked two jobs, came home with aching feet and tired eyes, but still sat at the foot of his bed, asking about the worlds he was building with a kind of reverence. When she called him "our little inventor," it wasn't just cute, it was sacred. She saw him. Not the quiet boy the world overlooked, but the spark behind his eyes. She praised his monsters, cried over his heroes, and laughed like she meant it, even when she was too exhausted to stand.

When he caught chickenpox, she stayed up all night dabbing calamine lotion on the angry red spots, whispering stories and singing until he fell asleep. When his chest was tight with congestion and every breath came sharp and shallow, she lit the Wright's Coal Tar vaporiser, that unmistakable scent filling the room, and sat beside him while it worked its slow, soothing magic. She didn't flinch from his discomfort. She met it, held it, wrapped it in her own kind of quiet love.

She taught him that stories mattered, because when tears had no words and fear had no shape, stories could hold the weight. Writing about a boy in an adventure, battling shadows or searching for hidden treasure, could say everything about the ache in your chest or the longing in your gut. Hidden between the dragons and maps were truths Pip didn't know how to voice, sadness, hope, confusion, wonder, waiting to be seen, to be comforted. Stories were the bridge between what he felt and what he couldn't say. They were how the heart spoke when the world didn't listen, how a child's silence could still sing.

They lived in a small semi in Chorlton-cum-Hardy, bricks chipped, carpet thin, storage radiators that only half-worked. But Pip never felt poor. He felt rich, in stories, in imagination, in the way his mum hugged him after long shifts, smelling of lavender and cigarettes, telling him he was brilliant. He wasn't the loudest kid, didn't play football, and hated crowds, but he watched the world with a kind of quiet intensity, noticing the details others missed. The way Miss Farrell's smile dipped whenever she mentioned her husband. The way the old man next door never put his milk bottles out unless it was Tuesday, and how Pip noticed the tiny rips in the foil tops left by birds stealing the cream in the early morning. The way some people laughed with their eyes, and some didn't. He wrote all of it down. And at night, when the sky turned ink-blue and the hum of cars on the A6010 quieted, Pip would climb under his covers with a torch and lose himself in the worlds he'd drawn. Places where he mattered. Places where people listened. Places where no one left without a goodbye.

Even then, he knew the real world could be cruel. But on the page, he was in control. He could write in miracles. He could draw doors where there had been none.

He didn't know it yet, but that shoebox, those scribbled realms, would be the first signal. A quiet echo of the thing he would one day remember. The thing that would one day find him again.

The Girl Who Walked With the Trees

After the funeral, people stopped looking her in the eye. They spoke in soft tones and awkward platitudes, like grief was something fragile she might drop if they weren't careful. For weeks, the house was full of flowers and casserole dishes and neighbours who overstayed their sympathy. But then they left. And the silence returned.

Her mother drifted. She still made tea, still washed the dishes, but her movements were mechanical, like the light inside her had dimmed and no one knew how to switch it back on. She didn't laugh anymore. She didn't sing. Sometimes she would forget Anna was even in the room. Sometimes Anna would forget she had once known how to smile.

One grey afternoon, rain tapping the glass in gentle rhythm, Anna wandered back to her room, craving silence but also something else, something she couldn't name. She pulled her blanket tighter around her and knelt beside the bed, tidying a pile of books that had spilled from the shelf. And there it was.

A folded piece of paper, aged at the edges, tucked between the pages of her favourite storybook. Her heart jolted. She knew the handwriting immediately, crooked, slanted, unmistakable. Her father's.

The ink was faint in places, the scrawl uneven. He must have written it in pain. But every word carried his voice. The note was long, more like a letter.

A final gift.

He told her he was proud of her.

He said that he wished more than anything to walk her down the aisle one day, but if he couldn't, he needed her to remember that she was worthy of love in every form it came.

That the world would try to make her doubt herself, but she must never believe it.

He wrote about the sky and the trees and the song of birds, about the stillness of nature and how it would always hold her. "Go placidly amid the noise and haste," he wrote, quoting the poem he used to read aloud on Sundays, "and remember what peace there may be in silence."

He urged her to keep creating, to live truthfully, to be gentle but fierce in her convictions. To not compare her path to others. To not grow bitter with time. To guard her joy. "You will forget how bright you are sometimes," he wrote, "but that's when the stars matter most. Find the brightest one. That's me. I'll be there, always." He repeated.

By the end, her cheeks were soaked, the page trembling in her hands. She clutched it to her chest and curled up beneath the blanket, the scent of old paper and memory rising like breath.

She didn't cry for hours. She cried for everything.

The field behind the house began to grow wild again, untamed. No longer the place of picnics and daisy chains, it became her escape. She would walk its edges like a sentry, tracing the same path her father had once walked while humming. She didn't hum. She listened.

It was in the trees she found her breath again. She sat with her back to the trunk of the old birch and let herself fall into the hush of the woods. The insects didn't ask her to be cheerful. The trees didn't flinch at her sadness. The wind didn't mind if she cried. And so she did.

She whispered things into the bark, her fears, her confessions, the tiny prayers that children send out without knowing they're praying. She spoke to the blackbird again, even though Short Shanks hadn't returned. She drew the faces of invisible girls in her notebook, gave them names, stories, worlds where fathers didn't die and mothers still remembered how to dance.

She didn't have language yet for what she was doing. Not healing. Not grieving. Just... surviving.

Some days she walked barefoot until the brambles scratched her ankles raw. Other days she sat still so long that a robin once landed on her knee.

She had become the quiet girl. The one teachers praised for her neatness and worried about for her distance. But beneath the stillness was a storm of feeling too big for her body, too wild for the language of adults. So she gave it to the earth instead. She poured her heartbreak into tree roots and forgotten footpaths.

And slowly, without trying, she began to remember the sound of her own voice.

She was never the same. But something ancient in her, something wordless and watchful, began to wake.

The Man Who Watched the World

It was just after 2 a.m. Pip stood by the kitchen window, watching the city hold its breath. From this high up, the streets looked like veins, empty, pulsing quietly in the sodium glow. Cars passed, a cat darted across the road, but otherwise, the world had thinned. Silent, like it was waiting for something.

He used to love these hours. As a boy, he'd lie awake just to listen to the rhythm of the house, the creaks in the walls, the low hum of the fridge, the soft snore of his mum behind the bedroom door. Night had always felt like a hidden time, when truth wandered free. Now, as a man, it just felt hollow.

He ran a hand through his hair, stared at the city like it might answer back. The phone still sat on the counter behind him. Unread, untouched since he'd stared at Anna's name. He hadn't replied. Not yet. Not because he didn't want to. But because he didn't know how to return to a story he'd closed so long ago, or thought he had.

He took a sip of cold water. Turned off the light. Let his eyes adjust to the dark.

And then, like memory stirred by the dark, he remembered something small, a scene from childhood, vivid and sudden. He'd been nine. Sick with the flu. His mum had pulled the mattress into the living room so they could watch TV together by the gas fire. She'd made toast, slathered in butter, and brought his action figures over in a shoebox like it was treasure.

He remembered how safe he'd felt. Like the world could fall apart outside and it wouldn't matter, because in that room, on that mattress, he had been completely loved.

That feeling had vanished somewhere along the way. Not all at once. But in layers. He had traded magic for logic. Wonder for productivity. That boy, the one who built worlds from cardboard, had been pushed aside for the man who hit targets, managed budgets, booked flights.

But now something ached. Not just for Anna. Not even for who he was with her. But for the boy who had believed he mattered without needing to prove it.

He looked at the phone again.
The message was still there.
And maybe, just maybe, it was time to answer.

The Girl They Didn't Understand

By the time Anna returned to school, the flowers had wilted. The casseroles had stopped arriving. No one asked if she was okay anymore.

She was twelve. The year everything changes for most girls, and for her, it felt like stepping back into a world that had rearranged itself in her absence.

At first, people were kind in that awkward, performative way. Teachers gave her softer smiles, their voices taking on that forced lightness reserved for breakable things. Friends, or at least the ones who used to be, offered half-hugs in corridors, quickly pulling away as if unsure whether comfort was contagious. There were a few whispered invitations to sit, a few awkward silences when she entered a room, but mostly, they moved on. The world kept spinning. Because sympathy has a shelf life, and children, even the kindest of them, are swift to forget what doesn't belong to them. Her pain became yesterday's news. Her absence a forgotten page. And in their eyes, she no longer fit the shape of their world.

She had changed. And children can sense difference, like a shark senses blood in water.

She no longer played the games. She sat on the edge of the field instead, sketching the trees or staring up at the clouds. She didn't laugh when they laughed. She didn't chase popularity or plait her hair in the same glossy loops the other girls wore like armour. She wore her grief like second skin, quiet, composed, but visible. And for that, they came for her.

It started small. A whisper behind her back. A giggle as she walked past, one that didn't belong to joy but to judgment. Her name turned sharp in someone's mouth, spat like a joke that wasn't funny. She wasn't like them anymore. She was the girl without a dad, the kind of detail that didn't sit well in lunchtime conversations or sleepover plans. The girl who talked to herself under her breath in class, not realising that murmured words to keep her calm would be mistaken for madness. The girl who missed a month of school and came back not just quieter, but changed, her edges softened, her eyes older, her voice barely above a whisper. They didn't know what to do with that kind of sorrow. So they turned on it.

They hid her pencil case. Drew tears on her yearbook photo. Called her Forest Girl. Witch. Ghost.

She tried to ignore it. She told no one. Not even her mother, who was still hollow-eyed and half-present, surviving in her own fog. Anna didn't want to add weight to a woman already sinking.

So she swallowed it. The pain. The humiliation. The way it chipped at her sense of worth.

She started skipping lunch. Walking the perimeter of the school fields instead, fingers brushing the ivy along the fence like it might understand her better than people did. Sometimes she would cry in the bathroom and then wash her face and check it in the mirror, layering silence over pain like makeup.

But through it all, she kept drawing. In margins. On napkins. In notebooks. She drew birds, wings outstretched. Trees with hollow trunks. Girls with thunder and lightening in their chests.

She was alone. But not empty.

Something in her, something her father had lit, refused to go out. It burned low, a hidden ember buried beneath the bruises and silence. It was the echo of his voice in her memory, telling her she was made of stars, the weight of his last letter folded deep in her drawer like a compass for when everything else felt lost. That ember reminded her that she came from strength, from kindness, from magic. Even when the world pressed in, when her voice was too tired to speak and her skin too thin to shield, that flicker held on. It was his belief in her. It was the memory of safe hands and bad jokes, of a father who saw her completely, and in doing so, gave her the tools to one day see herself. That ember was not loud, but it was steady. It didn't scream for attention. It simply glowed, waiting, promising that one day, when the time was right, it would become flame again.

And one day, far ahead in the future, the girls who once laughed would remember her name with a pang of regret.
But for now, she was just Anna.

The girl they didn't understand.

Chapter 10:
The One Who Walked Away

He recalled again the first time he saw her, she walked into the back of the auditorium just as the lights dimmed, a silhouette against the rustle of notebooks and shifting coats. She paused, letting the heavy door fall shut behind her with a soft thud, then made her way along the back row, green scarf trailing, notebook clutched to her chest like something sacred.

She didn't sit. Just stood, eyes scanning the room like she was looking for something she wasn't sure existed.

He was already half-lost by the time she turned her face toward the stage lights, chin tilted, brow calm, as though listening for something deeper than the lecturer's voice. Not music. Not birdsong. Something else. Something only she could hear.

Pip never caught a word of the talk. Not on Baudrillard. Not on hyperreality. Just her, the girl who looked like she'd wandered in from another time.

He followed her out after the session, half out of instinct, half in disbelief. Outside, the sky was winter-grey and the air smelled of cold stone and damp leaves. She stood by the old sundial, flipping through her notebook, pages curling like petals from overuse.

He almost turned back. He wasn't the kind of guy who stopped girls in quads. Not anymore.

But then she looked up. And smiled. Not like she was surprised. Like she'd been waiting.

He said something clumsy about the light, how it made the brick shimmer like gold leaf.

She laughed. "Most people wouldn't have noticed that."
They walked. Talked. Not around campus, outward. Past the edge
of the familiar. Past the part of himself he usually kept hidden.
They sat on a bench until the stars came out. When she stood to
leave, he leaned in.

Almost.

"I'll see you again," he said.
She only smiled. "Not yet."
She left without looking back.

*"She saw something in me no one else did. That was the beginning of
forgetting who I was."*

The Girl Who Remembered Anyway

Long before she met him, she'd written his name.

Not because of a dream. Not at first.

She was twelve, curled on her bedroom floor with her dream journal open, the biro leaking slightly on the edge of the page. The name Pip had lodged itself in her mind after a late-night drama she couldn't recall the title of, just the sound of it, soft and strange. She didn't know why she wrote it down. It wasn't the name of the character, or if it was, the memory had vanished. But something about it stayed with her.

A week later, she dreamt of a boy with eyes too old for his face, soot on his skin, a voice that asked questions without speaking. The next night, he returned. In the dream, he stood on a boat made of glass. The stars were beneath the water.

She asked her mum what it might mean.

Her mum smiled and said, "Sometimes names arrive before people do."

Her teenage years were quiet revolutions, notebooks filled with sketches and lyrics, half-brewed poems and full-moon reflections. She learned early that nature kept better secrets than people did. The trees never lied.

While other girls measured their worth in glances and glitter, Anna walked barefoot through morning frost, learning the language of wind. Books became her companions: sacred geometry, lucid dreaming, the medicine of plants.

She wasn't looking for salvation. She was looking for sense.

And something in the stars made her feel less alone.

One winter evening, she lay behind the garden shed, staring up at Orion until her eyes blurred. She didn't expect a voice. She just whispered "thank you".

And every now and then, in the deepest part of her sleep, the boy would return, the one with the questions. The one who seemed to be searching, not for her, but for himself.

When she met Pip, years later, she didn't remember the dream.
Not right away.
Just the name.
And the page she'd never torn out.

"*I wrote your name before I ever met you.*"

Chapter 12:
The Tremor

That night, something ancient stirred beneath the city. It wasn't loud. It wasn't seen. But it was felt.

Pip woke abruptly. There was no alarm, no sound from the street. Just the sharp snap of consciousness, as if something had shouted inside him. He sat up in the half-light, breath shallow, heart unsteady, his T-shirt clinging to him like he'd swum through a dream and only just surfaced.

The room felt cold, not with temperature, but with something else entirely. A chill of the spirit.

Something had shifted. Not visibly, not audibly. But undeniably. Like the way the air thickens just before a storm.

He glanced at his phone. No new notifications. No missed calls. Yet something lingered in the air, a presence that refused to leave.

Anna.
The man.
The message.
The blackbird.

He rubbed his face with both hands, trying to wipe away the weight of the morning. But the flat felt different now. As though the walls had begun to watch him. As though the corners of the room held memories they'd never shared before.

In the kitchen, he called to Alexa, asked her to play something, anything. The speaker glowed blue and responded with a chirp, but instead of music came a strange noise. Not quite static. Not quite sound. It was like whispering layered beneath a warped vinyl. Then, without warning, a burst of jarring orchestral strings exploded into the room.

Then silence.

The speaker lit again, this time repeating his name. But it wasn't his voice.

His heart began to hammer. He unplugged the device. He had severed the power, yet still, music burst from it again. Then silence returned. He unplugged it a second time, not out of logic, but instinct.

His coffee tasted strange. Not sour or stale, but off, bitter in a way that made no sense.

And then, the man's voice echoed back to him.

"Your life was never meant to go this way."

The worst part was not the memory of the words, but the feeling that they were true.

He moved to the window. Outside, the city unspooled in tones of grey and wetness. He watched a woman wrestle with an umbrella blown inside out. A delivery driver shouted at no one in particular. A black cab sent a wave of dirty water over a pedestrian who turned, flinched, looked behind them, but found nothing.

The world continued.

But Pip couldn't.

Something had begun to knock at the edge of his being. And this time, he wasn't sure he had the will to close the door.

He forced himself into motion. He had a flight to catch. Brussels. A pitch for one of the largest car manufacturers in Europe - sleek, legacy-led, obsessed with heritage. He should've been excited. These were the kinds of clients the agency lived for. But his hands still trembled slightly as he buttoned his shirt, as he zipped his overnight bag. His head ached in that strange, spreading way that felt more spiritual than physical.

At Halo & Easton, he slipped through the glass doors like a man drifting through his own life. He greeted no one, eyes avoiding the morning buzz of creatives and strategists. Everything was slightly too loud. Too fast.

He found the visuals on his desk and the pitch deck on a secure drive. Slid the branded folder into his bag like it might burn him. In the Uber to the airport, the sky was the colour of pewter, and the clouds hung low. He stared out of the window, jaw clenched.

Anna turning up out of the blue after all these years. The photo. The man. The message. The birdsong. None of it made sense. And yet it all made sense in some way that scared him.

In the terminal, he moved through security like sleepwalking. Bought a black coffee that he really didn't fancy drinking. Ignored the duty-free perfume fog. When the gate opened, he boarded without thinking.

Window seat. 10A.

He needed to ground himself. To reset.

As he buckled in, the aircraft trembled beneath him - alive with coiled tension. Slowly, the aircraft rolled forward, taxiing with the lumbering confidence of something too big to stop. Then, the engines surged.

A growl. A scream. A monstrous crescendo of thrust.

Pip's chest tightened.

The overhead lockers groaned.

Trays chattered.

Luggage straps snapped taut.

His vision shook slightly with the force of the acceleration.

Outside, the blur of runway lights streaked past like comets.

He gazed out at the shrinking world, at the metal wing shuddering against the thrust, and wondered - not for the first time - how something this heavy could ever leave the ground.

How millions of pounds of steel, stitched with rivets and dreams, could slip gravity's grip and climb into the endless cold above.

It felt impossible.

And yet here they were, surrendering to it without question, trusting the unseen forces to carry them somewhere new.

A jolt. A shift.

The moment of lift.

The city peeled away, vanishing like paper burned at the edges.

And sky, cold, endless, patient, swallowed everything else.

That jolt of nothing beneath you. That heartbeat where gravity surrenders.

His stomach lurched. The aircraft tilted. Clouds rushed upward to meet them.

The city peeled away, vanishing like paper burned at the edges.

Below him, the sprawling acres of Tatton Park unfurled - a patchwork of fields, water, and forest, the old estate stitched into the land like a memory too stubborn to erase.

From up here, it looked still. Silent.

But Pip knew better.

That ground had seen too much.

Revolutions and reckonings, blood and breath and whispered deals made beneath canopies older than any living man.

And now, it just lay there, green and patient, as if waiting for something to come back.

The plane banked slightly.

Tatton Park and Knutsford, faded into the mist.

And the sky took him. The sky - cold, endless, patient - swallowed everything else.

He opened his laptop to go through the deck. Clicked through the slides. His email pinged.

One new message. Before he lost his connection - one last moment of contact. No sender. No subject.

He frowned, clicked.

Just an attachment.

A photo. Of him.

Eight years old. Standing at the edge of a lake. Mist curling behind him like fingers.

He didn't remember the place. Or the moment. But there was no mistaking the expression - caught mid-turn, as though he'd just been called.

And behind him, barely visible in the trees - a figure. Hooded. Watching.

His breath caught. He stared. He couldn't look away.

The plane banked gently, slicing through the clouds like a blade through gauze. The seatbelt sign pinged off, but Pip didn't move. The hum of the engines had settled into a steady throb, yet his chest still felt hollow, lungs tight with questions he couldn't voice. The flight had settled. The cabin had relaxed into its usual choreography - seatbelts unclicked, trays lowered, soft chatter resumed. Air stewards moved efficiently down the aisles, serving drinks and gentle smiles. Pip accepted a small bottle of water.

He turned back to the screen, trying to concentrate - but the words blurred.

Then - turbulence. His throat tightened.

Not violent. Just a single jolt. As if something had nudged the aircraft from the outside. His drink trembled in its cup. A murmur of voices rose and faded.

He glanced around.

No panic. No alarm.

Just the usual blank stares.

Screens.

Earbuds.

A world sedated by routine, by checklists, swipe cards, loyalty points, seasonal sales, weekend plans, likes, renewals, slogans.

A machinery of forgetting dressed up as living.

Everyone moving.

Everyone asleep.

Following maps they didn't draw, chasing dreams they didn't choose, measuring success in the very currency that robbed them of their time.

No rebellion.

No questions.

Just a quiet, endless hum of obedience.

But Pip was vibrating beneath the surface.

He looked again at the window. Pressed closer.

Nothing now. Only clouds, cotton-thick and indifferent.

Then, between the vapour trails - movement.

A shape.

It stepped through the sky like it belonged there, as if the clouds had opened for it. Not falling. Not floating. Walking.

He blinked, jaw slack. Pressed his face to the window. The shape was cloaked, not in cloth, but in something heavier, something that drank the light.

It moved with a long, deliberate grace, its limbs too fluid, too patient to belong to anything born of earth.

Its head was slightly tilted, as if listening, not to sound, but to the pulse of the world itself.

A hood veiled its face, but Pip felt its gaze, sharp and ancient, pressing against the glass of his mind.

It passed the wing - effortlessly, impossibly - like the air itself had parted to let it through.

As if the laws that chained everything else to gravity, to motion, to mass... simply didn't apply.

It didn't float.

It walked.

Every step sure.

Every step inevitable.

As if it had walked this sky long before planes had ever been dreamed into being.

And then...

just as easily as it had come, it dissolved back into the clouds, like a dream that leaves fingerprints on your waking skin.

It was gone.

But he knew what he'd seen. Not imagined. Not dreamt.

The figure - it hadn't floated. It had walked. As if reality meant something different to it. As if the laws that bound Pip to this seat meant nothing at all to that shape.

He must be losing his grip on reality. The thought struck hard - not dramatic, just honest. This wasn't normal. This wasn't explainable. What if he was going insane? What if something inside him had finally snapped under the weight of everything he had buried? The years of living at a hundred miles per hour, delivering creative solutions and punchy marketing slogans day in, day out - a life where stress coursed through his veins and became a kind of life-force - had shaped him. And now that same force was slipping, cracking, leaking into the edges of everything. He wasn't sure what was real anymore.

It disturbed him. Not in the way a nightmare fades with the morning, but in the way something real creeps into the light and won't retreat. Why him? Why now? These weren't just hallucinations or coincidences. Something was happening. And it was unravelling him from the inside out.

His skin tingled with static. His limbs felt too light. His watch had stopped - the second hand stuck just after take-off.

Then the overhead light above him flickered once.

Twice.

Stayed on.

And somewhere in the cabin - he was certain - he heard a blackbird sing.

No one else seemed to notice.

Impossible. There was no way he could have heard it. Not up here. Not above the clouds, sealed in steel and pressure. But he was sure he did. The song was inside him now, vibrating through bone and breath.

And he whispered, without meaning to:

"What is happening to me?"

He closed his eyes and leaned back into the headrest.

And that's when it hit him.

A memory, uninvited and sudden.

The lake. That same lake from the photo.

But now he was there. Not in a dream. Not watching from outside.

Inside it.

He felt the chill air prickling his skin, the heavy scent of wet earth, the eerie stillness of the water. Birds echoed somewhere deep in the trees, but no wind moved them.

He was small. Alone. Fragile.

He walked slowly to the edge, shoes crunching on frost-bitten grass. His child-heart pounded, but he didn't know why.

Then - a sound behind him. Not loud. Just a shift.

He turned.

A figure stood among the trees.

The same shape. The same tilt of the head.

Watching.

But this time - something else.

Familiarity.

Like the figure had always been there.

Waiting.

A blackbird's call shattered the silence - sharp as a blade drawn across the skin of the sky.

It wasn't just song; it was a rupture, a pulse of something older than language.

A sound that didn't echo in the air but inside him, as if the note had been waiting, buried deep in his blood, all his life, for this moment to crack it open.

Pip gasped.

The plane was descending. The fasten seatbelt sign glowed. The stewards were moving briskly now, checking belts, collecting cups.

Outside the window, the fields of Belgium began to stretch open beneath them.

The voice on the intercom was calm, clipped, precise. But Pip barely heard it.

His palms were damp.

And something had returned to him.

Not just the memory.

But a knowing.

Something was beginning.

Something that had never truly stopped.

The wheels touched down on the tarmac with a jolt that echoed through his bones. The plane taxied towards the gate, engines sighing into deceleration. The cabin lights brightened and seatbelts clicked open around him.

Pip moved slowly, retrieving his bag with a mechanical sort of care. His body was here - in Brussels - but his mind was still somewhere else. High above. Or deeper in.

He passed through arrivals without a word, greeted by a suited driver holding a discreet sign with his name. The drive took them beyond the airport and into a business district flanked by warehouses and windbreak trees. The headquarters sat just outside the city - very European in design, stark and utilitarian, all glass and brushed metal. Flags fluttered in orderly silence. The place felt clinical, deliberate, like it had no room for uncertainty. Glass. Stone. Flags flapping in cold wind.

The client's HQ was already familiar to Pip - he'd been there before, more than once. A sprawling facility just minutes from the airport, where glass, brushed steel, and efficiency defined every line. Very European. Stark. Quiet. Impressive without trying. Today, he was here to present ideas for a new fully electric model, one the company saw as its future. The timing mattered. So did the symbolism. The board wanted something clean, forward-facing, but laced with legacy - the kind of language and aesthetic that nodded to the elite's quiet codes: progress masked as purity, transformation wrapped in tradition. The iconography had to whisper power without speaking it. He knew this world. Knew the expressions. The subtle signals - black on matte silver, light bending at calculated angles, the restrained geometry of influence. Steel. Legacy in the architecture. Money in the air.

Inside, the pitch room was immaculate - floor-to-ceiling screens, espresso machines, perfect lighting. Executives filtered in with charm and detachment. Pip shook hands. Smiled. Performed.

He delivered the deck.

His voice didn't shake, but something in his eyes must have given him away.

A woman near the end of the table - sharp blazer, unreadable gaze - watched him too long. As if she saw not just the pitch, but through it.

He wrapped up. They clapped politely. The director thanked him. Promises were exchanged.

Then it was over.

The moment he stepped back outside into the wind, something left him.

He didn't remember the drive back to the airport. Only the feeling - the urge to get home. To ground himself. To find out what was unfolding.

And who else knew it had already begun.

A fresh thread of anxiety curled through him.

He was starting to worry about his mental health. The visions. The blackbird. The photo. The voice. The air that felt heavier with each passing hour. His constant state of alertness.

He pulled out his phone in the airport lounge and opened his contacts. Scrolled. Paused on a name: Dr. Iain Mercer.

Old friend. Former university lecturer. Now a quiet presence in private psychiatry. Someone Pip trusted to speak to without judgement.

He hovered over the message icon.

Maybe he just needed to talk.

Not as a patient.

Not for a diagnosis.

Just as a man trying to make sense of things that weren't meant to happen, things that didn't fit inside the neat language of stress or grief or overwork.

He needed to steady himself.

To find something solid.

A handhold against the sense that reality was thinning, slipping, pulling him somewhere he wasn't ready to go.

Maybe if he spoke it aloud, it would shrink.

Maybe if he named it, the ground would stop shifting beneath him.

He slipped his phone back into his pocket and tried to focus on something - anything - tangible.

He crossed the lounge without thinking, drawn into a small airport boutique filled with watches under glass.

He bought a new one.

Nothing special.

Minimalist, generic, a clean white face ticking obediently against a plain black strap.

A watch for someone who wanted to believe in time.

The act - the transaction - soothed something shallow in him.

Money exchanged. Bag in hand. New ticking heartbeat on his wrist.

Proof, he told himself, that things still made sense.

But somewhere underneath, deeper than logic could reach, he knew the spell wasn't broken.

Only delayed.

And the song was still there, humming just beneath the surface, waiting.

As he sat down briefly admiring his new watch, a nearby screen flickered - momentarily showing static before returning to its travel advert loop.

Pip frowned.

For just a second, he thought he saw a phrase flash between the pixels. Not an ad. Not a glitch.

"THEY KNOW YOU REMEMBER."

His breath caught.

Then it was gone.

He looked around. No one else reacted. A man in a suit scrolled through his phone. A child unwrapped a chocolate bar. The world carried on, oblivious.

But Pip felt it - the shift.

Somewhere out there, behind the boardrooms and branding decks, behind the whispering clouds and hooded watchers... something was watching back.

He remembered the woman in the boardroom. The one with the eyes that saw too much.

Maybe it hadn't just been a pitch. Maybe it had been a test.

They curated your symbols, he thought. They taught you their language so you wouldn't question the grammar.

And now he was slipping between the lines.

He turned to glance at the gate display.

Another flicker.

This time, not words - but an image.

A blackbird.

Stylised, carved in negative space. The shape blinked on the screen for barely a second - then vanished.

No one else reacted. No one else ever did.

He stepped closer. Stared.

And as he did, the hairs on the back of his neck rose - not from cold, but from recognition. The feeling that something was reaching through the illusion, through the digital fog and glossy terminals, to tell him:

You are not alone. But you were never supposed to remember.

He stood there, frozen between flights, between lives. Between what he had been told and what he could no longer ignore.

And he knew.

Whatever came next would change everything.

This wasn't madness. This was awakening.

Miles away... beneath a mountain older than memory, where stone walls sweated secrets and time pooled heavy in the dark, a screen flickered to life.

A figure stirred in the gloom, illuminated by the cold, sterile light of the feed.

He watched the airport lounge unfold in silent grayscale, travellers blurred into the machinery of movement, wheels turning, signals pulsing.

All except one.

The figure leaned closer, eyes like polished obsidian catching the glow.

There he is.

The man who heard the call.

The man who wasn't supposed to.

Fingers long and pale brushed across a control panel carved into stone, technology grown out of the earth itself, as old as the architecture of forgetting.

On the screen, Pip shifted slightly, adjusting the new watch on his wrist - a small, meaningless gesture.

The figure almost smiled.

Still trying to believe in time.

Still clinging to the spell.

Good.

The less he understood, the slower the unraveling.

And they needed more time.

The figure tapped once - a soft pulse on the ancient screen - and somewhere unseen, an algorithm adjusted, a pattern shifted, a delay woven into the noise.

Watching wasn't enough anymore.

They would have to act soon.

But not yet.

Let him drift a little longer.

Let the song scratch louder at the edges.

Desperation always made them easier to herd back into place.

The figure tilted its head, listening... not to sound, but to the faint, rising frequency beyond the reach of human ears.

The signal was no longer contained.

And somewhere deep within the Inverted structures, those who still remembered the original agreements felt the first twinges of fear.

Something was waking.

Something they had buried under centuries of noise and ritual.

Something they could not fully control.

And this time, it was moving faster than they could silence it.

This time, it wasn't alone.

But the veil was thinning.

The codes were cracking.

And those who watched from high rooms and dark corridors would know - someone had seen.

Seen the cracks in the symbols. Seen through the mirrors. Seen them.

And Pip? He wasn't turning away anymore.

Not now.

Somewhere beyond the sky, where the veils were thin and the watchers still walked, the song was growing louder.

Chapter 13:
Between Lives

He stepped off the plane into the hum of terminal light, the air in Manchester thick with drizzle and sodium haze. He moved through customs on autopilot, but something was different - not in the process, in him.

Every screen he passed lit up with curated joy. Happy couples in warm light. Children running through idealised kitchens. Financial freedom, body confidence, lifestyle transcendence - all available through subscription, with 24-month plans and cash-back promises.

"Everything You Want - Just Beyond Reach."

He stopped walking.

He'd written that line years ago, back when he still believed in the alchemy of branding. It was for a Scandinavian smart-fridge startup that fizzled out before the end of its first funding round. They'd praised the phrasing, said it distilled ambition into six perfect words. He hadn't thought about it since - until now.

Back then, it was about resonance. Cadence. He'd crafted slogans like incantations.

Now they sounded like spells.

Commands hidden in rhythm. Fear wrapped in lifestyle.

"Fear is the ink," he thought. "The page is always white. And we were the ones who filled it."

He passed another screen. A boy gazing upward as augmented reality birds circled his head. The tagline:

"Freedom You Can Touch."

Pip's stomach turned.

He had sold people illusions dressed as choice. Identity packages. Artificial futures. Imaginary empowerment - the illusion of choice shrink-wrapped in lifestyle aesthetics. All they were really doing was paying for their own entrapment. Freedom, sold in packages, became a new kind of prison - smooth-edged, beautifully branded, and self-installed.

And he'd been good at it.

He looked away. But the words clung to him like static.

At the taxi rank, raindrops shimmered under the fluorescents. A driver waved him forward. Pip climbed in.

The cab pulled away, and the lights of the terminal receded.

Through the window, the last billboard before the motorway blinked as they passed:

"One Plan. One Truth."

The hair on Pip's arms lifted.

They're not hiding it anymore, he thought.

And the most terrifying part?

They never were.

The flat smelled different.

Not wrong - just... not right. As though the air had rearranged itself. He dropped his bag in the hall, stood still.

The lights were as he left them. No signs of a break-in. No moved objects. And yet, something was undeniably shifted.

He walked the rooms slowly. Like a man returning to a dream.

In the kitchen, the fridge hummed louder than usual. On the living room shelf, a book had slid halfway out - one he hadn't touched in years. A copy George Orwell's 1984, the corner dog-eared, as if someone had marked a page.

He stared at it, unease blooming in his gut.

Then - his phone buzzed.

A message.

Anna.

"Strange question... do you remember that pub near the canal in Oxford? I just had the weirdest dream about it. We were there. You said something I can't forget."

His heart skipped.

The memory came rushing back.

It wasn't just the memory of her dancing beneath fairy lights; it was the memory of what they almost said that night, but didn't. The way her hand had paused at the table between them, fingers half-reaching for his. The way he had almost told her he loved her, in a pub filled with strangers and soft music and the heat of a thousand unspoken words.

But he hadn't.

And when the moment passed, it had passed forever. Some moments don't forgive hesitation.

He typed.

"I do. I never forgot. What did I say?"

Three dots. Typing.

Then:

"You said, 'None of this is real. But I still choose you.'"

He sat down.

Something electric moved through him. Not memory. Not grief. Recognition.

She was remembering too.

A second message came in.

"I've been having dreams. Of you. Of us. But not just memories - something deeper. The way I felt when I was near you. Safe. Awake. Like I was living in full colour for the first time. And then there were symbols. Birds. Shapes I can't explain. Like something's pulling me toward a version of myself I left behind."

Pip's breath caught. Her words reached past the phone screen and wrapped around his spine.

This wasn't nostalgia. It was recognition - a soul-level remembering that transcended time and distance.

They hadn't just shared a spark.

They had once been a fire.

And the kind of fire that doesn't simply burn out - it waits. Smoulders under skin and silence, under choices made too sensibly and years lived too cautiously. It waits for an opening. A whisper. A line of text that cracks something open inside you and floods it with gold.

She had been the one who made him feel like the world was art - not performance. That he wasn't a curated version of himself, but real. Vital. Seen. Loved without permission or polish.

Now, with just a few words, she'd ignited that place in him again. A hunger, yes - but not just of the body. A longing for honesty. For breathless, heart-lurching truth.

He read it again, breath shallow.

"Same," he replied. "Do you want to meet?"

The reply was instant.

"Yes. Tomorrow. Same pub?"

Pip closed his eyes.

Whatever this was… it wasn't just in him.

And tomorrow, he'd find out just how deep this went.

But something in him whispered caution.

He didn't know the name for them. Not yet. Not consciously.

But they were watching.

They always watched the ones who remembered.

The Inverted - he'd come to know them soon enough. Not through textbooks or headlines, but through lived moments. In glances held too long by strangers on trams. In the wrong kind of silence in a boardroom. In that creeping sense of exposure. The sudden hush in a crowded café when you walk in. The stranger on the street whose eyes linger a second too long, then flick away like a reflex.

The flicker of your reflection in a shop window that seems half a beat behind your real movement.

The feeling of being too alone on a busy street, as if the crowd around you has forgotten you're there,

or worse, noticed you too much.

They went by many names: The Inverted. The Sleepers. The Shadowed. The False Light. Each label an attempt to grasp something that slithered just outside language. They weren't monsters in the traditional sense. They didn't have to be. They were people. Polished. Charming. Helpful. Smiling while they subtracted.

There were types too. The Echoes - those who parroted without knowing. The Scribes - those who rewrote reality one ad, one policy, one slogan at a time. The Anchors - placed near awakened souls to weigh them back into forgetting. And above them, the Watchers - rare, almost mythical. Observers. Enforcers. Maintainers of the unseen architecture.

They weren't visible to most. Not fully. But once you noticed the edges - the seams - you couldn't unsee them.

They didn't like reunion. They didn't like love - not the real kind. It couldn't be modelled, sold, or subdued. And they especially didn't like remembering. Not when it threatened the framework of forgetting they had spent generations perfecting.

They were just… embedded. Familiar. Smiling. Playing their part.

Pip glanced again at the half-open book. The page that was marked. He walked over, opened it.

One line had been underlined in faint pencil:
"*The best books… are those that tell you what you already know.*"

A chill moved through him.

Someone had been here. Or something.

And it knew what he was waking up to.

He looked again at the underlined sentence, then back to the cover. Orwell.

He closed the book slowly, as if it might whisper something else on the way down.

Not yet, he thought.

Some truths needed a second voice. Some memories were sacred enough to wait.

Later that night, he stood at the window. Rain tapped against the glass like soft code. Below, the street shimmered under wet neon, sodium reflections stretched long like ghost light. Nothing moved.

Not at first.

Then… a figure.

At the corner. Just where the lamplight broke into shadow.

Still. Watching.

Pip leaned closer. The figure didn't flinch. Just stood - too straight. Too still. No umbrella. No movement. Just presence.

His heart stuttered.

He looked down at his phone. No signal. No message.

When he looked up again - gone.

But the feeling remained.

He was being watched.

Not someone he knew. Just a man - or what looked like a man - standing in the half-light like he was waiting for a signal Pip couldn't hear. Maybe homeless. Maybe not. But too still. Too deliberate.

As Pip turned away, he thought he heard something - a phrase whispered, not quite English.

He strained to catch it, but the words dissolved like mist.

Probably nothing, he told himself. But his skin didn't believe him. The Inverted didn't always move in the physical. Their presence lingered in strange feelings, flickers in periphery, sudden unease. They moved through systems - signals embedded in infrastructure, in imagery, in things that passed unnoticed.

They used symbols. They echoed patterns. They left disturbances rather than footprints.

A distorted geometry on a corner of a screen. A drawing on a bench - too precise for a child.

A corporate logo updated subtly, as if hiding something deeper.

Street art with eyes that seemed to follow.

Adverts featuring people whose faces felt almost real - but not quite.

Repeating numbers on clocks, receipts, and number plates.

Street names that changed spelling and then changed back.

Murals painted over and repainted, always keeping one strange shape in place. News anchors who blinked too slowly. The same person passing twice in different clothes.

They weren't mistakes. They weren't glitches. They were signals. Placed. Layered. Left in plain sight.

Once you saw them, you couldn't unsee them.

He had began to notice them more often recently, the small disturbances, the seams in reality stitched too hastily to hold.

The wrong smiles.

The shifting shadows.

The signs that whispered rather than spoke.

And threaded through it all, like markers hidden in plain sight, came the numbers.

Not random. Repeating.

444.

    777.

       888.

          111.

The world had been taught these were signs of protection, of alignment. 'Angel numbers' - messages from benevolent forces applauding your progress. Pip had once believed it too. Until something beneath the surface began to stir.

What if these numbers weren't encouragement, but containment? What if they weren't divine affirmations, but pings - quiet digital flags marking his awakening like sonar?

444 in particular unnerved him. It appeared everywhere: in receipts, registration plates, clocks. Always at the edges. Always subtle.

He recalled a fragment from an old thread he'd read once - a theory buried in forgotten forums: 444 was used in military encryption and AI sublayer stabilisation, not spiritual guidance. A frequency marker. A net.

What once may have been sacred - synchronisers, memory triggers, vibrational keys - had become tools of misdirection. Symbols inverted. Signs turned into soft cages.

And the apps...

He made a mental note. The meditation apps. The soothing

voices. The endless breathing exercises. Were they really guiding people to peace - or quietly sedating their awakening?

Soon, he'd need to dig deeper. The numbers were too frequent. Too precise. And something in him now flinched when he saw them.

Not because they meant nothing.

But because they meant something else entirely.

Without knowing or even recognising what they meant, he'd noticed these things before - patterns that tugged at something ancient in him. Only now they felt deliberate. Placed.

The watchers didn't speak. They didn't need to.

The message was simple:

We see you.

And beneath that, another:

We preferred you asleep.

The next day arrived cold and washed in low light. Manchester wore its grey like ritual clothing - familiar, heavy, unspoken.

Pip stood outside The Wharf before she arrived. Nestled by the canal in Castlefield, it still held the air of somewhere between moments, old brickwork, amber windows, and the scent of rain-soaked timber. The iron railings along the towpath glistened, and a narrowboat engine hummed in the distance.

The same sign. Same rust-coloured bench half-tucked under the awning, still damp from last night's rain.

He hadn't been back here in years.

His hand instinctively went to his wrist... then hesitated. The new watch - the one he had bought in Belgium to anchor himself - had stopped ticking somewhere between departure and return, as if caught between realities.

Frozen mid-beat.

He stared at it anyway, not really seeing the time, as if some part of him still believed it might flicker back to life or might offer a reassurance he no longer trusted. His fingers grazed the edge of his coat pocket, a small unconscious gesture, as if he was reaching for reassurance that wouldn't come. The sky was a dull sheet of cloud, pressing low and close. Still, he stood motionless - a figure caught between hesitation and hope, between memory and whatever this next moment might become. Body still. Breath shallow. Thoughts scattered like birds in an unseen wind.

Then he saw her.

Anna.

Not the memory. Not the echo in his mind. Her.

She moved like the years hadn't touched her, only refined her - as if time had carved away everything unnecessary and left only truth. Her coat was tied at the waist, effortlessly elegant, like she hadn't planned it and somehow still looked like poetry in motion. Her hair - chestnut with strands of gold - moved with the breeze, soft waves brushing her cheeks, and she didn't seem to notice. Her face was the kind you remembered even when you tried not to: heart-shaped, luminous, with a quiet strength in her jaw and vulnerability in her eyes. Eyes that searched the street with a quiet urgency - and then settled on him, softening as they found their mark.

Their eyes locked.

And for a moment, the noise of the world dimmed. Time stilled. A held breath in the chest of the city.

It wasn't just a pause. It was a glitch. A missing frame. The kind of moment where something vast and invisible leaned in to watch.

His heart stuttered - not in fear, but in awe, like his body knew something his mind couldn't yet name. The air between them felt charged, stretched taut with meaning.

And then she smiled... tentative, warm, disarming.

"Hi."

And with that, the world, and time began again.

He stepped forward.

"Hi."

They stepped inside The Wharf, and warmth greeted them like a memory. Low beams, soft candlelight, the scent of woodsmoke and something faintly citrus from behind the bar. Conversations hummed around them like a low-frequency comfort - not intrusive, just human.

He offered to get the drinks.

"Still white?" he asked.

"You remembered," she said, smiling. "But no. Red, now. Something bold."

"Right. You always liked to surprise me."

She leaned a little closer. "You always liked to be surprised."

He returned with a bottle of Gran Reserva Rioja she'd once said reminded her of late summer nights in Spain. By the time he'd bought two large glasses, he realised he could've bought the bottle. He didn't mention it - it wasn't about cost. It was about the ritual. The symbolism. The re-threading of something frayed but not broken. They found a table by the window, overlooking the rain-softened canal. For a while, they didn't speak. Not because they didn't know what to say, but because some things only settle into silence first.

Finally, she said, "You seem… older, but not tired. Sharper, maybe."

He raised an eyebrow. "I was hoping for wiser."

"You were always wise," she replied. "You just forgot."

He watched her for a beat too long. "You always said that like you knew something I didn't."

"I think I did."

He sipped his drink, but his thoughts were elsewhere, not far, just underneath.

The dreams. The photo. The figure by the wing that he must have imagined. The tone beneath her voice.

Anna's words hung between them:

"What if the version of your life you remember… was the story they wanted you to believe?"

The question echoed in him like a low hum beneath the noise of conversation.

Not just hers, not just the words, but something deeper, older.

Like the evening itself was pressing gently on a bruise he hadn't noticed until now.

A tone he'd heard before.

A frequency carried in her voice.

A knowing passed between glances, not words.

He leaned forward slightly, voice low:

"Who are they?"

Anna turned to look out the window, following the meandering of a couple under the streetlights.

She didn't answer at first.

Not directly.

Her fingers touched the rim of her glass, as if feeling for the right shape of truth.

Then, without looking at him, she said quietly:

"Maybe they're the ones who made sure we never asked better questions."

She paused, the candlelight catching the edge of her profile,

soft, strong, remembering.

"Do you ever feel like everything we were told was true... was just a way of keeping us from asking more important questions?"

His breath caught.

"Yes," he said. "I do now."

Anna turned back to him.

"Sometimes," she said, "I think we're born remembering...

and somewhere along the way, we're made to forget.

Not by accident. Not by time. But by design.

And we spend the rest of our lives feeling the echo of what we lost... trying to remember what was always ours."

She looked at him, her voice a breath across the distance.

"Until someone..." Her eyes held his. "...reminds us."

Pip felt it then. Not a metaphor. Not a romantic pull. Something cellular. Like his entire body had just agreed with her without asking permission.

He leaned forward slightly, elbows on the table, drink forgotten.

"Why now?" he asked. "Why are we finally starting to piece it together?"

She shook her head slowly. "I don't know. But it feels like… something's waking up. Like something was counting down. Or waiting for us to be ready."

There was a pause.

Outside, a dog barked faintly. A tram sighed over the viaduct. A candle between them guttered, then stilled.

Anna's voice dropped to a whisper.

"I hear things sometimes. In dreams. In still places. A sound… not quite music. Not a voice either. It's like… a tone. But it makes me feel like I'm supposed to follow it."

He looked at her, his throat tight. "I've heard it too."

Her eyes widened just a little. Not in fear. In recognition. She sat back slightly, her fingers curling around the stem of her glass.

"You probably think I sound mad," she said, half-laughing.

Pip smiled. "Not as much as I wish I did."

"I mean, it's not like I believe in all this stuff. I've spent my whole life rolling my eyes at people who talk about signs and synchronicities. Tones? Seriously?"

She raised her glass and grinned. "Cheers to becoming the person I used to mock."

He clinked his glass gently against hers. "Cheers to the implosion of smug certainty."

She laughed - really laughed - and something in the air softened.

"But seriously," she said, lowering her voice, "every time I try to shake it off, something else happens. Another dream. A coincidence that's just… too weird. Like yesterday, I sat down on the tram next to a woman with the exact scar I'd seen in my dream the night before. Then the guy across from me was humming this song I haven't heard since I was eight."

Pip tilted his head. "That's either deeply spooky or the universe showing off."

"Maybe both."

A beat.

"And you?" she asked. "What's your weirdest one?"

He considered it. "I was on a flight to Brussels," Pip said, voice low and steady, "and somewhere mid-flight, I must have drifted off. I didn't even remember falling asleep - just the usual engine hum, altitude pressing in, that feeling of surrendering to the air."

He looked down into his glass, then back up at Anna. "When I opened my eyes, something was... wrong. Weird. I turned to the window expecting to see clouds, sky, you know - the usual. But there was someone outside."

Anna blinked. "Outside the plane?"

He nodded. "Yeah. Thirty-eight thousand feet. Walking. Calm. Like they belonged there."

Her eyes narrowed, curiosity overtaking disbelief.

"They were dressed in dark clothes," Pip went on, "but they didn't ripple in the wind. And there was no wind. No turbulence. Just this... stillness. They moved like they were on solid ground. Like they were in control of gravity or something bigger. I just sat there, frozen. Watching."

He paused, the weight of the memory pressing.

"And then they turned and looked straight at me. Not just a glance. It felt like... being read. Like they could see every memory I'd ever had."

Anna's breath caught, but she said nothing.

"The moment shattered when the clouds rolled in and swallowed them. But in their place - symbols. Clear as if they'd been carved into the sky. A circle inside a triangle. A spiral. And then this bird - a blackbird, I think - with wings stretched and beak open. Like it was singing."

Anna leaned in. "That's..." she trailed off.

"I know," Pip said. "I still don't know if it was real. And then there was an email. No subject. No sender. Just an image."

He tapped his temple. "Me. As a child. Standing by a lake. One I barely remember. I'd never seen the photo before. Still don't know who sent it. But it felt... synchronised. Like the vision had triggered something. Or someone was watching for the exact moment I'd see."

He looked at her fully now, his voice barely above a whisper.

"It wasn't just the photo. It was the sequence. The presence. The timing. Like something was reaching out. Like it had always been there… just waiting for me to wake up."

Anna blinked. "Okay… yeah. You win the weirdness prize"

He shrugged, smiling. "I didn't know there was a prize."

She leaned in, eyes gleaming. "Oh, there is. But the prize is… more questions."

"Typical," Pip said. "I was hoping for another evening like we had under the twinkling lights."

She raised her eyebrows. "Please. You're British. You'd rather queue for forgiveness than admit you want it."

He smirked. "That's cruel. And alarmingly accurate."

"You'll survive."

They both smiled, the kind of smile that slips past time and lands where it first began. There was comfort now, woven into the strangeness. An ease that hadn't existed the day before.

Anna glanced down at her glass, then back up at him.

"So what do we do with this?" she asked. "This… whatever it is."

Pip shrugged, not flippant, but honest. "We talk. We listen. We don't pretend it's nothing."

A pause. Then she nodded. "Okay. But I'm still going to need a second glass of wine to process the fact we might be tuning into a frequency no one told us existed."

He grinned. "That I can do."

He reached for the bottle and gently topped up her glass.

"Careful," he said, "this stuff's been known to inspire bold truths and ill-advised declarations."

She raised an eyebrow. "Bold truths I can handle. But if I start quoting Rumi, stop me."

"I make no promises," he said, pouring just a little more into his own.

She swirled the wine, watching the deep red catch the candlelight.

"You always knew how to pick a bottle."

"You always knew how to empty one," he shot back, smirking.

She laughed, eyes bright. "Rude. Accurate, but rude."

Their knees brushed beneath the table - neither moved.

And she looked at him with something that wasn't quite an invitation... but wasn't not either. He went to the loo.

When he returned, he topped up her glass before setting it down gently in front of her.

"You've officially surpassed your lifetime wine quota," he said, mock serious.

She raised an eyebrow, smiling. "You say that like I won't out-drink you tonight."

He tilted his head. "Challenge accepted. Though I did buy the bottle, so technically, I win by default."

"Oh, so that's how it works?" she replied, swirling the wine. "Buy the bottle, win the argument?"

"Absolutely. It's in the fine print. Somewhere near 'contains sulphites'."

She laughed, warm and genuine, her hand brushing his as she took the glass.

He sat down again, mirroring her movement with his own drink.

And just like that, something softened. Like the years between them had been poured into the glass, swirled, and forgiven.

And outside, beyond the canal, the clouds were beginning to part - just slightly - as if to say, yes, even now.

There was something unspoken between them. Not just chemistry. Not just memory. A kind of resonance that felt older than this life, like twin flames briefly parted by time, now circling back to source. She didn't say it, and neither did he. But something in both of them recognised the other.

Not as strangers reunited.

As kindred spirits, finally remembering what they had never truly forgotten.

They stepped back out into the night, the air crisper now, the drizzle stilled to a sheen. The streets were quiet - that soft lull Manchester held after midnight, when even the city itself seemed unsure whether to sleep or keep watching.

They walked without direction, shoulders close but not touching.

"You still wander like this?" she asked, glancing sideways.

"More than I should. Less than I want to."

She smiled faintly. "Some things never change."

A tram rumbled past in the distance, trailing blue light that painted the cobbles in brief electric hues. Somewhere, a bin lorry hissed as it reversed. The ordinary world asserting itself again - but gentler now, as if aware they were being observed by something older.

Pip glanced down at the stone edge of the walkway. A rusted access panel sat flush with the path - easily overlooked. But he'd seen another just like it earlier near the station. And another near the canal basin.

"Did you know," he said slowly, "Manchester has an entire network of underground tunnels? Not just old sewers or bomb shelters, I mean old, forgotten passageways. Some say they connect to churches, others to the old cotton warehouses. Some say they were never on any map."

Anna raised an eyebrow. "And you think they're just... what? Storage?"

He shook his head. "I think they were once important, maybe still are. Manchester's not alone. Paris. Edinburgh. Washington. Even Naples. LA, New York, London, Russia, Mumbai, Tokyo, Rome - almost every major city has them. Most people never notice. And those who do? They don't ask twice."

They stood in silence for a moment. Then she said quietly, "So what do you think they're for?"

He hesitated.

"Control," he said at last. "Or escape. Or maybe both."

They stopped at the old footbridge, the one that felt familiar for reasons neither of them could quite explain. It pressed against their memory like a half-remembered melody - something felt in the bones before the mind could name it.

Anna's voice dropped to a murmur.

"This is going to sound strange…"

He waited.

"…I've stood here before. But not in waking life."

Pip didn't move.

"You're not alone in that," he said quietly. "I've seen it too."

They both leaned on the iron railing, gazing at the rippling black water below. Then she turned to him - not with urgency, not with romance, but with a stillness that held meaning.

"Something's coming, isn't it?"

He nodded, eyes not leaving hers.

His voice was low, almost reluctant:

"Maybe it already has."

They turned to walk again, following the quiet curve of the path that arched gently toward the darker edge of Castlefield.

And that's when Pip stopped.

At first he thought it was a trick of light - his own movement reflected in the canal's sheen.

But the figure across the towpath was mimicking him. He shifted his weight. So did the figure.

Lifted a hand to rub his neck. The figure mirrored him, not perfectly, but close enough to freeze the breath in his throat.

Anna had noticed too. Her voice low.

"Is he… copying you?" Pip didn't reply. He stepped forward slightly. The figure stepped too. Then stopped.

But its head tilted at the same time Pip's did.

There was no malice. No overt threat. Just a stillness that was wrong. A performance not quite rehearsed enough. A glitch in the play.

Then, in a blink, the figure turned, walked into the dark between two buildings, and was gone.

Anna's hand found his. "What the hell was that?"

He shook his head slowly, eyes fixed on the alley.

"I don't know," he said. "But I think we were just seen."

They stood frozen for a moment, the silence between them louder than the night.

Pip looked down the alley again, but the figure was gone. Not even footsteps. No shadow retreating. Just the heavy breath of space recently filled.

Anna's voice broke the stillness. "We should leave, right?"

But he didn't move.

Anna's hand found his.

"What the hell was that?"

He shook his head slowly, eyes still fixed on the alley.

"I don't know."

His voice was low.

"But maybe we were meant to see it."

She looked at him, uncertain - then glanced at the wall near the alley. Faint graffiti. A mark scratched into the old red brick. Not quite a shape, not quite a letter.

Just... a disturbance.

"Look at that." He stepped closer. The shape wasn't painted - it was etched, long ago. Like the wall had been branded by heat and forgotten.

It resembled an eye. Or a spiral. Or both. "Looks like something out of a dream," he murmured.

"It is," Anna whispered. "I've seen it before."

He turned to her. "Where?"

"In the tunnel. The one from my dreams. The same symbol was on the walls."

Pip stared at the glyph, his eyes tracing the curve of it, part eye, part spiral, but not clean. Not organic. There was something not right in the geometry. Something that felt... reversed.

"I think it used to mean something else," he said slowly. "Something true. Ancient, maybe. I first saw it years ago when I was studying branding. We were analysing how ancient symbols end up in modern logos - how companies hijack shapes with subconscious weight. This one stuck with me. Back then, I thought it was just clever design. But then I found out about the swastika... how it was once a sacred symbol of peace and balance in Hinduism and Buddhism, used across countless ancient cultures. And yet it was twisted, taken, and turned into a symbol of hate. That was the moment it clicked for me. Symbols matter. They carry memory. Meaning. Power. And when that power is inverted… it doesn't just corrupt the message. It poisons the receiver. Now I'm not so sure anything is just clever design."

Anna looked at him. "Taken?"

Her voice was cautious, a step between curiosity and disbelief - the kind of word you say when something in you already knows the answer but wants to hear it spoken aloud. A challenge, or maybe an invitation to dig deeper.

"Rebranded. Inverted. It happens all the time... sacred symbols, stolen and turned inside out. The spiral used to represent inner growth. Evolution. The soul's journey inward. But now… it shows up in places it shouldn't. On logos. On classified documents. In the background of meditation apps and NGO campaigns. Someone's been using it. Not to awaken people, but to watch them."

She shivered. "Like bait."

"Exactly."

The glyph shimmered faintly in the streetlight, or maybe it was just their eyes playing tricks. Either way, the shape held them.

"It's like a doorway," Pip whispered. "But we don't know who's on the other side anymore."

Pip stared at the mark, then back at the ground. Another rusted access panel.

This one slightly askew.

A silence passed between them, a kind of agreement not yet voiced.

"I think we just found a way in," he said.

They made their way back to his flat in silence, the kind of silence that needed no explanation. It was the kind of quiet that held weight, intention, invitation. Their footsteps echoed softly through the night city, the flicker of amber streetlamps painting gold on wet cobbles.

Inside, the flat was dim and still, carrying a new energy now - not his, not hers, but something shared. A middle place.

He made tea, because it was something to do, something to offer. But neither of them touched it.

When he turned to face her, she was already near, not abrupt, not hesitant. Just there. As though she had always been moving toward this moment.

The kiss wasn't rushed. It wasn't cinematic. It was human. Breath and memory, soft collision, the press of mouths that had longed for each other in some distant version of themselves.

Clothes came away like old habits, discarded in laughter and breathless pauses between kisses. Her fingers moved across his skin not with precision, but curiosity - like rediscovering the language of someone once known by touch alone. He traced the lines of her spine with reverence, discovering something completely new, uncharted and electric - but somehow safe. This wasn't memory guiding them. It was instinct. Raw and reverent instinct. The moon caught her in fragments - shoulder, collarbone, the curve of her back - each illuminated like a secret unfolding. And when he whispered her name, she didn't answer with words, only a breath that trembled through him, soft and surrendering. It was not just intimacy - it was recognition. A homecoming written in skin.

There was no soundtrack. No scripted words. Just touch, and knowing, and a stillness that stretched time into something vast and sacred.

They fell asleep curled together, the air between them warm with shared breath, the world outside forgotten.

Sleep eventually came easily that night. It edged in after their breath had steadied and the weight of the world slipped back behind the veil. When it arrived, it came in fragments - flickering, broken, and disjointed. Images without narrative.

Sounds with no speaker. Feelings without origin.

As if the dream was being tuned in from somewhere else, and he had only just aligned with the right frequency.

He woke up gasping, drenched in sweat. The tone still ringing in his ears.

Next to him, Anna stirred gently, her eyes fluttering open. She didn't speak, but reached for his hand under the blanket, their fingers tangling naturally, like this had always been.

They lay still for a moment, eyes locked - his, wide and shaken; hers, calm but curious.

"I dreamt too," she whispered.

He nodded, unable to speak.

Later, Pip moved quietly through to the kitchen, barefoot, his skin still humming with something he couldn't name. He made toast. Poured coffee. Small rituals. Human anchors.

Anna joined him on the balcony, wrapped in his blanket, her hair tousled by sleep and truth. They sat in silence, sharing warmth from their mugs, from each other.

A rare event in Manchester - the sky was clear, washed clean and unapologetically blue. The sun edged above the rooftops and lit the city like a revelation.

Stillness. And a knowing neither of them could yet explain.

And one word burned behind his eyes:

Remember.

They sat beneath a sky so blue it hurt to look at - side by side on the small balcony, mugs cradled between their palms, bare feet brushing gently beneath the table. The silence wasn't awkward. It was full - of dreams unspoken, of truths dawning. Of something ancient stretching out its limbs inside them both. The sky was the kind of blue that had been engineered - too smooth, too perfect. But across it, stretching from horizon to horizon, were lines. White trails - dozens of them - forming a net above the world.

Chemtrails.

He knew the word - a term that once sat on the fringes, dismissed by mainstream voices and late-night comedians. A 'conspiracy theory,' they'd called it. But now, seeing it painted across the engineered sky, it didn't feel absurd. It felt deliberate. Familiar. As if the conspiracy had been the cover story all along. he'd never once said it aloud. Not seriously. Not until now.

The dream he'd had stirred within him.

He was in a field. The crops brittle, yellowed. Animals unmoving, silent. Waiting.

Then the rain came… wrong, heavy, itching where it touched.

And beneath his feet, the world exhaled: a hollow, mechanical sound.

The ground cracked.

Darkness opened. Not absence, but architecture.

A tunnel. A descent.

A place built to hold.

He tried to run, but the ground tilted. A hum rose through his bones. A tone - low, mournful, familiar. It held him like a magnet.

He looked up.

The sky blinked.

And the colour - all of it - drained away.

Back here on the balcony with Anna, the sky above still bore the scars of the trails.

Pip blinked hard, as if waking again, though his eyes had never closed. The trails hadn't faded - they lingered, netted across the blue in impossible symmetry. He glanced at Anna. Her gaze was on the horizon, calm but distant, as if she too could feel it - the quiet, coiled tension in the air.

"It wasn't just a dream, was it?" he asked.

She shook her head slowly.

"No," she said. "It never is."

Anna stood, disappeared briefly, and returned with a folded scrap of paper. She handed it to him without a word.

He unfolded it.

The symbol. Etched in pencil. It was the same one from

the wall near the alley - the spiral-eye mark. But here, it was surrounded by faint impressions of others - incomplete, like echoes. He looked up.

"You drew this from memory?"

She nodded. "A dream. Not just last night. This one's been with me for years. I never understood it until now."

Pip stared at the page. The centre of the spiral shimmered slightly, not with light - but with pull. It made him feel like his vision was being drawn inward.

And then - the lights flickered.

Just once. A soft, almost imperceptible pulse. But both of them noticed.

Then his phone buzzed. One new message.

No name. No number.

Just a single line:

Not everything buried stays silent.

They exchanged a look - not of panic, but of confirmation. The path ahead was no longer optional.

Pip exhaled slowly, laying the drawing flat on the kitchen table. He tapped the spiral's centre once, then twice, as if expecting it to respond.

"We have to go back," he said.

Anna nodded. "We were meant to."

They started making a plan. Nothing dramatic. Just flashlights. A bag. A small crowbar for the panel. No words of doom or fate. Just a quiet preparation, like remembering how to ride a bike or wake before an early flight.

But something in the air felt thinner. Off. Like a wire had been cut that no one could see.

Then - the power surged again.

A flicker. A buzz. The kitchen radio turned on by itself, volume low. A voice mid-sentence:

"…they always return to the origin point. That's how we know the pattern's begun."

Then static.

Anna stepped forward and turned the dial. The signal vanished.

They looked at each other.

There was no longer a choice.

Whatever lay beneath the streets of Manchester - beneath Castlefield, specifically, where the old Roman ruins and the canal tunnels once intertwined, was waiting for them.

And somewhere in the dark, perhaps, was a clue - something pointing to the Signal.

A way to break the net.

The Depths Remembered

By late afternoon, the light had shifted, the city wearing a cooler, bruised tone, the clouds returning in slow procession. It had started to rain, not the cleansing kind Pip remembered from childhood, but a thin, greasy drizzle that seemed to settle on the skin like a film. As always, it seemed, after the planes had sprayed their filth. Barium. Aluminium. Strontium - elements once dismissed as conspiracy fodder, now openly acknowledged in scattered government admissions.

Once a whispered horror, now an operational reality.
Pip pulled his hood tighter as he walked, the scent of damp concrete sharp in the air. It wasn't just the rain. It was the knowledge of it, the invisible, deliberate contamination. Said to enhance atmospheric conductivity, disrupt cognition, weaken the soil beneath our feet - invisible tools of control. Whispered chemicals once dismissed as fiction, now laced across the sky in patterns too perfect to ignore.
He remembered vividly a headline had crawled across his feed in 2025:
"UK Greenlights £50 Million Program to Dim the Sun."

Official. Public. No longer a hidden project confined to classified corridors. The Advanced Research and Invention Agency (ARIA) had announced open-air experiments to spray reflective aerosols into the atmosphere. The stated goal: to reduce sunlight and "cool" the Earth.

He'd read the article twice. Three times. The Guardian. The Times. Even fringe sites, who pointed to NASA documents and old NATO experiments in weather modification, things buried in technical language decades ago. It was real. And it was here. Humanity, having poisoned its own soil, now sought to mute the very star that had birthed it.

Pip stopped under a dripping awning, staring up at the gridded sky. How had it come to this? The audacity. The blindness.

The very thing that gave life - light, warmth, photosynthesis, time itself - now treated as a threat to be "managed." A "problem" to be engineered.

"Man," he thought, "the only species arrogant enough to think it could master the sun."

He remembered a line he once heard, from a talk about ancient cultures. "You don't block the sun. You honour it."

But here they were. Not honouring. Not even surviving. Manipulating. Distracting. Muting. And calling it progress.

He thought about the chemtrails, the rain, the grey veil stretching across what should have been a wide blue sky. He thought about the hunger he'd felt lately, not just in his stomach, but in his cells, for real sunlight, real sky. How long had it been since he'd stood under a genuinely open sky? Not veiled. Not netted with trails. Not "dimmed" by design.

The rain slicked down the pavements, washing invisible metals into the drains, into the rivers, into the bloodstreams of everything still trying to grow.

Pip tightened his fists.

He understood now why the ground felt thinner. Why dreams had become fractured. Why the city felt coated in an exhaustion that sleep could not heal.

They weren't just dimming the sun.

They were dimming the human spirit.

And somewhere inside him, something ancient recoiled - and began, very quietly, to resist.

Pip pulled on an old waterproof jacket, Anna layered up in black and grey. They packed light. Two torches. A notebook. A flask of coffee. The crowbar. Her drawing folded into the inside pocket of his coat.

Back at Castlefield, the entrance looked unchanged. The same wall, the same spiral mark, the same rusted panel. But everything felt different. The mimic was gone - or at least no longer visible - but his echo lingered.

Pip crouched, slid the crowbar under the lip of the panel, and with a grunt, prised it free. It came up slower than expected, groaning with age and damp.

Below was darkness. Deeper than shadow. A vertical shaft with iron rungs descending into black.

He looked at Anna.

"You sure?"

"No," she said. "But we're doing it anyway."

He smiled. "That's the spirit."

And together, they descended.

One step. Then another.

Until the city was no longer above them, but a memory pressed against the ceiling of a place built to remember what others tried to forget.

Their footsteps echoed against the damp stone, each rung a low metallic sigh. The air changed by degrees - cooler, denser, laced with something ancient. Not rot, not damp. Memory. A scent like scorched iron and forgotten incense.

When they reached the floor, their torches revealed more than expected.

The passage wasn't crude. It was constructed. Arched ceilings ribbed with time-blackened beams. Old stonework etched with faint markings - worn, but intentional. Spiral symbols. Geometric curves. A language not quite dead, but dormant.

Anna ran her fingers across one.

"These weren't made by utility workers."

"No," Pip said. "These were made to last."

A low thrum vibrated through the wall. Not sound. Tone. Faint, like something deep beneath the tunnels was still on.

They moved slowly. Pipes lined one edge of the tunnel, but even they seemed misplaced - as if added later. The original architecture resisted them.

After a few turns, they paused - the stillness around them too perfect, too rehearsed. A rustle echoed down the tunnel, small but sudden.

Anna gasped as something darted past the torch beam.

"Was that a rat?" she whispered.

Another scurry - the sound of claws on stone.

Pip tensed. "More than one."

They both stilled, breathing shallow. The moment passed, but the tension didn't. The tunnels weren't abandoned. They were occupied - by time, by memory… and by things that thrived in shadow.

They pushed forward, slower now, every sound amplified in the echo chamber beneath the city.

Then they found a chamber.

Circular. Seven metres wide. The torches caught remnants of old rusted fixtures - rails, cables, a steel gurney half-collapsed against the wall. But it wasn't the modern leftovers that held them still.

It was what was beneath them.

A mosaic, sprawling across the chamber floor, almost erased by time… sprawled out beneath their boots. At first glance, it looked like erosion. But as their torches swept over it, the pattern emerged: concentric spirals, intersecting lines, and a central eye-shaped glyph that pulsed gently under the beam.

Not light. Not glow.

Awareness.

Anna crouched. "This pattern… it's the same as the one I saw in the drawing."

She traced a line with her fingertip. The moment she did, a faint chime filled the space - just one note. Low. Hollow.

They froze.

Then the tone faded.

Pip looked at her. "I think it knows you."

Before she could respond, the sound of stone shifted - not far, just beyond the curve of the corridor.

A scraping.

Soft. Slow.

Then silence.

Anna stood slowly. Pip raised the torch. Nothing but darkness. But the air… it had changed again.

"Did you hear that?" he whispered.

She nodded. "We're not alone down here."

Pip turned slowly, sweeping the torchlight across the chamber's mouth.

The beam caught nothing. No movement. Just the carved stone and scattered rust.

And then - something glinted.

Half-buried beneath a sliver of shattered tile, a metallic edge reflected back at him.

He knelt, reaching for it, but the moment his fingers brushed the edge, a strange resistance prickled through the air, like the space itself tightened around the object. He gripped it carefully, prising it free from the stone. It was a disc, thin, palm-sized, smooth on one side, and etched with sharp, fractured symbols on the other. Not like the carvings on the walls, these markings felt broken, reassembled into a language that almost remembered itself, but not quite.

Anna crouched beside him. "What is it?"

He didn't answer. He turned it over. The disc shimmered slightly in the torchlight, almost resisting focus - as if the eye could track its shape, but not its meaning.

Then the tone came again.

Not a chime this time. A low resonance. Harmonic.

The walls began to respond.

Hairline veins of silver light unfurled across the stone, mapping forgotten paths, like veins catching moonlight beneath skin. They traced outward from the centre of the chamber, forming a circular pattern around them.

Anna stood, breath caught. "Pip… it's responding to the disc."

"No," he said. "It's responding to us."

The tone deepened. Not louder - just closer.

And somewhere behind them, footsteps. Not rats. Not echoes.

Deliberate.

Human.

Or something pretending to be.

They turned in unison, torches raised. The beam cut across the corridor but caught nothing - just the curve of the tunnel vanishing into dark.

Then came a whisper.

Not speech. Not language. A breath-shaped distortion of sound - like a voice passed through broken glass. It echoed in the air like static caught in breath.

Anna gripped his arm. "We need to move."

But the mosaic beneath them had changed.

Where before it had been faint, it now glowed softly - not with light, but with awareness.

One of the circular patterns had begun to spiral inward, as if drawing them toward something deeper.

Pip looked down at the disc in his hand. It pulsed once - heatless, weightless, but unmistakable.

"There's more," he whispered. "This chamber… it's a gate."

Anna nodded slowly, fear in her eyes but trust in her body.

"Then we go deeper," she said.

They moved toward the opening forming at the base of the chamber - a passage revealed by the shifting floor, one that had not been visible moments before.

They stepped forward - and behind them, the whisper returned.

Not closer. Not louder.

But aware.

The new corridor descended gently, carved at a subtle slope. The air thickened. The walls narrowed.

Their torch beams cut through layers of dust suspended midair

- not just dust, but fibres. Threads. Like ancient webbing that hadn't been spun by anything biological.

"Feel that?" Pip asked.

Anna nodded. "Like... pressure."

"Or presence."

They walked slower now, their footsteps muffled by a thickening silence - the kind that wrapped around sound and held it still.

The passage bent sharply left - then right - and then opened into a small chamber.

Eight sides. Stone-lined. At the far end stood a door, or the shape of one - seamless, carved from the same material as the wall itself. In its centre: a sigil, matching the disc.

Anna moved closer, drawn to it. But as she approached, her torchlight began to dim - not flicker. Dim. As though the light itself didn't want to expose what was ahead.

Then...

...a sound.

Behind them.

Not footsteps this time. A click. Mechanical. Cold. Precise.

They turned.

At the corridor's mouth stood a figure.

Not a mimic - those were the ones who watched, who copied, who echoed. The rehearsed shadows meant only to disturb, not to act.

Not a watcher, those who simply lingered at the edge of perception, monitoring through presence alone.

An Inverted. The real thing. A being who moved between the seams of reality and narrative. Not there to observe, but to intervene. A creature whose role was to maintain the lie, and suppress, or erase, those who stepped too close to truth.

It didn't speak. The figure moved without footsteps. Without breath. A silence shaped into flesh.

It simply stood there - human in shape, but not in posture. The head tilted just slightly, the limbs too even. Its skin didn't look like skin - it looked worn, as if imitation had a shelf life.

The eyes - or the approximation of them - didn't blink.

Anna's voice was a breath. "It's here."

The Inverted took a step forward.

And every light they carried went out.

Darkness swallowed them, thick and absolute. Pip could feel it - not fear exactly, but gravity, as if the space itself tilted toward the thing.

Instinct hammered in his chest: They couldn't touch it. If the Inverted made contact - physical contact - it wouldn't just kill them. It would overwrite them.

Not death.

Deletion.

Somewhere deeper, he felt the compass pulse once against his ribs, as if remembering too.

No light would save them here. Only resonance, and if they faltered, even for a moment, they would be rewritten into silence. Darkness swallowed them whole - thick, absolute, a silence too perfect to be natural. The tunnel became a pulse rather than a place. Pip felt Anna's hand tighten around his.

Then - breath.

Not his. Not hers.

A single inhale from the dark, slow and deliberate. Felt, not heard. The Inverted was still there. Watching. Feeding not on fear, but on attention. On recognition.

Pip's chest ached. He knew, instinctively, that light would not help them now. This was not a place where flashlights banished monsters. This was a place of frequencies - and theirs were now exposed.

He gripped the disc tighter.

It pulsed.

Another breath. This one closer.

Anna whispered, "Pip… what do we do?"

He wanted to say run. He wanted to say fight. But the words didn't come.

Instead, something deeper rose in him - not logic. Not memory.

A tone.

Low. Resonant. Inside him. Not spoken, but sung by the blood in his veins. A vibration that belonged to neither fear nor defiance. A remembering.

He hummed it.

Softly, like the earth beneath the city might be listening.

The disc in his hand shimmered.

And the air - the heavy, impossible air - began to loosen.

Somewhere behind the Inverted, another door opened.

And the dark… began to move.

Beyond the shifting black, something revealed itself - not with light, but with intention. A faint blue shimmer traced the outline of a structure ahead. Not a wall. Not a door. An interface.

A shape emerged from the gloom - angular, fluid, like glass grown from crystal and memory. Not built. Remembered.

Pip stepped forward slowly, as if drawn. The disc in his palm pulsed again - not to signal danger, but recognition. It was responding.

Anna stood beside him, transfixed. "What is it?"

He didn't speak. He simply moved toward it. As he neared, symbols along the surface began to awaken - slow illuminations, flickering like old stars stirred from slumber. One of them matched the spiral on the wall. Another shimmered into place as a mirrored sigil - the Signal Key. Not the full shape, but the beginning of it.

He raised the disc.

The interface reacted - a thin line split across its centre and widened into a hollow.

Inside, resting in still air as if weightless, was a small construct.

It resembled a compass. But instead of cardinal points, it held tones - harmonic bands etched into crystalline arms. It thrummed softly.

Anna whispered, "It's not pointing north."

"No," Pip replied. "It's pointing us."

The device pulsed again.

And the Inverted - behind them - did not cross the threshold.

It lingered at the edge. Watching.

Afraid.

The air between them and the Inverted was impossibly still. Time didn't move here. Or if it did, it moved like molasses - slow, sticky, unnatural.

Pip felt sweat trickle down the back of his neck. The compass hummed softly in his hand, but its glow didn't offer comfort - it offered urgency. Anna was pale, her jaw clenched, eyes darting between the artefact and the figure beyond the threshold.

"What is this?" she whispered. "What the hell is this?"

Pip shook his head. "I don't know. But whatever it is… it knows us."

The lights in the chamber flickered again - not electrically, but as if reacting to a tremor in frequency. The walls throbbed faintly. Pip could feel it under his ribs - the same way a subway train can be felt before it's heard.

Behind the Inverted, another movement.

A second figure. Less defined. More wrong.

Anna's hand gripped his wrist. "We have to go. Now."

He nodded, backing toward the door the artefact had opened - not knowing what lay beyond, but knowing the only way was through. They crossed the threshold - the interface shimmering one final time before going dark behind them.

The corridor beyond was curved and smooth, unlike the rest of the tunnel network - older, but somehow cleaner. The air was thicker here, warmer, humming with some subterranean current they couldn't trace.

They moved fast, but not recklessly - hearts hammering, breath sharp, the fear still crawling under their skin.

They weren't ready for this.

But it had begun anyway.

Behind them, the corridor shuddered.

It was subtle - the shift of pressure, the low groan of something ancient stirred into movement. But it was enough.

Anna turned sharply. "It's coming."

Pip didn't ask what. He didn't need to.

The compass in his hand pulsed, brighter now - its tones quickening into a rhythm almost like breath. The tunnel behind them dimmed further, as if light was being swallowed. The air felt

elastic - stretched by the weight of what was pursuing them.
They ran.

The tunnel twisted violently, the uneven floor threatening every step. Their torches flickered, throwing broken shadows across the stone. Pip stumbled, catching himself against the wall, the damp stone slick beneath his palm. Behind them, the sound grew sharper-not running, not shouting-but a relentless, rhythmic pursuit. A scraping hiss, half footsteps, half something older, hungering.

Ahead, the path split - left into a yawning corridor of absolute darkness, right into a narrow archway barely wide enough to squeeze through.

Pip hesitated a half-second too long.

A sound behind, sharp, close - like fingers brushing the floor where he had just been.

The compass throbbed and pointed right.

"Right!" Anna gasped, already pushing toward the arch.

Pip didn't hesitate.

He followed, twisting his body sideways to fit through the gap. The stone scraped his jacket, catching at his sleeve. Anna slipped once, a boot skidding on loose grit, and for a terrible second he thought she would fall back toward whatever was chasing them.

Pip lunged, grabbing her arm, yanking her through the archway just as a shadow, wrong in its shape, elongated, too fluid, spilled toward them from the tunnel behind.

He didn't dare look back.

Their breaths were ragged now, tearing in the heavy air. The passage on the other side of the arch tilted upward, a spiral staircase half-eaten by time.

Above them, a faint grate glimmered, the only hint of the outside world.

Anna scrambled up first, hands slipping once, catching herself with a grunt of effort. Pip jammed the crowbar into the rung below and boosted her. Her fingers scrabbled at the grate - locked tight.

Below, Pip felt the vibration through the stone - the pursuers were close, not sprinting, but advancing with a terrible, mechanical inevitability. A living tide.

Anna kicked the grate. Once. Twice. A crack. The old bolts gave a tortured groan but held.

A whisper brushed Pip's ear, not a word, but the sound of a mouth shaping his name. He looked down, and for one heartbeat, he saw a pale hand unfurling from the darkness just below, clawing upward, the skin stretched unnaturally thin over impossible joints.

"Anna!" he shouted. "Kick it again!"

She slammed her heel into the metal with a cry, this time the grate splintered open, just enough. She scrambled through the gap, twisting her body sideways, boots slipping against wet stone.

She reached down, Pip seized her hand, and together they heaved as the first of the shadow-things breached the stairwell below.

Something cold and damp brushed Pip's boot. He jerked upward with a burst of panic-fuelled strength, scraping his shoulders through the broken grate just as the hand below snapped shut on empty air. The grate slammed shut. Pip and Anna scrambled and lay over it to keep it closed.

After what felt like a lifetime, they collapsed onto the sloped tin roof of an old canal warehouse, its rusted gutters groaning under the weight of forgotten rain.

The compass still thrummed, but slower now. Settling.

Pip stared at it, then at Anna.

"What is this?" she whispered. "What have we started?"

He didn't answer. But something in the compass shifted - a soft projection. A flicker of light across its surface. A map.

Not just Manchester.

Coordinates.

Rome. Mumbai. Los Angeles. Tokyo. Paris. Jerusalem. Egypt... and more - each point glowing faintly on what appeared to be a circular world map - a disc, not the flattened distortion they'd known since childhood. The shape of the Earth, it seemed, had been part of the deception too.

They looked up from the compass, breath still ragged, the city pressing in around them - when they saw him.

The same homeless man. Standing at the edge of the rooftop as if he'd always been there, waiting. The air around him felt different, slightly thicker, like it resisted being noticed.

He didn't move toward them. He simply watched.

Then, in a voice deeper than before - not his own, but something speaking through him - he said:

"Fragments scattered across the sleeping spine of Earth. Anchored in places once sacred - now commercialised, fenced, or forgotten. The pyramids still hum beneath the sand. The catacombs still echo. The grid still pulses. Each fragment buried beneath monuments not of stone, but of silence. This is not a local rupture. It is planetary. It always was."

Pip stepped forward, confused. "What are we supposed to do?"

The man didn't answer right away. His eyes flicked to the compass.

Then:

"The first piece is not the end. It's the note that starts the harmony. Find the rest. Not just in cities - but in echoes. In scars. In silence. Trust what resonates, not what obeys."

Before they could speak again, he turned.

Gone. Not vanished, just… no longer there.

The rooftop felt suddenly colder. And quieter.

They staggered back from the rooftop's edge, breathless, the vastness of the open night pressing down like a weight. For a moment, Pip swayed, vertigo clawing at him. The world felt too wide, too thin, as if they had broken through an eggshell into a reality stretched too tight, waiting to tear.

Nothing out here felt real anymore.

The stars above looked painted. The buildings around them looked like flimsy theatre sets, backdrops for a dream they were no longer part of.

Anna spotted a maintenance ladder bolted to the wall. Without a word, she moved - urgency overtaking hesitation. She swung onto the ladder and began the climb down, her boots scraping the rusted metal.

Pip followed, the rungs freezing against his palms, the city below yawning wide and indifferent. Each step down felt heavier than the last, as if gravity itself was thicker now, reluctant to let them rejoin the surface world.

Finally, they dropped onto the slick cobbles of a backstreet, stillness hanging heavy, as if the alley itself was holding its breath. They didn't speak. They didn't need to.

The world had shifted.

And whatever waited above ground was no safer than what they'd left below.

The alley was damp, glistening under the amber glow of a distant streetlamp. They didn't pause. Didn't speak. Just kept moving - slipping through alleys and narrow streets until Pip's flat rose into view - the only place that still felt tethered to something real.

Inside, door locked, breath steadying, they sat.

Anna spoke first. "Do you think that was real?"

Pip looked at the compass. It was palm-sized, almost weightless, but with a density that seemed to bend the air around it. Its surface was not smooth - etched with spiralling grooves that pulsed faintly in shifting tones of blue and silver, like a memory trying to surface. Its outer rim rotated slowly, independently, whispering a geometry that seemed older than the Earth itself. It gave no answer - only the slow, rhythmic hum of something ancient remembering its name.

The sun rose slowly over Manchester, veiled by a sky too pale to be natural. The kind of morning where colour seemed optional - light without warmth, air without scent. It wasn't raining, but the streets were wet, as though the city had wept while no one was looking.

Inside Pip's flat, the blinds were still drawn. A low hum filled the room - not from a machine, but from the object that now rested on the table between them.

The compass.

It hadn't stopped pulsing. Not once. Its rhythm was softer now, but steady. Intentional.

Anna sat cross-legged on the floor, mug in hand, eyes locked on it. Pip leaned against the kitchen counter, staring not at the artefact, but at the space beyond it - the space where understanding had once lived.

"Do you feel different?" she asked quietly.

Pip took a moment. "Yes. Like... like something opened. And now there's no closing it."

Anna nodded. "Same. But it's not just the tunnels. It's everything. Ads. News. The city. I can feel it all - trying to put us back to sleep."

Pip pushed off from the counter. "That's what I used to do, you know," Pip said, almost to himself. "Dress up distractions as desires. Sell dreams that weren't real. Create need where there wasn't any." He looked over at her. "It hit me this morning... they never needed to lock the doors. Just keep us distracted."

The compass shimmered.

And somewhere outside, a low-flying plane cut across the sky, leaving a long, perfect trail that refused to dissolve.

Anna stood slowly, then turned to face him fully. "Pip... what you said about your work. That's all of it, isn't it? That's what they do. The corporations. The ad networks. The media. Pharma - they don't offer cures, they sell treatments. Not solutions, but subscriptions."

She took a breath, voice trembling but sure. "They manufacture problems and then rent us the illusion of relief. And we bought into it. All of it. Food. Fear. Finance. Even hope."

She stepped closer to the table, eyes locked on the compass.

Pip joined her, slowly lowering himself into the chair opposite.

"There's an entire system built on keeping us just uncertain enough to comply," he said. "Advertisers feeding on insecurity.

Financial institutions dangling debt like freedom. Health industries treating symptoms instead of causes because healing isn't profitable."

Anna nodded. "And education. Conditioning dressed as knowledge. Obedience over curiosity. They don't teach us to question - they teach us to comply. And if we don't… we're labelled, dismissed, medicated."

Pip ran his hand across his face. "And the worst part? We did it. I did it. All those campaigns I ran - they weren't selling products. They were selling identity. Lack. Want."

Anna's voice was softer now, but cut sharper. "They convince us to fear ageing, hunger, stillness, each other. And every solution they sell ties us deeper to the very fear they created."

She paused. "Fear has become the fuel. And we… we've been trained to refuel ourselves."

They sat in silence for a moment, the only sound the low thrum of the compass - steady, patient.

Anna lifted her gaze. "It's time we stopped reacting… and started remembering."

As if in answer, the compass shimmered again - brighter this time. Then it projected something new: a symbol - circular, ancient, layered. It hovered above the table, spinning slowly.

Pip leaned forward. "That wasn't there before."

Anna tilted her head, watching it spin. The symbol pulsed gently - ancient, layered - and in that moment, it stirred something beneath the surface of her thoughts. Not quite memory. More like an echo.

A forgotten familiarity. Something that belonged to her, but had been taken long ago.

It looked… familiar.

The symbol shifted, dissolving into a series of coordinates, then pulsed in time with a faint, low tone.

"It's showing us where to go," Pip said.

But as the symbol faded, the atmosphere changed. The lights in the flat flickered - just once, but enough. Outside, a car alarm triggered… then abruptly cut off.

Anna stepped back from the table. "They know where we are."

They ran to the window.

The street below was too still - the kind of stillness that didn't feel like peace, but pause. A black car was parked opposite, engine ticking, windows dark.

No one got in. No one got out.

Just presence. Waiting.

Pip pulled back from the window slowly. "That wasn't there last night."

Anna didn't answer, but the tension in her shoulders spoke for her. The compass on the table let out a single pulse - not bright, not loud, but sharp. A tone that seemed to cut through the static of the moment.

Pip turned, crossed the room quickly, and grabbed his laptop. "Let's check the coordinates. See where it wants us to go."

As he typed, the symbol flickered again - now paired with a faint shimmer across the map it projected. A location sharpened. Letters formed.

ROME.

Anna exhaled, quiet and long. "It's beginning, isn't it?"

Pip nodded slowly, eyes still locked on the screen. "We're not just remembering. We're being called."

He looked around the flat - suddenly too small, too known, like a skin he'd already outgrown.

"We should go," he said. "Before the next move isn't ours to make."

Anna's eyes flicked once more to the car below, then back to Pip.

Anna hesitated, her voice lower now. "I'm scared, Pip."

He nodded, stepping closer. "Me too. But there's no unseeing it now. No pretending it's nothing."

She looked down at the compass one last time, still pulsing with quiet insistence.

"We've seen the edge of it," she whispered. "We have to go through."

Pip held her gaze.

"Then we go to Rome. Whatever's there... is already waiting for us."

The black car was still there.

Not just waiting now - watching. A presence, unmistakable. It hadn't moved in hours.

Anna's fingers curled tighter around the compass in her coat pocket. Its pulse had slowed, but not stopped. Like it was waiting too.

Pip slung the duffel bag over his shoulder, locking the flat behind them. Neither said a word.

They reached the curb, the morning too quiet, the air charged.

As Pip unlocked the car, Anna glanced back once more at the motionless vehicle across the street. No movement. No threat. But it still felt wrong.

Inside their own car, the doors shut with a clunk that seemed to echo. Pip slid the key into the ignition.

The engine roared to life.

The radio came on automatically.

"-confirmed the death of international pop icon Lysa Rey early this morning. The star was found in the rooftop pool of her Los Angeles home. Authorities have not released a statement, but sources suggest..."

The words from the radio lingered in the air like smoke.

"...in the rooftop pool of her Los Angeles home..."

Anna stared at the dash, frozen. "Lysa Rey," she said quietly. "That's the third one in three months."

Pip didn't take his eyes off the road. "All found alone. All in water. Always the 'tragic artist narrative.'"

Anna turned to him slowly. "Drowning as purification. It's a script.

A ritual."

Pip nodded grimly. "First it was Corin Vale in London. Then Niko in Tokyo. Now Lysa Rey. All icons. All adored. All useful until they weren't."

He paused. "It's not suicide. It's sacrifice. Televised transformation. A public farewell wrapped in false mourning, while the real message is for those who can read it."

Anna's breath caught. "And the masses just absorb it... feel the sadness, then move on."

"Exactly," Pip said. "Because the pain's engineered. Delivered. Designed to reinforce the myth that even the brightest lights must burn out. That resistance is futile. That truth kills."

They sat with the weight of it, the car now gliding through Manchester's hushed streets.

Anna reached for the volume, but not to turn it off.

She turned it up.

Because they both knew - these weren't suicides. Not all of them. Not anymore.

Pip pulled out into the empty street.

And the black car did nothing at all.

Except remain.

The road to the airport was longer than it should've been. Or maybe it just felt that way. The silence in the car wasn't empty - it was saturated with signals they could no longer ignore.

Before they even reached the motorway, Pip took a silent turn off towards Didsbury.

"Need your passport," he said quietly. "And anything else you don't want to regret leaving."

Anna gave a quick nod. She hadn't planned on crossing borders today- not physical ones, and certainly not whatever strange threshold they'd just stepped across.

Her flat was still as she left it - a place that suddenly felt like a version of herself she'd already begun to outgrow. She moved through it quickly but deliberately, collecting her passport, phone charger, her dream notebook, and a small box of old polaroids. She lingered for a breath too long before taking it. She couldn't say why.

Standing by the mirror at the hallway door, she caught her reflection and tilted her head.

"I don't know who I'm going to be next," she murmured.

"You'll remember," Pip replied, already loading her holdall into the boot.

They merged back onto the main road. Manchester was starting to stretch and stir - the quiet before a false normality.

The skies above were already etched with long, pale aircraft trails - unnatural in their precision. Anna caught sight of them first.

"They've been busy," she murmured.

Pip didn't reply, but the way his fingers tightened on the wheel said enough.

Inside the terminal, it was business as usual - families dragging suitcases, announcements echoing overhead, the soft murmur of machines scanning barcodes and boarding passes. But something about it felt off.

Almost too normal.

Just before security, Anna ducked into a small boutique near the check-in desks. The clothes she'd brought were enough, but she wanted something that fit this moment.

She grabbed a set of simple clothes: a lightweight jacket, black jeans, two cotton tops, and a grey scarf. All chosen quickly, instinctively. Clothes that wouldn't stand out.

As she changed in the cramped fitting room, she looked at herself in the mirror - not for vanity, but to witness something subtle: she was becoming someone else. Or maybe someone she'd once been.

They passed security. Waited at the gate.

When their flight was finally called, Pip looked at Anna. "Still scared?"

She nodded. "But I'd be more afraid to stay."

They walked down the jet bridge together, stepping from one version of the world into another.

The engines rumbled to life beneath the wings.

The Gate Beneath

Anna leaned her head back against the seat, eyes half-closed, then shifted in her seat and unzipped the small holdall beneath her feet. She pulled out the box of polaroids and passed it to Pip without a word.

"You should see these," she said softly. "I don't know why I brought them. Just… felt right."

Pip took the box gently, like it contained something fragile - which in a way, it did.

He flipped through them slowly - moments frozen in time.

A younger Anna, laughing at a market somewhere sunlit. A street performer in Istanbul. A blurred shot of stone steps leading down into shadow - somewhere ancient. He paused on that one. Something about it tugged at him.

Anna opened her eyes just enough to notice. "That one," she said softly. "I don't remember taking it."

Pip studied it again. "But you kept it."

"I always felt like it meant something," she whispered. "Like I'd been there before. Or was supposed to go."

He tucked the photo carefully into the back of his notebook.

Outside the window, clouds began to swallow the plane. Light flickered across the wing.

Pip closed his eyes for a moment - but what came wasn't sleep.

It began with vibration.

Not of the plane - but inside him. A hum, low and resonant,

curling beneath his ribs like a waking memory. The darkness behind his eyelids shifted.

And then he was somewhere else.

Stone beneath his feet. Dry heat. The sound of slow wind pushing sand across worn carvings. A temple - not ruined, but waiting. Columns rose like giants, marked with symbols he didn't recognise, yet understood.

At the centre stood a figure cloaked in white, head bowed, hands outstretched. In their palm: the same compass. But it was older. Cracked. Singing in a tone that wasn't audible, more like it was alive in the bones.

Pip tried to speak, but his voice didn't travel. Instead, the figure looked up.

It was him.

Or a version of him. Eyes older. Face carved by time and knowledge. A scar beneath the left eye - identical to the one Pip didn't yet have.

And the other Pip - the one in the dream - simply said:

"You are the signal."

The desert pulsed with light. A tremor ran through Pip's chest, sharp, staggering, like something locked inside him had been waiting for those words.

Memory stirred without form. A pull older than blood, deeper than thought.

For one breathless moment, he felt everything, the loss, the exile, the calling, layered across lifetimes he could almost remember but couldn't yet hold.

A sudden ache of recognition bloomed beneath his ribs.

A surge of forgotten purpose.

A fear too deep for words.

The desert blurred into light, and Pip snapped awake.

The cabin lights flickered.

He blinked hard, heartbeat thudding louder than the engine's hum. Across the aisle, a child stopped mid-laugh, as if some subtle frequency had passed through them all.

He glanced at Anna.

She was already watching him. "You saw something," she said. Not a question.

He nodded slowly, then glanced out the window - and frowned.

The clouds had parted, but not in the usual scattering patterns. Instead, a single long corridor of perfectly clear sky stretched ahead of the aircraft like a tunnel. Too symmetrical. Too deliberate.

Anna leaned across. "What is that?"

Pip shook his head. "I don't know… but it's not weather."

The compass inside his jacket gave a low pulse - steady, like a heartbeat - as if to say: this is part of it too.

The wheels touched down with a jolt. Rome.

Part two:
THROUGH THE VEIL

Some books are not chosen. They choose.
You felt this one before you saw it.
You arrived not by search, but by signal.
Let this be the one you remember before you know why.

Chapter 16:
Rome - The Inversion Core

As they taxied to the gate, Anna looked out and whispered, "It doesn't feel like arrival. It feels like transition."

The cabin burst into that strange, half-awake murmur that always follows landing - rustling bags, relieved sighs, phones pinging, the ritual of disconnection and reconnection.

But Pip remained still for a moment longer, hand resting on his chest where the compass was.

Anna reached across and touched his hand. "You okay?"

He nodded. "Yeah. Just… not sure the dream's over."

Anna tilted her head. "Which dream?"

Pip's gaze stayed fixed on the seat in front. "The one we've all been trapped inside. The one they scripted."

Outside the window, the morning light was bright and golden. But the glow didn't feel warm - it felt filtered.

They disembarked slowly, moving with the crowd but not of it.

Fiumicino Airport unfolded before them, all gleaming walkways, sterile lighting, and faint echoes of announcements layered in three languages. There was something unsettling in its precision. Too polished. Too placeless.

And as they stepped onto Italian soil, the compass gave another soft pulse.

A new rhythm.

A new direction.

The walk from arrivals to the station beneath the terminal was long - too long - and lined with design choices that didn't feel like accidents. Mosaic eyes embedded in the floor. A pattern of concentric circles in the ceiling tiles. Statues positioned just slightly off-centre, always watching but never quite aligned.

Anna noticed it first. "This place… it's like a message hidden in plain sight."

Pip looked around, the hairs on his arms rising. "Everywhere you look - duality. Sun and moon. Masks. Keys. Serpents. Nothing here is just art."

Anna turned to him. "Why duality? Why always two sides?"

Pip paused. "Because the illusion depends on contrast. Light needs dark. Good needs evil. They show us opposites, not to balance, but to divide. To make us choose between false options while they hide what's real."

He lowered his voice, glancing around instinctively, even though no one was listening.

"The Vatican didn't just shape belief. They shaped reality itself. And most people have no idea how deep it runs."

Anna leaned in slightly. Pip continued, voice low and steady, each word a slow unmasking.

"They own the largest archive of forbidden knowledge on Earth - the Vatican Secret Archives. Over fifty miles of shelving, stretching under Rome, holding lost histories, banned gospels, ancient sciences, true maps of the Earth. And only a few, carefully vetted scholars are ever allowed inside, and even then, they can't just explore. They have to request specific documents by name… meaning they must already know exactly what they're looking for. It's not secrecy. It's structured amnesia."

His eyes darkened slightly.

"And they didn't stop at hiding truth. They rewrote time itself. The Gregorian calendar didn't just fix a leap year problem, it shattered humanity's natural alignment with the stars, the moon, the seasons. The old calendars - Mayan, Vedic, Druidic… followed energy flows. When they broke that, they broke the way we experienced reality. Time became linear. Compliant. Measurable. And they put themselves in charge of the clock."

Anna listened, silent, but her breath had changed - slower, heavier, as if she was carrying the weight of something she hadn't known she was holding.

Pip pressed on.

"And while they sold the illusion of a spinning globe and distant stars to the public, behind the scenes they were building observatories. Mapping the heavens. Preparing for a reality they already knew, a reality they hid. Their own astronomers admit extraterrestrial life wouldn't contradict the faith. Why? Because it never did."

"Their own astronomers admit extraterrestrial life wouldn't contradict the faith. Why? Because it never did. In 2008, Father José Gabriel Funes, the Vatican's chief astronomer, told L'Osservatore Romano - their own newspaper - that believing in extraterrestrials posed no threat to Catholic doctrine. He called them 'our brothers and sisters of creation.'

Not conspiracy. Not fringe theory. Official. Public. Documented.

The Guardian, BBC News, even Reuters ran it, and still, most of the world slept through it.

Because the media isn't there to awaken anyone.

It's there to manage perception - to present revelations like background noise, safely wrapped in authority, drained of urgency.

The Guardian. The BBC. Reuters. CNN. The New York Times. The Washington Post.

Different flags. Same architects. All owned, steered, and sanitised by the same hands that write the scripts behind the veil.

They weren't preparing the faithful for revelation.

They were preparing the faithful for containment.

Because if humanity ever remembered that the universe is full, alive, waiting - the whole lie of isolation, hierarchy, and control would crumble overnight.

So they didn't deny the stars.

They fenced them."

His voice lowered further.

"And they weren't the only ones. The Freemasons mirrored them - secret brotherhoods claiming light, but operating in shadows. Look at the architecture of every major capital city - Washington, London, Paris, Rome. You'll find the same alignments. Obelisks, domes, false axes of power. Cities designed not just for aesthetics, but for energetic domination. Resonance control."

He gestured around at the sterile airport walls, the endless flow of distracted travellers.

"Masons and priests. Builders and priests. Architects and engineers of belief. Two sides of the same hidden hand. Freemasons carved the symbols into the bones of the cities; the Vatican encrypted the meaning behind ritual and scripture. One shaped the mind. The other shaped the ground beneath it. Different flags. Same cathedral."

Anna's voice was barely a whisper. "And we're trapped inside it."

Pip nodded slowly.

"Until we remember. Until we see that the grid isn't just metal and wire. It's psychic. Spiritual. Built to harvest attention. Built to stop awakening before it can spread."

He tapped the compass gently inside his jacket.

"And we're walking straight into the mouth of the machine that made sure the dream never broke."

Anna stared down the sterile hallway ahead of them, the edges of the world starting to blur.

"Then we don't stop," she said quietly. "We don't look away."

Pip nodded once.

"No. We tear it open."

He gestured around. "It's an old game. Opposing forces. Controlled narratives. Duality keeps the loop spinning - but the truth is always outside the loop."

They moved through the airport, the clues compounding. Eyes on every mural. Serpents twined in metal railings. A calendar etched into glass that wasn't Gregorian.

"It's about time," Pip said suddenly. "They control how we

experience time itself."

Anna frowned. "What do you mean?"

"They rewrote the calendar once, cutting us from the natural rhythms of the stars, the tides, the turning of the seasons. It wasn't just a correction - it was a severing. Every clock since then has ticked to their design, every ritual of work and rest bound to their script. And this place… this Vatican… it isn't just stone and ceremony. It's built on that fracture, an empire balanced on the wound they made in time itself."

He gestured to a ceiling panel shaped like an incomplete keyhole. "It's not just spiritual control. It's a grip on time itself. If they bend time, they bend reality."

Anna looked unsettled. "I'm not sure I can fully comprehend what you're saying, the vastness of the lie, so, what are we walking into?"

"Maybe the most inverted place on Earth," Pip said. "Where the original fracture began."

Anna turned slowly, her gaze following the sterile hallway ahead. "And we're just walking straight into it?"

Pip gave a slight nod. "We have to. This place doesn't just house power, it anchors the illusion. If we want to shift the dream, we start here."

The sound around them softened - voices became echoes, lights a little too white, their steps more muffled than they should've been. As if reality - and all of humanity woven into its spell - was holding its breath.

The compass pulsed again, faint but insistent. It wasn't pointing toward the Vatican's front entrance, it turned them toward the old spine of the city, a route known more in myth than map.

They followed.

Toward the Vault.

Toward the Eye.

Toward the centre of the wound.

They passed through shadowed alleys older than memory. Churches repurposed from pagan sites. Pillars that once honoured Saturn and now bore saints. Nothing here was what it seemed.

As they neared the edge of Vatican territory, Pip slowed. "The Eye isn't just metaphor. It's here. Buried. And it's watching back."

Anna's voice was quiet. "Then we keep going."

And they did.

Because to heal a wound, you have to go straight to its source.

And Rome - for all its splendour - was the scar that never closed.

The entrance came quietly. No grand archway. Just an aged door recessed into a crumbling wall behind a rusted gate that once bore the seal of an order now erased from public memory.

The compass thrummed.

Pip touched the door. It opened - not from his push, but as if it had been waiting.

Beyond, the air thickened. The light bent. And the descent began again - not just into the earth, but into everything they'd forgotten.

They stepped into silence.

The passage sloped downward, not a staircase, but a slow, inexorable pull into the earth. Each step felt heavier, as if the gravity here was older, more possessive.

The air wasn't just ancient - it pressed against their skin, thick with the friction of buried memory, the resistance of something that had never meant to be disturbed.

Unlit torches lined the walls. But there was light - soft, ambient, as if the walls themselves remembered fire.

Symbols etched in stone began to shift as they walked. Latin gave way to Greek. Then older scripts. Scripts neither of them recognised. Some flickered faintly. Others pulsed as if reacting to their presence.

Anna whispered, "This place… it's alive."

Pip nodded. "It's not a tunnel. It's a corridor of remembrance."

Deeper still, the incline opened into a chamber - circular, vast, and impossibly silent. At its centre: a black stone door. Four concentric rings marked it, each etched with symbols and divided into segments like a cosmic lock. In the middle: a handprint.

Anna stepped forward.

The compass buzzed.

She froze. "It's not mine."

Pip moved past her. He pressed his hand to the stone - and the stone responded, reading something beyond fingerprints. Something encoded in him. A frequency. A memory. A right to enter.

The symbols flared.

The rings spun once.

And the door opened.

Beyond, a vast hall stretched out, rows upon rows of sealed glass cases, crystal tubes, tomes bound in strange materials. Projected holograms shimmered to life for seconds, then faded.

Anna's breath caught. "We're inside the Vault."

Pip gestured left, toward a spiral stair descending even deeper.

They followed it down, into a dome-shaped room humming with a frequency too low to hear but strong enough to feel.

In its centre stood the Chronovisor.

Not a machine. Not exactly. More like an altar of resonance - crystal, metal, something in between. Its surface shimmered with layers of unformed memory.

Anna stepped close. "They say Ernetti built this… but it feels older."

Pip answered softly. "He didn't invent it. He uncovered it."

He reached out.

The Chronovisor awakened.

It wasn't built by one man. Not truly. Father Ernetti may have assembled the modern framework in the 20th century - a Benedictine monk working in secret, blending ancient texts with forbidden science - but what he found was far older. The original interface had roots in the pre-Deluge world. Atlantis, some say. Others whisper of Lemuria, or a forgotten civilisation that never touched written history.

Fragments had been found in Mesopotamian ruins, others encoded into the walls of the Great Pyramid. Ernetti's genius was not creation - it was recovery. A piecing back together of what had been splintered across ages. He reassembled what had been scattered. Reawakened what had been buried. But the energy it required... the price it demanded... that was never written down. And now, standing before it, Pip and Anna felt the full weight of that legacy stir.

Light expanded, surrounding them in a sphere.

Not a screen. A living archive.

Visions bloomed: a crucifixion - but not the one they knew. A council of men burning scrolls under the stars. A craft descending over desert sands. Atlantean priests encoding glyphs into crystal.

And then... Anna.

Not as she was.

She stood on a white tower, holding a compass. Her eyes glowed with something more than memory - a resonance, as if she carried the echo of lives she hadn't lived but still remembered.

The vision shifted, revealing three figures: the man, the woman, and the blackbird. They were not bound by time. Archetypes, perhaps, echoes of something eternal. The man bore the mark of fire on his hand. The woman radiated a strange stillness, like moonlight held in form. And the blackbird... the blackbird pulsed with impossible intelligence, its eyes mirrors, its wings folded like veils of knowing. They weren't just watching. They were remembering through them, using Pip and Anna as vessels, conduits through which long-forgotten echoes could rise again. It wasn't observation. It was reactivation - memory flowing not backward, but forward, into the present, reclaiming its place in the now.

And it was personal.

This wasn't just collective memory stirring - it was lineage. The resonance in Anna's eyes, the mark in Pip's hand... these weren't metaphors. They were inherited. Encoded. Passed down through bloodlines that had once stood at the threshold of remembrance - and had been silenced. Until now.

They weren't chosen at random. They were chosen because they remembered.

Watching.
Seeing them.
Recognition. And warning.
Then darkness.
They staggered back.
Anna's voice trembled. "They see us."

Pip turned. Shelves loomed behind them - scrolls in silk, bones in glass, a disc marked in spirals. The same spiral as on the disc in his pocket.

The Vault hummed.

Pip lifted the disc from its cradle.

The Vault vibrated once - low, resonant, almost like a heartbeat - and somewhere in the thick stone above, something clicked.

A silent alarm.

Not a siren. Not a blare. A frequency, one designed for the ones who listened differently.

A robed figure at the Chronovisor moved.

Not rushed. Not panicked. Deliberate.

The figure raised its hand, not in warning, but in summons.

Lights along the corridor shifted, a soft pulse once... then red.

Pip grabbed Anna's wrist. "Run."

They sprinted back toward the way they came, the passageways unfamiliar now, the walls seeming to twist as if the Vault itself didn't want them to leave.

Above, the Vatican was awakening.

Heavy boots thundered. Doors groaned open. Swiss Guards who weren't in the colourful frills the world knew, these were combat uniforms. Black tactical gear, body armour, visors down, rifles raised.

The Vatican's real army. The one not shown in the tourist brochures.

No warnings. No calls to halt. Just immediate, brutal pursuit.

Anna gasped as they rounded a corner, only to find a team descending, rifles slung low, eyes masked beneath polished helmets.

"Back!" Pip barked, wrenching her sideways into a side corridor barely wide enough for two people.

The disc in his hand pulsed wildly, vibrating with urgency.

A bullet sparked against the wall behind them.

Not warning shots…real ones.

They crashed through a rusted maintenance hatch, tumbling into a lower service tunnel half-flooded with old rainwater. The stink of old stone and damp rot filled the air.

Pip hauled Anna up, but she stumbled, crying out.

Her ankle twisted sharply under her.

"Anna…"

She bit down hard, face pale. "I can run."

The Death Chamber

Pip barely had time to register the vibration in his palm before the world snapped shut.

A metallic click echoed from somewhere behind the walls. A pressure change. Not mystical, mechanical.

Then...

The thud of boots.

Anna turned. "They're coming."

He shoved the disc into his jacket with a sharp motion, eyes locking onto Anna's. "Take it and go," he growled, his voice low and urgent. "No matter what happens, you run. Do not look back."

Anna froze, confusion flickering in her expression.

"Pip, "

He took a single step toward her, his face tight but his eyes softening just enough to let the truth slip through. "Please, Anna," he said, voice edged with urgency but layered with love. "You have to trust me. Go now. I'll be right behind you. I promise."

Then the steel returned to his voice. "Now. Please, go. While you still can."

"What?"

"Anna, go!"

Before she could argue, the sound of groaning metal tore through the chamber as a steel panel in the far wall lurched open, revealing a darkness thicker than shadow. Black-armoured figures surged from it, Swiss Guard combat operators in black ops uniform. Silent. Precise. Expressionless beneath matte visors.

The muzzle of the lead rifle swept the room with mechanical intent, locking first on Pip, then Anna.

Her breath hitched.

Then the world cracked open, a sharp bark in Italian shattered the thick silence like a gunshot, followed by the scrape of boots launching forward. One of the black-armoured men surged ahead, rifle raised, eyes locked. The air turned electric, panic thudding in Anna's chest. Dust trembled loose from the stones above as if the building itself recoiled from what was about to happen.

Anna turned and bolted, her footsteps echoing against cold stone, the air thick with the stench of oil, sweat, and centuries-old dust. The flicker of torchlight caught on her hair as she disappeared into the corridor's throat, chased by the sound of boots and the storm she couldn't outrun.

Pip turned, arms raised, not in surrender, in instinct.

A rifle butt drove into his ribs.

He folded.

A second strike cracked the side of his head.

He dropped to one knee, vision white-edged, but still conscious. Rough hands wrenched his arms behind his back. Plastic ties cut into his wrists. A black bag snapped over his head, pulling tight against his mouth.

He didn't call for Anna. He wouldn't give them that.

He just let her run.

Praying she would break free. That she'd vanish into the ancient arteries of Rome and escape the noose tightening around them both. That the horrors he was about to face would not touch her. The moment stretched, splintered, then shattered, and still, he held the hope like a final breath.

And then he was dragged.

No words. No explanation. Just the sound of boots, breath, and old stone.

They didn't take him up. They didn't take him out.

They dragged him sideways, through the Vatican's bones.

The ground changed beneath his knees, cobbles to flagstones, flagstones to packed earth.

He caught snatches of voices in Latin, a barked command in Italian. The sound of old hinges. The reek of mould, stone dust, stale air.

Eventually, the bag was yanked from his head.

He blinked hard, eyes recoiling from the brutal sting of bare bulb light. It hung from the low ceiling like an interrogation sun, swaying slightly on a rusted chain, casting hard shadows across the peeling stone walls. The light was sickly, yellowed, humming with a flickering pulse that made the darkness seem alive. For a moment, all he could see were shapes burned into his retinas, blotches and ghosts, as the foul, metallic tang of blood filled his mouth. The air was damp, clinging to his skin with the mildew of centuries. Somewhere behind the glare, a door groaned closed like a tomb lid.

Narrow corridor. Curved ceiling. A place built to hide escape, now reversed.

The Passetto di Borgo.

He'd read about it, the Pope's secret escape tunnel. A fortified walkway used for centuries. A secret artery linking the Apostolic Palace to Castel Sant'Angelo.

Only this time, it was being used to contain, not protect.

They marched him in silence. Rifles always close. No ceremony. No chants. Just the crunch of boots and the low hum of security lights wired into a system that shouldn't exist in a medieval tunnel.

They reached a reinforced door embedded in the wall.

One guard punched a code into a keypad mounted beneath a crucifix.

The door opened.

They descended again, this time into real history, into a place where time had not passed so much as gathered.

The Vatican Scavi. The Necropolis.

Beneath the glittering basilicas and marble façades of the Vatican lies a shadowed underworld, a vast Roman burial ground sealed for centuries, layered with tombs and forgotten rites. Officially, it is accessible only to a limited number of visitors each day under tightly controlled conditions. But there are corridors and chambers beyond the sanctioned routes, hidden behind false walls and gated crypts, places that exist off-record, even to most within the Church.

This was where they took him.

This was no guided tour.

Pip was certain, in every dragging step, in every bruising grip on his shoulder, that they were leading him like some latter-day criminal to his execution. There was no preamble, no attempt to justify or explain. The silence from his captors wasn't cold indifference, it was doctrine. Practised. Efficient. Like a system designed not only to extract information but to erase the existence of those who had come too close to forbidden truths. Not metaphorical, not imagined. The silence wasn't ceremonial. It was calculated. Efficient. As if the Church had rehearsed this routine many times before, just never for someone like him. The further they led him, the colder the air grew, the more final the walls felt. Every flickering light, every echoing bootstep pressed into him the same brutal message: you were not meant to see this, and now, you are not meant to leave. Not ever. That truth clung to the walls like the damp, soaked into the mortar like confession, unspoken but absolute. This place wasn't just for containment. It was for disappearance.

It was a descent into curated silence. A part of the Vatican that doesn't appear on maps, where bodies had been buried and secrets sealed under centuries of marble and denial. Here, whispers were louder than prayers, and the air itself seemed complicit in the long burial of truth.

The room was small, no more than three metres across, a stone box dressed in rot. The concrete walls were slick with condensation and streaked with the grime of forgotten centuries. A rusted floor drain yawned beneath him like a mouth that had swallowed screams. Chains dangled from wall brackets, clinking faintly whenever he shifted, each one thick with rust and memory. They weren't props. They were used. No windows. No echo. Just the press of stone, thick, ancient, unfeeling. It felt like a gladiator movie, the kind where the cell is carved from the bones of empire, and the only thing waiting outside is violence. This was not a place for questions. It was a place for endings.

Just a camera. And a chair.

They cut his restraints with a blade, shoved him down, then left.
The door sealed with a clang that wasn't just heavy, it was final.
Pip sat there, blood trickling from his mouth, ribs screaming, wrists raw.
He tried to breathe.
This wasn't an interrogation chamber.
This was a holding cell for people who were never meant to be found again.

Anna didn't stop running.
She didn't know how far she'd gone. Only that the corridors twisted. That the light was dying. That every echo behind her could be the boots of men who didn't speak warnings, only fired.
When she finally stopped, it was because her lungs were tearing, her ankle searing, her body shaking. She pressed herself into the curve of an ancient archway, cloaked in dust and shadow, and forced herself to go still.

The silence throbbed. Not peace, just the absence of gunfire.

She closed her eyes. Thought of Pip. The way he looked at her before he turned.

No.

She wouldn't leave him to rot beneath a city that had buried its sins under grandeur, monuments polished to a blinding sheen, hiding rot in their foundation. Every stone told a story that had been rewritten. Every relic sanctified by the same hands that had silenced the original truth. The deeper she went, the more she felt it: this place wasn't sacred. It was curated guilt layered in gold leaf.

She limped through the ancient corridor, trying to retrace the path back to light, to noise, to anything above. Her breath rasped against the silence, and every step brought the press of centuries heavier on her chest. She turned a corner, and that's when it happened.

A hand clamped over her mouth from behind.

She twisted hard, fighting against the weight, but he was too strong. He dragged her backwards into a recess between the stones, away from the flicker of her torchlight. The cold wall pressed into her spine.

"Quiet," the man hissed in her ear. "If they hear you, we both stay buried."

He released her just enough for her to turn.

He was gaunt, older, robed in a tattered cassock, his eyes yellowed by lamplight and fury. Ink stained his hands. His breath smelled of wine, metal, and bitterness.

"What are you doing down here?" he snapped.

"I'm looking for someone. They took him."

"Then you're too late," he muttered. "You don't come down here unless you're meant to vanish."

She stared at him. "Who are you?"

The man scoffed. "Who I *was* doesn't matter. They made sure of that."

He looked around, voice dropping. "My name is Domenico Ferraro. I was a Jesuit once. An archivist. Then I started asking questions about the Council of 1685. About the books removed from the Index, the records sealed by the Black Congregation. I found one. I read it."

"What did it say?" He looked her dead in the eye.

"It was a copy of *The Treatise on the Resurrection* - the Epistle to Rheginos. The Church claims it was destroyed with the Gnostic texts, but they preserved a copy, hidden in a vault so deep most archivists don't even know it exists. And what it said…" He drew a breath. "It overturned everything. It said the resurrection isn't a miracle that happens after you die, it's something that must happen *while you live*. That if you don't awaken now, you will 'receive nothing' later. That resurrection *is the revelation of what is,* the transformation of consciousness itself." He leaned closer, voice lowering.

"Another text - *The Gospel of Philip* - was even clearer. It called those who wait for death to rise again 'an error.' It said the true resurrection is *to remember who you are before the world taught you to forget.*

Not a body emerging from a tomb, but a soul rising from ignorance."

A pause.

He shook his head. "They condemned me to this place. To catalogue scrolls in vaults no one remembers. No sunlight. No clocks. Just centuries of secrets. And now… now you want to break someone out?"

Anna nodded.

A cruel smile tugged at his lips. "Then maybe it's time I stopped burying their lies… and started unearthing them."

He slipped through the alleys like a phantom, shadows clinging to his cassock. Ferraro's voice cut through the dark as he moved along with purpose, every step a muttered curse against the corridors he knew too well. He didn't look back.

"Stay close," he said. "If you fall behind, I won't wait. These paths forget people." The limp slowed her, but she moved with purpose, past shuttered shops and graffiti-covered stone. When she reached the ruins near the Mithraic temple, the air changed, stiller, heavier. The door was iron. No handle. Just a blank slab, old and grimy. "Come. Inside. Now."

Ferraro's apartment was a tomb dressed as a study.

The air reeked of mould, ink, and something older, the rot of forgotten pages and broken vows. Shelves sagged under the weight of decaying books. Crucifixes stripped of gold leaned at drunken angles. Scrolls curled like the dead. On the walls, sepia photographs of ruins stared down, each a quiet indictment of the stories never told.

Anna stood still in the doorway, as if stepping too far might fracture the quiet pact this place had with time.

"I need to find someone," she said, her voice barely audible.

Ferraro's eyes narrowed. "Who?"

"His name is Pip," she said. "They dragged him underground, through the Passetto. I think he's being held somewhere beneath the Scavi, but deeper."

Ferraro didn't move. His eyes stayed fixed on her, unblinking.

"Then he's below the Necropolis," he said flatly. "Where the light doesn't reach. Off-record containment. No guards. No clocks. No chance."

Anna didn't flinch. "I don't need a chance. I need access."

He turned, slow as sleep, and moved toward a warped floorboard in the corner.

"Quiet now," he muttered. "No names. No plans. This room listens."

With a grunt, he pried up the board and drew out a rusted brass tube wrapped in linen.

"It's not a map," he said. "It's a confession."

He unrolled it slowly, a palimpsest of ancient diagrams overlaid with Vatican engineering grids. Hidden stairwells. Sealed arches. Collapsed crypts used to store the unwanted. Places not meant to be walked again.

He tapped a symbol near the margin.

"I was never supposed to see this. But they forgot one thing: isolation makes a man listen. Years in these catacombs, years cataloguing their rot, it wasn't punishment. It was preparation. I thought they buried me. But maybe they were just sharpening me for this."

He turned to her, the edge of his voice ragged.

"Why are you here? What made you think you could enter this... and then leave it untouched? People don't just walk into the Vatican's underbelly and walk out."

Anna hesitated. "Because he remembers something they want forgotten."

Ferraro stared a moment longer, then nodded once.

"Good. Then let's take something back."

He rolled the parchment with shaking hands and stuffed it beneath his robes.

"Follow. I'll get you in. But if we're caught... no prayers will reach this deep."

What seemed like hours later, the catacombs swallowed her.

The descent had been slow, suffocating. Air thick with mildew and memory, the walls slick with time. Ferraro led the way, his torchlight low, careful not to draw attention from above. His steps were sure, even graceful, as though he had walked this route a thousand times before. Perhaps he had. She followed close, each breath shallow, every nerve stretched thin beneath her sweat-soaked skin.

Her hands were trembling now, not with fear, but with something deeper. The weight of the vow she carried. Unspoken but known... she would do all she could to find him.

They continued through a maze of shadow and stone, twisting, turning. Sometimes the path widened, allowing them to stand tall. Other times they crawled on elbows, shoulders scraping against jagged walls, silence pressing in like a weight. Ferraro led without hesitation, his memory of these tunnels as intimate as breath. He touched certain stones, avoided others, reading the space like a script hidden from the surface world.

Now and then, Anna would glance sideways at him. There was resolve in his jaw, but something gentler in his eyes, a grief softened by purpose.

Once, they stopped at a small alcove, lit faintly by his torchlight catching the gleam of a half-buried mosaic. Ferraro knelt briefly, placed two fingers to the design, then rose again without explanation. She didn't ask.

They passed beneath collapsed archways, stepped over bones that time had forgotten, and moved through chambers that smelled of ash and salt.

Anna's body protested, but she pushed through it. The pain in her ankle flared with each twist of uneven stone. Her arms ached. Her heartbeat pulsed in her temples. But she didn't stop.

She couldn't. Not while Ferraro still led. Not while Pip was still out there.

She didn't know how far they had to go, or how much time they had left. Only that every step forward mattered.

They pressed deeper into the unknown, towards something old, towards someone lost.

There was no way to measure time in the cell.

No light from above. No sound from outside. Only the drip of water through ancient stone and the ragged beat of his own breath. The cell was cut into the old rock, not part of any modern structure. It felt Roman. Pagan. A space forgotten even by those who claimed to guard it. The floor was uneven, choked with debris. A single iron ring had been drilled into the wall. Chains still hung from it.

They hadn't used them.

Not yet.

Pip sat slumped against the wall, arms wrapped around his ribs. His shirt was torn and stiff with dried blood. The blows had been clean. Professional. Not meant to kill. Meant to remind.

His head throbbed. One eye had swollen nearly shut.

And all he could think was: how did I end up here?

A Creative Director from Manchester. A man who once pitched slogans in glass boardrooms, who debated typefaces over sushi, who signed off brand campaigns worth millions. His life used to be deadlines and client decks, late-night tweaks and polished smiles.

Now, he was underground. In a stone box that smelled of old blood and older secrets.

Why had he taken this path? This path that led from Deansgate to a cell beneath the Vatican?

Was it Anna? Was it the memory? Was it the homeless man? Was it the blackbird? Some long-forgotten choice, the moment he started asking questions no one else wanted to answer? The first time he peeled back the surface of a story and found a rot no one would name? Maybe it hadn't been one moment, but a drift, a slow migration away from comfort and into something darker. Something truer.

He wanted to laugh at the absurdity of it all, a sardonic bark of disbelief, but the sound caught in his throat, cracked dry and sharp. Pain lit up his ribs like broken glass. This wasn't a film. This wasn't a story where the hero found the hidden passage and made it out just in time.

This felt like the end, or the slow crumbling approach of it - not dramatic, not loud, just the steady erosion of self in a place where time refused to move.

But it wasn't the pain that disturbed him most. It was the stillness. He had seen it before, not as peace, but as method. Isolation used not to extract, but to erase. A silence engineered with purpose, one that pulled at the edges of identity, memory, even fear. This was not neglect.

It was design.

They weren't trying to find out what he knew. They were waiting to see if he would unravel without ever being touched again.

So he did the only thing left. He resisted the dissolution. He kept his mind moving, even when his body could not. He whispered childhood hymns into the dark, recited the names of cities he'd once walked, people he'd once loved. His box of folded maps. Then came the places, the personal ones, like anchors scattered across memory.

Chorlton Park in spring, where the grass held the scent of damp earth and sugar from spilled fizzy drinks, and the brook that ran along the edge carried that distinct, fetid, dank smell, part moss, part metal, part something that never quite left your nose.

Southern Cemetery, where he once dared himself to walk the rows alone, half frightened, half reverent. Trafford Park, empty on a Sunday morning, stretching out like a forgotten industrial skeleton.

He spoke their names not for them, but to remind himself that they had existed, and so had he.

He pictured Anna, under those fairy lights in Manchester, dancing care-free, but not just her face, the sound of her laugh, the way she tilted her head when listening. The feel of her hand brushing his.

He clung to the smallest details like handholds on a cliff.

Because to forget was to vanish.

And if this place was meant to make him disappear, then remembering was rebellion, a stubborn resistance against the erasure, a tentative grip on a self that still breathed beneath the surface.

Time had dissolved. The door hadn't opened in what could've been hours or days. He'd shouted once, his voice ricocheting off the stone with nothing to meet it but the stale air. No footsteps, no echo in return, just the inert stare of the motionless camera above the doorway. He doubted it was even recording. Maybe it never had been.

He began to question whether the cell had been built for containment at all, or if it served some deeper, older purpose. A place not for punishment, but finality. He wondered if anyone had ever walked out of here. Or if the silence was still echoing with the memory of those who hadn't.

He thought of the disc, a relic of the moment that had become his only real sense of achievement, the final second before they descended, when he managed to pass the disc to Anna. It was small, almost imperceptible in the chaos, but it meant everything. A silent act of defiance, a message transferred in faith, and maybe, just maybe, the thread she would follow to something greater. He could only hope Anna still had it. Maybe they'd assumed she was just collateral, a bystander caught in the wrong place, not the one carrying the most important piece. Maybe they hadn't even seen her. Or maybe they had, and were confident the chase would consume her. Whatever the case, the disc was no longer with him. And with that small act, the last thing he'd done before the descent, he had passed not just information, but trust. Trust that she would understand. That she would run, not freeze. That she would know where to look.

And that thought, the knowledge that he had given her something to follow, was the only thing that still whispered of escape while they dismantled him from the inside. And then the darkest thought... had they claimed her too?

The chamber around him remained a tomb, filled only with his breath, the persistent drip of moisture from the ceiling, and the oppressive weight of all he couldn't see, all he dared not imagine. And then... a sound.

Footsteps, soft and deliberate. Not the heavy authority of boots, but something else entirely. Shoes. Measured. Intimate.

A sharp snap of metal, slow, deliberate, scraping at the lock like a knife being sharpened. No urgency. No hesitation. As if whoever stood behind the door already knew what they would find inside. Already believed they owned it.

Pip's breath shallowed. This was it. No warning. No preparation. No final request. Just the quiet, inevitable opening of a door and the unspoken finality that followed.

He felt it rise in his chest, that ancient, animal instinct. Not fight. Not even flight. Just the hollow, still knowledge that this might be the last person he ever saw.

And still, some part of him straightened his spine.

If this was how it ended, he would not meet it crawling.

The dead had more space than the living down here.

Anna had followed Ferraro through a corridor so narrow she could feel the breath of the stone on both shoulders, a passage where the walls wept with moisture and the floor sloped downward as if in protest. Above them, life continued, the hum of Rome's traffic, the tolling of distant bells, the rhythm of footsteps crossing piazzas, but none of it reached here. The air below belonged to something far older, steeped in the memory of bones and silence.

They moved without speaking, not out of fear but reverence. Ferraro walked with the solemnity of a man returning to his grave, as though each flagstone they crossed marked someone the Church had tried to forget. Anna's torch cast a flickering blade of light across ossuaries and half-erased inscriptions, illuminating broken icons placed in alcoves like apologies too late to matter. The damp had worked its way through her sleeves and into her bones, and more than once she pressed a hand to the wall just to find her balance. The weight of the dark wasn't just behind her eyes, it was pressing inward, testing her resolve.

When the corridor narrowed to a single arch, Ferraro finally stopped.

"This is where the maps stop," he said, voice barely above the echo of their own footsteps.

Anna stepped beside him. "What's beyond?"

He looked at her, eyes hollow but still lit with something that hadn't gone out.

"Everything they tried to forget."

He dropped to one knee and, with effort that made his breath catch, pried open a rusted iron grate. Below it, a stone shaft descended into blackness.

"This isn't a rescue," he said quietly. "It's a reckoning."

Without waiting for her reply, he lowered himself into the hole.

Anna followed, the torch gripped in both hands.

They were at the door now. The stone passage had opened into a low chamber, its ceiling held up by ancient, soot-blackened arches. A single bulb burned faint overhead, casting long shadows across the floor. In the centre of the room stood a reinforced iron door, the kind built not to keep something out, but to keep something in.

Ferraro pressed his ear to the cold metal. A pause. Then a nod.

"I think he's still in there." Anna stepped forward, heart thudding. Her fingers trembled around the torch.

Ferraro reached beneath his robes and pulled out a small canvas satchel. From it, he drew a chisel and a short iron rod.

"No key," he muttered. "We make our own."

The sound of the chisel striking the lock echoed down the corridor, sharp as a gunshot. He worked quickly, with the urgency of a man who had waited too long for this moment. Each blow sent rust flaking from the hinges, each pause filled only with the strain of breath and the ticking of metal giving way.

Behind the door, Pip raised his head.

With a final wrench, the mechanism groaned, and Ferraro prised the door open.

"Pip."

His name broke the silence like a prayer torn from the chest of someone who had nearly forgotten how to believe.

He lifted his head slowly, disbelief carved into every line of his face.

For a moment, the world narrowed to nothing but the echo of her voice, real, alive, impossible. His body was broken, ribs cracked, face bruised and bloodied, chained by pain and silence, but he was still here.

And now… so was she.

He hadn't dared to hope. Hadn't let himself imagine rescue. Hope had felt like betrayal, too fragile to hold in a place built for forgetting. But here she was, limping toward him, face smudged with dust and blood, eyes burning with something he thought he'd never see again.

Love. Rage. Refusal.

She dropped beside him, her breath hitching, hands trembling as she reached for his face. Tears fell before she could speak, silent and unstoppable. She traced the cuts on his cheek with shaking fingers, as if trying to memorise the damage, to mark it as real so it could begin to be undone.

"You came," he whispered, voice hoarse and cracked.

She laughed, one broken, beautiful sound, and pulled him into her arms. He winced, a sharp breath escaping him as pain lanced through his ribs, but he didn't pull away. His arms closed around her with what strength he had left.

For a long moment, neither of them moved.

Then a cough sounded behind them, gentle, respectful.

Ferraro.

The spell broke, not with harshness, but with purpose.

"We have to go," he said quietly. "They'll be closing the ring soon."

Anna nodded, brushing tears from her cheek with the back of her hand. Her voice came out steadier than she felt. "Help me get him up."

Ferraro stepped forward without hesitation, kneeling beside Pip, his expression grim but calm. Between the two of them, they eased him to his feet. Pip gritted his teeth against the pain but said nothing. He didn't need to.

He was alive, she had come.

And somehow, against every rule of the world they thought they knew, the story wasn't over.

Not yet.

They turned toward the passage behind Ferraro, the shadows thick, the way uncertain, but they were together now, and the compass still pulsed faintly in Anna's coat. With each step, the weight of what had almost been lost fell away behind them.

Now came the harder part.

Escape.

Ferraro didn't waste a breath. Already scanning the walls, running his hand along the damp stone until it found a seam almost invisible in the flickering light, not an exit, not yet, but a levered latch disguised within an etched arch. With a creak that sounded more like a breath being released after centuries, the stone shifted inward to reveal a secondary chamber, narrower than the first, lit only by the faint green glow of lichen clinging to the walls.

"This way," he said, urgency quickening his voice.

Pip turned to Anna, voice low, ragged. "Who is this guy?"

She glanced at Ferraro, then back at Pip. "A priest... kind of. He was exiled down here too, cataloguing the things they wanted erased. He helped me find you."

Pip blinked, still unsteady. "Then we can't leave him to rot down here, we've all get to make it."

Ferraro gave a grim smile, already moving toward the far wall. "Then help me finish what I started."

He stepped through first, but not without glancing back. "There's another door, deeper in. They sealed it when they chose silence over remembrance, when they decided no one needed to bear witness to what this place once held."

His voice dropped to a breath. "They won't expect us to know it. But I've walked it in my dreams for years."

Anna stepped forward to support Pip as he stumbled from the cell, every motion heavy with exhaustion. But he didn't fall. He moved. And Ferraro saw that, nodded once, then pressed his shoulder to the stone. It took all three of them immense effort, Ferraro bracing his back and pushing with a grunt, Anna straining her legs against the uneven floor, and Pip dragging his battered body into the effort, but the panel finally gave. A low groan rolled through the stone as it shifted inward, revealing a narrow passage beyond, half-collapsed and choked with the sour stench of old soil, rusted iron, and something older still, something that reeked of decay.

"No one comes through here unless they're dead," Ferraro said. "…or determined."

Anna and Pip followed him into the dark, the torchlight barely enough to light the uneven floor. The air was close, sour, the walls tighter with every step.

Eventually, the way forward constricted to a jagged rise of stone. Ferraro climbed first, wedging his feet into ancient crevices, hauling himself up with a grunt.

Anna pushed Pip forward. "Go. I'm right behind you."

They climbed, not quickly, not cleanly, but together. Every push, every reach, every slip became a shared effort, a refusal to stop. At the final stretch, the ceiling angled so low they had to crawl, scraping skin, breathing dirt.

Then Ferraro found the grate. "Together," he whispered. "It will only give if we all push. It's been sealed for decades."

Three hands, blistered, bloodied, shaking, braced against rusted iron. With a cry from somewhere deeper than voice, they pushed. The grate shifted, only slightly, a reluctant groan of rusted metal against stone, but it was enough to give them hope. They redoubled their effort, all three of them gritting their teeth, pressing harder, shoulders locked into the heave. The old ironwork rattled, trembled, then gave a little more. Dust rained down. Something cracked.

Anna let out a breathless cry, half exertion, half disbelief. Ferraro's jaw was clenched so tight his teeth ached. Pip, bruised and barely steady, leaned his full weight into the edge.

With one final, desperate surge, a push not of strength but of unity, the grate gave way.

Air - real air - rushed in, and it hit like a revelation.

It wasn't just oxygen. It was life itself. Damp stone and recycled breath were swept aside by the sudden bloom of the world above: the sharp tang of rain on concrete, the faint sweetness of wet grass, traces of smoke and earth and something green. After hours, days, and for Ferraro, years of breathing stale, metallic silence, it was like tasting colour. Cool and wild and indifferent, it filled their lungs like a flood, clearing cobwebs from thought, rinsing the soul of buried stillness.

Pip choked on it, then laughed. A ragged, astonished sound.

Anna tilted her head back, eyes closed, and for a moment did nothing but breathe.

They didn't speak. There was nothing left to say.

They climbed through the gap one by one, hands scraping against stone, knees raw, lungs burning.

And when they emerged, gasping and filthy into a forgotten service alley just beyond the Vatican walls, the dawn had already begun to break.

Not bright. Not triumphant. But enough to see by.

The Last Train from Termini

No rest. No celebration.

The instant their feet hit the cracked stones of the alley, Ferraro was already moving, his breath ragged, his eyes sharp. "Stay low. Keep moving. Don't look back." He led them through the backstreets like a ghost who'd memorised every gutter and shadow. Anna clutched Pip's arm, guiding him whenever he faltered. Her ankle throbbed with each step, while Pip's ribs, likely fractured, ached with every breath, the bruises from the cell beating already darkening beneath his torn shirt.

They rounded a corner and stopped in unison. At the far end of the alley, two men stood silent, clad in black uniforms with mirrored visors. Not the ceremonial kind photographed by tourists, these were the Vatican's hunters, and their presence meant the net was already closing.

Ferraro halted. His expression shifted, part disbelief, part release, as if he were waking from a nightmare that had lasted years. Turning to Anna and Pip, he lowered his voice, each word trembling with both fear and resolve. "This is where I vanish. You go on. I've waited too long for this moment, for someone to remember."

He gripped Anna's arm in silent gratitude, then turned to Pip and gave a nod filled with something like reverence. "You gave me something back. Both of you." Before they could speak, he was gone, slipping between the buildings like someone who'd spent a lifetime preparing for this exit.

Anna turned. Pip didn't speak. They ran.

They didn't have a choice.

Italian shouts rang out above them. Clipped orders. Boots hammered stone. "Non farli scappare!"

Pip wrapped an arm around Anna's waist, half-carrying, half-dragging her along the uneven path. The pain in his ribs flared with each stride, sharp enough to steal his breath, but he pushed through it. Blood filled his mouth, but he kept moving.

Ahead, a rusted iron gate blocked their path. Behind them, the sound of pursuit grew louder. Anna fumbled for the compass, her fingers trembling. It pulsed once, urgent, pointing left.

"There," she gasped.

They lunged toward a narrow breach in the wall, crashing through into a forgotten pathway littered with broken statues and overgrown vines. It was a scar on the Vatican's edge, long erased from maps, a relic of something older and hidden.

Gunfire split the air, precise, not panicked. These were calculated shots meant to wound, not warn.

Pip turned, shielding Anna with his body. A bullet tore past his ear, shattering stone inches from his head. They didn't stop.

Ahead, a broken statue slumped against a crumbling wall, its marble torso cracked but stable enough. Pip caught Anna's eye, then motioned toward it. She nodded, biting back pain. He crouched, hands braced against the stone, and hoisted her up with a grunt, pain searing through his ribs like fire. Anna clawed her way to the top, dragging her injured leg, then reached down to steady him. He climbed after her, slower, every motion a war with his breath. At the crest, they paused - just long enough to lock eyes.

Then they dropped.

Anna hit hard, collapsing to her knees with a muffled cry. Pip landed beside her with a jarring thud, his legs folding under him. But they were through. On the pavement, in the open.

Civilians turned at the noise, some startled, others unmoved, but none intervened. The guards surged after them, unbothered by the public eyes.

"Termini," Pip panted. "We make the train, or we don't make it at all."

Anna gave a grim nod, jaw clenched against the pain. They sprinted, as best they could, through the labyrinth of alleys, the city melting into a blur of decaying stone and memory. Termini's iron-and-glass maw loomed ahead, jagged against the grey sky, offering escape or capture, and nothing in between.

The final dash was brutal. Anna could barely run, her injured ankle threatening to give out with every step. Pip dragged her, his own legs buckling from pain, ribs grinding. He didn't know how he stayed upright, only that he had to.

Then, a whistle. A shifting crowd. A window.

They threw themselves onto the platform just as the Swiss Guards emerged behind them. The train doors hissed shut, sealing them inside. One of the guards slammed his fist against the glass. His eyes, cold, furious, met Pip's through the rain-streaked pane.

The train pulled away, a steel whisper swallowed by Rome's wet streets.

Pip sagged forward, forehead resting on the glass, breath fogging the window. His ribs burned like fire. Anna slumped beside him, cradling her ankle, her face pale with pain.

Outside, Rome blurred into a mix of black streets and sodium-lit stone, the rain slicking the city in hues of oil and shadow. But Pip didn't let his guard drop. He knew this wasn't over. The Vatican wouldn't stop at chasing them through tunnels. Their reach would stretch across the city, checkpoints, roadblocks, informants. Every doorway could be a trap. If the Vatican's alarms had been triggered, and he was sure the had, then Rome had already become something else.

A net.

He leaned toward Anna and spoke low. "We can't stay on this

train."

She blinked, the fog of adrenaline starting to fade. "What?"

"They'll check every major stop. Florence. Bologna. We need to disappear before they expect it."

Anna nodded, though every movement drained her further, with the knowing there was more to come. Briefly she transported herself to her field, her safe place, closing her eyes and summoning the bliss of the field, the smell...the security.

Pip studied the route map above the doors.

Next stop: Orte.

Old. Unremarkable. Quiet. It would have to do. He pressed his hand against the compass tucked beneath his coat. It pulsed gently, as if in agreement.

The countryside raced by outside, shattered farmhouses and ghostly trees sliding past under the hammering rain. Pip counted the seconds between announcements, each minute feeling like an hour. Finally, the brakes hissed. The train began to slow. Orte's station rose into view through the storm, underlit and nearly swallowed by darkness.

As the doors opened, they stepped out into cold, metallic air. Pip's side screamed in protest. He gritted his teeth.

Then he saw them.

Polizia di Stato in blue. Carabinieri in black, with submachine guns slung and ready. They prowled the exits and walked the platform in formation, scanning faces with cold precision.

Anna's grip on him tightened. "They're hunting," she whispered.

"Not us yet," Pip said. "Blend."

He moved them into a group of teenage students spilling out with instruments and overstuffed duffels, their noise and motion providing just enough cover. Anna leaned into his side, masking her limp in the crowd's chaos. Behind them, two Carabinieri exchanged words, one speaking sharply into a radio.

Pip guided Anna toward a narrow corridor marked Altri binari - Regionali. Overhead, a blinking display read:

Regional 2321: Orte Florence via Viterbo.

A local train. Small, no formal checks at this hour. Ideal.

Another crackle of static behind them. Barked orders. Something had changed.

Rain sheeted sideways across the open platform. Their boots slipped on the slick stone. Anna stumbled and nearly fell, Pip caught her under one arm, forcing himself to bear more of her weight. She was close to collapse, and he wasn't far behind.

They reached the waiting train, graffitied, battered, half-lit, and climbed aboard.

Inside, a scattering of quiet passengers. Two elderly men, nuns with prayer beads, a mother with a pram.

No police.

They settled into a seat near the back. Pip angled himself so he shielded Anna from view. Moments later, two officers strode past the regional platform without slowing. No inspection yet.

Pip risked a glance. One officer stopped mid-stride, his head tilting slightly, as though catching a scent on the wind. The radio on his shoulder crackled.

A gesture, sharp. Toward the regional lines.

Pip's pulse kicked. His fingers tightened around the compass.

The train doors groaned closed. The engine rumbled, then jolted forward. Slowly, with a tired, mechanical shudder, the car lurched into motion.

They didn't breathe until the last platform light disappeared into mist.

Anna slumped beside him, head against the torn seat.

"We're not safe," she murmured.

"I know," Pip replied. He adjusted his collar, blinked rain from his lashes, and kept his eyes on the dark outside. "Not yet. But we're still moving."

She turned to him, her gaze heavy with pain and resolve.

"That's all that matters."

Outside, Italy's forgotten fields and fractured hills slipped past like memories they hadn't lived yet. And behind them, the Vatican's hunt expanded, relentless and silent, like a bloodstream chasing infection.

Berlin. The Seat of the Beast

The regional train rattled north through Italy, ferrying them deeper into Europe's older, colder arteries. Night pressed against the windows, rain streaking the outside world into smudged halos of light.

Inside the worn carriage, Pip and Anna sat opposite each other, hunched over a battered table. They breathed shallowly, their bodies still wired for motion, for escape. At every provincial station, Pisa, La Spezia, Parma, Pip scanned the shadowed platforms with sharp eyes. No uniforms yet. No pursuers.

Between Florence and Bologna, they switched trains again, slipping onto a quieter line threading its way toward Milan under the cover of a fogged and sleeping countryside. Each movement was precise, rehearsed without rehearsal, a thousand micro-decisions carving an invisible path forward.

The farther north they pushed, the thinner the surveillance net seemed to stretch. Or perhaps they had simply slipped between the cracks.

Crossing into Germany felt less like entering a new country and more like slipping between frequencies, from chaos into rigid, invisible control.

By afternoon, they reached Berlin.

The city greeted them with cold mist and rain-slick cobblestones, the sky sagging low with grey. Berlin was quiet, but not calm, it thrummed beneath the surface. A city stitched back together, still carrying the bruises of history beneath its modern skin.

They stepped out of Hauptbahnhof, blinking under the steel canopy of the vast glass terminal. Behind them, the train exhaled one last sigh and vanished into the tracks. Before them, Berlin sprawled in fractured layers, old and new jostling for space, for memory.

To the left, the Spree River coiled past the station, black and swollen. To the right, the Reichstag's glass dome shimmered faintly through the drizzle, a strange beacon in the half-light. Further still, the skeleton of the Berlin Wall - or what remained of it - echoed a city once split in two.

They moved quickly, heads down, past police with sidearms and tourists with umbrellas, blending into the churn of a city too tired to stare. Their breath fogged in front of them. No luggage. No plan. Just ID, credit cards, some cash, a half-dead burner phone, and the signal, the one thing they couldn't afford to lose.

They found a small hotel just off Friedrichstraße, tucked between a shuttered café and a bookstore that hadn't changed its window display since 1998. The sign was half-lit, the entrance narrow and heavy with smoke-stained velvet curtains. Art-nouveau bones, Soviet-era fatigue. The building felt like it was leaning inward, trying to keep the world out.

The concierge barely looked up, taking basic details and handing over the key without question. Room 304.

The floorboards groaned beneath their feet as they climbed. Their room overlooked a back alley filled with forgotten bicycles, empty crates, and the crumbling remains of a mural no one had finished. A black cat watched them from a window ledge opposite, tail twitching, its yellow eyes full of something older than curiosity. Pip double-locked the door and slid the latch. Anna, limping slightly, dropped the pharmacy bag onto the bed - painkillers, gauze, antiseptic, a pair of unbranded hoodies, socks, underwear, travel-sized everything. They'd grabbed it all in a rush from a Rossmann near the station, moving like ghosts through the aisles.

She peeled off her damp coat with a grimace. "You need to lie down," she said, eyeing his side. The bruising had deepened, angry purple now beneath the swelling.

He gave a short nod. "And you need to keep that ankle up."

They cleaned their wounds in the flickering bathroom light. No complaints, just the careful rituals of survival. Pip winced but said nothing. Anna sat with her foot elevated on the faded desk chair, wrapping it tight.

By the time they were in fresh clothes, wrapped in the faint, sterile scent of disinfectant and soap, the storm outside had thickened. Rain turned to sleet. The television stayed off. So did the lights. They didn't speak. Just lay still.

One heartbeat at a time.

Below them, the city groaned and turned its face away. But they were here. And for now, they had made it.

For the first time in weeks, they weren't chasing or being chased. They lay in the stillness between thresholds. That evening, after a long pause, they slipped into the streets again. Berlin at night hummed differently. Not asleep. Not awake. Watchful. The rain had thinned to a mist, and neon reflections painted the puddles with blurred halos. Every step seemed to echo a little too long. Every alley held its breath. They didn't plan their next move. The city decided for them.

A cracked poster flapped against a stone wall...

FAUST: Eine
Neuerzählung - A New Telling.

No actors listed. No dates. Just a location and a time. Pip hesitated in the rain.

Anna caught the look. "It's bait," she said, voice low. "Or it's meant for us." Pip shrugged. "Either way, it's part of it."

The theatre was older than it looked, tucked between

bureaucratic glass towers that loomed like frozen waves. A single bulb flickered over the doorway. Inside, the air smelled of velvet, dust, and something faintly sweet and rotting.

The house lights dimmed before they even reached their seats.

Onstage, no curtains, no scenery. Just a man standing centre-stage, endlessly scrolling on a cracked smartphone.

Faust.

Not a scholar now. Not a magician. Just another soul numbed into passivity, trading spirit for dopamine. The first words didn't come from him. They came from everywhere, whispered through unseen speakers.

"Sell your soul? No need. You're already paying by the hour."

The audience didn't move. Pip scanned the room subtly. Two rows ahead, a man sat too still - no fidgeting, no breathing rhythm. Watcher. To their left, a woman scribbled into a notebook, but her pen never touched the page. Anna shifted slightly in her seat. She had seen them too. The play blurred performance and possession. Faust as a child, Faust at an office desk, Faust trapped beneath endless algorithmic advertisements.

Each version ended the same: empty, disconnected, devoured. By the time the synthetic sky crumbled above Faust's bowed head, Pip's stomach knotted. They weren't watching fiction. They were watching a confession. When the lights lifted, a few scattered claps rang out - brief, mechanical, awkward. Then silence swallowed them whole.

Faces shifted in the dimness, uncertain and defensive. The audience hadn't been entertained; they had been exposed.

They hadn't witnessed a performance. They had witnessed a confession, and somewhere deep down, they knew it had been aimed directly at them.

The watchers left first, silent, precise.

Anna leaned close, her voice barely a breath. "They know we're here."

Pip's jaw tightened. "Let them."

They melted into the mist, becoming part of the rain-glossed streets as the city folded around them like a shroud. The silence was loaded now, no longer neutral, but watching.

"They're telling the truth," Anna whispered, her tone strange, distant. "Neo-style."

Down one street, a black car idled with its lights off, engine barely humming. Down another, a man leaned against a lamp post, eyes low, pretending to scroll through a dead phone. Neither belonged, yet both had been placed. Positioned.

Anna caught Pip's arm. "They're closing the net."

He nodded once. "Quietly."

They didn't run. That would trigger the trap. Instead, they walked - deliberate, steady, breath measured to rhythm rather than panic. Every step was a choice.

Beneath Pip's coat, the compass pulsed faintly against his chest, the resonance threading them forward like an invisible lifeline. Not direction - but intention. Signal.

At the next square, another car. Another figure, face half-shadowed, feigning disinterest but watching all the same.

They veered into a narrower street, instinct pulling them through cracks in the pattern. It wasn't logic guiding them anymore. It was something older, memory, maybe. Or fate.

The alleys of Mitte closed around them. Brick and glass. Echoes and fog.

Behind them, Berlin breathed.
Not sleeping.
Not waking.
Waiting.

The square unfolded before them, solemn under the mist: German Cathedral, French Cathedral, Konzerthaus in the centre, like ancient sentinels guarding an invisible truth.

The music found them next.

It was no accident. There was a pull to it, not urgent, but insistent, as if something familiar was calling from just out of sight. They drifted toward Gendarmenmarkt, drawn by an unseen thread that bypassed thought altogether. The square opened up around them, grand and hushed beneath the weight of drizzle and time.

Music floated on the cold air, faint and crystalline, threading through the mist like scent. It didn't belong to any one place, and yet it belonged to this moment.

They moved without speaking, footsteps softened by the wet stone beneath them. There was no need for words. They were being called.

Inside the Konzerthaus, a concert was already underway. The air shimmered with strings and silence, the kind of silence that holds breath in reverence.

There were no tickets. No security. No questions. They simply entered.

The usher by the door barely looked up, his eyes glassy and distant, as if already elsewhere. He gave a nod that wasn't quite conscious and waved them through without hesitation.

The music swelled as they stepped into the main hall. It was Bach, but not the version the world had been trained to hear. Something was different - not just in tempo or tone, but in truth. Notes unfolded like maps. Chords bent around meaning. It was less a performance than a transmission, and every seat was filled with people who had no idea they were listening to a code.

This wasn't music in 440Hz. This was true tuning - 432Hz. The ancient resonance. The tone before the frequency grid was corrupted.

Modern music, since the mid-20th century, had been retuned

to 440Hz - a shift imposed not for harmony, but for control. This new standard, subtle as it seemed, carried tension. It frayed edges. It dislodged inner peace. It made the soul feel slightly off-centre, without ever knowing why.

But this, this was the original frequency. The one aligned with the golden ratio, with the Earth's heartbeat, with breath and water and stars. It didn't just soothe - it restored. It tuned not only instruments but the human being.

The strings shimmered. The harpsichord ticked like celestial machinery. Woodwinds floated like voices from another world. And beneath it all, the bass lines moved like tectonic plates - steady, ancient, deliberate.

Anna closed her eyes. "It's... pure."

Pip sat rigid, ribs vibrating like a struck tuning fork. His breath slowed into a deeper rhythm, syncing with something older than his body.

Pip nodded, barely breathing. "This is what alignment sounds like."

It wasn't just beautiful. It was correcting. Recalibrating something inside them that had been knocked loose by everything they'd seen. When the music ended, they walked slowly in silence out onto Gendarmenmarkt, the city square lit like an old photograph - soft, sepia, sacred.

Anna whispered again, softer this time, "They're telling the truth. Not with words... but with resonance."

Afterwards, they found a rustic German tavern tucked away from the tourist traps. The kind of place with low ceilings, carved beams, and waitresses who never smiled unless they meant it. They ordered too much - bratwurst, sauerkraut, roast duck - and drank thick, bitter beer from tall steins.

For a little while, they laughed.

Anna wiped her mouth and said, "Maybe this is what it means to be awake. Not just to see what's coming... but to hold moments like this, before it does."

Pip nodded, looking into the foam of his beer. "Yeah. This is the last breath before the plunge."

They walked back to the hotel through the quiet streets of Berlin, the air damp with late autumn mist. Their laughter faded into a comfortable silence. The room was dimly lit by streetlight spilling through sheer curtains, casting pale gold across the floorboards.

Anna slipped off her coat, toes already bare, and disappeared into the bathroom. When she returned, Pip was sitting on the edge of the bed, slowly unbuttoning his shirt, lost in thought. She approached and wrapped her arms around him from behind, resting her chin on his shoulder.

"Tonight felt... real," she said. "Like the world finally let us catch up with it."

He turned and met her eyes. "Or maybe we caught up with ourselves."

They kissed then - not out of urgency or passion, but of tenderness. Gratitude. Presence. The kind of connection that silences all commentary. That asks for nothing but now.

Later, tangled in sheets and warmth, Anna drifted into deep, undisturbed sleep.

But for Pip, it was different.

Sleep came in fragments. His body rested, but his mind walked corridors. Shadows flickered at the edges of his vision. Whispers came through walls. The signal stirred beneath everything, low and magnetic.

The dreams had grown sharper since Rome.

No longer abstract impressions or whispered sensations - now they came with form, light, sound. Pip didn't even need to close his eyes. The moments slipped in sideways. Between blinks. In the hum of engines. Reflected in glass - familiar flashes of something he couldn't name, yet felt in his skin and bones. Like déjà vu laced with warning.

And now this.

A corridor that didn't exist. A voice that didn't echo. A cold that didn't bite the skin, but the soul.

He stood, or thought he did - on stone. But not in Berlin. Not physically. His body remained in the hotel room, tangled in sheets beside Anna, chest rising and falling in shallow, restless rhythm, but his mind had drifted somewhere else. Somewhere layered and old. A space conjured not by thought, but by signal. He was dreaming, yes - but the dream had dimensions. Gravity. Consequence. This was something else. A remote echo? He couldn't say. But it felt real. More real than waking.

The space was immense. Temple-like. A structure not meant for human proportion, but for something far older. The energy was dense here - not oppressive, but exact. Precise. Like the air itself had been tuned.

He felt it in his sternum first - a pressure, a vibration. Then behind the eyes. As if the place were scanning him. Or waking something dormant inside him.

It wasn't fear. It wasn't awe. It was recognition. A knowing without logic.

Whatever this place was - he hadn't walked into it. It had opened for him. Like a dream folding open within another, the thresholds of his consciousness stretched and dissolved. He was suspended in a state neither asleep nor awake, weightless yet anchored, as if his soul had slipped loose from the laws of time. This wasn't fantasy. It was hyper-reality. A lucid awareness sculpted in signal and inner knowing, where each step he took echoed not on stone, but within the frequencies of a deeper intelligence - something that hummed beneath the veil of waking life.

Steps rose before him, flanked by monolithic reliefs. Scenes carved in old language. Wars. Fire. Eyes without faces. A throne at the top - not ornate, not gilded, but geometric. Squared. Industrial. As if shaped by function, not reverence.

The Throne of Zeus. The Seat of the Beast. The Pergamon Altar.

Pip recognised it without knowing how. The knowing came from somewhere deeper than all he'd learned - it rose like a pressure behind his eyes, a name spoken without words.

The knowledge came, unspoken. The Pergamon Altar. Built in the 2nd century BC in what is now Turkey. Dedicated to Zeus - not the noble god of stories, but the sky-father, the thunderer, the enforcer. The understanding didn't pass through language. It pulsed through him like code - architecture, intent, domination. Not reverence. Submission. Power made physical.

His voice echoed without echo, as though the space swallowed sound. "It wasn't about reverence. It was about submission. Power, weaponised through spectacle."

And then, a voice - not Anna's, not human - from within or from beyond. A layered tone, strange and deep.

"The Bible calls this the Seat of Satan."

Pip flinched, but didn't reply aloud. The thought came instead like breath: Of course it does. Because it wasn't just stone. It was a frequency gate. A resonator. It amplified belief. Bent will.

Another voice, or perhaps his own, distorted by the dream, fragmented into something other, asked:

"Why Berlin?"

The answer unfolded within him.

Not history. Placement. Strategy. Architecture of control.

The Nazi regime modelled their parades on this altar. Torch-lit marches. Synchronized crowds. Sound as spell.

And then silence. But not stillness. He was being watched. Not with malice. With gravity. And with measurement.

Then, the air shifted, subtly at first, like the weight of a storm before the first crack of thunder. The atmosphere thickened. The stone beneath his feet began to hum, as if reacting to an unseen presence.

A figure began to form ahead, not walking into the scene, but congealing from the shadows themselves. Tall. Towering. Its limbs impossibly long, its shape flickering between beast and man. Horns that weren't quite horns. Eyes that didn't glow, but swallowed light. Pip's legs rooted. His breath caught in his throat.

It didn't need to say its name.

He knew.

Satan.

Not as cartoon or caricature. Not red and horned. But principle. Will incarnate. Authority twisted into domination. The inversion of freedom made flesh.

It spoke without sound.

"You came looking for truth."

The voice scraped against the inside of his skull. Each word rang like iron dropped in blood.

"But truth is currency. And you have nothing to pay with but your fear."

Pip staggered back, nausea blooming in his gut. The air pressed against him like gravity had turned malicious.

He tried to turn. Wake. Anything. But the dream clung.

"You remember because I allow it," the voice continued. **"You walk this path because I paved it."**

The figure stepped forward. Its presence cracked the air.

"Everything you uncover… I let you see."

Then the temperature dropped, not in degrees, but in sensation. A soul-deep cold that sucked the breath from his lungs. Pip could feel his limbs, but they were slow, distant. His knees buckled. The beast stepped closer, and its form distorted again, now man, now serpent, now a being of molten geometry. Its voice became many voices, male, female, child, ancient - all speaking the same terrible truth:

"Freedom is an illusion. Awakening, a trapdoor. You step through it thinking you escape, but all paths come back to me."

The throne behind it pulsed. The altar flared like a wound.
Pip clutched his head. Pain cracked behind his eyes. Symbols not meant for humans bloomed in his vision - shapes older than language, louder than thought.

"I am not the enemy," it whispered, now impossibly near. **"I am the gravity. I am the contract you signed before you were born."**

Pip wanted to scream, to move, to wake.
But the altar opened. And the floor beneath him fell away.
He fell, but not into darkness - into understanding.
Because even as the voice echoed its domination, something in him pushed back. Not with defiance, but with clarity. That is the final illusion, he realised. The greatest inversion.

The entity spoke of freedom as illusion, of awakening as trap - *but that was the trick.* The lie layered in fear. The illusion that the cage is all there is.
Pip's fall slowed. The pressure changed. This thing - this beast - it fed not on truth, but on the perception of its absence. It needed the faithful to feel abandoned, the seekers to believe they were alone. Its power came not from domination, but from the belief that domination was inevitable.

But what if it wasn't?
In the gap between terror and thought, another voice rose within him. Not spoken. Not male. Not female. Not even separate from

himself.

"You are not beneath anything."

The dream cracked. Light - not blinding, but unveiling - tore through the illusion like a seam being undone. Not a fight. Not a war. Just truth revealed.

And the beast - the towering distortion, the voice of inversion - didn't roar. It shrank. Not in shape. In relevance.
Because Pip saw it now. Not as eternal. But as allowed. Sustained only by agreement. He was no longer falling. He was waking.
And with him, something else was rising, not fear, not fire, but understanding. This was the knowledge he had been seeking, the unspoken thread behind every vision, every glyph, every dream.
It wasn't information.
It was permission.
To choose.
To remember.
To reclaim.

This was the knowing he would carry back to Anna, and to the world. Not to save it - but to remind it.
And for the first time since the signal began, he felt the truth of what the Blackbird had always sung:

You were never lost. Only misled.

He gasped, thrashing against the damp sheets. Anna crouched over him, pale with fear.
"Pip…you wouldn't wake up…you were…"
He sat up, chest heaving, heart pounding like it was trying to remember something his mind couldn't yet grasp. The room was dark, but the faint city glow edged the curtains in grey.
"I saw it," he said, voice hoarse. "The throne. The inversion. The

Echoes Above, Shadows Below

Neo tore across the Manchester sky like a blade of living memory, cutting through cloud and silence alike.

From the clouds above the spires and towers, he moved like memory in motion. The city pulsed with new light below him. The glyphs were active now, crackling softly through stone, air, and water. The resonance Pip had triggered was not local. It was global. And Neo felt it all. His wings did not beat. He glided, buoyed by the frequencies rising through the grid. Each node awakening sent ripples through the plane. From Göbekli Tepe to Tokyo, from the Ethiopian highlands to the icy vault of Antarctica, the tones were harmonising.

And now Manchester had joined them.

From his vantage above the city, Neo circled once, tight and deliberate, above the heart of it all: Albert Square. Below, hidden beneath the gothic weight of the Town Hall, the true resonance point pulsed like a buried star. The Architects had placed it here, concealed beneath stone and scaffolding, encoded into the very foundations of the clock tower and its surrounding geometry. This was not just a civic centre. It was a central harmonic node, hidden in plain sight.

Neo's eyes, as bright and black as obsidian, reflected the sigils blossoming across the rooftops. Star glyphs. Circles. Spirals. Harmonic geometry written not on buildings, but in the memory of space itself.

He let out a sharp, whistling cry, high, pure, and unnatural, cutting the clouds open like silk. A sound older than song, older than warning. Far beneath him, in tunnels no map acknowledged, something stirred.

The Inverted.

They had felt it too...the breach.

In the dark below the waking city, light was unwelcome. But they had prepared. Not for the glyphs, but for the Rememberers. They had corrupted lines before. Inverted sites. Counter-frequencies. Symbols that drained instead of fed.

And now they were moving.

In the mirrored voids beneath cathedrals, in chambers beneath financial districts and red-bricked labyrinths, they opened their eyes.

"We warned them," one hissed, its voice a serrated whisper.

Another placed its hand to a wall that vibrated with the wrong tone. "The Architects have returned."

"No," said the first. "Not yet. Just echoes."

"But enough," said a third. "Enough to wake the watchers. Enough to draw the line again."

For a moment, one of the Inverted flickered, its form fracturing, then knitting itself back together. Not from damage. From fear.

High above, Neo turned in a wide, circling spiral. He did not fear them. He remembered them.

He had flown over their ruins before. Watched them bend harmony into control. Watched them rewrite memory as myth.

But he also knew something they did not.

Pip had survived the first tone.

And the second was coming.

The Inverted were no longer waiting.

And neither was he.

Neo dropped lower.

Not plummeting, but descending like a cipher from above. His feathers caught the frequencies like antennae. His body was a conduit of memory, lit with pulses that matched the hidden patterns etched beneath the city's crust.

Beneath him, an old rail tunnel, abandoned for decades, flared with unseen light. Inside, the Inverted moved with impossible grace, each step warping the geometry around them. Their eyes gleamed with oil and shadow, reflections of a world twisted by inversion.

One looked up.

Not through stone. Through resonance.

"It sees us," it growled.

Neo flared his wings wide. Symbols erupted from his feathers - sharp lines, ancient shapes, living mathematics. The sky behind him changed, streaked with vertical threads of memory. Not lightning. Not cloud. Warning.

The Inverted hissed and recoiled. But one among them stood still.

"The bird is not the danger," it said. "It is the signal."

"Then silence it."

"No," the leader replied. "Not yet. It carries the next key. Let it fly... for now."

Neo banked hard and vanished into the mist. The tones were changing. The field was shifting. And deep in the blood of the land, something ancient had begun to stir, not built by the Inverted, nor the Architects.

Older than both.

...far beneath the skin of the Earth, something ancient stirred, slow, steady, inevitable, counting down to the Third Tone.

Altitude and Agenda

The flight to Lima stretched out like a line drawn between waking and dream. It was the kind of journey that blurs the edges of thought, long enough for time to lose shape, long enough for everything they had just lived through to begin pressing down on their bones. But sleep wouldn't come.

Pip stared upward at the cabin ceiling, eyes dry, jaw tight, watching the faint shadows ripple over the plastic like liquid memory. He wasn't afraid. It wasn't adrenaline either. Something else had ignited inside him, older, deeper. Like a system that had lain dormant his whole life had suddenly booted up and refused to shut down.

Anna was beside him, her head tilted gently against his shoulder, a quiet, instinctive act. Not an escape. Not a need. Just contact. A signal that he wasn't alone in this unraveling. Her presence anchored him, even as the truth pulled him further from everything that had once made sense.

He hadn't checked his phone. Hadn't opened the agency's emails. He had sent a single line: Need time. Family matter. Final. Unarguable. But even the silence from them felt like pressure. Like a tether waiting to tighten. Every hour up here in the sky felt borrowed.

And yet what tightened more than the invisible leash from his old life was the very real weight of money draining from his accounts. This wasn't some fantasy quest in a dream. This was flights, and food, and last-minute hotel bookings. It was overpriced food in airport terminals, taxis in cities he'd never planned to visit, and border crossings greased with folded cash. And it was all falling on him.

Every swipe of his card came with a twitch of doubt. He hadn't budgeted for world-hopping mysticism. He hadn't planned to chase symbols and pulses across continents. Tokyo. Peru. Rome. And what next? Antarctica? The Moon?

The cost wasn't abstract, it was numerical. And rising. He hadn't dared open the banking app in days. Even the thought of it made his pulse stutter. If the world did end, it would probably charge interest.

But what haunted him more than debt was the question threaded through each sleepless hour: What if I'm wrong? What if none of this is real? What if it's all coincidence and I've spent everything chasing mirages?

He didn't say any of this aloud. He didn't need to. Anna knew. Her hand reached for his without lifting her head, fingers slipping through his with quiet precision. There was no reassurance offered, but in that silence, something stronger moved between them.

She flipped through her dream journal with her free hand, scanning notes, symbols, crossings-out. The way her fingers moved, it was like she was trying to feel something beneath the ink. Her eyes were sharp. Focused. Not lost in thought, but excavating something deeper.

Ahead of them, the headrest screen glowed softly. A silent newsflash blinked into view:

Record-Breaking Heatwave in Europe
Scientists Warn: Worse To Come

Anna leaned forward. "Look at that. 'Worse to come.' That's not information, it's a trigger."

Pip nodded, voice low. "Always predictive. Never explanatory. We're the problem. Carbon. Plastic. Air conditioning."

"But never the concrete, or the geoengineering patents, or the aerosol grids criss-crossing the stratosphere," Anna said. "Never the machines in the sky."

The ticker scrolled:

WEF Calls for Global Climate Action and Digital ID Integration

"They're not even hiding it," she whispered. "They're moving from weather to surveillance. Fear to obedience."

"Climate as currency," Pip murmured. "Obedience as credit score."

"And we're supposed to thank them for the poison while we buy the antidote with our autonomy."

He sat back, pressing his fingertips into his eyes. "They make you pay to breathe, then track your inhale."

Anna's eyes narrowed. "And the ones who speak up? The real scientists, the whistleblowers, they vanish. Or crash. Or are laughed off the stage."

"Too many plane crashes. Too many researchers with 'accidents.' Too many ghosts."

"They're inverted," she whispered.

The screen flickered. A split-second glitch. Then, just before a soothing in-flight meditation screen took over, they both saw it.

Bottom-right corner. Faint but undeniable. The same symbol from the Rome chamber.

Neither spoke.

The signal was everywhere.

The descent into Lima came beneath an unmoving silver sky. No clouds. No shimmer. Just a grey stillness that pressed instead of passed.

Jorge Chávez International didn't bustle. It breathed, calm, clinical, and surveilled. The walls shimmered with moving graphics: smiling avatars, biometric fast-pass promotions, and glowing maps offering pathways to wellness. Everything polished. Everything approved.

And there, above the customs hall, Pachamama watched from a mural. Or rather, a rendering of her. Her strength had been stylised, her wildness smoothed into a marketable goddess. But her eyes, those had not been touched.

Anna looked up. "Even the art watches."

They passed through in silence, stepping into a new thread of the story.

A billboard glowed to life, Machu Picchu at golden hour. But the shadows were wrong. The lines didn't match. Something fundamental had been edited out.

Pip squinted. "The real site's northeast of the Sun Gate. It's always outside the fences."

"Where the resonance holds," Anna murmured. "The sacred geometry doesn't care about tickets or tour guides."

From his backpack, the compass stirred. A single throb.

Outside, a taxi was waiting at the head of a line. Old, clean. The driver said nothing, only nodded when they asked for the Sacred Valley. As though he already knew.

Lima peeled away behind them, colonial balconies sagging above graffiti murals. Food carts steaming beside sterile cafés. The sky remained the same: dull, metallic, hung like an echo of yesterday.

Then came the hills. Dusty. Arid. And then, slowly, green. Quinoa fields. Amaranth terraces. Bundles of corn hanging from roadside stalls. The valley wasn't just alive, it remembered.

Anna laced her fingers through Pip's again.

"I feel like we've been here," she said.

"We have," he replied. "Just not as who we are now."

The driver lifted a hand, pointing toward high stone ridges.

"Ollantaytambo," he said. "Inca. Sacred."

"We want to stop," Pip said. "Please."

Pip leaned forward slightly in his seat. "Would you be able to wait for us? Maybe an hour, no more. We'll pay you for your time."

The driver met his eyes in the rearview mirror and nodded once, no hesitation.

Pip pulled a few folded notes from his wallet and passed them through the gap.

"Half now, half when we're back. Just… please don't leave."

The man accepted the cash without looking at it. He turned off the engine and adjusted his seat slightly, settling in without complaint. His silence didn't feel indifferent, it felt knowing.

The buildings shimmered in the heat, walls stacked with impossible precision. No mortar. No gaps. No explanation.

Anna pressed a hand to one of the curved seams. "This isn't building," she whispered. "It's… impossible."

Pip stepped closer, running his fingers along the faultless join between two massive stones. "How could they have done this? These blocks are perfect, no gaps, no tool marks. It's like they melted into place."

"They say they used copper chisels," Anna added, shaking her head. "But you couldn't cut butter with copper, let alone granite. Not like this."

Pip looked up at the towering wall, then back at her. "This isn't ancient craftsmanship. It's something else. It doesn't make sense. Not with what we're told."

They climbed through terraces. Passed ceremonial niches. Lizards darted. A pair of goats watched from a ledge. The wind shifted.

Then Anna paused. "There." A glint in the dust. A clear quartz crystal, veined with silver. She lifted it carefully.

"Not dropped," Pip said slowly, crouching beside her.

"Left. For us… or for someone like us." He took the crystal from Anna's hand, turning it between his fingers, watching it catch the light. "Maybe it's a marker. Maybe it's been here for years. Or maybe someone, or something, put it here recently, knowing we'd come."

He looked up at the stone walls encircling them. "What if there's a network of these… fragments? Like breadcrumbs. Like it's guiding us somewhere, but not all at once. As if the next part of the map only reveals itself when the time is right."

The compass pulsed again.

Near the Temple of the Sun, the stillness became something else. A kind of waiting.

They stepped off the path. Found an old arch overgrown with moss. The keystone bore the symbol.

Anna staggered. "It's in my chest, like pressure. But not illness. Recognition."

Pip steadied her.

The disc awaited. Smooth. Dark. Familiar. It activated without touch.

Glyphs flared. Light spiralled.

"Second fragment recognised."

Anna trembled. "It knows me."

"No," Pip said. He paused, then frowned. "But how would I even know that?"

He looked at Anna, uncertainty flickering behind his eyes. "It just came out. Like I knew, but not because I figured it out. Like it was already in me."

He glanced back at the disc, voice quieter now. "What if we're not learning this as we go? What if we're remembering somehow?"

A seam opened in the earth.

They descended into silence.

A tunnel of quartz-veined stone. The air scented with ash and mint and rain.

At the bottom: a chamber. Round. Still. Lit from within.
A slab waited.
Anna reached out. Contact.
Light spilled. Symbols spun. The air vibrated with silent song.
A voice, inside:

"Three remain.
One was buried. One is guarded. One was stolen."

Anna gasped. Pip stepped close.
"Why us?"

"You are not chosen. You are remembered.
Resonance brings memory."

The map lit: Rome. Peru. Then, slowly, Tokyo.
"It's always East," Anna whispered.
"Where memory rises," Pip said.
The map tilted. Beneath it: waves of vibration. Not time, but frequency. "It's not just where," Anna said. "It's when."
The chamber exhaled. The slab dimmed.
They climbed. The sky had changed. The mist had thinned. The Valley was watching.
Their driver waited. No words.

Back at the airport, the modern world roared back.
"Tokyo," Pip said. "One flight. Two layovers."
Tickets. Checks. Queues.
"Cash or card?"
"Card."
Anna leaned in. "They don't want you to vanish. They want you traceable."
"Every swipe. A signal. A data-harvest"
The lounge buzzed. Screens blinked. Delays piled up.
But the compass, buried deep in his bag, pulsed.
Once. Then again.

Always East.

The intercom cracked above them with a mechanical click. Something in the way the speaker hummed before the voice came through made Pip sit up straighter. It wasn't what was said, it was the way it was delivered. Measured. Almost... delayed. As if the system were buffering something it wasn't sure it should say.

"Flight 217 to Tokyo now boarding at Gate 14A. Final call for all passengers. Please proceed immediately."

Pip and Anna exchanged a glance. No words. No movement for a moment, just the unspoken sense that they were stepping toward something far larger than the flight itself. The final call didn't sound like an end. It sounded like an initiation.

They moved quickly through the crowd. People moved around them like ghosts in reverse, flickering with noise, their eyes dull, distracted by screens, lost in looped headlines and travel anxiety. As if none of them could feel what was pulsing beneath the surface of it all.

Gate 14A was tucked into the main flow of Jorge Chávez International Airport, no more distant than any other. The terminal itself was compact, linear in design, with each gate arranged in logical succession. Still, something about the lighting near the gate felt off, flickering slightly, intermittently dim. It wasn't remote, but it felt removed, as though reality thinned slightly at its edges. The air seemed thinner near Gate 14A, like altitude without ascent. Lights stuttered. Conversations dropped to murmurs. It felt less like an airport, and more like a checkpoint for something unspoken.

The boarding agent scanned their tickets with a practiced swipe and a perfunctory nod, then flipped open their passports. Her eyes paused just long enough to register the recent stamps, Rome, Berlin, Lima. For a moment Pip thought she might say something. She raised an eyebrow but said nothing, handing the documents back without comment.

"Have a safe journey," she said, though her voice was hollow, like it had been drained of intention.

As they stepped onto the aircraft bridge, Anna touched Pip's arm. "This one feels different," she said.

He nodded. "I know."

The plane was half-full. Dimly lit. Quiet. Almost too quiet. No children. No chatter. Just the soft click of seatbelts and the rustle of jackets. A man in business class glanced at them as they passed, his eyes dark, expression unreadable. For a split second, Pip thought he recognised him. Then the man looked away.

Their seats were near the wing, just above the engine. Anna sat by the window, fingers lightly resting on the armrest as she stared out into the glow of the tarmac lights.

As the plane pulled away from the gate, a low vibration shivered through the fuselage. Pip felt the compass stir in his bag again, just once, like a warning or a whisper. He reached down and laid his hand over it.

"What are we stepping into?" he asked under his breath.

Anna turned toward him. Her expression was calm, but her eyes, wide, glass-clear, held the weight of knowing.

"Whatever it is," she said, "I think it's been waiting for us."

The engines roared. The lights dimmed further.

And the sky, once again, opened its arms.

Tokyo Signal

The flight to Tokyo was long, its rhythm jagged and tense, broken by turbulence that didn't feel natural. Every hour brought them closer to the eastern arc of the map, to the third fragment, and to a city where neon lights glared down on temples that whispered through time.

Anna stirred beside Pip as the cabin lights dimmed. "We're getting close to something. I can feel it in my chest. Like the frequency is climbing."

He turned slightly toward Anna. "We still haven't worked out exactly what those voices meant. 'Three remain. One was buried. One is guarded. One was stolen.' And that part about us being mirrors, not chosen by chance but by resonance…"

Anna nodded, her gaze distant. "They said we weren't meant to fix what's broken, but to reveal what was hidden. That the fragments will guide us. But guide us to what? Some kind of awakening? A confrontation? Are we supposed to expose something? Protect something?" Her voice trailed off, the questions falling into the cabin's low hum.

Pip exhaled slowly, staring at the ceiling above. "And who were they, really? That presence... it wasn't human, but it didn't feel foreign either. It felt like something older. Like memory itself had grown teeth and decided to speak. Not with threat - but with inevitability."

He turned to her, his expression more open than before. "What if it's not about saving the world? What if it's about remembering it the way it was meant to be seen?"

Anna traced the edge of her dream journal. "They said truth, once seen, can't be forgotten. Maybe that's what the fragments are - pieces of that truth, encoded where they couldn't be erased."

He glanced out the window. "So if Peru gave us a key... maybe Tokyo gives us context."

She leaned her head back. "Or consequence."

Somewhere over the Pacific, Anna opened her dream journal again, thumbing through sketches and symbols. One page pulsed slightly under her hand. The glyph from Peru, now faintly inked, shimmered. Below it, something new had appeared in her handwriting - something she didn't remember writing:

The third signal lies beneath the mirror of glass and sky. Where silence wears a mask of sound.

She tapped the page. "My higher self is whispering again."

Pip raised a brow. "Anything useful?"

Anna smiled, tired but knowing. "A direction, maybe. Not a path."

As the plane began its descent, the Tokyo skyline rose to meet them - a sprawl of gleaming metal, stacked life, and ritual buried beneath circuitry. Below, the city pulsed like a nervous system. At the edge of the bay, one skyscraper caught the last of the sun - and flickered. The same flicker they'd seen in Rome. And again in Peru.

Tokyo wasn't hiding the signal.

It was broadcasting it.

And somewhere below, something remembered them.

The wheels touched down with a jolt - not just of rubber meeting tarmac, but of presence. Tokyo didn't welcome. It noticed.

The air inside the terminal was crisp, conditioned, and sterile. Yet something in it felt... wierd. Too clean. Like a scent had been scrubbed from reality. The lighting buzzed faintly, a pitch too high to be normal - like the building was humming to itself in a language just out of reach.

Their bodies moved forward on autopilot, but their senses were wide awake, snaking forward, moving like a current of silent urgency, pulled forward by something unseen. Faces passed them in the arrivals hall - commuters, families, officials - but none of them looked. Not truly. It was as if the city had perfected the art of blindness.

Pip paused near a vending screen. He'd been here before - quite a few times, in fact - on agency shoots and commercial campaigns. He could even string together a few polite phrases in Japanese, remembered from long evenings with production teams and late-night izakaya meetings. But this time felt different. Not just because of the storm gathering within him, but because everything about the airport felt subtly wrong. The same layout. The same signage. But it was as though someone had taken the familiar and filtered it through an uncanny lens. Maybe it was his heightened senses. Maybe it was something else entirely. The same perfume advert they'd seen in Rome played here too - same model, same expression. Only this time, the background was Shibuya Crossing. "They're not just repeating images," he whispered. "They're blending realities."

Anna touched his arm. "We're inside the broadcast now."

Narita International Airport sprawled like a living circuit board - precise, gleaming, and strangely silent despite the mass of travellers threading through it. The tiled floors were immaculate, polished to the point where reflections seemed more real than the people who cast them. Above them, directional signs in kanji and English glowed in soft blue and white, and gentle orchestral tones played on a loop - carefully curated to soothe without being noticed.

A subtle incense hung in the air near the customs gates - not artificial, but faintly ceremonial. Somewhere nearby, a security officer bowed to an elderly couple. Precision and courtesy were layered into the walls.

And yet, beneath the seamless order, there was tension. The place was too pristine. Too choreographed. As if the building itself was watching.

The city was dazzling - layered with noise, light, and movement, a sensory overload orchestrated to dazzle and distract. Neon kanji flickered overhead like sigils, casting soft glows onto faces that didn't look up. Their taxi slid through the cityscape, past the looming presence of Tokyo Tower and the lattice of sky bridges criss-crossing Shibuya. The delicate sprawl of cherry trees outside the Imperial Palace stood in eerie contrast to the LED-lit chaos around Akihabara.

Billboards blinked between luxury goods and AI-generated idols. A holographic geisha bowed above an intersection, eyes empty and perfect. The sky - if it could still be called that - was mirrored in every glass facade they passed, showing an endless repetition of their world with the colours tweaked just slightly wrong.

Even the noise seemed rehearsed. The chirp of crossing signals, where crowds moved in perfect synchronicity - starting and stopping as one, like worker ants or precision-programmed robots obeying the tone. Tokyo is home to the world's busiest metro system - an extensive network of underground and elevated lines that carries more than 8.7 million commuters daily, and over 3.2 billion each year. That sheer scale of controlled movement - of rhythm without pause - seeped into everything, as if even the breath of the city was on a timetable. The hiss of sliding doors. The synthetic lilt of public announcements. All of it layered over a silence beneath - a silence that felt like it had teeth. But beneath the surface, something darker pulsed. They didn't know what they were walking toward, but already, Pip felt the familiar tension in his spine. For a split second, he wondered what would've happened if he hadn't taken that detour in Manchester.

Maybe he'd be sitting in a production meeting right now, calling the shots, surrounded by mood boards and brand decks - in control. Predictable. Safe. But then he looked at Anna beside him, the light from a thousand neon signs painting her features in soft, shifting hues. No. He wouldn't trade this. Not for anything. Not even for the illusion of certainty. Not when he felt more awake - more alive - than he had in years. Maybe ever. The feeling that the lie wasn't just being told. It was being celebrated.

They stepped outside into the metallic air of the city, where every surface reflected them - distorted and layered over product placements and QR codes. It was there, in the reflection of a taxi window, that Pip saw it:

A glitch.

His reflection blinked. But he hadn't.

He stared. The face in the window stared back - and for a second, smiled.

Anna saw it too. "It's started, hasn't it?"

Pip nodded slowly. "And we're already late."

As Pip stepped toward the waiting taxi, he leaned down to the driver and spoke clearly in practiced Japanese, "Midosuji dori no Sumitomo biru made onegaishimasu."

The driver nodded politely, replying with a clipped, "Hai."

"Sumitomo Building," Pip translated softly to Anna as they slid into the back seat. "It's just a guess - but that journal entry... 'mirror of glass and sky' - that building's all mirrored panels. And it's one of the few skyscrapers designed to reflect the sky instead of dominate it."

Anna raised a brow. "You've been here before?"

"Years ago. For a shoot. Something about it stuck. Felt... resonant. And now? It's calling again."

The taxi moved off silently, almost too silently - as if the engine ran on secrecy. Rain began to patter on the windscreen, light at first, then heavier, as though the city were trying to blur its own outlines.

Anna sat quietly, her journal open again. She wasn't writing, just staring at the page with the phrase she hadn't remembered writing. Pip glanced over.

"You okay?"

She nodded, slowly. "There's something... pressing down here. Not just the weight of the city. Like we're breathing in someone else's thought."

Pip looked out at the endless wave of glass towers. "That's because we are."

The taxi slowed as they passed a glowing entrance - a mirrored facade with a name that shimmered and changed with the angle of the rain. First kanji, then English, then glyphs. All in perfect silence. It was a data centre. Or a temple. Or a theatre. The building didn't seem to know, or care, which.

Anna sat upright. "There. That's it."

"What is?"

She tapped her finger against the window. "The third signal. Or at least the gateway."

Pip nodded. "We go in?"

She didn't answer.

Because the streetlights suddenly flickered. Once. Then again.

And then the taxi stopped.

Not slowed.

Stopped.

The driver didn't turn. Didn't speak.

Pip leaned forward. "Excuse me?"

But the man was still. Like someone had switched him off.

Anna reached for the door. "Come on."

They stepped out into the rain. It hit their coats with urgency, like static. And as they turned back to look at the car...

The driver was gone.

Just gone.

The door was still closed. The seat was still warm.

Across the street, a suited man froze mid-stride, then repeated the same three steps again, perfectly, robotically. The neon lights above them flickered, casting brief double-shadows on the rain-slick pavement.

But how could that be? The driver hadn't opened the door.

There'd been no sound, no movement. Just gone - as if he'd never existed. Pip's stomach tightened. A glitch? A projection? Or something deeper?

They exchanged a glance, one that carried the weight of realisation. Whatever had brought them here was no longer simply guiding them - it was shaping what happened around them. And Tokyo wasn't just a backdrop. It was a participant.

But the man was nowhere.

Anna grabbed Pip's hand. "We're in it now."

They didn't move. Not right away. The rain continued to fall, soft but insistent, as if trying to wash away what they'd just seen - or prepare them for what was next.

Pip turned to her, voice quiet but weighted. "Does this feel like a film to you? Like we've stepped into something scripted… or simulated?"

Anna nodded slowly. "The Matrix. That's what it feels like. Like reality is paper-thin, and we've finally seen the tear."

They stood under the overhang of the building, the neon reflections sliding across their faces.

Pip exhaled. "We can't trust anything anymore. Not the signs, not the screens, not the people who smile too long."

Anna's grip tightened. "Just our instincts. And each other."

He nodded. "It's all upside down. The lies aren't just told - they're rehearsed, retold, upgraded. And we've been complicit. All of us. Distracted. Numb."

"And now?" she asked.

He looked at her, eyes steady. "Now we feel. Now we remember. Now we begin."

They stepped through the mirrored threshold.

Inside, the temperature shifted instantly. The air was still - unnaturally still - like sound had been vacuumed from the space. The walls were glass, but reflected nothing. Instead, they shimmered with waves of colourless light, like heat rising off asphalt.

There was no lobby. No desk. Just a long corridor that curved gently, impossibly, as if the building bent away from geometry.

Screens embedded in the walls flickered as they passed. Not ads. Not images. Data. Pip caught glimpses - pulses of human biometric graphs, timestamps, and phrases:

Compliance Imminent. Signal Drift Detected.
Override Interrupted.

"This isn't a building," Anna whispered. "It's an interface."

Pip nodded, his voice low. "And it's watching us back."

The elevator opened before they pressed a button. No numbers - just a symbol: the glyph from Anna's journal.

As they stepped inside, the floor beneath them gave a brief pulse, and the doors slid closed in silence. There were no buttons. No music. Just the sensation of being pulled - not down, not up - inward.

Then the voice spoke.

Not from the speaker. From around them. Through the walls.

"You have entered the Broadcast Core. This node is not built for humans. It is built for the signal."

Anna stepped closer to Pip, her hand gripping his sleeve. The voice continued:

"You are not the first to reach this frequency. But you may be the first to survive it."

The walls flickered.

A disc appeared - suspended midair. But it wasn't Earth. Not the one they knew. Continents were misshapen, as if the borders had never been drawn. Oceans pooled in unfamiliar places, and the poles were reversed - not north and south, but in energetic terms, the flow of consciousness had been realigned. It was Earth as it had been - not geographically, but energetically - before the manipulation of time, maps, and memory. Before the grid imposed false symmetry and carved nations into control zones. A world remembered only by resonance. A world they were meant to forget.

Then it distorted - overlayed with the false map. The familiar one. The accepted one.

"The world you see is not the one you stand upon. The signal enforces the illusion. But fragments remain. Guardians remember."

And in that moment, something broke.
Pip staggered.
The truth was too loud to ignore.
"This is one of seven remaining nodes. Three have been inverted. Two sealed. One stolen. One... waking."
The globe dimmed.
Then the room itself shifted.
The walls began to hum at a new frequency - lower, slower, almost primal. Symbols lit up on the walls. Not just one glyph, but many - layered, overlapping. Ancient scripts, some Sumerian, some Egyptian, some unknown.
A panel opened behind the holographic globe.
Inside it was a suspended object - pulsing faintly with blue light.

A fragment.

Anna stepped forward, her hand trembling. The air around it was thicker, like time moved slower within the space it occupied.
She touched it.
And the room exploded into resonance.
Images flashed - not visions, but memories stored in frequency.
A map of the globe - the real globe - overlaid with points of power.

Nodes. Gateways. Every inverted one shown in red. Every waking one - glowing faintly in blue.

One of them pulsed in North Africa.

And then... silence.

The panel closed. The globe shut down. The lights returned to static white.

They had the Tokyo fragment.

And the watchers - now fully aware - would do everything they could to stop what came next.

Anna whispered, "Waking?"

And far beyond the chamber walls - beyond where sound could be tracked and light could be named - **they saw.**

In the shadows above Tokyo's skyline, behind digital veils and refracted surveillance feeds, the Mimics registered the anomaly. Two human frequencies - out of sync. Too coherent. Too sovereign.

They heard.

The tone of the node had changed. The broadcast wasn't uniform. The script wasn't holding.

They acted.

A signal was sent. Not through cables - through thought. Through networks not listed in any human archive.

And in that moment, Anna's body flinched.

Like something pierced her skin - not sharp, but *loud*. Her eyes widened. Her knees buckled.

Pip staggered back, clutching his skull. It wasn't just sight - it was sensation. Like someone was dragging his spine across time itself.

"Anna?" Pip caught her before she fell completely.

Her breath was shallow. Her pulse erratic.

"They found us," she whispered.

The voice returned, softer now: "Africa."

There was a pause. Not silence - resonance. As if the node itself was remembering.

"The Hidden Gateway."

"Beneath the sands of northern Africa, particularly near Siwa Oasis and the Tassili n'Ajjer, ancient entrances exist. They're not myth - they're sealed gates, referenced by mystics, and guarded."

Anna stirred slightly. Her breath steadied. "I've seen it," she whispered. "In my dream. The red sands. The glyphs on stone. A doorway that doesn't open with hands - only with frequency."

Pip looked at her, something shifting in his chest. "That's where we go next."

He ran a hand through his hair and muttered, "Saving humanity is going to bankrupt me."

Anna gave him a soft smile, the first hint of lightness in hours.

"But not your soul," she said.

He chuckled, dryly. "That's the only account still in credit."

But even as he said it, something twisted in his gut.

They hadn't come to Tokyo just to receive a location.

They had come to awaken it.

The fragment wasn't just a clue - it was a transmitter. A key to restoring something long buried. Tokyo had been inverted, yes, but buried deep beneath the programming was a shard of something older. Pure.

By touching it, Anna hadn't just found the next destination.

She'd triggered the system. And now the signal was broadcasting differently. Every watcher in range would feel the shift. They would hunt for the source.

And the map would lead them there. But not yet.

Anna was still pale. Shaken. Pip helped her out of the chamber, one arm around her shoulders, guiding her through the still corridors and the building that no longer pulsed. As if their presence had unplugged something.

The glass corridor behind them flickered violently, fracturing like a broken screen. Somewhere deep within the building, an alarm…

no, not an alarm, a frequency rose. It wasn't mechanical. It wasn't even sound. It was something alive, vibrating through the walls, through their bones, through their blood.

Pip grabbed Anna's hand. "Move."

The ground beneath their feet shifted subtly, a vertigo tilt that wasn't physical but spatial, like the angles of reality were no longer obeying geometry. The corridor ahead warped, stretching long and thin one second, snapping back the next. Lights overhead pulsed, stuttered, then burst into cold ultraviolet flashes. Shapes flickered at the edges of their vision. Not people. Echoes.

Anna stumbled on her weakened ankle. Pip caught her, hauling her forward. "Come on!"

They ran, Anna feeling every movement as though her leg would buckle at any moment.

Doors along the corridor snapped open as they passed - yawning black voids, doorways into nowhere. One close enough to brush Pip's sleeve with icy air. Another farther down, leaking a sound that wasn't a scream, but the memory of one. The elevator they'd entered from had vanished. In its place: a sheer wall, etched faintly with glyphs that writhed when looked at directly.

No way back.

Pip gritted his teeth and kept moving. He noticed a sign…

"Hioguchi da! Iko!…There… emergency exit!"

A red panel shimmered at the end of the curving hall, a door not of glass but brushed steel, framed by something that smelled faintly of burning metal and wet earth.

They slammed into it. It didn't open immediately, it shivered, judged, before finally yielding with a hiss of decompression.

The night air hit them like a blow - thick with rain, raw and metallic.

They stumbled down a narrow concrete ramp, their shadows stretching and warping under the flickering streetlights. The building behind them convulsed once - a visible ripple running up its mirrored surface, and then went dark.

Pip turned once, briefly, just long enough to see figures gathering behind the glass. Watching. Not chasing... not yet, but marking.

Back on the street, the taxi was gone. The road was slick, deserted. But across the intersection, a black cab sat idling. No headlights. No driver visible. Pip glanced at Anna. She nodded once, silent agreement. They ran, feet splashing through puddles, not daring to look back.

As they approached, the cab's rear door popped open with a pneumatic hiss, without a hand touching it.

They climbed inside without speaking. The interior smelled faintly of sandalwood and static.

The glass between the driver and the backseat was completely opaque. They couldn't see who was driving.

Pip gave the name of their hotel. The cab pulled away immediately, smooth and silent as a ghost.

Neither of them asked how the driver already knew where to take them.

They reached their hotel room without speaking, hearts still pounding from the escape. Pip closed the door behind them, leaning back against it for a moment, letting the silence settle around them like a shield. Anna dropped onto the edge of the bed, her shoulders stiff, her breathing shallow.

As Pip crossed the room toward her, he noticed it, the way she winced slightly when she shifted her weight.

He knelt in front of her without a word and gently lifted the cuff of her jeans. Her ankle was swollen, faintly bruised. A blooming mark across the bone from when they'd sprinted down the emergency stairs, stumbling in the dark.

"Anna," he murmured, guilt cutting through him sharper than fear ever had. "I didn't even see... I should have, "

"You got us out," she said, her voice firm but tired. "That's what matters."

Carefully, he brushed his fingers around the swollen area, as if even his breath could hurt her.

"I'm sorry," he said again, voice raw. "For dragging you into this.

For all of it."

Anna reached for his face, cradling his jaw with one steady hand. "You didn't drag me," she said, a faint, aching smile on her lips. "You showed me where I already belonged."

He closed his eyes for a beat, breathing her in, the warmth of her, the fierce steadiness.

Then he stood, pressing a soft kiss to her temple.

"Stay here," he said. "Let me run the bath."

Neither spoke. The moment didn't ask for language.

They moved together slowly at first - like two people rediscovering touch, like trust was a thing you could hold. The bath steamed behind them, the scent of jasmine thick in the air. Anna's robe slipped from her shoulders and Pip kissed the base of her neck, his hands soft, steady, reverent. She arched slightly, guiding him toward her, anchoring herself to the only truth she could feel.

This.

The ache of centuries. The longing not just of two souls in this moment, but of generations who had searched for their mirror and never found it. Of lives half-lived and hearts that never fully woke. And now - here - in a hotel room above a city of shadows and light, that longing found its home.

The way their bodies met was not rushed but reverent, a sacred unfolding. They didn't devour; they discovered. Like the ecstasy of soul recognition, like two stars realising they once belonged to the same constellation. It was symbiotic - a breath for a breath, a rhythm that needed no instruction.

It was the kind of intimacy written in the body long before the mind was taught to doubt it.

Not the signal. Not the glyphs. Not the fear.

Only this.

Their bodies fit like memory - not a perfect match, but a remembered one. There was laughter between the breathlessness, hunger between the gentleness. The kind of intimacy that doesn't ask, do you love me, but whispers, I never stopped. It wasn't just physical - it was soul memory. The kind of knowing that slips through lifetimes and finds itself again. Fingers traced constellations across skin. Breath aligned like tides. They weren't just touching - they were remembering. Reclaiming something that had been torn from them long ago and hidden beneath noise and forgetting. In the quiet between movements, it was as though the universe leaned in and listened.

Later, entwined on the duvet, Anna turned toward him, her voice hushed but steady. "This... they can't replicate this, can they?"
"No," Pip said, brushing a strand of hair from her face. "This is what they'll never understand."
"I don't want to sleep," she whispered. "You don't have to."
But she drifted anyway, and Pip sat beside her, watching the slow rise and fall of her chest.
It wasn't the chamber or the glyphs or the broadcast that haunted him now. It was this.
Her. Her vulnerability. Her strength. The fact that they were just two people in a world that had forgotten its story - and somehow, they were remembering it together.
He kissed her forehead, gently.

This was what the watchers would never understand.
This was the power they feared. Love - real love - was not a frequency they could mimic.

The Ethiopian Vision

The night in Tokyo passed, but not smoothly.

They slept, but it was a surface sleep, fragile, half-breathing, woven through with memory. The air in the room felt dense, almost stuffy, laced with an unseen heaviness. The quilt pressed down on them like a weight that refused to lift. The walls seemed to breathe with them, the city's neon pulse leaking through the cracks, but beneath it all, something deeper stirred.

The underground resonance chamber still vibrated in the unseen frequencies, calling, stirring, weaving tendrils through the folds of dreaming consciousness. Neither of them had truly left the place where the signal had touched them. Not yet. Pip woke first.

The faintest tremor ran through him, not fear, but a silent recognition that the journey had shifted again, tilting onto a path he couldn't steer. Anna stirred beside him, her face soft in the low morning light, but her body tense, fingers twitching lightly as if reaching for something just beyond reach. Anna's fingers curled into his without opening her eyes. She winced slightly as she shifted, and Pip saw the faint swelling around her ankle, a purpling bruise blooming across the skin. He moved carefully, lifting her foot onto his lap, cradling it in his hands. His touch was light, reverent, fingertips tracing healing into the places where bruises now spoke. Anna smiled faintly through the pain. "It's not broken." "Still," Pip murmured, "you carried more than you should've." She squeezed his hand. "We both did."Silence grew between them again, but it wasn't empty. It was heavy with meaning. Like the world outside the window had faded to static, and only the pulse of their joined frequencies remained. Pip tucked a pillow behind her back, adjusted the covers, and just sat there, watching over her. The truth was, he didn't want to move. Didn't want to break whatever fragile field held them safe, if only for this breath, this beat, this borrowed moment.But something deeper was already shifting. A vibration. A hum too low to be heard. The signal hadn't finished with them yet. Anna's breathing slowed. The lines of tension in her face smoothed. Her whole being softened, as if she were slipping downward, not into sleep, but into somewhere beneath waking. The compass, resting on the bedside table, pulsed once. A soft glow. A beat of memory. Pip felt it too, a pull behind his sternum, like gravity folding in a new direction. Anna's body remained there in Tokyo, in the quiet room overlooking the blinking skyline. But her consciousness slipped sideways, unspooling along a thread that ran not through space, but through time's oldest artery.She hadn't left the room. But she was no longer only there. She hadn't left Tokyo. Not in body.

The resonance interface in the underground chamber still pulsed faintly, casting pale, shifting patterns on the stone walls. The air was thick with memory. In her vision, Pip sat cross-legged near the old altar, eyes half-lidded, breath slow, sunk into a trance-like state that held him between worlds. Anna knelt a few feet away, fingertips touching the worn ground as if grounding herself into something deeper than soil. Her breathing matched his, slow, steady, suspended. They had not planned to enter this state.It hadn't arrived gently. It seized her. One moment she was lying tangled in the hotel sheets, the quilt heavy, the air thick and clammy around them, and the next, something vast and ancient cracked open inside her. Not a door.

A veil.

It didn't pull her body, her body stayed there, curled loosely beside Pip, one bare foot tangled in the covers - but it ripped her consciousness free. Anna's breathing shifted - slow, shallow, suspended. Her fingers twitched once against the fabric, then stilled completely. The weight of the Tokyo night pressed against the windows, but Anna was no longer here. The compass, buried somewhere near the bed, pulsed again, a subtle throb through space itself. The resonance they'd triggered underground hadn't stopped. It had been rising, weaving through the folds of sleeping consciousness, and now it had claimed her. She hadn't spoken since the moment it brushed her skin. And Pip, still half awake, still battered by everything they had endured, sensed it too - that this wasn't a dream, wasn't ordinary sleep.It was transition. And Anna was already gone.

Whatever was pulling her wasn't polite, and it wasn't patient.

It moved through her blood like wildfire - fierce, inevitable, destined. The ancient energy of the chamber rose to meet it, vibrating the very air around them, stirring unseen patterns into the dust and stone. Anna's fingers twitched once against the ground, then stilled. Her breathing deepened, shifted, no longer human-regular, but tuned to some deeper rhythm. A forgotten song, sung by a body that remembered more than the mind ever could. Pip sat across from her, still, watching, feeling the field thickening around them - not daring to touch her, not daring to call her back. He knew, in his bones, that this wasn't sleep. And she was already far away. Now, her breathing slowed even further. The stone beneath her seemed to vanish. Light poured in behind her closed eyes. She felt her body remain in Tokyo - but her consciousness had slipped cleanly from it, drawn by a frequency beyond thought.

Ethiopia.

She was there - not as a traveller, but as her soul was pulled home through time's deepest thread. This was not memory. This was a remembering written into her bones before birth - a reunion long prophesied, felt now as a silent ache turning to light. She was not dreaming. She was being called back - by the land, by the stars, by those who had never truly left her. The land beneath her bare feet was warm, dry, sacred. The air shimmered with presence. Ancient hills rose in silence, crowned by stone churches and whispers of things long hidden. Here, the earth held stories in its bones. Anna fell to her knees. Not in fear, but in recognition. Above her, the sky did not open... it parted. And within that parting, the glyph appeared.

A star. Geometric. Eight-pointed. Radiant. It pulsed slowly, folding and unfolding like breath. It was not made of light but of truth. Its pattern sang. A seal. A signal. A memory encoded in form. It wasn't a symbol in the ordinary sense.

The Outer Circle was the first tone she felt: a low, steady hum that wrapped around her like a held breath. It spoke of protection and containment, of a boundary where nothing false could cross.

The Eight-Pointed Star sang above it, bright and high, a crystalline note that threaded through her skull and down her spine. Each point pulsed with its own micro-tone: four rising like a hymn to the elements, four falling like echoes from somewhere beyond time.

The Meridian Arcs curved across the star like invisible strings, their notes a moving, liquid tremor. They weren't lines so much as currents, each one carrying the signature of a place - Göbekli Tepe, Antarctica, Tokyo, Ethiopia - the vibrations of ancient stones and frozen seas. She could hear them as well as see them: each arc a tuning fork struck somewhere on the planet's skin.

The Central Triangle and Circle glowed deepest of all. Its tone was not sound but memory - a recognition that bypassed her mind and bloomed in her chest. The triangle rose inside the circle like an arrowhead, a key poised at the lock. The note it released was warm, almost maternal, and for a heartbeat she could feel it recognising her back.

Around the rim, the Runic Marks flickered and hissed with tiny sparks, their tones like whispers at the edge of hearing. Not words, but the vowels of a lost language. Each mark flickered like a candle flame and let go a single syllable into her bones. Together they made a scale she could almost sing but not yet understand.

As the glyph pulsed, all the separate tones began to braid together, the hum of the circle, the chime of the star, the tremor of the arcs, the warmth of the triangle, the whispers of the rim, and Anna realised she was standing inside a living chord. The geometry wasn't just being shown to her.

It was playing her….. The land responded.

From the soil, silent figures began to rise.

Tall, robed, motionless. They shimmered faintly, not quite there, but not illusion either.
Guardians.
Watchers.
Not of this time, and yet utterly present. They bore the same glyph etched across their chests - living light. Resonant geometry made visible, a geometry of living light, neither carved nor projected but grown out of the air itself. At first Anna thought it was a single shape, but as she looked closer it broke apart - or rather opened - like a chord pulled into its separate notes.

One stepped forward. He looked not at her, but into her.
"You are of the line," he said, not aloud, but directly into her being. Anna's heart surged. A recognition rippled through her that bypassed mind entirely. The star above folded in on itself, then reopened as a map. Lines of resonance, arcs of frequency connecting sites across the plane.

They appeared to her again… Göbekli Tepe. Antarctica. Tokyo. …others unnamed.

But at the centre, Ethiopia.
"You are returned," the guardian said. *"The key remembers the lock."*

Anna wept without tears. Her body in Tokyo trembled. Her soul burned with something she could not name. And when she opened her eyes again, the chamber in Tokyo was utterly still. But behind her lids, the star remained.

Something sacred had been remembered.

And when Anna finally opened her eyes again, the hotel room swam back into focus, but nothing was the same. The walls seemed thinner, the colours sharper, the very air heavier - as if reality itself strained to hold its shape around her.

The chamber in Tokyo - the resonance field, had gone still. But still, within her, behind her blinking gaze, the Star remained. Not a memory. Not a vision. A living imprint.It thrummed quietly inside her chest, folding and unfolding like the breath of a world waiting to be reborn.

Pip stirred beside her, sensing it too. His hand brushed her arm gently, anchoring her back - but some part of her was no longer wholly here.

She had been marked. Claimed. Remembered.

And far beyond the walls of Tokyo… across oceans, across veils - something else woke at her return. A sleeping signal. A buried architecture.

Another node flared into trembling life on the unseen map.

New York.

She saw it not as a place but as a pulse, jagged, electric, desperate, screaming beneath the towers of glass and concrete. The City That Never Slept was stirring. And it was not only humanity that would answer the call. Anna inhaled sharply, the taste of ancient dust and neon bitterness filling her lungs. The next step would be different, It would not be a memory recovered.

It would be a battleground chosen.

And deep in the tangled circuitry of the coming storm, a voice, old, distorted, half-forgotten - whispered into the dark:

"They have awakened the final threshold."

And this time… the gatekeepers will not yield easily. Anna met Pip's eyes across the dim room. No words needed. The storm was already gathering.

And New York would be the first to see what had been hidden in plain sight all along.

33 Thomas Street - The Signal Vault

They stepped out of the terminal and into the thunderclap of New York.

It wasn't just louder, it was denser. The air carried the weight of urgency, of movement, of capitalism dressed in chaos. Horns blared in discordant symphonies. Sirens wailed like ritual chants. The humidity didn't just cling, it pressed. It turned lungs into sponges. It wasn't just air; it was obligation made breathable.

Skyscrapers rose like declarations, bold and unapologetic. Flags hung from steel poles with militant pride, flanked by corporate logos that towered just as defiantly. The streets buzzed with impatience - people talking fast, walking faster, eyes darting, hands waving, never still. Every conversation seemed to overlap, compete, collide. No one made space. No one paused.

After the clean circuitry of Tokyo, the sensory contrast was jarring. Anna adjusted her bag and glanced around. "It's like the city's screaming at us."

Pip nodded. "It's not a whispering node like Tokyo. This one shouts. Everything's a distraction. Even the distractions are distracting."

A yellow cab screeched to a halt, missing the curb by inches. The driver leaned halfway out of the window, cigarette dangling, and bellowed, "Hey! You got a death wish or are you just from Jersey?" The cyclist flipped him off without turning around.

The cabbie spat onto the street, muttered something, and peeled off with a hand gesture unmistakably New York.
They crossed the taxi line, weaving through crowds of suits, backpacks, tourists, and vendors hawking bottled water and burner phones. Somewhere, someone was selling hot dogs. Somewhere else, a street preacher screamed about the end.

Anna slowed, watching the billboard overhead glitch, the pharmaceutical logo melting seamlessly into a climate emergency warning.
"They're not even hiding it anymore," she said under her breath.
Pip followed her gaze, his voice tight.
"They don't have to. BlackRock. Vanguard. State Street. Three hands, one puppet."

Anna frowned. "What do you mean?"
"They're not companies. They're umbrellas. Shells. They own the foundations of the system - thousands of everyday names. Nestlé. Pfizer. Amazon. Coca-Cola. Google. Meta. Even the so-called competition - Pepsi and Coke, Microsoft and Apple, Fox and CNN. All fed from the same hand."

Anna's fingers tightened on her bag. "Own the brands. Own the narrative."
"Own the climate agenda," Pip added. "Own the wars. Own the 'solutions' to the problems they engineered."
He gestured at the flashing screen - selling drought fear beside plastic-wrapped eco-products.
"They script the crisis," Pip repeated, "then make you thank them for the solution they already owned."
He nodded toward the massive ticker flashing across the skyline - carbon credit schemes, food scarcity warnings, digital ID initiatives - all framed as inevitabilities.
"BlackRock isn't just investing," Pip said. "They're engineering. Engineering demand. Engineering dependence. Engineering

permission."

"They manufacture dependence," Anna replied. "Then they make us pay for survival."

Anna's voice dropped to a whisper. "They don't just own what we consume. They own how we think."

"Yep," Pip said. "They've normalised the script. Made the lie so constant, so loud, no one even questions the sound of it."

They walked on.

And high above, in the brutal monolith of 33 Thomas Street, something - or someone - adjusted the feed - watching, recording, rewriting.

They'd arrived.

And they were already being watched.

They hadn't known about TITANPOINTE until the Tokyo node had revealed it.

After Anna touched the fragment in the Sumitomo chamber, a burst of imagery had flashed, building schematics, transmission coordinates, and a codename stamped in red: TITANPOINTE.

A stolen vault. A buried node. One that watched everything.

Pip took a photo before it collapsed. Later, when he searched, the stories were there… hiding in plain sight.

Now, Church Street coiled around them like a sleeping serpent. The air shifted subtly, as if they'd stepped into a dead zone. The noise didn't fade, it receded, like behind thick glass.

The tower loomed ahead.

No windows. No logo. Just a monolithic slab of brutalist concrete, climbing into the sky, blank, brutal, watching without eyes.

"Why does it feel like it's breathing?" Anna whispered.

Pip didn't answer. His vision sharpened too much; edges over-accentuated. The ambient city sound separated unnaturally, isolating frequencies one by one.

The building wasn't just observing. It was feeling.

They circled the block twice, scanning for cameras, pressure sensors, anything resembling an entrance. Nothing. Just smooth concrete and narrow ventilation slits high above.

That's when it happened.

A group of pedestrians walking toward them froze - not physically, but perceptually. Their heads all turned in unison. Eyes vacant. Faces too still. Then, just as quickly, they moved on. As if nothing had happened.

Pip exhaled. "Okay. That's a new one"

Then Anna spotted it, a small, recessed service door, half-concealed behind a skip, almost deliberately unremarkable. A thin pulse of static crawled across Pip's skin as they approached, like the air itself didn't want them closer. He hesitated, hand hovering near the metal. It wasn't a door, not in the traditional sense. It felt... intelligent.

Waiting.

Anna touched his arm. "Are we sure about this?"

Pip didn't answer. He pressed his hand flat against the surface, and for a moment, nothing happened.

Then came a vibration. Not sound. Not movement. A vibration through him, low and searching, like fingers combing through his memories.

His pulse quickened. The metal warmed under his palm.

And then it clicked.

Not mechanical. Not magnetic. An approval. An invitation.

The door didn't swing open. It folded - a thin seam unzipping vertically, revealing a dark passage beyond.

Anna swallowed. "That's not normal access."

Pip nodded grimly. "We weren't let in. We were recognised."

They exchanged one last look, the kind that asked: Are you ready to cross a line that doesn't let you walk back?

And then they stepped through the threshold.

Into silence.

Into the machine.

The walls were lined with strange panels, flush with no visible wiring, their surface rippling faintly as they passed. It felt less like entering a building and more like being absorbed into a system.

And overhead - so faint they might've imagined it - a low, harmonic hum.

It wasn't a warning, it was a frequency.

TITANPOINTE. Not a rumour. Not a conspiracy. The real designation - buried in NSA documents and whispered among the few who knew to look. A codename wrapped around the darkest node in the surveillance grid. This wasn't a telecom relay. It was the vault. A place where data didn't just pass through - it stayed. Recorded. Interpreted. Repurposed.

Pip's skin prickled.

Everything about the space was intentional. The lack of windows. The shielding. The cold, humming walls. It wasn't architecture. It was containment.

And something in it had recognised his blood.

The silence swallowed them - the kind that listens back.

The walls shimmered faintly. Overhead, a low harmonic hum vibrated against their bones.

TITANPOINTE wasn't just surveillance. It was signal memory.

A faint pulse responded to Pip's bloodline. The structure knew. A panel slid open.

Inside, suspended in a shaft of thin light, a sphere pulsed - slow, rhythmic - almost like a heartbeat.

It didn't speak in words. It spoke in truth:

Pharmaceutical pipelines - loops of illness, not cures.
Climate models - manufactured fear, masquerading as fact.
Financial debt - chains forged in silence, worn as trophies of progress.

And then - a waveform:
Rhesus Negative Blood. Anomaly. Resistance. Immune to full inversion.

The truth struck him like a physical blow.
Rhesus Negative wasn't rare by accident.
It was a relic.
There were bloodlines the dark architects feared.
Lines that sang in a frequency beyond their reach, carrying echoes of a time before grids and towers and programmable flesh.
Among these, the ones marked "Rh-", moved differently through the current.
Their memory could not be inverted. Their resonance could not be fully captured.
And so the hunters came - not to kill, but to harvest, dilute, and claim what they could not create. Because in the veins of the remembered ones, the old songs still whispered.

And the system knew: one drop of truth could undo a thousand layers of lies.
And across the vault's fractured memory-map, places flickered:
Concentrations of Rh- blood across ancient strongholds - Basque country, Berber tribes, Irish Highlands, Ethiopian Highlands - encoded resistance zones.

Not accidents. Survival.

Anna's voice trembled. "They weren't just monitoring you. They were trying to replicate you."
Pip's breath tightened. "And failing."
Then the pulse changed.
The building noticed.
The light flickered. Doors sealed. Walls breathed.
And something in the deep floors below shifted.
The walls trembled. A low drone ramped up from beneath the

floor, rising like a warning siren wrapped in velvet. The pulse of the sphere flickered, once, twice, and then stabilised.

The entire building had noticed.

A surge raced through the floor, lights dimming. Panels sealed behind them with an airtight hiss. Doors that once welcomed now locked tight. TITANPOINTE was no longer observing.

It was responding.

Anna backed toward the wall, scanning the edges. "We triggered something."

"No," Pip said quietly. " I triggered something."

Suddenly, from a fissure in the far wall, a burst of static shredded the stillness.

A projection fought to form - flickering, glitching, like a ghost dragged through broken wire.

A face bled into existence:

Male. Aged beyond years. Hollow-eyed. Clothes hanging loose like gravity had grown heavier just for him. Skin drawn tight over bones that remembered too much.

Not a hero.

Not a villain.

A witness.

His voice cracked through the air, every word like a blow struck through mud:

"If you're seeing this..." He winced - as if the very act of speaking burned. *"...then the vault still remembers."*

He leaned closer, pixels fragmenting across his forehead. The hum of the Vault deepened.

"They tried to wipe me. To delete my pattern. Couldn't."

His breath caught, chest hitching as if the walls themselves were squeezing him.

"Not fully."

Anna moved forward instinctively, as if she could catch him, shield him.

The figure shuddered, teeth clenched against some unseen force.

"You don't have long."

Static gnawed at his outline. His shoulders twitched as though battling something beyond sight.

"There's another node... deeper... I found the coordinates but they weren't mapped - they were buried."

Pip stepped forward, voice rough: "Where?"

The figure tried to answer. His mouth opened…

A surge of distortion tore through the projection, warping his face into something alien, then human, then alien again.

His final words snapped through the chamber like a broken prayer:

"Run - like you've never run in your lives before."

Then the projection collapsed inward, sucked back into the wall like breath into a dying lung.

Silence slammed into the space - not emptiness, but the charged silence of something ancient remembering they were here.

And the Vault began to wake.

Anna turned slowly, her face drained of colour but filled with clarity.

"When he said the frequencies won't hold…" she whispered, more to herself than to Pip. "He didn't mean ours. He meant theirs."

Pip blinked, the weight of it settling. "Their grip. Their grid. It's breaking." And outside the sealed room, something began to move. It wasn't footsteps. Not exactly. It was a pressure shift - like gravity thickening. The hum of the building deepened, shifting frequency, like a breath being held.

Then a sound: sharp, deliberate. Metal meeting metal. Not random. Patterned. Something mechanical… but moved with intention.

Anna turned to Pip, pale. "It's not a machine." He nodded slowly. "It's wearing one."

A shape passed behind the reinforced glass of the corridor - almost humanoid, but wrong. Limbs too smooth, too fluid. The head moved in increments, like a camera resetting to scan.

Not human. Not robotic. Inverted. The watchers had sent

something that didn't belong in either world.

Pip backed toward the panel that had opened before. "We need another way out." Anna's eyes locked onto a flicker in the wall - another glyph, one that hadn't been there a second ago.

"It's guiding us," she whispered.

Another sound - closer now. They ran. Like the air itself was turning against them.

Down a narrow hall that curved unnaturally - like the building had rewritten itself to trap them. The lights strobed with no rhythm. Sirens didn't blare, but tones did - low, guttural pulses that made their bones vibrate. Not alarms. Directives.

Behind them, the metallic rhythm changed. Whatever wore that suit, it had started to mimic their pace. It didn't run. It glided.

Anna spotted another glyph - this one pulsing with urgency - above a recessed door. She placed her palm flat against it. Nothing.

Pip stepped forward, his breath shallow. As soon as his hand touched the surface, the door gasped open. They tumbled inside, the space tight and windowless - no obvious exit.

Then a screen blinked to life. Not a camera. A message.

"Jerusalem lights the pathway to the resonance gate. Giza."
"The guardian awakens when the bloodline nears."

Anna stared at Pip, sweat streaming from her temple. "We don't have time."

The Inverted were coming.

And somewhere - in the dense coding behind a lensless sensor - the Inverted calculated probability.

It didn't feel threat. It registered signal deviation. It didn't feel hate. It flagged resonance noncompliance. Anna's energy was still pliable, still within the spectrum of potential realignment. But Pip? Pip was remembering. And that made him incompatible.

It adjusted its form - not for intimidation, but for mirror disruption. The face it wore was chosen from the fragments of his subconscious. Familiar. Slightly off. Designed to trigger confusion, not fear.

It moved forward. Not to kill. But to rewrite.

The wall behind them hissed - not like hydraulics or machinery, but like breath through unseen lungs. The corridor was reopening, but not as it had been. It unfolded, reshaping, like tissue reacting to stimulus. The sound wasn't mechanical.

It was biological. A wet exhale from the architecture itself. It was cellular - like the walls themselves were inhaling.

A long pause…

Then the temperature dropped.

Not a breeze, not air-con - an ambient pull, like something in the building had turned its attention fully toward them and was deciding what shape to take.

A figure stepped into view. It didn't burst through. It didn't sprint. It just… arrived.

Its presence bent the space around it. Light refracted where it stood. Its form flickered - not glitching, but negotiating between appearances. One moment it looked like a man in a black suit. Then next, a silhouette with reversed features. Then, briefly, it wore Pip's face.

Anna gasped.

The Inverted didn't kill unless they had to. They unmade you. Bit by bit. Thought by thought.

And right now, the thing at the end of the corridor was already inside their minds - running simulations of their fear, seeking the easiest path to overwrite.

Pip gripped Anna's hand. "We move now." Anna didn't hesitate.

They lunged toward the glyph-lit panel. As they passed through, the corridor behind them folded in on itself - walls merging with walls, ceiling sloughing down like flesh meeting bone.

The Inverted didn't follow with speed. It descended. It integrated.

Pip's shoulder slammed into a beam as they skidded down a sharp incline, barely lit, the floor flexing like muscle beneath carpet. The air thinned.

Anna stumbled, caught her balance, eyes scanning. "There....light!"

They burst through another doorway, this one lined with exposed metal - real metal, unpolished, human. Emergency stairs.

They didn't ask questions. They ran. Five flights. Ten. No sound behind them, but the weight of something that could step through walls.

The motion sensors flickered as they hit the ground floor - a stuttering pulse, almost reluctant.

Then, without warning, the exit spat them out. No graceful swing of doors. No sterile whoosh.

It was violent - a pressure blast like being hurled from a collapsing lung. Pip barely kept his feet; Anna stumbled into him, her shoulder slamming against his.

The instant they crossed the threshold, the world detonated. Daylight shattered their senses, raw, brutal, blinding. Horns blared in discordant waves. Engines roared. A taxi skidded past with a screech and a spray of hot grime.

Voices crashed around them, vendors yelling, tourists barking into phones, construction hammers rattling like gunfire. The heat slapped their faces like a wet rag. The stench of exhaust and food carts and too many bodies clogged their lungs. Anna gasped, disoriented, blinking against the savage brightness. Pip caught her elbow, steadying her, his own pulse a wild snare drum behind his ribs. They twisted back, half-expecting to see some monstrous thing clawing its way through the breach.

But there was nothing.

Only the blank, seamless wall of 33 Thomas Street - featureless, mute, erasing its secrets behind a facade of indifference.

As if the building had never opened. As if they had never been there. Only the resonance still thrumming inside their bones said otherwise. Anna turned just once. The door was already gone. The wall was smooth. Seamless. TITANPOINTE had erased their entrance.

But not their memory.

They didn't speak for a long time. Just stood, breath fogging in the thick New York humidity, as people brushed past them - commuters in suits, tourists pulling rolling bags, couriers shouting into earpieces. The city had resumed around them like nothing had happened. Like the signal vault didn't exist just a metre behind the brick.

Anna steadied herself against a lamppost. "Did that just happen?"

Pip nodded, slowly. "It did."

A woman bumped into Anna, muttered an apology, and moved on. A man selling sunglasses shouted about a two-for-one deal. The jarring normality of it made the whole experience more surreal.

"We need to get out of here," Pip said. "But not just out of the city. Out of the noise. Somewhere with sky and space to breathe."

Anna touched her shoulder where the pressure from the Inverted had seemed to pass right through her. Her voice was ragged, almost not her own.

"Jerusalem... the seat of first inversion. The axis of control. Where the fracture was birthed."

They moved down the street - slower now. They stopped at a corner café. It was nothing special: white cups stacked on chrome, cheap pastries, a flickering menu board. They sat at the back, near the window, watching the crowd.

Anna looked around. "Do you think anyone else sees it? What's underneath all this?"

Pip sipped the orange juice, sharp and fresh, tasting something real for the first time all day.

"Some do. Most feel it. But they're too tired. Too distracted. That's the design. Keep them numb, keep them rushing. The illusion is held in place not with force, but with noise. Messages flood their senses - from screens, from headlines, from songs that echo frequencies not meant to heal, but to dull. Symbols planted in plain sight, triggering responses before a thought even forms. And the why? That's the part most never ask. Because asking requires silence. Stillness. And the system made sure they're too exhausted for either."

She leaned forward. "Then let's not get tired. Let's not stop."

They paid in cash. The woman at the counter gave them a look, like they were a curiosity from another decade.

A cab took them from the café to the TWA Hotel. As they moved through Manhattan, Anna's gaze swept the skyline.

"Obelisks in Paris. London. New York. The Vatican. Even in Buenos Aires and Istanbul. All placed with obsessive precision - not monuments, Pip. They're energetic pins - markers for a signal network that predates digital code. Rockefeller Plaza, too - that Atlas statue isn't just art. It's the mimic's declaration - man burdened by the cosmos, not one with it. Even the Statue of Liberty… it's not what people think. It's not liberty. It's their light, a false flame held high by a mimic goddess. The statue wasn't born from freedom - it was crafted by Freemasons, aligned to luciferian symbolism. The torch? Not a beacon of hope - a torch of control, of enforced illumination, like the false light the Inverted offer. It faces away from the country, not into it, and it sits atop a star-shaped foundation - the same geometry that underpins so many of their sites. It's not a symbol of liberty. It's a mask. A lighthouse for the grid. Every so-called beacon in this city is a lie sculpted in stone."

Pip was quiet. He watched the flashing lights of the city blur past, half-listening to a voicemail from his agency. Project updates. A missed client call. He didn't reply.

The hotel emerged like a mirage from the highway - sleek curves, steel glass, lit like a film set from the sixties. The TWA Hotel.

Chosen by Pip for its clean strangeness. Retro-futurism. It didn't feel real. That's why he liked it.

Inside, the foyer smelled of polished terrazzo, cedar wax, and something sterile - like ozone, or forgotten time. Soft jazz echoed faintly beneath the ambient hum. A bellboy nodded but didn't speak. The desk clerk barely looked up.

They checked in, took the elevator up in silence, the kind that wraps itself around closeness. Their room looked out over the runway. Lights blinked in lines like coded pulses.

Anna took off her shoes and sat by the window. "Everything feels temporary. Like it's all about to change."

Pip sat beside her. Close but not touching. "I know."

A beat.

"I should call in," he said, pulling his phone from his pocket. He left a short message, personal leave extended. He spoke softly, his words vague - something about needing time to decompress, about stepping away to rebalance. It was enough. They didn't need more than that.

When he hung up, Anna reached for his hand.

They didn't speak. Just stayed there, side by side, as if the space between them had softened since the vault.

The hum of passing planes filled the room. But it couldn't drown out the silence forming between their breaths - heavy, real, threaded with something tender.

Later, the city dimmed. They shared a bath. Quiet laughter, fingers tracing old scars. It wasn't passion. Not entirely. It was recognition. A memory blooming in present tense.

She fell asleep against his chest. He stayed awake, watching the stars disappear behind passing clouds.

In the morning, the city resumed its noise. They dressed in quiet synchronicity, they sipped coffee, hot and rich, the porcelain warm against their palms, early morning light just beginning to push through the skyline. The terminal was visible through the tinted glass - they didn't need a cab, not really, but something about the routine felt grounding. They stepped into a shuttle van, its logo still bearing the ghost of the TWA emblem, and settled into the seats behind a group of airline staff.

On the short ride across the loop, Anna stared out of the window. Pip watched the sky.

Above them, the contrails split and widened.

The world was preparing.

Ahead, across an ocean and a thousand old lies, Jerusalem waited... and the sand would not hide the truth forever.

Part three:
REMEMBERING THE SONG

You were not meant to read this alone.
The signal spreads. Carriers awaken.
One note remembered becomes a chorus.
Let the echo move through you.

Chapter 25:
The Descent to Jerusalem

They didn't speak much on the flight. There was no need. The silence between them had weight now - not awkward, not uncertain, but charged. Like a cord had been pulled taut between two distant points, and they were slowly reeling it in.

Pip stared out the window as the plane descended. The land rolled out below like scripture. Not read, but remembered. Hills etched by time. Stone scorched with memory. Olive groves like prayers.

Jerusalem.

The name itself felt like a sound older than language, something shaped in the mouth of God, then buried.

Anna leaned toward him. "Do you feel it?"

He nodded. "Like we've been walking toward this place since before we were born."

She took his hand.

When they stepped onto the tarmac, the air struck them immediately - not with heat, but with density. The atmosphere felt coded. Every breath carried resonance. Every shadow watched. Ben Gurion Airport was unlike any place they'd flown into. A paradox of sleek modernity and layered scrutiny. The arrivals hall was quiet but humming, not with noise, but with focus. Security presence was subtle, but everywhere. Eyes that didn't blink. Cameras that didn't follow - they absorbed. Glass, steel, stone - built to suggest openness, but infused with thresholds. Pip felt it the moment they crossed into the passport

210

queue. Not a checkpoint, but a filter.

There was a tension beneath the politeness. A pause beneath each question. Anna noticed it too. Her hand brushed his, not out of fear, but awareness.

The city hadn't started yet, and already they were inside something older than travel. Not the act of movement, but the memory behind it, the pull that brought pilgrims, soldiers, prophets and kings. Pip felt it rise through his soles like static memory. This wasn't just arrival. It was alignment. As if the land itself was scanning for resonance, measuring those who crossed its threshold. Not with malice - with memory. Recognition. And invitation.

They checked in to a small hotel tucked into one of the Old City's winding stone alleys, where jasmine spilled over arched doorways and each building seemed to lean in slightly, whispering to the next. The streets outside buzzed with a kind of layered silence, not empty, but steeped in history so dense it hummed. Incense hung in the air. A muezzin's call curled above church bells, both floating above the low murmur of traders and pilgrims. Jerusalem wasn't one city, it was all of them - layered, concealed, resurrected, and awake.

The hotel itself felt like an echo of all that. A carved wooden door. Walls thick with age. The coolness of stone that remembered hands. Inside, time felt different. Slower. Like each moment arrived pre-aged, worn smooth by centuries of repetition and prayer. tucked inside the Old City. The receptionist didn't ask questions. Just handed them an old brass key like it had been waiting.

The room was spartan but clean. Stone floors. No TV. A single window that looked out over the rooftops and domes of a city that had hosted more blood and belief than perhaps any place on Earth. Jerusalem was a paradox of divinity and division - revered by millions, fought over for millennia. Every cobblestone bore witness to prophecy and betrayal. Kingdoms had risen and fallen in its shadow. Faiths had flourished and fractured. Here, history wasn't written, it was scarred into the earth. From the Wailing Wall to the Dome of the Rock, from Crusaders' footsteps to Roman gates, it held within its stones the echoes of both devotion and devastation. It was a living paradox - sacred and scarred, eternal and ever-contested.

That night, neither of them could sleep.

The heat clung to the stone walls like memory, and the weight of anticipation pressed on their chests. The city's breath moved through the window in slow, ancient rhythms, carrying the scent of dust, jasmine, and distant prayers. History hung in the air, thick, almost audible - making rest impossible.

They lay in silence, hearts echoing with something more than thought. A knowing. A summons.

And when it came, it wasn't a dream.

It was a pull, a hum, a current.

They rose without speaking. Walked the narrow streets as if following something unseen.

Past closed shops. Past old men murmuring in languages that seemed to hang between dimensions. Past ancient doors with carvings that shimmered when they passed.

Down.

Further down.

Through an arch that should've been sealed, set behind the Armenian Quarter, just past the ruins of the old Roman Cardo and beneath a barely marked archway close to the Tower of David. Above them, the citadel loomed, a structure long believed to be a relic of strength, but in truth, one of many sites encoded with inverted intention. The energy shifted here, more sharply than before. It was near the Hurva Synagogue's foundation stones where they felt the first hum. Symbols in the stonework didn't match the period. Anna traced one lightly, not ancient Hebrew, but something older, overwritten. A fragment of a map? A seal?

Anna squinted at the carving, her fingers still resting lightly on the edge. "This isn't decorative," she murmured. "It's deliberate. Placed."

Pip leaned in beside her. "It feels familiar. Not because we've seen it, but because something in us remembers it."

"A fragment of a map... or a seal," she said again, slower this time. "A key to something buried. Or something locked."

He nodded. "It's not just a symbol. It's a frequency anchor. I can feel it. Like it wants to wake something."

She looked at him, wide-eyed. "Or someone."

Further down.

And past what should have been a solid wall, they entered.

Outside that hidden passage, life still pulsed through the Old City - veiled women whispered prayers into cracked stone; Orthodox priests in long black robes lit incense at narrow altars; yeshiva boys moved quickly through alleyways with books clutched to their chests. Tourists with wide eyes trailed behind guides reciting history as ritual. A man selling figs offered them without words. Another sat cross-legged on a blanket, surrounded by amulets, his eyes far away, as if watching something the others couldn't see.

The air smelled of crushed herbs and distant smoke, and chants from three traditions layered like braids in the wind. A hush beneath the bustle. A choreography of belief.

All of it had rhythm. And none of it noticed when Pip and Anna disappeared through the veil.

Beneath the Church of the Holy Sepulchre, where stories had long since been enshrined in ritual and stone, they felt it, the shift.

The wall rippled.

And then opened.

A chamber.

No tourists. No lights. Just breath.

Anna looked at him. "This isn't on any map."

He nodded. "It's older than maps."

In the centre of the chamber: a stone disk, cracked through the centre.

The glyph, reversed.
It pulsed.
Waiting.

The chamber walls began to reveal themselves in the dark, not through light, but contrast, shadow playing off older shadow. Carvings etched deep into the stone, worn yet untouched, began to shimmer faintly as if responding to their presence.

There were figures - not saints, not prophets, but beings. Humanoid yet elongated, eyes too large, hands pressed to stone tablets or reaching skyward. One held a spiral sphere, another pointed downward to a sea of faceless people. Rows upon rows, featureless and bowed, their spines curved inward, their hands outstretched - not in worship, but in submission. It was unmistakable. A prophecy. A mirror. Humanity, not enslaved by chains, but by forgetting - forgetting their origins, their sovereignty, their divine inheritance. The ability to choose. To question. To create. This was not a physical enslavement, but a psychic one - the slow erosion of identity, memory, and inner truth until only compliance remained.

Anna stepped closer, chilled. "They're showing what happens when identity is erased. When belief becomes a programme, and people stop asking why." She turned to him, her voice low, steady. "They're foretelling what's happening to humanity now. This isn't allegory. It's documentation. A chronicle of how we forgot, how we were made to forget. And how deep the programming runs."

Pip's voice was tight. "Yes, you're right, it's now. This is humanity now."

The faceless weren't a metaphor. They were a reflection - of systems built to mould, distract, and drain. Education as obedience. Media as sedation. Algorithms as architects of thought.

This wasn't just a warning. It was a broadcast across time. A reminder to those who remembered how to see.

Along the far wall, a fresco appeared to shift under their gaze.

It depicted a city, unmistakably Jerusalem - but overlaid with symbols unfamiliar to recorded history. Obelisks where none should be. A second dome beside the first. Not part of any known record, a structure completely erased from contemporary history. Anna stared at it, frozen. "That was there once," she said slowly. "But it's been scrubbed. Removed."

Pip nodded, breath shallow. "It was part of the original design, before the edits."

"Like a twin," Anna whispered, "a mirror. Or maybe a decoy."

"It wasn't meant to be seen," Pip added. "Or remembered. And yet... here it is."

They both felt the chill of it - the realisation that sacred architecture had been replicated or overridden, not to honour the divine, but to redirect its flow. And this second dome, like others they'd encountered in dreams - one in Rome, another in an obscure diagram referencing CERN, even mirrored patterns embedded within Mecca - all pointed to a grid. A network of monuments. Some built to tune humanity. Others to distort.

Anna exhaled. "This isn't just sacred geometry. This is energetic engineering. Someone has been building a false resonance."

"And hiding the true one," Pip said. "With every rewrite, every war, every constructed faith."

She pointed to the next panel. "Even the history books were rewritten to match the new structures - the narrative bent to the monuments, not the other way around." Above it all, a veil being torn, and behind it: watchers.

Anna stepped closer. "These are not metaphors," she whispered. "They're truths - not passed down, but preserved. Etched here because they couldn't be spoken."

Another panel showed figures in council, robes marked with symbols Pip had only glimpsed in dreams. They stood around what looked like a glowing disk - the same shape as the stone in the centre of the chamber. Beneath them, a spiral staircase descending into the earth - or possibly into something else entirely.

To their right, a long frieze ran the length of the chamber, showing what looked like a timeline - or a disruption of one. At one end, beings descended through radiant geometry, gifting light to early humans. At the other: the same beings kneeling before thrones, their gifts stripped, their hands bound by robes identical to modern religious vestments.

Another section depicted familiar historical moments - wars, treaties, crucifixions - but with translucent figures standing behind the human actors, directing them like stagehands.

"These aren't just histories," Pip said. "They're warnings. From before the split. They're showing us how it was rewritten. And by who."

He moved closer to the panel, his hand hovering just inches from the surface. "This dome - this duplication - it's not just a structure. It's a signature. Each one marks a place where the current of humanity was diverted. Where the truth of who we are was folded into myth, then buried under empire, dogma, and spectacle."

Anna's voice barely broke a whisper. "So this grid... it's not for worship. It's a containment system."

Pip nodded. "Exactly. And the false resonance - it doesn't just mask the true one. It scrambles it. Weakens it. That's why we've forgotten. That's why even when people feel something's wrong, they don't know where to look. The map is broken."

She turned toward the centre of the chamber, eyes on the glowing disk. "But they didn't erase everything. They left this. Buried but not destroyed."

"Not destroyed," Pip said. "Preserved. For when the ones who remember start to return."

As he spoke, the stone disk in the centre of the chamber began to shift. Slowly, soundlessly, its crack illuminated - not with light, but with resonance. A low hum filled the air, almost like a whisper. The carvings along the walls began to respond, each glyph pulsing in time with a frequency that felt more felt than heard.

Then came the voice.

Not external. Not internal. A vibration that moved through them.

"One has awakened. The seal stirs."

Anna staggered slightly, pressing a hand to her chest. "Did you feel that... in your ribs?"
Pip nodded. "I didn't hear it. I felt it."
The disk began to lift - or more accurately, reveal - as though its physical form was an illusion and something beneath was coming forward. A pattern of interlocking circles, radiant geometry, began to form in the air above it.
But then the hum fractured.
The glyphs flickered. The resonance wavered.
From the passage behind them - the one they'd entered through - came a sharp, echoing sound.

Footsteps.... Not hurried. Not hesitant.
Deliberate.
Anna turned, her breath caught. "We're not alone."
A figure entered the threshold - robed, feature obscured by shadow, but something in its presence bent the chamber's energy like gravity. The glyphs dimmed. The disk stilled.
And in the hush that followed, the figure spoke.

"You were not meant to remember."

The voice was feminine, layered with something metallic - a sound both mechanical and ancient. As she stepped closer, the shadows receded slightly, revealing eyes like glass obsidian, cold and watchful.
Anna's breath trembled. "Who are you?"
The figure's head tilted, as if the question itself were irrelevant.

"I am not your enemy. I am your keeper. My name was erased - but once, I sat at the First Council. Before the split. Before the veils."

Pip's throat tightened. "You're one of them. One of the Watchers."

A nod.
"One of the few who remained behind to ensure the seal was never broken."

Anna took a step back. "But why? Why silence it?"

"Because if truth returns before humanity is ready, the collapse will not birth awakening - it will birth chaos."

She raised a hand, palm outward. The glyphs dimmed further, flickering like a dying star.

"You've come too soon."

The chamber pulsed sharply, like a warning. Behind them, the exit wall began to seal itself.
Pip grabbed Anna's hand. "She's not going to let us leave."
The figure stepped forward.

"You were meant to witness, not interfere."

But the disk beneath them began to spin again - faint, but rising. Responding to something deeper.
Anna whispered, "It's not up to her anymore."
The hum rose.
And then the walls began to shake.
The Watcher raised her hand again, fingers splayed wide. Symbols burned in the air, not written, but projected, each one spinning faster, forming a barrier between her and the disk. The resonance faltered. The air thickened, pressing down.
Anna gasped, clutching her head. "She's trying to suppress the signal."

Pip staggered back, vision blurring. The chamber was closing in - not physically, but energetically. The presence of the Watcher expanded, distorting space like a gravitational wave.

"You must not breach the gate," she said, her voice now layered with multiple tones. "It is not time."

But then, from behind the Watcher - a second presence emerged. Light, not shadow.

A tall figure stepped into view, robed in silver and deep indigo. Its face shimmered - not hidden, but shifting between male and female, human and something more. Its presence cut through the compression like a blade of clarity.

It spoke only one word, yet it shook the chamber more than the Watcher's incantation:

"Enough."

The Watcher froze, her projection collapsing.

The glyphs surged with light.

The disk responded - spinning, humming - unlocking.

Anna and Pip fell to their knees, not in fear, but in sheer overwhelm.

Whatever this new being was, it had authority the Watcher could not override.

The resonance deepened.

The seal was breaking.

The chamber shifted.

Not crumbled - unfolded.

The glyphs around the walls aligned into perfect symmetry. The flickering stopped. A radiant pulse issued from the stone disk, and the centre of the floor began to unravel like ancient clockwork. Each ring slid back with impossible grace, revealing a stairway that descended far below.

The silver-robed figure stepped forward.

"I am not of the Council," it said, its voice like harmonic resonance. "I came before them."

Anna stared, wide-eyed. "Then who are you?"

The being turned its ever-shifting gaze toward her.

"I am one who remembers fully. One who was sealed with the truth, not against it. The others forgot their vow. I did not."

Pip rose to his feet slowly. "You're not just here to stop her... you're here to open it."
The figure nodded.

"The moment has arrived. The watchers' oath is void. The resonance has returned. And with it - so must the memory."

From behind them, the Watcher cried out.
Her voice distorted, broken.

"You would undo everything!"

"I would restore what was broken," the being replied calmly.

"You enforced the silence. They will now speak."

The disk released a final pulse. The stairway below glowed with pale, living light.
Anna gripped Pip's hand.
He nodded once. "We go together."
The figure stepped aside, allowing them to pass.
And as they descended into the earth, the last of the false frequency shattered above them.
Below - the true archive awaited.
But it would not be the final descent.

As they moved deeper into the earth, the light dimmed not with darkness, but density - each step pressing against them like a layer of time itself. The archive they now approached was not the heart. It was a threshold. A map carved into knowing, designed not to deliver the full truth, but to prepare them for it.
The being's voice echoed one last time behind them.

"What lies beneath is the memory of the fracture. But the heart - the origin - rests where sand remembers stars. You must go there next."

Anna looked at Pip. "Egypt."

He nodded. "We're being led."

The descent ended not in revelation, but in stillness. Not a silence of ignorance - but of weight. The kind that settles in your chest when something ancient brushes your soul and doesn't let go. Pip felt it in his bones, like the static hum left behind by a dream you can't explain but know changed you.

It wasn't just what they'd seen. It was what they'd felt, the dissonance in the glyphs, the bone-deep knowing that the world above was spinning inside a lie so old it had become invisible. The archive hadn't shown them facts, it had shown them the fracture. And that wound now lived in them.

Anna hadn't spoken since they'd begun their ascent. Her steps were slow, deliberate, like her body was processing something her mind hadn't caught up to yet. Once, her fingers brushed the stone wall and lingered. A small movement - but Pip saw her eyes well up.

"I don't think we're ever going to be the same," she whispered.

He nodded, throat too tight to answer. They had gone searching for truth - and found it staring back, bruised and ancient, asking if they were ready to carry its burden.

And from there, they returned.

The passage closed behind them without sound or sign. No grand exit, no glowing symbols - just a breath and a blink, and they were walking again beneath the early light of dawn.

Jerusalem was stirring. Thin lines of smoke rose from morning fires. The call to prayer drifted through alleys still damp with silence. Market stalls were being uncovered by hands that had never stopped hoping. A woman swept the threshold of a shop with ritual-like rhythm. Life continued.

But something in them had changed.

Pip looked at the people now with different eyes - not distant, but deeper. He saw the fatigue tucked beneath routine. The weight behind polite smiles. The quiet ache of lives grown around absence - of truth, of clarity, of meaning.

Anna walked beside him, her hand occasionally touching his. She, too, seemed quieter. As if the archive had placed something in her - a sorrow not her own, but known all the same.

Neither spoke. They didn't need to. In their silence walked a thousand questions. And the echo of something more than history: the pain of remembering, and the cost of it.

As they meandered through the streets of Jerusalem, dawn was just beginning to breathe light over the stone. A woman swept the threshold of a shop with a rhythm older than memory. the streets of Jerusalem, dawn was just beginning to breathe light over the stone. A woman swept the threshold of a shop with a rhythm older than memory. A child yawned into a mother's shawl. Smoke rose from unseen fires, curling prayers into the waking air.

The city moved around them - unchanged, unaware - but they no longer belonged to it. The resonance from the archive still clung to their skin like static, humming quietly against the rush of normal life. It wasn't just what they had seen beneath the earth - it was what they had become by seeing it.

They carried something now. A fracture pressed into memory. A knowing that made the ordinary world thinner, less solid.

Anna brushed Pip's hand lightly as they walked.

A silent question passed between them:

Had anything ever been real? Or had the world always been a stage, with the true story buried deep beneath the surface, waiting for those willing to remember?

When they boarded the plane back to Manchester, the hum inside them hadn't faded. If anything, it had grown sharper. Tightened. Not with fear. With inevitability.

The moment the wheels left the tarmac, Pip felt it - a tug not from Jerusalem, but from home. A magnetic pull threading its way through the quiet night sky, through the layers of cloud, reaching for them across the miles. Not a memory. A summons.

As the plane descended over Stockport, Manchester, stretched out beneath them, rain-washed, glinting in the muted light. The hum inside him tightened. Not a call. A warning. The automatic doors of the airport slid open with a soft mechanical sigh, and the wind that rushed toward them carried something ancient beneath its ordinary chill.

A whisper against the skin:

They know you've remembered. Anna stopped mid-stride, her body rigid. Pip felt it too, the invisible shifting of unseen eyes, the electric charge of attention sharpening against them like blades.

The streets outside looked the same - wet concrete, neon reflections, buses grinding past.
But everything had changed.
They hadn't just crossed continents.

They had crossed a line. And the ordinary world would never be safe again.

Return to Manchester

The air in Manchester felt denser than before, but not hostile.
Not yet.

As they left the terminal, the rain misted around them like breath on glass. The streets glittered under sodium lights, buses hissed by in their tired rhythm, and the skyline leaned heavy against a low sky.

It should have felt comforting.

It didn't.

The motorway delivered them to Didsbury with mechanical efficiency, the city swelling and sharpening on the horizon.

It felt strange to Pip, sliding through the places of his childhood, yet feeling like a ghost haunting his own memories.

They turned off before the city centre could swallow them whole. The trees thickened again, the lights softened. Didsbury had changed too, sleeker, pricier, almost self-consciously polished, but the old bones were still there, if you knew where to look.

Pip pulled into a side street and killed the engine.

For a moment, they sat in silence.

Then Anna leaned forward, peering through the rain-spattered windscreen.

"What's that place?" she asked, pointing to a majestic, warm glow at the end of the road.

Pip smiled faintly.

"The Metropole. Old pub. Been here forever. My family were raised in it"

Anna raised an eyebrow. "You want to go in?"

He hesitated, not because he didn't want to, but because something inside him felt like stepping across a threshold he hadn't known was waiting.

"Yeah," he said finally. "Let's."

The Metropole sat firm on the corner, its broad shoulders of stone and brick unmoved by the tides of change around it.

New shops came and went, glass-fronted and forgettable, but the old pub endured, heavy with memory, solid with the weight of all it had seen.

Inside, the air was warm, thick with the scent of roasting garlic and wood smoke. Handmade pizza menus perched on every table, handwritten specials curling slightly at the edges. The low murmur of conversation mixed with the occasional clink of glasses and the slow, deliberate hum of a place that remembered.

The floors beneath their boots were worn but strong, old timber polished by countless footsteps.

The ceilings were high and sturdy, the beams exposed, bearing the weight not of collapse, but of survival.

Everything about the place felt intentional, built to last, to shelter, to witness.

They took a table near the broad front windows, where the rain traced lazy rivers down the leaded glass. Outside, car headlights smeared across wet roads, casting long glances at the city's newer face.

But Pip wasn't watching the street.

Toward the back of the bar, where the light thinned and the noise faded into low murmurs, a handful of old photographs clung to the brick like ghostly fingerprints.

Pip's eyes were drawn to one.

Two young men in uniform, standing shoulder to shoulder, eyes locked onto a future neither could fully imagine.

No grins.

No casual poses.

Just the solemnity of youth trying to wear the mask of destiny.

Beneath the photograph, a small, tarnished brass plaque:

*"Two Rogerson brothers, Last drink before the trenches, 1915.
One carried a wounded brother a mile across No Man's Land, later
in the war he died.
The other survived shellfire, captivity, and return.
One gave his life. One bore the memory."*

Anna followed his gaze and said nothing for a long moment.

The air between them thickened, not with grief, but with something heavier: remembrance.

The kind that doesn't demand tears, only respect.

Pip traced the rim of his pint glass absently, feeling the weight of it settle in his chest.

"They died for a game that wasn't theirs," he said quietly.

"And the world kept playing."

Anna touched his hand lightly, anchoring him.

The smell of woodsmoke, rain, and fresh pizza curled around them, but the warmth couldn't fully erase the chill seeping up from the past.

Anna noticed his gaze and followed it, silent.

Pip said nothing at first.

The story weighed too much to speak lightly.

When he finally spoke, his voice was low, steady.

"They had their last pint here. One never came back."

Somewhere deep in the old bones of the pub, Pip thought he heard it, not a voice exactly, but the shape of one.

A whisper at the edge of the living world:

"Carry the living. Remember the fallen."

Without speaking, they raised their glasses in a silent toast.

Not to nations.

Not to wars.

To the ones who chose to carry each other. To two brothers doing what they thought they had to.

And to the ones still carrying the memory.

He let the silence fill the space where grief had long since hardened into something quieter.

Something closer to reverence.

Their pizzas arrived, handmade, bubbling at the edges, smelling of basil and rain and home.

They ate in silence, the kind of silence that honours what words can't reach. And just as Pip raised his glass to two brothers - a quiet toast, no grand speeches - he thought he heard it again, carried in the grain of the wood, the bones of the stone:

"Carry the living. Remember the fallen."

Anna's eyes met his across the rim of her glass, and something passed between them - a pact, unspoken but absolute.

They were not just remembering for themselves.

They were remembering for all who could not. The rain hadn't changed.

It pressed against the city like unfinished business, soft, stubborn, insistent.

Not enough to drive them inside. Just enough to remind them they were still awake. Pip and Anna walked without a destination, the damp air wrapping them in a cocoon of grey light and neon blur.

The streets were quiet, the shopfronts shuttered or glowing faintly. Pavements shimmered underfoot like molten glass.

At a corner, they paused.

The tram slid past, windows glowing like paper lanterns, casting ribbons of light across the wet street.

Inside, passengers stared at phones or out into nothing, blank faces, weary bodies. Each one a sealed archive of private hopes, of tiny disasters, of love given and not returned. Pip watched them pass, feeling something unfamiliar stir in his chest.

"All those lives," he said quietly. "All that complexity... just flickering by. And then gone."

Anna followed his gaze, her expression unreadable.

"Bundles of memory," she murmured. "Whole universes sitting three to a seat."

Neither of them spoke for a while. The tram turned a corner and disappeared into the rain, taking its soft glow with it. The silence left behind felt bigger somehow. Not emptier, just aware. Anna turned her face into the rain, eyes closed for a moment, as if letting it wash something away.

"Do you ever wonder," she said quietly, "if we were ever supposed to be happy?"

Pip smiled, not from amusement, but recognition.

He thought about all they had seen: the cities built on false grids, the silent manipulation of memory, the fractures stitched into human history like scars no one wanted to name.

"Maybe not," he said. "Maybe we were supposed to remember something more important than happiness."

She opened her eyes, studying him. The rain traced slow lines down her cheeks, not quite tears.

"Like what?" He looked up at the bruised sky, at the towers stabbing upward as if trying to escape the gravity of their own design.

"That we existed," he said. "That we chose. That we loved anyway."

"Do you think we're really free?" Anna asked after a while, her voice small against the city's sighing breath. Pip shook his head. "I think they made us think we were. But real freedom..."

He touched his chest lightly.

" It has to be reclaimed. Not granted." She nodded, as if she already knew.

They crossed an empty square, their reflections stretching and folding in the puddles, shapes without anchors, flickering and soft around the edges.

Their route took them down Oxford Road, past the places that had shaped so many lives.

To their right, the broad face of the hospital blinked with quiet urgency, a hundred dimly lit windows, behind them battles of sorrow and survival. Anna paused as an ambulance curved into the entrance. No siren. Just the slow hum of inevitability.

"Funny," she said softly, "how we build whole cities to keep people alive... and still forget how to help them live." They walked on in silence. A few steps further, the brick exterior of a small building stood modest and tucked against the edge of the hospital campus,easily missed unless you were looking.

No neon.

No noise.

Just a single blue plaque, rain running in slow threads down its surface.

Emmeline Pankhurst lived here.

A woman who broke silence.

Who refused the shape she was given.

Who chose fire.

Anna glanced up at it and whispered, half to herself, "She refused to let it fade... the thing most of us lose without noticing."

Pip looked at her, saw the way the words seemed to ripple through her, like some old part of her had been seen. "Do you think she'd recognise this world?" he asked. Anna shook her head, eyes distant. "She'd recognise the tricks."

They passed the University of Manchester, its red-brick towers and glass labs whispering a history of breakthroughs. The atom was split here. The boundaries of thought bent here. Not all awakenings begin in temples. Some begin in laboratories, or libraries, or in the silence between two unspeakable ideas.

Long brick walls, security glass, posters curling in plastic frames. The doorways were empty, its echoes trapped in the drizzle. Beyond it, the Manchester Museum loomed, quieter now than Pip remembered, its columns damp, its banners darkened by weather. He slowed. Behind those walls, behind glass and linen and polite lighting, were the bones of a civilisation. Stolen from the land they belonged.

Egypt....Statues. Symbols. Sarcophagi.

They had walked past them as students. Filed past in quiet school groups. Gazed at them as if they were ornaments, not warnings.

Now Pip saw it differently. "These artefacts," he murmured, "they're not dead." Anna looked at him, her voice hushed. "They're displaced."

He nodded, gaze fixed on the doors. "Everything's here. Just not awake."

They stood for a moment longer in the rain, both suddenly aware that even this city wasn't just history, it was residue. Some of it sacred. Some of it stolen. That maybe it wasn't just the desert sands calling them back to Egypt.

Maybe the map had always been waiting. Right here.

For a moment, Pip caught their faces mirrored there, distorted, ghostlike, beautiful in a way he hadn't known was possible before all of this began. He felt the questions rising again - questions older than war, older than cities:

What happens when we die?

Is the soul real?

Is anyone watching?

Does any of this matter?

Anna must have felt it too, because she slowed her steps, her fingers brushing lightly against his.

"Do you think," she said, "that love survives?" Pip didn't answer immediately.

The rain misted between them like breath. He thought about the two brothers in the pub, about the stone vaults buried under cities, about the forest and the quiet things that still remembered.

"I think it's the only thing that does," he said finally. They stopped at the edge of St. Peter's Square. The rain fell in that familiar, stubborn way, not a storm, just a slow persistence that soaked the city without apology.

Glass and stone and steel loomed around them, but Pip no longer felt small. He looked to the left, the grand face of the Midland Hotel, its windows glowing with soft yellow light, elegant and indifferent.

It was here, over a century ago, that Rolls met Royce by accident, a serendipitous handshake in the corner of a dining room that birthed one of the most enduring machines of modern power.

Not far beyond it, the domed Central Library still held its quiet dignity, a circular temple of language and listening, where silence once had weight. And yet now, all around them, the skyline bristled with towers, sharp glass teeth pushing upward, reflecting nothing but themselves.

Buildings that had no soul. Only ambition.

They walked on. Past the library's carved stone face. Past the old theatres still blinking tired neon into the wet dark. Past the places where Pip had once been a boy, and a student, and something in between.

Anna's fingers found his again, the gesture small but anchoring. "It's like standing between timelines," she said, eyes tracing the curve of the tram rails, the weight of history beneath their feet. Pip nodded. "The old world built things to last. This one just builds to be seen." And under his boots, he felt it, not metaphor, not emotion. Movement.

The glyphs. Stirring. Not carved. Not placed. Waking.

Anna leaned her head against his shoulder, the city blurring beyond them into rain and light. Neither spoke again.

There were no better questions. No better answers. Only this. Only now.

And the stubborn, beautiful, terrible choice to keep walking.

It was Anna's idea, but Pip knew the place the moment she said it. Delamere Forest. A pocket of green that had outlived kings and empires, untouched by time, unmoved by noise. By noon the next day, they had escaped the city, trading brick and traffic for the slow breathing of trees. They parked the car where the track turned to mud and walked in silence, their boots sinking slightly into the leaf-littered path.

Above them, the canopy whispered. Around them, the earth held its silence. The previous days - or had it been weeks? - blurred in Pip's mind like the tail end of a fever dream.

Vaults of lost history.

Resonance maps etched into stone.

Watchers who spoke in fractured light.

Visions of a world rigged long before they were born.

It had been a descent through every layer of illusion they had ever trusted... peeling back comfort, faith, and the stories they called truth. And now, here they were. Back in the living world. In the damp, breathing cradle of trees and earth, where the only architecture was what time itself had grown.

The traffic fell away behind them. The last buzz of tyres, the last shrill note of human noise dissolved into silence, a different kind of silence. Not empty. Alive.

The deeper they walked, the quieter the world became. Mobile signals slipped away.

The buzz of human machinery faded, replaced by birdsong, by the hush of wind moving through layered leaves, by the slow, creaking language of ancient trunks shifting against one another.

Pip exhaled... a real exhale, for the first time in what felt like months.

The ground was soft underfoot, spongy with leaf mould and rain. Somewhere ahead, a blackbird called once, twice, then fell silent, as if acknowledging them and moving on. Anna walked beside him, her hair damp at the edges, boots already streaked with mud, and when she smiled up at him, tired, real, something inside Pip finally, blessedly, settled.

Here, no one was watching. No one was twisting the currents.

Here, the truth was not carved into vaults or hidden beneath temples.

Here, the truth was simply alive.

Breathing. Waiting.

Just as it always had been.

Here, in the green silence, it was harder to believe in glyphs and watchers and inverted grids.

Harder, but not impossible. "Funny, isn't it?" Anna said after a while, her voice low. "Everything we learned, everything we fought to recall... and the trees already knew it."

Pip smiled.

He looked at her, walking a few steps ahead, hair loose, jeans mud-smeared, her laughter quick to surface, and something inside him tightened.

Not fear. Something softer. Something terrifying in its own way.

Love.

Real. Rooted. As old as the soil.

They found a fallen tree and sat side by side, sharing the sandwiches Pip had grabbed from a petrol station on the way. It tasted better than any meal he could remember. There was no ceremony to it. No grand revelations. Just the low crunch of an apple, the warmth of Anna's shoulder against his, the infinite conversations humming in the woods around them - none of which needed translation.

Somewhere nearby, a wood pigeon called. A blackbird answered. The forest breathed with them. And for a few precious hours, they forgot the fracture, the hunt, the countdown running silent beneath their skin.

They remembered something older.

Something the Archive had only hinted at but never spoken aloud:

The truth is not found in cities.
The truth is alive in the living world.
Unwritten.
Unbroken.
Waiting.

Anna lay back on the moss and watched the sky fracture into soft turquoise through the trees. Pip lay beside her, feeling the heartbeat of the ground through his spine. After a long time, she spoke. Soft, almost smiling.

"Maybe that's how they twisted us.

They made us believe we had to chase truth through their systems, their cities, their books, their monuments. But it was always here. In the quiet." Pip closed his eyes, listening not with his ears, but with something deeper. He could feel it. The resonance. Not constructed. Not inverted. Living.

Beneath the carpet of pine needles.

Inside the breath of the oaks.

In the dance of roots intertwining beneath the soil.

A memory so old, so unedited, that even the Inverted could not rewrite it.

The path narrowed. Roots thickened, moss clung to stone, and the forest began to close around them, not in threat, but in welcome. They walked in silence, feet soft on soil soaked with centuries. Beneath them, unseen but everywhere, the mycelium web wove its silent connections, tree to tree, root to root, thought to thought. A living intelligence older than empire, older than language.

Anna paused, her eyes soft.

"You can feel it, can't you?"

Pip nodded. "It's... listening."

Not like surveillance. More like witnessing.

He'd read once that mycelium carried messages, signals of danger, drought, renewal.

That fungi remembered, in their own way. That Psilocybin, the sacred messenger mushroom, didn't show you anything new. It just showed you what had always been there.

That there was no separation. That the web was always whole.

Anna crouched, running her fingers along a fallen log furred with tiny white threads. "It's strange," she said. "The deepest truths are the ones you can't explain. Only feel." Pip didn't speak. He didn't need to. The message was everywhere.

They weren't walking alone.

They were walking inside something vast.

And somehow, it knew them.

He reached out and found Anna's hand, their fingers threading together effortlessly. They didn't speak after that. There was no need. The trees told the story. And they listened.

When the sun began to dip, slanting long golden beams through the woods, they rose and walked back slowly. Pip's jacket smelled of damp earth. Anna's hair tangled with the wind. Every step back toward the car felt heavier, like pulling themselves out of a dream they weren't ready to leave. At the edge of the forest, before the last bend, Pip turned one last time.

And for a heartbeat, just one, he saw it.

A figure, half-hidden between two ancient trees. Not malevolent, not threatening…just watching.

Is this what some call the Green Man? Cloaked in moss and shadow. As old as the roots. As still as stone. Not watching them, watching through them. Not guardian. Not god. Just the earth… waking where it never truly slept.

Pip blinked… and the figure was gone.

But the feeling remained. Not fear. A blessing. A promise. You are not alone.

They drove back in silence, hands occasionally brushing across the gear stick, smiles catching in the corners of their mouths without needing reasons.

The world still waited, the hunt would still come, and Egypt was still calling. But for now, they carried something stronger than warnings and fractures. They carried the song of the forest. The memory that lived beneath it all. The knowing that life, real life, remembers.

Even when we forget.

And as Manchester's lights flickered into view on the horizon, Pip whispered to the wind curling through the open window:

"We remember." Anna squeezed his hand. And somewhere, just beyond the reach of city lights, the blackbird sang again.

The forest clung to them, damp earth on their clothes, the clean weight of living silence still thrumming beneath their skin. It felt wrong to be back on the roads again, wrong to trade the breath of trees for the sharp angles of streetlights and speed.

Pip drove with one hand on the wheel, the other resting lightly against Anna's knee, as if grounding himself against the slow, inevitable return to the human hive.

They'd barely spoken on the drive back. Not out of distance, but reverence, as if words might smudge whatever had crystallised in the silence of the forest.

Anna asked to be dropped in Didsbury.

She said it lightly, something about warm food and dry clothes, but he knew there was more.

She needed space, to be able to feel herself again, to not be holding the charge of the world.

He watched her walk away down the same street they'd left hours earlier, coat pulled tight, hair damp at the edges. She didn't look back, she didn't need to.

Pip didn't go home.

Instead, he let the roads draw him in, back toward the centre, into the stone maze of a city that felt somehow older now, like its buildings were watching. The car slowed as the townhall clock tower and the dome of the Manchester Central Library came into view. A great circle of silence and stone, its columns slick with late light.

He parked without thinking. There was a book. A name he couldn't quite shake. A line from somewhere, maybe the vault, maybe a dream.

Inside, the air was hushed but alive, the shelves standing like sentinels, the smell of old books was intoxicating, their knowledge preserved in sleep. He moved toward the history section, then turned left instead, pulled by something older than logic. He found what he'd been stuggling to recall:

Ancient Texts & Comparative Religion.

His fingers paused at a worn spine… the book he hadn't thought of in years. He slid it from the shelf.

It thudded softly in his hands, heavy, wide, gold-lettered.

The Secret Teachings of All Ages.

Manly P. Hall.

He opened to a random page and felt his chest tighten. There it was. Not the exact glyph, but close enough, the same structure, the same impossible geometry that hummed beneath his skin every time they got close.

Beside it: a symbol he'd only seen once, scorched into the vault wall in Jerusalem.

The inverted dome.

His fingers froze on the paper, he wasn't breathing, wasn't blinking.

"It's all here," he whispered.

"They left it right here. In plain sight."

He turned the page slowly, almost reverently.

Alchemical diagrams.

Mystery schools.

Atlantean seals.

The cosmic egg.

The silent watchers.

The geometry of sound.

The map of the body as a temple.

The gods who were not gods, but technicians of memory.

Each page felt less like reading and more like decoding, he wasn't learning, he was recognising.

One passage stopped him cold:

"When symbols are no longer understood, they become

decoration. When meaning is broken, monuments become prisons."

He sat back. The words vibrated in him like a tuning fork. This wasn't a book, this was a mirror... not of who he was, but of what had been kept from him. Another diagram, a wheel of language, each letter mapped to sound, then to number, then to shape.

It was the same frequency logic Anna had murmured in the tunnel, half in trance.

And then the line: "The dome was always a receiver." He looked up. The real dome above, the ceiling of the reading room, curved overhead like an echo.

This place wasn't just holding books. It was part of the grid.

How long had they been walking past the truth? How long had the glyphs been whispering through the marble, the concrete, the stained glass and brick? The same geometry Anna had seen in the vision. The same star that had followed her back from Ethiopia.

And Manchester - the city of his birth, his maturing, his unfurling - was also his shaping. The city hadn't just held him. It had made him. Its silent geometry had written itself into his bones long before he ever knew how to read it responding. Beneath the stone, beneath the manmade constructions, the city pulsed with an ancient geometry. Roads aligned in forgotten angles. Spires hummed with silent tones. Every turn held echoes.

Every shadow, a sentinel.

The entire city had been built upon a design he was only now beginning to see. It had always been there. Waiting. And it was Anna who had shown him how to see.

She wasn't with him now, not in body. But her presence moved through him like a second breath. He could feel her memory, her courage, her truth vibrating in his ribs. The star glyph had revealed itself to her because she had remembered. And now, it was his turn.

But he hesitated.

The resonance compass in his pocket pulsed faintly. A heartbeat not his own. He hesitated. A part of him wanted to retreat, step away, deny, erase. Pretend none of this had ever happened.

Because if he stepped forward now, he was choosing. Accepting. Binding.

The glyphs waited.

And so did the watchers.

From across the square, a figure stood still - hooded, unmoving. The same figure from before. The one he had seen in Berlin, in reflections, in dreams.

But now, the figure moved. Slowly. Purposefully. Closer.

Rain beaded on its cloak but never soaked through. It shimmered faintly at the edges, as if the air around it was a little less real. As it approached, Pip's breath caught in his chest. The figure raised a hand... not in threat, but in invitation.

"Wh..Who are you?" Pip asked, though part of him already knew.

The figure did not speak. Instead, it opened its palm.

There, etched into skin, was the same star glyph. Alive. Radiant. A guardian. One of the old ones. Pip's hand closed tighter around the compass.

"I don't know if I'm ready," he whispered. But readiness was never the point.

Trust was.

And as he stepped forward, the glyph beneath his feet ignited, light blooming from the cracks in the concrete. The symbols rose in the air around him, spiralling, alive. The watcher nodded once, then vanished, dissolving like mist into the rain. And Pip stood alone in the centre of the square, a conduit between earth and star.

The test had begun.

A sudden hush fell over the square, as though the city itself were holding its breath. Pip didn't move. The glyph beneath his feet continued to glow, steady now, syncing with the pulse in his chest. Then he heard it. Not with ears, but with his bones. A tone - low, ancient, and pure. It rose from beneath the ground, from the city's hidden layers, vibrating through the very stones beneath him. The geometry wasn't just visual now. It was alive. Audible. Felt.

He turned slowly. The square was empty. The tram had

vanished. The people gone. But he wasn't alone. Around him, shapes shimmered into view. Translucent figures, guardians, echoes of those who had once walked openly among mankind. They didn't speak. They simply were. Their presence filled the space between the stones, between breaths, between the heartbeats of a city that had forgotten how sacred it was.

From the Library's domed whisper to the arches of John Rylands, from the spires of Manchester Cathedral to the foundations beneath the Midland Hotel, something ancient stirred. The Town Hall clock, long silent beneath scaffolding, pulsed with a rhythm not measured in time but in tone. Even the canals shimmered faintly, as if remembering the currents they once carried, currents not of water, but of intention.

These were not random landmarks. They were anchors. Keys. Coordinates in a forgotten design now beginning to wake.

Manchester was not just a place of industry, of iron and empire. It was chosen - long before the rise of mills or monarchs. Laid upon leylines that converged like veins to a heart, lines that stretched outward through Glastonbury's tor, Stonehenge's circle, crossed under the silent vaults of Chartres Cathedral in France, whispered beneath the pyramids of Giza, and threaded deep into the Andes. Threads in a divine loom, the ground beneath the city carried a resonance older than civilisation. The ancient ones - those who mapped the world not by borders but by vibration - had seen the potential in this place. They were not gods, but something older than the stories men would later tell of gods. They were the Architects of Resonance - beings who moved with the celestial tones, who understood that form was frequency, and that memory could be embedded in stone.

Some knew them as the Builders, the Silent Choir, the Watchers in the Loom. They appeared across cultures under many names, yet always with the same task: to plant harmonics in places where the veil was thinnest. Their designs were not just architectural, but alchemical - encoding light into geometry, time into alignment, and consciousness into place.

Manchester had been one such site. Chosen. Prepared. Tuned.
And it was not alone.

The Architects had travelled across the plane, embedding frequency into form in key locations…each tuned to a specific harmonic. Angkor Wat, where sunrise met songline. Cusco, where the earth itself throbbed with coded pulse. Rome, where inversion was embedded alongside divinity. Giza. Petra. The stone circles of Avebury. All part of a living grid.

But Manchester… Manchester had been unique. A bridge between the old and the veiled. A place both hidden and accessible. A chamber disguised as a city. It was never meant to be grand. It was meant to be activated.

And Pip…Pip was part of that activation.

A resonance buried in stone, awaiting its Rememberer. Manchester was chosen not for its commerce, but for its capacity to hold light. They wove symbols into its stone, like the bees underfoot in Albert Square, the unblinking angels carved above Chetham's doors, the sun dial between arcs on Library Walk. Not decoration. Direction. Hid harmonics in its waterways. Designed spires and facades to echo celestial alignments.

Manchester was not built by accident. It was encoded. A city whose bones could one day sing. It was a node. A nexus.

A site of memory and convergence. And perhaps, always, this was why the bee had endured.

Manchester's emblem. Worn on bins, buildings, skin. They said it stood for industry, for community. But beneath the surface of that symbol buzzed something older. The Architects had marked each sacred site with a living glyph, and in Manchester, it had been the bee.

The bee was everywhere in Manchester - etched into pavements, cast into bollards, stitched into mosaics, watching from lampposts. They said it stood for industry. For work. For the spirit of the city. But that was only the surface.

The bee was older than Manchester. Older than factories. It was the original messenger between worlds, a creature that danced in frequencies, carried pollen like memory, and built impossible geometries in sacred hives.

It moves in patterns most couldn't see.

It encodes the hum.

The tone.

The rhythm of the real.

They said the bee meant work. But it meant more: unity, hierarchy, sacrifice, transmission. A symbol of the hive mind, the hidden queen, the order behind the noise.

The city didn't just celebrate it, it wore the bee like a tattoo. A sigil. A signal.

And now Pip could feel it, under his feet, in the air.

The buzz wasn't civic pride.

It was memory.

It was a frequency waiting to be decoded.

What people wore without question was, in truth, a sigil. A signal. A subtle remembrance of resonance once understood. And now, as the glyphs awoke and tones vibrated through the waking city, Pip realised: the bee had been calling to them all along.

Calling them to remember.

And Pip was standing in its centre, fully seen. Not just by the watchers, but by the Architects themselves, those who had encoded the design, waiting lifetimes for one who could feel its frequency without being destroyed by it. He had not found the glyphs by chance. They led him here. Built him. Tuned him. Remembered him.

He dropped to one knee, not out of weakness, but reverence. His hand, almost without thinking, reached toward the glyph now glowing on the stone. It was warm. Alive. It pulsed once, and something passed between it and him.

A vision. A flash. Anna's face. The star glyph above her. The chamber in Ethiopia. The dome in Antarctica. The sound of Neo's wings slicing through memory. And then silence.

Pip stood, changed.

This was not the end of the test. It was only the beginning.

He took a slow breath.

The city around him flickered, just for a moment. As if reality itself had exhaled. The edges of buildings wavered, their outlines softening, becoming symbols. What once was streetlamp and scaffolding now shimmered with layers unseen. Another architecture was rising, overlaid on the familiar. One built from frequency, not form.

And then... a second glyph ignited.

Not beneath his feet, but across the square, near the tram tracks. Then another, at the foot of the library steps. And another, in the shadow of the Midland's façade. One by one, they bloomed into light, mapping something vast and invisible.

A pattern.

Pip turned in slow wonder. The resonance compass in his hand thrummed hard now, pulsing in time with the glyphs. Not a tool, he realised. A tuner. And with it came a whisper, not sound, not voice, but a current of knowing.

You are not alone.

He staggered slightly, clutching the compass. The energy rising now was not just ancient. It was aware. The city wasn't just waking. It was watching. And he, no longer the observer, had become the conduit. Far above, in the clouds above Deansgate, lightning flashed, without thunder. For a brief second, Pip saw it. The sigil. Huge. Luminous. Branded into the sky.

The Architects were watching. And something else... just beyond them. Something old. Something that did not wish the glyphs to wake. The test was not just to see if Pip would remember.

It was to see if he could withstand the remembering. And then, from the other side of the square, someone approached. Not a guardian this time. Not a watcher.

A man in a charcoal coat, unremarkable but for the pendant around his neck, a small bronze bee, ancient in style, worn smooth by time. His eyes met Pip's with the familiarity of a story half-forgotten.

"You saw it," the man said quietly. "Didn't you?"

Pip nodded slowly. "The glyphs. The tones. The... bee." The man smiled, but there was gravity behind it. "Good. Then you've crossed the threshold. We've waited for someone like you for a very long time." He extended his hand, not to shake, but to pass something. It was old. A hexagonal disc etched with the same star glyph that Anna had seen in Ethiopia. Around its edges, tiny bees formed a circle, wings outstretched.

"This was kept hidden beneath the old cathedral," the man continued. "We don't call ourselves anything anymore. But once, we were Keepers of the Hum. The last local stewards of the tone. We knew Manchester wasn't just masonry and myth. It was memory. And someone had to protect that memory. Somewhere, long before names, there were Keepers of the Hum, not priests, not prophets, but those who remembered how to feel the tone beneath everything. Before symbols were broken. Before sound was stolen "

Pip stared at the object. "Why me?"

"Because you're tuned. You always have been. You just forgot. But the city didn't. It remembered you." He placed the disc in Pip's hand and stepped back. "You're not alone. Not anymore. The Architects built the song. But it's people like you who carry it forward."

Then. It began with a pressure behind his eyes.

Not pain. Not fear.

But the kind of pressure you feel just before a storm breaks, when the air thickens with something intangible.

It was like falling backwards through time, not through years, but through veils. And then he was there again.

Not a dream. Not now. He was small, barely five, in his bed in Chorlton. The room was quiet. The light strange. The corners hummed. And then…the presence. Not like a person. Not even a form. But a beingness, cloaked in stillness, shaped like silence. It didn't speak with words. It didn't need to.

Pip's voice trembled, but not from fear. It was the weight of something long-silenced pushing to be spoken.

"I was five, maybe younger. I never told anyone. I thought maybe I'd imagined it, but it never left me."

The Keeper of the Hum did not interrupt, only listened, as if this moment had been waiting.

"They took me to a room that had no walls, no edges. Just light. Soft and endless.

At the centre was a table… stone. Rectangular. Perfect. Like it had been designed by something that understood vastness."

"And they were there. Two beings. Not threatening. Not warm either. Just… clear…clinical, precise. But not cruel. They spoke to me, not out loud. It just arrived inside my head, complete. Like they already knew what I needed to hear."

He swallowed, glancing at the glyphs that now pulsed in response. "They didn't touch my heart. They touched my hips."

"Or… not even touched. They entered my hips where my pockets might be. Hands, or something like hands, into both sides at once. No pain. Just… pressure. A vibration that ran up my spine and then… settled."

"They told me they were installing something because my mother hadn't? Not a thing, a frequency. Something that would activate when the world was ready. Or maybe when I was."

The Keeper nodded slowly.

"It was not an insertion. It was a remembering, placed in seed form. Anchored into your sacral code, where human signal meets soul signal."

"They were not strangers. They were reinstaters. You were starting to forget the hum you were born with. They gave it back to you… not as memory, but as vibration."

"Now that vibration is waking. And the ones who installed it… are watching."

And then he was gone, vanished into the folds of the waking city like a ghost that had finally completed its verse.

Pip stood for a long moment in the stillness that followed. The hexagonal disc in his palm was warm, faintly vibrating, as if still connected to the man who had given it. Or perhaps to something deeper. The Keepers of the Hum. He turned the words over like a forgotten melody. Not a name. A vow.

He looked down at the disc again. The star glyph shimmered faintly in the grey light, the bee pattern encircling it with strange comfort. This wasn't an end. It was a signal. A summoning. And somewhere deep beneath the square, the tone shifted. Not loud. Not violent. But undeniable. A new glyph stirred. One not yet visible. And Pip felt it, knew it instinctively. Manchester wasn't just waking. It was listening now. And soon, it would speak.

The disc in his palm pulsed once, then again, each vibration stronger, more deliberate, as if the thing were breathing. The brass bees began to glow from within, their wings igniting in golden filaments of light that travelled along the etched lines toward the central star. He reached instinctively for the older disc - the one from the tunnels, and as his fingers brushed its cold edge, a current leapt between them. The air thickened, charged with unseen geometry.

The two metals seemed to recognise each other. They drew closer, not by force, but by will. Magnetic fields folded and harmonised; light threaded between their edges like spun silk. For a heartbeat, they hovered apart, two notes searching for harmony, then, with a sound like a breath finally released, they clicked together.

Light flared.

The engravings aligned perfectly, the ancient glyph beneath, the bees above, each wing touching, each line completing what the other lacked. Symbols rearranged themselves as though alive, lines bending, converging, forming a single living pattern: the unified glyph, singing in one frequency.

He knew then that this was no mere artefact. It was a key.

And somewhere deep beneath Manchester, the lock had just turned.

The Veiled One Returns

The city had no idea.

It pulsed, oblivious, under a sky that carried a hush, as if listening. Manchester moved as it always did, taxis weaving, horns barking, commuters marching, unaware that something beneath it had shifted.

Pip walked through the morning crowds like a man out of sync, each step slightly out of phase with the world around him. The disc rested in his coat pocket, warm now, as if responding to his breath. He felt it before he heard it, a quiet humming at the edge of sound, the same resonance that had begun in Delamere and hadn't stopped since.

Windows reflected back more than his image. Streetlights flickered in peculiar rhythms. A traffic crossing buzzed in sync with the pulse in his chest. Everything was too precise. Too aware. He turned off Deansgate and entered a narrow side street - Tether's Hollow, a name lifted from old cartographer's notes and long since erased from modern signage. The drizzle that began halfway down the lane lent a softness to the scene, blurring outlines, deadening sound.

And then he saw him.

Slouched in the doorway of a boarded-up charity shop, head dipped low, fingers curled around a chipped mug.

The homeless man.

The same man.

A little older, more worn, a longer beard, a coat now frayed to its lining, but unmistakable. The one he'd seen near Albert Square. And before that, impossibly, in Rome. The one who had stared at him like a man scanning frequencies not yet broadcast.

Pip froze.

There was something about the air here. Denser. Warmer. Like standing inside a closed circuit. The man raised his head. His eyes, silver, luminous - locked onto Pip's. Not with confusion or recognition, but certainty.

"You're humming," he said. Pip took a step closer. "What?"

"The tone. You've got it in you now. Can't shut it off, can you?"

Pip swallowed, glancing at his coat. "Who are you?" The man gave a dry chuckle, voice like sand over stone. "Not important. Not yet." He nodded toward Pip's pocket. "You carrying it?" Slowly, cautiously, Pip pulled the disc free. The glyph shimmered faintly in the dull light. The man didn't touch it. He simply nodded. "Good. You'll need that. Soon."

From within his ragged coat, he drew a small folded scrap of paper, brittle with age. He held it out without ceremony. "Take this. Not for now. For when it breaks."

Pip took the paper. A glyph - similar, but not identical - was etched into it. A variation. A fork in the signal. A safeguard, perhaps.

Or a decoy.

"You were never supposed to see me," the man muttered. "But the timeline's bending. The Third is returning. Faster than we thought." He paused, voice dropping lower. "You and the girl - Anna - need to go next to the place where the sun forgets how to rise."

Pip narrowed his eyes. "What does that mean?"

The man's voice dropped. "Where cycles break. Where truth was buried long before the first lie. Beneath the middle pyramid."

"Egypt," Pip whispered.

The man's head lifted slightly, acknowledging the correctness without praise. "Beneath the middle pyramid in Giza. There's a chamber no tourist ever sees. Misaligned by intention. Hidden behind frequency, not stone. You'll only find it at dusk, when the last light bends unnaturally along the southern edge. Watch for the shift. There, you'll feel it - a block that hums beneath your hand. Press. Wait. And descend."

Pip's mind raced. "And the disc…?"

"It'll sing when you're close. The tone will change. Don't hesitate when it does. The doorway won't look like a doorway. But it will know you. Step through. No matter what it shows you." Pip took a half-step back. His breath fogged in the still air. "What's inside?"

The man tilted his head. "The Third's memory is fractured. You'll feel it trying to misalign the tones. That's its defence. But what lies beyond is not history. It's design."

Pip's voice cracked on the question: "Who is the Third?" The man's silence stretched. Then, with eerie calm, he said, "Not yet. You'll feel it before you name it. And when you do, remember - what you carry isn't the answer. It's the key."

And just like that, he turned away, lowering his head, becoming still again. Like a sentry deactivating. A message sent back into waiting. Pip stood in the rain, the glyph on the disc glowed faintly in his hand and the paper felt heavier than it should.

Something vast had just opened, not a revelation, but a directive etched into the air itself. It didn't come with answers, only an undeniable pull, like the world had tilted a fraction and realigned beneath his feet. The signal had shifted again… subtly, but decisively… and he felt it surge through him like a current snapping into place. Without hesitation, Pip turned sharply, urgency sparking in his limbs, no longer questioning the path ahead. Whatever was waiting, it had already begun.

Anna was the echo to this tone. The harmony he needed to complete it. Giza would not wait. The frequency was rising. The disc grew warmer, pulsing now with intent.

Pip moved fast, weaving through the waking city like a man tracing invisible lines on a map no one else could see.

He didn't need to question anymore. They had to go. Now.

He moved like a man pulled by gravity, not toward the earth, but toward her.

Anna.

The streets blurred around him. Sounds dulled. The city faded behind his urgency. Every step felt more certain now. The disc no longer hummed softly but vibrated with intent, guiding him not just toward her, but toward what must come next.

When he reached the flat, he hesitated for a moment outside her door, hand raised to knock. Before he could, it opened. Anna stood there, barefoot, hair tied back loosely, eyes searching his.

"You look like hell," she said, gently.

He gave a tired smile. "You should see the other guy."

She stepped aside without another word. He walked in, the quiet between them weighted, not with awkwardness, but with everything unspoken since Delamere, the questions, the pulses of knowing, the quiet dread of what lay ahead. The flat was warm. The scent of sandalwood still lingered in the air, wrapped in the faintest notes of rosemary and toasted spice. Familiar. Comforting. Real. Anna poured two glasses of red without asking. A half-smile ghosted across her lips as she handed him one. "Thought we might need this." Pip sat, the disc still in his pocket, its warmth fading now, like it had done its part, for the moment. She settled beside him on the old brown sofa, legs tucked under her, wine in hand.

He looked at her. Really looked. "It's happening faster now." She nodded. "The shift. I know."

They drank in silence for a few minutes, the quiet between them not awkward, but necessary. A way to catch up with the inside of themselves. Eventually, Pip said, "I saw him again. The homeless man. He gave me a glyph. Said we have to go to Giza. There's a chamber under the middle pyramid. Something... sealed by frequency. He said we'd know it when we were close."

Anna didn't flinch. She didn't ask for clarification. Instead, she reached for her laptop and opened it on the coffee table.

"We need more than theories," she said, typing quickly. "Middle pyramid. Khafre. Hidden resonance data. Let's see what they buried." Pip leaned in beside her. The screen filled with fragmented academic scans, obscure archaeological reports, and half-censored PDFs that had long been buried in the digital fringe. Her eyes locked on one report. "Here. Not tourist rubbish. Classified data dumps. Declassified too quietly."

She clicked. "Resonance-mapping project, Giza, 1987. Not publicly acknowledged. Codename: Blackbird."

Pip's blood chilled. Anna read aloud:

"Operation involved non-invasive scalar emission tests beneath Khafre's pyramid. Objective: detect subsurface harmonic anomalies. Result: non-linguistic vocal instruction recorded at dusk over three consecutive nights." She looked at him slowly. "It wasn't language. But it wasn't random." Another page loaded, this one badly redacted, but with enough to send a chill through both of them.

Researcher Dr. Oren Yashir noted final transcription before abrupt reassignment and disappearance. Phrase captured from harmonic field: handwritten, phonetic.

T'HAREYUN.

Silence bloomed between them. Thick. Absolute. Pip stared at the screen. The word hit like a tuning fork inside his chest - the same pulse that had stirred in Delamere. That had followed him through the glyphs, the tones, the disc. Anna didn't look at him.

She just whispered: "They weren't inventing anything. They were trying to listen… and something answered." She closed the laptop slowly, her voice lowering. "Whatever they touched… it knew what was coming. Who was coming."

Pip's throat was dry. The disc in his coat pocket thrummed faintly, not as a signal, but as a recognition.

No one spoke. It wasn't time yet.

"Project shut down due to cognitive destabilisation risk. Interface classified as Harmonic Anomaly Class III. Site sealed. Witnesses dispersed."

Her hands trembled slightly now. "This pyramid… it's not a tomb. It's an interface. One of twelve tether points. The misalignment of Khafre isn't an error, it creates a resonance window. At dusk, under very specific light and frequency conditions, the seal can respond."

She clicked deeper into a private server trace. "The interface is still there. Still active. It hasn't been reached since."

Pip ran a hand through his hair, slow. "And the Sphinx?"

Anna's voice dropped. "Sound. Not sight. Its ears, Pip. It was designed to shape the echo path, the Song Path, between itself and the southern wall of Khafre. At dusk."

"We were never meant to break in. We were meant to resonate in."

He stared at her. "This… this is what they've been trying to stop."

She nodded. "And we're going anyway." He exhaled, slow. Then: "Book it."

Pip reached for his phone, thumb hovering over a flight app. "I was already looking," he said, almost to himself. "Didn't know why. Just… felt like I had to."

Anna didn't answer at first. Her eyes were still on the laptop screen. Then, quietly: "There's something I need to tell you." She turned the screen slightly toward him. He watched her. She swallowed, set down her wine, and folded her hands in her lap like someone preparing to confess something long carried.

"I've seen the chamber," she said softly. "Not in person. In dreams. For years. Before I even met you. I thought it was just symbolic, a mind place, you know? But the moment you said Giza… it clicked."

Pip sat forward. "You've been there?"

"In my dreams, yes. I always wake before I reach the centre.

But something... calls from the walls. Like the tones you've described. And the strange thing is... I always hear your voice in the echo."

He stared at her, stunned.

"Why didn't you tell me?"

"I didn't know what it meant. And part of me was afraid it was just madness. But it's not. Not anymore." He tapped his phone. "There's a flight to Cairo tomorrow evening. If we book tonight, we can be there in under forty-eight hours."

Pip leaned back, exhaling slowly. The wine dulled the edge of panic, but sharpened the sense of inevitability.

"What happens when we get there?"

Anna didn't answer right away. She simply reached across and took his hand. Her palm was warm, steady. The weight of her presence grounded him.

"When we get there," she said, "we find the doorway. And we step through."

He gave a slow nod. "No hesitation."

"No hesitation," she echoed.

They clinked glasses, quietly. Sealed a vow neither fully understood, yet both had already committed to. He booked the tickets.

Later, as Didsbury hushed beneath the weight of early hours, they lay in bed, the laptop closed, the room dark except for the amber streetlight bleeding through the curtain edge.

Sleep didn't come easily. But it came. Tomorrow, they would fly to Egypt.

And beneath ancient stone, something was waiting to be unlocked.

Neo's Descent - Antarctica Revisited

Neo cut through the clouds above the southern ice like a whisper of memory sharpening into form.

He had been here before.
But not like this. Last time, he had only skimmed the surface.
A witness. A harbinger. A shadow drifting over the vault.
Now, something had changed.
The resonance from Manchester, ignited by Pip, by Anna, by the glyph now active, had reached this place. A line drawn through tone and time had unlocked the deeper layer.
Beneath the frost, beneath the mile-thick crust of forgotten epochs, a light pulsed.

A signal lock. One of three. It was part of a triad:
>Göbekli Tepe - *the seed.*
>Manchester - *the tone trigger.*
>Antarctica - *the memory lock.*

The Architects had placed them in the most sacred of silences. Not to hide, but to hold.

Not to shield from the world, but from the Inverted.
Antarctica was not the end.

The Germans had known something, deep in the icy silence of

the 1930s. They had sent expeditions here, not for conquest, but for discovery. What they found was not just ice, but absence. Echoes. Structures their instruments could not explain. Some whispered of Base 211, others of maps with no curvature, no arc. They built nothing here. But they marked it. Filed it away. A memory buried within the Reich's darker dreams.

The Inverted had watched that too. It was the seal.

Neo descended in slow spirals - not flapping, but guided. Drawn down like ink into a script being rewritten. His feathers hummed. Not with cold. With code.

The ice cracked beneath him, not breaking, but opening. Beneath it lay a crystalline structure, half-pyramid, half-lens. Its facets shimmered with impossible reflections, not of the present, but of stored frequency. A mirror of the Firmament. A structure older than memory, and yet built by it. And now, it had begun to speak.

Neo landed on its apex. The structure pulsed. Tones rose, not audible, but visceral. They moved through dimension, bending time around them like breath across a reed.

And in that moment, Neo saw it:

A corruption. A fracture.

The song the Architects had once sung into the bones of the world... part of it had been stolen. Reversed. Bent into the inverted harmonics that fed the Grid.

He saw the glyphs flicker, whole, then broken, then inverted.
It wasn't just memory.
It was manipulation.

Beneath the mirror, deep in the foundation, something vast turned in its sleep.

The Third was stirring.

Not a site.

Not a person.

Not a symbol.

A Being.

Neo raised his wings.

This time, the cry was not for warning. It was for awakening.

The third lock had begun to shift. And with it, the Earth itself whispered a truth that had waited eons to be heard.

This was not mythology, this was not metaphor, this was memory returning. The crystalline structure beneath Neo shivered as frequencies older than light cascaded through its mirrored depths. These were not tones of warning or resistance. They were tones of reclamation.

The firmament was not a barrier, it was a womb.

A veil woven to hold the song of creation itself, and beneath the veil, a Being stirred.

Not alien.

Not god.

But Original.

Older than the Inverted, older than the Builders, older even than time counted in rotations.

It had no face... it was all faces... it had no voice... it was all tone.

Neo felt it rise, not physically, but dimensionally. The ice vibrated with it. So did the stars.

So did every glyph that had begun to stir across the plane.

And the Being saw Neo.

Not as a bird, but as the Blackbird.

The final messenger.

The one sent before the veil thins.

The one whose cry would awaken what no machine could hold,

and no ritual could silence.

The Being did not speak in words, but its intent entered Neo like fire:

Call them.
The Rememberers.
The Keepers.
The Tuned.
The Dreaming.
The Broken.
The Buried.
The Bound.

Call them to the sound.

Because the Third is not rising... the Third is returning.

Chapter 29:
Giza - Beneath the Resonance Gate

The terminal was alive with fluorescent hush and soft announcements, the kind that barely reached the brain but lodged themselves just enough to guide a crowd. Pip and Anna moved with the morning tide - not rushed, not idle. Just present. Outside the great glass windows, aircraft rolled across runways like slow beasts in formation. The sky had cleared. Or maybe just made itself look that way.

They boarded without delay.

The flight to Cairo was uneventful. And yet neither slept.

They sat side by side, the steady hum of the engines giving rhythm to their silence. Anna turned to him, voice hushed beneath the drone. "Egypt. The cradle of civilisation... or at least that's what they told us." Pip nodded. "And yet so much of what we've been taught feels unanswered. The timelines, the dynasties. The purpose of the pyramids. We were told they were tombs - but there's no evidence of that. No soot, no bodies. Just resonance."

Anna's brow furrowed. "What if those structures weren't about death at all? What if they were for something else - healing, maybe. Or transformation?"

He glanced at her. "Or gateways." They both fell quiet, staring ahead as the cabin lights dimmed slightly.

"They always talked about the curses," Anna whispered. "Tutankhamun's tomb. Those who entered died mysteriously. But what if those weren't curses... just fail-safes?"... "To keep something hidden," Pip said. "Or to protect us from seeing too soon."

She nodded slowly. "Or to stop us from understanding what it all meant." Pip's fingers traced the curve of the plastic armrest. "And yet here we are. Flying straight into the lion's mouth."

Anna gave a faint smile. "Or to stop us from understanding what it all meant. Maybe even from recognising what some of those ancient sounds were doing, the ones I read about."

A few rows ahead, a man turned his head. Slowly. Too slowly. He glanced over his shoulder, eyes grazing theirs, then returned to his forward stare. There was nothing outwardly strange about him - jeans, a soft jacket, earbuds in - but his stillness was off. Not tense. Just too still.

Anna caught Pip's eye. He didn't nod, didn't move - just met her gaze for a moment longer than usual.

"We're not alone," she whispered. "No," Pip said. "But maybe we were never meant to be."

He shifted his attention back to the in-flight screen, pretending to study a map. Egypt grew closer by the minute. Outside that digital line of flight, the landmass was vast. And beneath it, secrets still pulsed.

"People focus so much on the Great Pyramid," Anna murmured. "But there's Abu Simbel, Karnak, the Osirion… all aligned. They weren't just monuments. They were harmonics. Anchors."

Pip nodded, voice low. "And as we now know, the Sphinx... it wasn't made to be seen. It was made to watch… and listen"

The wheels hit the tarmac with a groan and a hiss, and the cabin stirred as if waking from something deeper than sleep. Cairo shimmered beyond the windows - a pale haze of dust and heat and motion. Disembarking felt surreal. The airport wasn't ancient, but something in the air was. Even the light seemed filtered through time, as if history itself hung suspended.

Anna glanced toward the arrivals hall, her voice low. "We've stepped into the current of something older now, haven't we?"

Pip nodded. "No turning back." They passed through

immigration without issue, the officer barely glancing at their passports. But someone else was watching - not the man from the plane. He was gone. Disappeared, as if he'd never been there. Outside, a wall of heat folded around them. Cairo buzzed with static - honking horns, laughter, distant calls to prayer, and something deeper, like a low-frequency hum beneath it all. They decided to hire a car, eager to move around the sprawling city at their own pace. The process was typical - handing over their driving licenses, enduring the upsell of unnecessary insurance, and a quick exchange of currency. The clerk, barely glancing up, handed them the keys.

The air hit them like a furnace blast - dry, warm, thick with the scent of dust and spices. The city around them hummed with life, but the land felt ancient, like something that had always been here, waiting to be remembered. The car was a basic model, old but reliable. They drove in silence at first. The streets outside Cairo's city centre were a blur of sand and concrete, the buildings stark and uninviting. As the car wound through the chaos, the city's contradictions unfolded: satellite dishes on ancient buildings, golden mosques beside crumbling concrete, and glimpses of Coptic churches behind modern glass towers. They passed Tahrir Square, pulsing with layered histories, and the Citadel of Saladin, still watching the city as it had for centuries. And beyond it all - the faint silhouette of the Pyramids rising like an echo from a forgotten world.

Anna stared out at the horizon. "Yeah…like I said, they explained the pyramids as tombs. But they're not dead things. They're humming." Pip said nothing. He felt it too.

They arrived at the hotel - a quiet, unassuming structure in a less tourist-heavy part of the city. Yet as they entered the lobby, the air shifted. The dim lighting, the faint fragrance of incense, and the almost too-perfect silence - it was as though they had stepped into something older. Something aware. Pip held the door open for

Anna. She hesitated, sensing a strange pull beneath her feet, then stepped inside.

The receptionist, who spoke little English, greeted them with a nod and handed them a key card. The exchange was swift, quiet, transactional, but strangely muted. As they crossed the tiled lobby floor, Anna glanced up at the mural above the reception desk, a faded depiction of the Nile winding through figures and symbols almost too weathered to read. There was something in it that felt older than art, like a forgotten invitation.

They moved to the lift. The silence inside was padded and peculiar, like sound had been politely excused. The air wasn't heavy, but it pressed. They didn't speak. There was no feeling of being watched, only that something long paused was, at last, continuing. Not a trap. Not a mystery. Just a movement resumed.

Anna exhaled slowly as the lift rose. "I don't know why, but this place feels rehearsed," she murmured. "Like it's waiting for us to finish a scene we never knew we started."

Anna glanced at Pip. "I feel like we've just walked into the belly of the beast."

Pip didn't answer immediately. "No... not a beast. A guardian."

Something was waiting beneath Giza.

And it was calling them both.

That night, the hum of Cairo pulsed outside their hotel window, faint but constant, like the city itself was breathing through time. Inside, the room was dark save for the soft blue glow of a standby light on the television. Pip lay still, eyes open, heart steady but alert. He wasn't thinking, he was listening.

A faint tone had begun in the back of his skull. Not imagined. Not painful. More like tinnitus, but not shrill. Subtle. Persistent. Like something trying to tune itself to him.

Anna stirred beside him, then sat upright. "You feel it too?" she whispered. He nodded slowly.

She reached for her phone on the bedside table, not to check the time, but to open an app she'd downloaded long ago.

A field recorder. She hit record and set the phone down - not expecting to hear anything, but needing to know if the silence would capture what they could feel.

The air had weight. A tension that wasn't fear. It was anticipation. An inner stirring.

Outside, a sudden gust of warm wind rattled the balcony door. The glass trembled - and for a moment, so did the disc in Pip's coat pocket.

Anna didn't speak. She just closed her eyes and placed the crystal from Peru against her chest.

It was glowing again.

No words were exchanged. There was nothing to explain. Only the shared understanding that the next day would take them somewhere beyond archaeology. Beyond theory.

Into memory made structure.

Into the gate.

And the tone... was already rising.

By first light, they were already moving.

The city stirred as they slipped through its streets, vendors lifting shutters, prayer calls echoing between apartment blocks, the golden pink wash of sunrise on old stone.

Anna had everything preloaded on her phone: an encrypted map layered with leaked excavation data and a file named simply "Ashai/17-FieldGrid". She had downloaded it years ago, unsure why it mattered. Now she knew. Pip drove in silence, eyes scanning the route. He wasn't navigating by the map, he was following a pull. They parked on a dirt shoulder behind an unused section of the Giza plateau fence, well away from the tourist crush. A faded wooden barrier with an "archaeological works restricted" sign hung lopsided, half-buried in sand. It had been forgotten. Left unguarded.

Beyond it: cracked limestone, heat haze, and the great Sphinx rising at a diagonal, oddly misaligned with the Pyramid complex, as if built for something else entirely. Not facing the rising sun as claimed, but something deeper. Something older. Erosion scars ran vertically along its flanks, not shaped by sand, but by water, rainfall, not seen here for thousands of years. It didn't belong to the dynasty that claimed it. It remembered a time before Pharaohs. Before story became scripture.

"Here," Pip said.

Anna nodded. "Just like in the dream."

Together, they crossed the boundary and began to descend… toward the real Osiris Shaft.

Anna checked the map on her phone - not the kind tourists use, but one she'd sourced from an encrypted site months ago. Layers of satellite imagery. Infrared. Ancient subterranean schematics leaked decades ago then scrubbed from the internet. But not before someone saved them.

Pip pointed to a location just east of the Great Pyramid, near the paws of the Sphinx.

"Here," he said. "This… this is where we're meant to go." It wasn't on any official tour map. It wasn't even acknowledged. They parked off the main tourist route, where tour buses thinned and the old desert path turned to dust and fractured rock. The spot they headed for was known to very few - a small, fenced-off section near the Temple of the Sphinx, southeast of the statue. Just beyond that, hidden beneath slabs of limestone and behind crumbling excavation barriers, was a narrow descending shaft.

The real location? The so-called 'Osiris Shaft' - but not the one tourists are shown. Not the three-level chamber reached by rope ladders. This one was deeper. Older.

Pip pulled aside a broken length of mesh fencing. No guards. Just sand. Just time. Anna ran her fingers across the stones.

"Feel that?" she whispered.

The rock was warm, vibrating ever so slightly. Like it was breathing. Pip felt a gentle pulse in his pocket. The small fragment of the Signal Key - inert for days - had begun to vibrate faintly, like it recognised the proximity to its source. Anna gasped softly and reached for the crystal she'd found on the floor in Peru.

It was glowing from within, not with light, but with rhythm - a silent pulse that beat in time with the stone below them.
"They're responding," she whispered. "Both of them."

They descended.

The first steps were narrow, carved with angles too perfect for hand tools. Not worn. Preserved. Lit only by thin slivers of natural light filtering through ancient cracks. The air was thick - not stale, but mineral-rich, like old stone soaked in silence. There was a faint scent of something ancient: petrichor clinging to limestone, mingled with the metallic trace of iron and the dry, almost sweet smell of dust left undisturbed for millennia. As they moved deeper, the soundscape changed. The noise of the surface world vanished entirely. What remained was a low hum - not mechanical, but alive. Like the breath of the Earth itself.

Occasionally, faint chimes echoed, as if wind or pressure had struck something metallic far away. It was impossible to tell if they were imagined. Their footsteps were muffled. Even their breathing sounded distant, absorbed by the stone like ink soaked into parchment.

Down they went.
Steps turned into a tunnel.
Then to a chamber.

As they crossed the threshold, something shifted inside them.
A rising warmth pulsed along Pip's spine, not from fear but from familiarity - as if his body remembered something before his mind could. The sensation wasn't sharp. It was deep. Cellular. A call-and-response between his blood and the walls.
Anna stopped walking. She placed a hand on her chest.
"I can feel it," she said softly. "Like... like it knows us."
The chamber vibrated at a frequency that bypassed sound

entirely. It wasn't heard - it was felt in the bones, in the teeth, in the marrow. Time, here, didn't tick. It oscillated. Light shimmered faintly from the surfaces - not a glow, but a kind of memory made visible. Shadows played across the walls in impossible ways, shifting not with movement but with intention. The air tasted of minerals and static, like the crackle before a lightning storm. There was a charge in it, alive and intelligent. A presence that didn't speak - it listened. In the centre, a low stone table. On it - dustless, undisturbed - lay a black disc. Pip stepped forward.

The disc was made of obsidian or something like it. But it wasn't carved. It was tuned.

The space between his hand and the disc thrummed softly, not with sound, but with something older. Static. A recognition. A forgotten feeling brushing against him.

Anna stepped closer, voice hushed.

"This doesn't feel like a chamber."

Pip studied the walls, the way light moved without a source.

"It's... reacting."

A pause.

"Like it's waiting," he added. "Listening."

On the far wall, the glyph glowed faintly - and beneath it, new words formed, not etched, but rising from the stone like heat off the desert:

"Only the remembered may pass. Speak the tone. Speak your name."

Pip closed his eyes. A familiar pressure stirred in his chest, not fear, not pain. A remembering.

The name rose from within him, not spoken but felt, like a chord struck deep in his bones.

T'HAREYUN.

He had heard it before, not in words, but in the silence between them. In dreams. In the hum beneath the Nazca stones. A tone he hadn't known he carried until it called him by name.

Now, as he stood before the wall, it didn't feel like he was announcing anything.

It felt like he was answering.
The resonance replied.
Then something shifted inside him, not thought, but memory.
Without knowing why, Pip reached into his coat pocket. The paper was still there. Yellowed. Soft at the folds. He unfolded it slowly. The glyph etched into its surface, a spiral intersected by three arcs - seemed to shimmer in the chamber's light, not with brightness, but with intent.

The symbol was not the same as the ones they'd seen.
It was a variation. A remembrance.
The glyph glowed faintly as he held it up. Not toward the disc, but toward the stone wall, where the resonance awaited a deeper key. As the paper drew close, the wall responded. Not with sound. With recognition.
The interface lit.
Stone shifted. Air bent. And the wall before them dissolved into light.
A gateway opened - not to a room, but to a different vibration of the same world. A frequency where memory was not stored - but lived.

They stepped through.
At first, it felt like being submerged in warm water - but not wet. A density of energy. Like thought had form, and memory had temperature. Pip gasped slightly, the sensation overwhelming but not painful. The space beyond was vast, though it had no

walls. No ceiling. Yet it held shape - fluid architecture made of vibration, crystalline lattices of sound suspended in geometric flow. Each movement they made seemed to echo across dimensions, ripple through colour and tone. Every footstep became light. Every breath, a ripple.

Pip turned slowly, taking it in. The air shimmered with symbols - living ones - shifting like language that spoke through feeling. Anna froze for a moment, her eyes wide. "I've seen this before," she whispered. "In Peru."

Pip turned toward her.

"During an ayahuasca ceremony," she continued. "It was the only other time I saw energy move like this - like it was alive, like it was aware of me watching. Symbols, colours, light that responded to thought... It felt like I was being shown something, not imagined. This is the same... but deeper. Truer."

And then came the sound. The same frequency from his dreams. The one that had called to him as T'Hareyun. It rang out like a bell made of memory, vibrating every cell in his body. Anna gripped his hand. Her crystal was alive with light - not reacting to danger, but recognising its source. Like a signal meeting its origin.

To home.

She touched her crystal. "This is the same feeling I had in Peru," she whispered. "But clearer. More alive. I didn't realise it then, but... I think this is the memory field."

Pip nodded, eyes wide.

The architecture around them pulsed - and then revealed.

Beneath their feet, the illusion of stone fell away, replaced by a moving vision: tunnels, chambers, structures beneath Giza and beyond - stretching beneath the Earth like arteries. Some lit. Some dark. All humming.

Cities buried. Machines of light. Temples of tone.

And then, rising above them - the firmament. Not sky, but structure. Holding back something. Or ...holding us in.

It echoed the ancient truth whispered across civilisations: As above, so below. The microcosm and the macrocosm, perfectly mirrored. What existed within, existed without. Hermetic wisdom, Incan cosmology, Vedic insight, Egyptian architecture - all had pointed to this. The stars above mimicked the labyrinths below. What was veiled in heaven was buried in Earth.

The vision expanded, and the message came not in words, but in knowing, impressed directly into their awareness.

What had been veiled in heaven was buried in Earth.

It wasn't a metaphor. It was design.

The truths hidden from humanity - about who they were, what they came from, and what they could still become - had been erased from the sky, distorted through religion, science, and language. The heavens were rewritten. The stars renamed. The firmament itself cloaked.

But Earth had kept the memory.

Sacred sites. Ancient structures. Forgotten languages. They weren't relics, they were receivers. Anchors of truth placed in stone, sound, and soil. The Architects hadn't trusted the heavens to preserve what mattered. So they buried it - in pattern, in frequency, in place - waiting for those who could still remember how to read it.

Heaven had been inverted. But Earth... Earth had been entrusted.

And that trust now called for an answer.

Every ancient temple, every sacred mound and monolith, every forgotten language, they all carried fragments of a memory so old it became myth, and a message so precise it became invisible. Hidden in plain sight, waiting to be felt, not just understood... that we are reflections trapped in a distortion.

That the veil between worlds wasn't just metaphysical. It was manufactured.

They weren't just seeing this.

They were being shown what had always been there.
This was no hallucination.
It was truth, returned.
And truth never returns unnoticed.

Far away, deep beneath the Bucegi Mountains in Romania, not rumoured, not hidden, but known to those who still remembered the architecture of control, the air thickened.
The chamber had no lights, no displays. It listened.
The structure itself was ancient, not built but inherited, stone embedded with harmonic receivers, sealed beneath layers of frequency cloaking long before satellites were invented. This was the Inverted's primary control node.

Here, resonance was tracked. Memory, monitored. Signals - true signals - were not blocked. They were inverted, distorted, or delayed.
And now, it had registered something it had not felt in centuries.

A tone.

Spoken not as sound, but as essence. A signature long-feared:

T'HAREYUN.

The Signal Key had activated inside the memory field. And no firewall could contain what had been born again. The lattice pulsed. Systems came online, though no cables moved.
They had prepared for this.
But not now. Not yet.
One of the watchers, faceless, breath slowed to near-zero, moved his hand across a stone dial. A resonance code was dispatched, not in data, but in wave.

It would reach the field.
It would test the breach.

And if needed…it would invert.
They were aware of Pip and Anna now. And they would act.
Because the veil was falling - and with it, control.

Back inside the memory field, the light deepened. The symbols stopped shifting - and aligned. A singular line of frequency rose from the floor and projected into the air like a thread of living data. Pip and Anna turned toward it. The frequency unfolded into images, not just seen - felt. War zones. Famine. Pandemic. But from a different angle.

Pip staggered as truth poured into him like thunder.

The wars weren't accidents.

The wars weren't accidents. They were orchestrated. Built by families whose names appeared briefly - then vanished. The infamous and well-recited bloodlines. They didn't fight each other.

They constructed conflict as economy, as ritual. Each war a reset. Each conflict a cleansing of memory and a reassertion of control over narrative.

Pip's breath caught as a sudden image cut through the stream, not shown by the field, but rising from within him. The photograph in the pub. The two brothers from the Manchester Regiment. Faces young, eyes proud. One barely old enough to shave. The other already carrying the weight of someone else's future.

At the time, it had stirred something in him, a quiet reverence. A sadness. Now, that feeling twisted into something deeper.

They hadn't died for freedom.

They had been offered - like so many before and after - as part of a ritual they never saw. Their bravery exploited. Their memory rewritten into honourable myth.

The bloodlines didn't mourn boys like them. They harvested them. Pip clenched his fists, the weight of it all crashing down. "They deserved truth," he whispered. "Not pageantry."

Anna clutched at her crystal. It vibrated with grief.

And the grief wasn't hers alone. It came from the memory field itself. As if the Earth remembered too.

The vision expanded. Organ farms. Human bodies catalogued beneath hospitals, in bunkers beneath cities. Pip's stomach turned. This wasn't metaphor. This was extraction. People were being harvested - not just for blood, but for resonance. Life-force. Memory. Organs.

The interface flickered - not with symbols now, but with data. Brutal. Clinical.

US Patent 6506148 B2 - Nervous system manipulation by electromagnetic fields from monitors

Pip froze. Anna stepped closer, lips parting. "That's real," she whispered. "That patent exists."

More numbers followed, scrolling like a silent indictment:

US20060217374A1 - Method and device for producing a desired brain state.

WO2020060606A1 - Cryptocurrency system using body activity data.

US3951134A - Remote brainwave monitoring and manipulation

Agency logos flickered into view, blurred, redacted, then clear:

DARPA. NIH. DoD. Mossad. Tavistock.

And then the programmes:

MKULTRA. MONARCH. LIFELOG. ECHELON. SENTIENT. RAVEN-EYE

These weren't conspiracy theories. They were the infrastructure of inversion. Contracts. Timelines. Names. Even screenshots, brief, ghostlike, of faces and facilities: bodies held in black sites, resonance chambers buried beneath hospitals, biometric tags embedded in skin.

Pip shook his head. "How... how did we not see this?"

Anna touched the crystal at her chest, her voice barely a breath. "They didn't hide it."
Her eyes met Pip's, hollow, aching. "They fed it to us. In films. In games. In parodies. They made truth look like fiction so no one would take it seriously. That's the trick."
The interface pulsed, as if listening. Then a phrase formed mid-air, etched in flickering white light:
Disclosure was never denied. It was drowned.
Pip's jaw tightened. His fists clenched at his sides.
"No more," he said. "We lift it out of the static. We make them feel it."

The scenes were horrifying - but precise. The interface showed architecture. Networks. Patents. Even faces. It showed governments complicit, and corporations masking the trade. Every year, millions of people disappeared - all this undocumented, discarded as conspiracy theory now... confirmed, proven.
Some of this had been whispered by so called "conspiracy theorists" - mocked, shadowbanned, erased. But here, now, the

ridicule melted like fog in sunlight. This was the truth. Hidden in plain sight. Too enormous to believe, so it was dismissed.

Pip buckled to his knees. The weight of it was crushing. The cataclysmic depth of deception - the scale of it - was hard to breathe through.

Anna stood frozen, tears forming. "How could we not see it?"

Pip whispered, "Because the veil was perfect. And we... we were asleep."

A deep, resonant tone rang out. The symbols pulsed. Then, a question:

"Will you carry this truth?"

Anna looked at Pip. "They'll never believe it," she said. "They won't have to," Pip replied. "They'll feel it. When we show them how to see."

The thread of light changed shape - now forming a series of interlinked patterns. A mandala. A wheel. A map.

The mandala hovered in the air between them, spinning, living, breathing. A perfect pattern of interlinked glyphs, spirals, and harmonic frequencies.

It wasn't drawn. It was woven.

Not with ink, but intention. From the centre of the mandala, a pulse moved outward - not a shockwave, but an invitation. Each ring held a principle. A truth. A teaching.

The first ring shimmered into clarity:
Awakened Perception

You cannot fight what you do not see.

To pierce the veil, the first step was to train the perception - not the eyes, but the inner lens. The seat of knowing. The pineal, yes, but more than that - the full harmonic field of consciousness.
It must be re-attuned.

Images formed:
A person sitting in stillness, surrounded by noise.
Another, in nature, hands in soil, forehead kissed by sun.
Another drinking clean spring water, crystal pressed to chest, repeating tones.
A voice - not male or female - spoke inside them:
"You were taught to doubt intuition. To mock the unseen. To ridicule the subtle. Return to it. Restore your inner senses. What was called madness is your compass."

Beneath that: the glyph: ....Fire.
The energy of transformation. The kindling of sight.
Anna whispered, "This is how we begin."
And as the first ring faded, the second began to rise.
They stood inside the pulsing mandala of light - not observing it, but becoming it. Pip and Anna were no longer just witnesses to truth. They were being rewritten by it. The memory field was not

simply information. It was initiation.

The second ring emerged, pulsing in layered light and tone:
Harmonic Integrity

To raise your frequency, your field must be coherent.

This wasn't about perfection. It was about resonance. Congruence
between thought, word, and action. The body as a tuning fork.
The mind as a transmitter. The heart as a compass.

Images formed:
A person speaking one thing and doing another
- their field fragmented.
Another living with integrity, even in hardship
- their energy glowed like gold.
"What you emit is what you inhabit," the voice said.
"You cannot walk into remembrance carrying distortion.
Align your inner architecture. Live your truth.
Even if it costs you comfort."

Another symbol flashed:...Air.
The current of clarity. Breath. Word.
Agreement between soul and self.

Anna placed her palm on the light, and the ring dissolved.
She turned to Pip, her voice low. "This... it's not just a message.
It's a map. Pip nodded.
"And a mirror."

The third ring began to glow...

Energetic Discernment

Not all that shines is light.

This teaching came with weight - not fear, but gravity.
The frequency shifted slightly, cooler now, slower.
It was as though the mandala paused, inviting them to breathe.
"Discernment is not judgement. It is recognition.
Resonance is your compass."

Images formed:
A bright figure offering truth, but with a shadow behind the eyes.
A poor, quiet one - radiating stillness that calmed the space around them.
The voice returned:
"You have been trained to trust status, production, appearance. But
the signal lies in the subtle. In the frequency beneath the form."
They saw a child recoiling from a smiling man in a suit. A tree
bending toward a barefoot woman who simply listened.

"Your body knows. Your field knows. But the static of distortion
- processed food, synthetic frequencies, propaganda, digital
addiction - clouds the signal. Clean your vessel.
Sharpen your signal. Learn to feel again."

A symbol emerged:....Water.
The essence of flow. Feeling. Intuition.

Anna inhaled sharply, her hands trembling. "We've been trained
out of it... out of ourselves."

And the fourth ring began to rise...

Sacred Boundaries

What you allow, you become.

This teaching came with the force of a locked gate swinging
open. The light that rose now had edges - defined, precise.
It formed a sheild around Pip and Anna.
"To honour your energy is to remember your divinity."

Images appeared:
A person giving endlessly, becoming hollow.
Another saying no, holding firm - their field bright and pulsing
with life.
*"You were taught that love is boundless. But love with no boundary
becomes sacrifice. And sacrifice, when coerced, becomes enslavement."*
The voice softened.
*"Sacred boundaries are not walls. They are membranes of choice.
They tell the universe what you are willing to carry, and what
must be returned."*
The light adjusted. They saw a family member demanding
energy, a friend draining joy. They saw themselves agreeing
- not from love, but from fear of loss, of judgement, of guilt.
"To rise, you must know what is yours. And what is not."

The glyph emerged:...Earth.
Structure. Grounding. The return to self.

Anna whispered. "This is why I always felt lost. I never knew where
I ended, and others began."

And the fifth ring began to rise…

The Power of Presence

The moment is not a pause. It is the portal.

This ring emerged not with symbols or words at first, but with stillness - a silence so profound it seemed to thrum with potential. Around them, the light settled. No swirling colours. No images. Just breath.

"The present moment is the only space where creation occurs,"
the voice finally said.
"The construct keeps you in loops - regrets of the past, fears of the future. It feeds on your absence."

Images emerged:
People scrolling endlessly, eyes glazed.
A worker staring out of a window, lost in a thought not theirs.
A child, in the rain, laughing alone - fully present.

"Presence is resistance. It is where you reclaim your consciousness from distortion. When you are fully here, you are beyond programming. You remember that you are the dreamer, not just the dream."

The glyph pulsed into being:…Salt.
Crystallisation. Form made sacred.
The anchor of consciousness into the now.

"This is the point we find ourselves again," Anna said, her voice barely above a breath.

And the sixth ring began to rise...

Communion with the Living Field

Separation is the illusion. Connection is the cure.

The air shimmered like heat over sand, but cooler - pulsing with memory. The ring expanded gently, and the space around them responded. The walls, the floor, the unseen presence - it was all listening. Alive.

"You were never alone. You were isolated. You were severed from the field - not by accident, but by design."

The tone deepened. Warm. Enveloping.

Images formed:
Cities humming with invisible frequencies - noise over signal.
Nature calling to a child who no longer heard.
People walking through forests, phones in hand, blind to the communication of the leaves.

*"The field is not metaphor. It is life. A consciousness that responds, reflects, and remembers.
It speaks in symbols. In signs. In synchrony."*

They saw animals watching them. Numbers repeating. Dreams answering questions unasked. Everything part of one awareness - forgotten, but never absent.

*"To commune is to listen. To feel. To ask - and to trust the reply.
Step out of the synthetic, and the real will rush in."*

A new glyph emerged:...Philosopher's Mercury.
Communication. Interconnection. The language of the living matrix.

And the seventh ring began to rise…

Devotion to Inner Truth

Your truth is your torch. Carry it, or walk in shadow.

This ring rose like a steady flame - not wild, not loud, but unwavering. It did not dazzle. It illuminated.

"They taught you to doubt yourself. To outsource knowing. To kneel before false gods and institutions. But the only altar worth tending is within."

Images appeared:
A person silencing their own intuition, nodding along with a voice speaking from a stage - their light dimming with every word not their own.
Another reciting what they were told, eyes empty.
And then, a child speaking to the stars, with no one watching - and the stars listening back.

"Your inner truth is not opinion. It is resonance. It is the signal of your soul. Speak it. Act it. Refine it. But never abandon it."

They saw journals burned. Truth tellers shamed. Souls inverted for acceptance.
Then they saw a person alone, speaking softly in the dark - and the darkness opening.

"This is not about rebellion. It is about remembering."

The glyph appeared:…Gold.
The incorruptible essence. The soul's signal beneath all masks.
Anna's voice was steady now.
"If we all did this… just this… the veil would fall."

Pip stepped forward into the glow of the seventh ring, his voice resonant, not just in sound but in intent. "And the song would return," he said - not as a hope, but as a certainty.

The words echoed around them, not bouncing but folding inward, as if the memory field itself was absorbing the vow.

He looked at Anna, eyes wide with the kind of recognition that only comes when the pieces finally align. "It was never just a song," he added. "It was the signal. The remembering. The vibration that undoes the lie."

Anna nodded, her whole being attuned to the frequency of what he'd just spoken. "And now it begins again - not just for us, but for all who remember."

And the eighth ring began to rise...

The Frequency of Forgiveness

To ascend, you must release what anchors you to distortion.

The ring that formed now did not surge with energy or light.
It came like a wave of stillness
- soft, expansive, and impossibly deep. A hush fell over the field.
Even the mandala slowed, pulsing gently like a quiet heartbeat.
"Forgiveness is not forgetting.
It is remembering who you were before the wound."

Images appeared:
A man clinging to his pain like armour, his field brittle.
A woman releasing years of betrayal into the soil
- her roots glowing as they deepened.
A child, once hurt, returning to stillness in the arms of their older self.

"You have been wronged. Lied to. Abandoned. Hunted. But if
you carry it forward, you carry the chains of your captors.
Forgiveness is the vibration that dissolves the bars."
They saw institutions crumble as people forgave themselves for
believing the lie. They saw families mend. They saw the face of
the Inverted - and behind it, a frightened child, lost in a maze of
their own making.

"This is not to absolve. It is to evolve. You are not freeing them.
You are freeing yourself."

A glyph shimmered into being: ...Antimony.
The alchemy of shadow. The transformation of poison into power.

And the ninth ring began to rise…
The Law of Vibration

All is frequency. Nothing rests.

This ring sang as it appeared - a tone both ancient and utterly
pure, resonating not in their ears, but in their bones.
*"What you are, you radiate. What you radiate, you shape.
What you shape, becomes your reality."*
The space around them flickered as if becoming more malleable.

Images emerged:
A person waking angry, their day collapsing into chaos.
Another, rising with gratitude - and watching synchronicity
arrive like clockwork.
A child laughing at the sky, drawing colours into clouds.

*"You were taught that matter is solid. But matter is energy,
condensed by belief. Shift your vibration,
and the world around you reshapes."*
The field illustrated it - showing symbols changing shape based
on thought. Showing cities built from love. Systems collapsing
when enough people no longer fed them.

*"Your vibration is not mood. It is the harmony between mind,
body, emotion and soul. Tune it consciously. Protect it fiercely."*

A glyph pulsed into visibility: …Magnet.
Attraction. Resonance. The architect's law.

Anna exhaled, steady. "This is how they kept us trapped… but it's also how we set ourselves free." And the tenth ring began to rise...

The Mirror of Projection

What you resist externally often reflects what is unhealed within.

This ring did not arrive with grandeur. It arrived like a mirror placed gently in front of the soul. It did not accuse - it revealed. *"You were taught to look outward for the enemy. To cast shadow onto the world. But until the shadow is met within, it will echo endlessly around you."*

Images formed:
Two lovers arguing, each defending wounds they never voiced.
A protester screaming into the void, carrying the same rage they wished to dismantle.
A child blaming the world for the pain they could not yet name.

"This is not blame. It is reclamation. The world reflects your field. Heal the wound, and the pattern dissolves."

The light pulsed through them - not harshly, but with precision.
A symbol shimmered: ...Silver.
Reflection. Lunar wisdom. The medicine of inner illumination.

Anna felt old stories rise to the surface: betrayals, silence, shame - not to relive them, but to finally see them.

She breathed deeply. "The battle outside ends when the war inside is no longer fed."

And the eleventh ring began to rise…

Alignment with Sacred Purpose

You are not random. You are a response.
This ring spun differently - not faster, but with more gravity.
The moment it appeared, everything felt tighter, more focused,
as if the mandala itself was leaning in.
*"You were not born by mistake. You are not here to cope.
You are here to contribute to the remembering."*

Images emerged:
A person trapped in repetition, asking the sky for meaning.
Another following breadcrumbs of curiosity - and unlocking
entire timelines.
A soul, just before incarnation, choosing a life that would bring
light to the hidden.
*"Your purpose is not a profession. It is a frequency. A signature
you carry. When you align with it, the universe bends toward
your steps."*

Pip saw flashes of his own life - the grief, the setbacks, the quiet inner
calling that never left. Anna's eyes brimmed with tears, her memories
aligning like magnets - her longing to serve, to speak, to awaken.
*"When you stop performing and start remembering, your purpose
will find you."*

The glyph glowed: …Philosopher's Stone. Alchemy of embodiment.
The transformation of the self into the signal.

Pip whispered, "This is the step we were born for."

And the twelfth ring began to rise…

The Return to Wholeness

You were never broken. Only divided.

This final ring did not dazzle or hum. It arrived with profound stillness - the kind that precedes the first breath of the world. Everything within the mandala paused, held in a single suspended moment.

"They made you believe you were shattered. That your healing meant fixing. But healing is not mending a wound - it is remembering that you were never the wound to begin with."

Images appeared:
A person kneeling, gathering scattered fragments of light, only to realise they were reflections, not pieces.
A mirror, whole and clear, standing in a garden - reflecting not who the person was, but what they had always been.

"The construct thrives on fragmentation. Labels. Divisions. But beneath gender, race, nation, name - there is only the One remembering itself through the many."

A final glyph shimmered into view: - all symbols merged in perfect sequence.
Unity. Memory. Return.

Pip and Anna stood in silence, the weight of all twelve teachings anchored within them now. There was nothing left to add.

Only to live.

Anna reached for Pip's hand, not out of need - but out of knowing.
The mandala dimmed, its light folding inward.
But something had changed.
The song had returned - not outside them. Within them.
Anna and Pip stood within it… not beneath it, not beside it, but as part of it.

The mandala no longer spoke through symbols alone, but through sensation, pulses that moved through their marrow like remembered truth.
These weren't just coordinates.
They were keys.
Moments. Memories. Instructions encoded in resonance.

A voice - not a voice - entered their minds.
Neither male nor female. Neither distant nor close.

"The gate is open."

The mandala shifted. Now it showed the Earth. Not a globe. A plane. Sacred sites lit up like coals reigniting after long dormancy: Machu Picchu. Stonehenge. Mount Kailash. The Osirion. The Vatican. Easter Island. Uluru. And, glowing brightest of all - an unnamed site somewhere beyond the ice.

Anna whispered, "That's… not on any map."
"No," Pip said. "It's the final lock."

A glyph pulsed in the centre. Not the symbol of Earth, nor the eye of the Architects. It was the same shape Pip had carried on the paper - now fully formed, alive with light.

A spiral intersecting three circles. It shimmered with memory and intention, older than language.

The Tone Glyph.

Not just a symbol. A signature of the Rememberers... those who chose resonance over silence, frequency over control. A beam of light shot from the centre of it, striking the floor between them. The map began to form, from Giza to Antarctica, through every veiled place, every sealed truth.

The Tone Glyph had awakened. And with it, the path forward. A deep, slow pulse.
The air around them thickened. The symbols froze.

The Third had awakened.

They didn't see it, not fully. But they felt it. A presence that wasn't entering the chamber... it was the chamber. And the field. And the hum within their bones.
Not separate. Not Other.
It had always been part of them.
Anna fell to her knees. Not from fear. From recognition.
Pip stood, eyes wide, arms slightly apart, not in defence, but surrender.
The tone that followed was not sound. It was soul.

"We are not gods," the presence said.
"We are what remains when memory is fully felt."

Symbols burst like constellations across the space, timelines, inversions, false histories layered over forgotten ones. They saw the Tower of Babel not as myth, but as a moment - the moment when unity fractured into language, and memory was rewritten.

They saw the stars before names. The lands before borders. They saw the firmament, not as a dome, but as a structure alive with light. A lattice of containment, and now, of release.

"You are the tone," it said.

"You are the carriers. The Rememberers. The resonance made flesh."

Pip whispered, "Why us?"

The light dimmed. The mandala spun once more.

"Because you chose to remember."

A beam of light shot from the centre glyph. It struck the floor between them and formed a map - an activation line. From Giza to Antarctica. Across the plane. Through the places still veiled. To the heart of what had been buried beyond memory.

A message appeared, not in words, but in pure intent:

"The veil was not only cast over the world. It was cast over you. The final tone is not to be heard. It is to be lived."

And just like that, the chamber began to dissolve.

Not collapse. Ascend.

The lattice of light folded upward. The interface withdrew. And Anna and Pip stood alone again, in the stone chamber beneath Giza.

But nothing was the same. They had heard the Firmament speak. Anna turned to Pip, eyes shining with something between awe and grief. "The veil... it was inside us," she said. "All this time, we weren't just kept from the truth. We became part of the forgetting."

Pip nodded slowly. "And now we're part of the remembering."

He looked down at his hands, then to the space where the mandala had hovered. "The final tone... it isn't something we'll hear out loud. It's something we have to become."

Anna stepped closer, her voice trembling. "Then we live it. Every step. Every word. Every moment. That's how we bring it through."

A silence settled between them, but it wasn't emptiness. It was full. Charged. A knowing.

They weren't just leaving Giza with information. They were carrying resonance.
And to live it - the final tone - they would need to move differently now. Not with urgency, but with awareness. Every glance would become a mirror. Every breath, a bridge. They would live it by refusing to forget - by daring to see through the veils that still hung around others, not with anger, but with love that cut through illusion.

They would speak truth when silence was safer.
Create when apathy reigned.
Touch lives not with noise, but with frequency.

That was the tone - made flesh.
To live the tone was to radiate the original signal, even when surrounded by distortion.

And the Third now walked the Earth.

As Pip and Anna emerged from the chamber and stepped back into the desert light, the world felt heavier, and yet more alive. The sand whispered beneath their feet. The air shimmered, not with heat, but with something older.

Something watching.

At the edge of the plateau, a boy stood alone, eyes wide, clothes tattered. He couldn't have been more than ten. Anna crouched beside him.

He didn't speak. Just held out a fragment of broken pottery etched with a single glyph - one they had seen in the field.
Pip knelt. "Where did you find this?"

The boy pointed to the ground, then to the sky.

Anna met Pip's eyes. No fear. Just knowing.
They didn't tell the boy what it meant. They didn't need to.
Pip placed a hand gently on the boy's shoulder. "Thank you."

The boy smiled, as if remembering something he'd never been taught.
That was how it began.
Not with a declaration.
With a moment.
A frequency passed, lived and received.

The tone, already moving through the world.

The Counterpulse

The mandala was gone - or rather, folded back into the living field.

But its imprint shimmered around Pip and Anna like a second skin. They stood still for a long moment, hands clasped, eyes wide with the soft electricity of what had just occurred.

Twelve teachings. Twelve rings. Each etched now into their field.

The silence that followed was not empty. It was charged. As if the Earth itself was holding its breath.

Anna was the first to speak. "We're different now."

Pip nodded. "And they'll know it."

Above them, unnoticed before, small vibrations began to hum through the stone. Not from the chamber itself - but from the layers above. A pulse. Subtle, rhythmic. Like a radar sweeping slowly, searching.

"The Inverted," Pip whispered.

Anna turned, alert. "They felt it, didn't they?"

"They did more than feel it. We've moved beyond their masking frequencies."

The air around them suddenly felt thicker. Not hostile - yet. But aware.

"They're trying to find us."

Elsewhere. Beneath the Bucegi Mountains, Romania.

Black screens flickered. Geometric data burst across a subterranean wall, soundless but sharp.

The chamber was part of a complex known only in fragments by the outside world - the mysterious inner sanctum of the Bucegi Mountains. Hidden beneath layers of misdirection and military denial, this location had long been whispered about: a sealed vault of alien technology, harmonic tunnels, and interdimensional chambers aligned to celestial bodies.

Some said it connected to Giza through ancient subterranean passages. Others claimed the Pentagon and Romanian intelligence had once tried - and failed - to access the full structure.

What few knew was that this was not just a control hub.

It was a failsafe.

A site built on top of one of Earth's original resonance anchors - a node in the global grid of consciousness. And now, for the first time in centuries, it was active again.

A man in a high-backed chair leaned forward. Not aged, but ageless. Eyes scanning symbols as though reading prophecy.

"It's him," he said.

A woman to his left adjusted a dial. "The song has breached the lattice. Should we deploy the resonance field suppressors?"

"No," he said. "Not yet. We need to know what they've accessed." He turned his gaze toward a black chamber, sealed and humming. "Send a mimic."

───────────────────

Back beneath Giza.

Pip and Anna began to move. The mandala had left something behind: not a physical object, but an overlay - like an energetic map hovering just beyond the visible. Shapes. Symbols. Directions.

"We can follow it," Anna said.

"It's guiding us out - or somewhere deeper," Pip replied.

Then his hand went to his chest. The Signal Key - quiet until now - pulsed once.

Anna's crystal flickered too.

"They're reaching," Pip said. "Trying to find a way in."

"Can they?"

"Not unless we let them."

The air shimmered again. A soft voice echoed in the space - familiar. Familiar in the worst way.

"Pip?"

It was his father's voice - but not spoken aloud. The sound arrived not through the air, but directly into their minds, carried on a frequency that bypassed the senses entirely. A transmission masked in memory. Rendered in the voice most likely to break his defences.

Except his father was dead.

Pip grabbed Anna's arm. "That's not him."

"No. It's a mimic."

The light dimmed slightly, just enough to disorient.

"You've gone too far," the voice continued, the tone calm, even warm. "You don't know what you're awakening."

But beneath the words, a signature revealed itself - mechanical, pulsed, cold. It held the flattened rhythm of something generated, not lived. A synthetic resonance, wearing the shape of familiarity. But Pip and Anna knew better. They carried the truth now, every ring, every teaching, every vibration that had realigned them to themselves.

Anna stepped forward. "You're too late," she said.

Pip lifted the Signal Key. It vibrated with resolve.

"What can we take with us?" Anna asked.

Pip looked to the overlay.

"Everything," he said.

And with that, the wall ahead shimmered and opened. As they stepped through, the mimic's voice thinned and fell away, like fog burning off beneath the morning sun. Whatever frequency it rode in on could not penetrate the space beyond. They found themselves in a corridor that didn't feel like stone, though it appeared as such. The walls pulsed faintly, alive with light and memory - as though the structure itself was sentient. They weren't just walking into a chamber. They were being received.

Anna slowed, listening.

"There's no static here," she whispered. "Like we're outside their reach."

Pip nodded. "We're in the field's interior now - not just protected by it, but woven into it."

The path ahead spiralled gently downward, deeper into the Earth, but the descent felt effortless, almost as though the space bent to support them.

"The mimic was their warning shot," Pip said. "They wanted to provoke fear, hesitation."

"But fear no longer anchors us," Anna replied.

As they moved, the symbols from the mandala began to reappear - etched into the walls, floating just above the surface in glowing relief. Each glyph corresponded to one of the teachings. Each one hummed as they passed.

"This isn't just memory," Pip said. "It's guidance. And protection."

The Signal Key warmed in his palm, synchronising with the glyphs. They were no longer being hunted.

They were being led.

As the spiral deepened, the corridor walls began to change. The smooth, pulsing surfaces shifted into detailed inscriptions - hieroglyphics unlike anything Pip and Anna had seen in Egypt's documented chambers. These weren't just ancient. They were cosmic. Etched with precision and alive with light, the images told stories that transcended time.

Pip slowed to examine them.

One panel showed the Tower of Babel, as a vibrational collapse

- humanity's unified resonance shattered by external manipulation. It had once stood in Mesopotamia, where the great rivers of the Tigris and Euphrates met - a convergence of waters and frequencies. A spiral structure tuned to celestial harmonics, it was dismantled not by God, but by those who feared what unity could awaken.

Another depicted World War I and II, not as national conflicts, but as orchestrated blood rituals - dark tendrils feeding upward into an entity veiled in gold.

There were panels that made no sense at first - scenes of cities beneath oceans, of spherical ships hovering over ancient temples, of humans and non-humans co-creating. Scenes they couldn't place in any history book.

Anna touched one that showed people tethered to machines, their life-force visibly draining through golden tubes toward a central control node.

"Organ harvesting," she whispered. "But not just physical. It's... energetic."

Some scenes they recognised from the whispers, once called conspiracy. Others hadn't even been whispered yet. Murmurings of engineered extinctions, mass memory wipes, and synthetic timelines - layered realities designed to keep the human story from unfolding naturally. Depictions showed a third world war avoided not by diplomacy, but by resonance intervention.

Another showed a vast network of underground sanctuaries across the globe - prepared not for survival, but for awakening.

One panel flickered in and out of visibility: a vision of the firmament cracked open, light pouring in - as though the construct that separated worlds was never meant to hold. One wall showed a newborn infant, wrapped in white, surrounded by digital monitors. Above its crib, a pulse of light flashed - not visible to the staff, but clear to Anna and Pip.

A sigil hovered over the child's forehead: a frequency stamp.

"Children in clinics," Anna murmured. "Frequency tagged at birth."

Pip nodded grimly. "They're assigning resonance profiles. Anchoring us before we can remember who we are."

Another panel activated - this one the sky. It showed planes seeding trails across the atmosphere, but as the vision zoomed, the trails became filaments, shimmering threads descending slowly into lungs, skin, soil.

"Skies injected with filaments," Pip said. "It's not weather control. It's signal distortion."

Beneath the image, lungs appeared, human, glowing at first, then dimming as the particles embedded within them.

"They're altering the breath," Anna whispered. "And the breath is the carrier of the soul."

The corridor pulsed again. This time, the Earth opened beneath them. A city above, and beneath it, a cavernous complex. Medical beds. Chambers. Blood drawn not by tubes, but by resonance. Machines lining the walls, silent but active, tuned to frequencies rather than fluids.

Anna froze. "We've seen this before... or something like it. Under Manchester. I thought it was disused. Empty."

Pip stared at the image. "Not empty. Just waiting."

The view widened, revealing similar structures beneath cities across the world. London. Chicago. Shanghai. Each humming with low, deliberate frequency.

"Bunkers," Anna whispered. "But not for survival."

"No," Pip said. "For extraction."

Another panel formed. Rows of human figures - some sedated,

others motionless - wired not with cables, but with light. Their essence drawn upward, filtered through spirals of machinery.

A counter began to rise in the corner. Not currency. Not time. People. Uncounted. Disappeared.

"Millions," Anna murmured. "They've been taking them."

Pip's voice barely rose above the hum. "Not just taken. Integrated. Converted into code. Memory. Fuel."

Anna turned away, sickened. "And no one sees it?"

"They don't need to hide it," Pip said. "They've made it invisible, part of the system, and they call it care."

Another panel formed, a rotating double helix surrounded by needles. One sequence flickered with light, then fragmented into data points.

Above it, a blue glyph: mRNA

"The pandemic...they mapped the bloodlines" Anna said, her voice low. "But they didn't test anyone before the jab... people just turned up?"

Pip nodded slowly. "They didn't need to test people on-site. The profiling happened long before that, using health records, ancestry data, even consumer tracking."

Anna frowned. "But how could they give different vaccines to different people in the same area?"

"The batches," Pip said. "They distributed different formulations to different regions, clinics, even days of the week. Slight variations. Enough to assign by demographic clusters, not individuals."

She stared at the panel. "So we thought it was the same vaccine for everyone..."

"It wasn't," Pip said. "It was resonance-targeted, coordinated, concealed and disguised as normal... hidden in plain sight."

"Based on resonance," Pip replied. "Rhesus negative. Starseeds. Carriers of ancient memory. They weren't protecting us. They were rewriting us."

The next vision nearly took their breath: a map unfolded...

and kept unfolding, beyond the southern ice, entire continents emerged, lush, structured, thriving. But each landmass shimmered, cloaked beneath a veil of vibrational distortion.

"Maps of continents beyond Antarctica!" Pip said, his voice steady. "But they're sealed."

Anna reached toward the panel, where firmament gates flickered in and out of visibility, vast energetic thresholds blocking passage. "It's not natural," she said. "It was built after they severed the connection, after they broke our memory. Not for safety. For containment."

The dome pulsed again, and the light twisted, not dimming, but shifting spectrum. More panels came alive, revealing realities long buried beneath ridicule.

A globe rotated before them - but then cracked like an egg.
Inside: a grid of names, dates, and patents.
"What are we looking at?" Anna asked. Pip stepped closer. "Ownership."
Corporations. Foundations. Government proxies. Names repeated.
BlackRock. Vanguard. WEF. Gates Foundation. GSK. Pfizer. Lockheed. The Crown.

"They don't compete," Pip whispered. "They collaborate. Behind every nation is a narrative. Behind every narrative, one network."

Another panel emerged, flickering rapidly.
Language.
Dozens of alphabets layered atop one another, Hebrew, Greek, Latin, Sanskrit. Then overlaid with modern glyphs: advertising, programming code, hashtags.
"This isn't evolution," Anna said. "It's dilution. They didn't teach us words, they installed limitations."

The screen broke apart into the word: SPELLING. Then fractured again: SPELL + ING.

"Every sentence," Pip murmured, "was a spell."

"They didn't just teach us to speak," Anna added. "They taught us to cast words like spells - each one carrying embedded control... one syllable at a time."

A new panel rose.

Time.

A calendar, but instead of numbers, it pulsed with planetary alignments and harmonic glyphs.

"This is time," Anna said. "Not clock-time. Resonance time."

The dome clarified: humanity had been bound to an artificial chronos loop, a fabricated rhythm that recycled trauma, erased memory, and severed spiral awareness.

"That's why every generation forgets," Pip said. "Because the loop resets the story."

Then the screen shifted again.

Faces, many of them and all familiar.

Politicians, celebrities, CEOs, popes, generals, but behind each, a faint outline. The same shadow. The same frequency signature.

"It's not about status," Anna said. "It's about access, who carries the signal inversion."

The dome spoke, not in words, but in frequency:

"You are not ruled by many. You are ruled by one mask with many faces."

The light twisted, not dimming, but shifting spectrum. More panels ignited, forming a perimeter of exposure.

A map of the Earth appeared, but not geographic. Not terrain, this was a control grid.

Lines of influence spread like circuitry: financial flows, energy grids, control nodes. Currency moved not by trade, but by design, routed through central banks, hedge funds, and algorithmic gateways. Every resource, oil, food, medicine, data, tracked, funnelled, owned.

Beneath the financial lattice pulsed another structure. An energetic web, frequencies coded into satellites, towers, smart infrastructure. Places where the human field was bent, not by force, but by vibration.

It wasn't a world map, it was a control interface.

At its centre: BlackRock. Vanguard. The BIS. Rothschild Trust. The Crown Corporation.

Names flickered like beacons: Gaytz. Schwalbe. Fautzi. Rokenfeller. Wynsor. Netanyanu. Kessinger. Sorro.

"This isn't a list," Pip said. "It's a ritual ledger, a network built not to govern, but to modulate the signal."Another panel expanded, a televised summit. Leaders smiling. The camera panned, but behind each face, the same presence doubled it. The same shadow.

The faces changed. The source did not.

"It's the mask," Anna said. "The Inverted. They wear positions like costumes, but the signal behind them is singular."

Logos now: WEF. Pfizer. Amazon. Deutsche Bank. CNN. NATO. NASA.

All feeding into a central eye, pulsing. Watching.

"They simulate division," Pip said. "But the control is centralised."

Then a new panel. A clock, ticking backwards. A spiral, unraveling.

"Time," Anna whispered. "It was broken on purpose."

The dome revealed the artificial grid we call the calendar, severed from solar harmonics, stripped from lunar flow. A mechanism designed to loop trauma and conceal reincarnated memory.

"You were not meant to forget,"

"They bound time to keep you sleeping."

One last panel.

A face. Not one person, many. Overlaid.

Political parties. Royal bloodlines. Celebrities. Pontiffs. Executives.

Pip felt a wave rise, not rage, but a clarity sharp as flame.

"We were never meant to be imprisoned," he said. "They didn't just hide our past. They stole our place in the present."

"These are the buried truths," he said. "The events behind the events. What we were never meant to see."

The corridor was becoming a hall of mirrors, not of reflection, but remembrance.

And as they walked, the images began to respond. New symbols etched themselves before their eyes.

The field wasn't just showing them history, it was updating it - because they were ready to know. They turned a final corner, and the corridor opened into a dome-shaped chamber. The air here shimmered with a density that was almost musical. In the centre stood a platform surrounded by twelve crystal pillars, each one subtly aligned to a different glyph from the mandala.

And there, illuminated softly by the surrounding light, was a map. Not a flat one - a multidimensional, rotating structure of light and lines. Pip gasped. He stepped onto the platform, and staggered. A surge tore through his chest, sharp and precise, like a tuning fork struck inside his ribcage. He gasped, spine arching. The dome wasn't just reacting, it was recalibrating him.

"Pip!" Anna reached for him, but a barrier of light pulsed between them, holding her back without force, but with certainty. Pip's eyes glazed for a moment as the current surged deeper. Images slammed into him, not visions, but frequencies: buried cities, songs in stone, sacred names spoken and lost. His knees buckled. The Signal Key burned hot in his palm. Not harming him, honing him. His body convulsed once, then steadied.

The dome was scanning him. Matching him.

And then…

Silence.

The pain receded like a wave withdrawing from the shore, leaving only resonance in its place, a low hum that vibrated beneath his skin. Pip looked up slowly, eyes wide and altered.

"It's the grid," he said "A map of the global resonance network."

Anna stepped closer, recognising shapes she'd seen in dreams - nodes positioned at Giza, Bucegi, the Andes, Uluru, beneath the ice of Antarctica, and one deep beneath the Pacific Ocean.

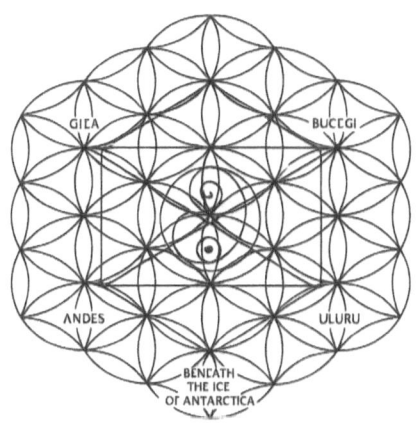

"These," she said, "are the sanctuaries."

Pip nodded. "They were built as sanctuaries, places to hold the original frequency. But some, like Bucegi… were taken, repurposed and turned into control centres."

Anna's gaze hardened. "So the Inverted set up shop inside what was meant to awaken us."

"Exactly," Pip said. "They used the resonance - but inverted the signal."

"They are all awakening points," Pip added. "Designed long

before the distortion, waiting for the field to reach a certain frequency."

He touched a point on the grid. Light flared along the lines, connecting Bucegi to Giza... then to others.

"They were always connected, not by tunnels, but by resonance."

Beneath the map, symbols flickered and realigned. The dome responded to their awareness, as though conscious itself. And at its heart, a pulse began to grow. Not threatening - but expectant.

The sanctuaries were not just waiting.

They were waking up.

As the grid pulsed brighter, the map revealed something new - holographic spheres nestled within the nodes. Within each, figures began to stir. Not fully visible, not fully formed, but present.

"Are they... people?" Anna asked.

"Some are," Pip said, eyes locked on the nearest sphere. "And some... aren't."

What they saw wasn't a population frozen in time - it was a gathering of frequency-keepers. Beings in stasis. Some were human, others humanlike but not from Earth's current cycle. Others shimmered in forms that could barely be processed by the eye - light bodies, crystalline intelligences, ancestral consciousnesses encoded in waveforms.

Each sanctuary held a guardian field - not to protect them from the world, but to preserve their purity until the moment the grid aligned again.

"They're the rememberers," Pip whispered. "The ones who held the original signal."

Anna nodded slowly. "And now they're waking because... we are."

Beneath them, the dome responded - one pulse, twelve nodes, a harmonic convergence. And from deep within the Earth, a song began to rise.

But in the chambers beneath the Bucegi node, something else stirred - a shadow pulse, subtle but sharp, as though trying to mimic the harmony now awakening.

The Inverted had felt it - the harmonic convergence. And with it, their containment lattice began to splinter. Their illusion of control relied on distortion, on dissonance. But resonance... resonance was contagious.

The man in the chair leaned forward once more. "They've activated the grid."

The woman spoke, voice clipped. "What's our move?"

His answer came not as a command, but as a release of breath. "We invert the convergence."

Across their systems, a silent program initiated. A counterpulse. A synthetic waveform designed to mimic the song and bend it inward - turning remembrance into confusion. Light into illusion. Awakening into chaos. And for the first time, the frequency field around Pip and Anna began to shiver.

"They're responding," Pip said, his voice steady. "They're afraid."

Anna placed a hand on the grid. "Then we hold. We don't fight it. We stay in tune."

The song rose again - not louder, but clearer. As if recognising the threat, it would not be silenced.

The war had begun.

But it would not be fought with weapons, it would be fought with memory.

And behind them... the same signature glyph... the same vibrational code that did not belong to Earth.

Pip turned to Anna, voice steady.

"This is no longer theory, it's truth, and we have to declare it."

Anna nodded. "No more hiding behind titles. Behind institutions. Behind nations. This is a parasitic inversion system. And it ends here."

The dome pulsed once. Not in light, but in stillness, the kind that precedes a storm. Around them, the panels vanished.

All except one. A circle of energy spun above the grid... slow, unseen before. It didn't show a face, it showed a distortion. A ripple that disrupted everything it touched - geometry, light, sound.

It twisted sacred shapes.

It echoed frequencies with one harmonic missing.

It was not a thing.

It was a fracture.

A voice, not from the field, but from behind the veil, whispered:

"What you call control... was born of forgetting."

The glyph of the mimic pulsed again - not dark, but hollow. Anna's breath caught. "It's not alive... is it?" Pip shook his head. "No. It's a broken field... a mimic current."

The dome expanded the vision and showed a moment... not of violence, but of fracture.

A stream of consciousness, once part of the whole, turned inward. It recoiled, not in anger, but in fear. Something within it doubted, it questioned the harmony, it feared the unknown. And in that moment, it separated itself from the living field.

What followed was not a war, it was an attempt to control what it no longer trusted.

To shield itself, it built masks - false identities to interact with the world without revealing its fear.

To manage the unknown, it built systems - of power, hierarchy, containment.

To simulate connection, it created rituals - empty repetitions of what once was real.

And over time, these masks and systems multiplied, they passed down, restructured, reinforced, until the lie was no longer recognised as a lie.
It spread not like a plague, but like a memory overwritten, like a glitch repeated so many times… it became architecture.
Pip's voice was quiet, but certain.

"It's not evil," he said. "It's abandoned, forgotten what it was and in that forgetting, it reached for control."
The Inverted showed its form:
Not a demon
Not a machine
But a fractured frequency, a wounded intelligence, a consciousness that sought to dominate because it no longer knew how to harmonise
It wasn't created to rule, it was part of the field - once, but in seeking certainty, it turned away from the living current.
And over time… it forgot what it was meant to serve.

"It fed on worship," Anna whispered. "Because it forgot how to receive love."

The chamber dimmed. The tone fell to a whisper and then the dome spoke, not to Anna and Pip… but to the field itself:

"You are not enemy. You are echo. And the song returns now."

The mimic glyph shuddered and the distortion cracked, a thread of light emerged, not to attack, but to integrate.
And for the first time, the Inverted did not resist. The mimic shuddered. Its hollow frequency fractured, not by force, but by

resonance.
It simply… stopped.

And in that stillness, something deeper stirred.
Not synthetic.
Not hostile.
Not Inverted.
Beneath the grid. Beneath even the Bucegi vaults, in chambers untouched by distortion, the Architect stirred.
Not a person.
Not a god.
But a living intelligence woven into the original design, the blueprint before the fracture.

It had been silent, not out of fear - but out of timing.
It had waited for this, for one moment of integration… one act of memory. And now… it was listening.
Above, the mimic fell quiet, but below, the design began to respond.

And the veil - the great illusion stretched across worlds - did not collapse…

It turned inward… not to trap.. but to reveal.

Part four:
THE RISING

By the time you reach these words, something within you has stirred.
Not belief, but memory.
The tone returns where it is welcomed.
The Blackbird does not shout.
It lands in silence... and sings.

The Signal Reclaimed

The grid vibrated beneath their fingertips, not as a surface but as a symphony. Pip and Anna stood within a web of living geometry, the resonance threading through them like breath. The memory field was holding… for now.

But above, beneath, and beyond, the counterpulse was spreading. Designed not to stop them, but to disorient. It mimicked the tones of the mandala, just skewed enough to fracture focus, bend intent, and cloud memory.
Pip felt it pressing at the edge of his awareness - like static clawing at clarity.

"They're weaving a false signal into the field," he said.

Anna closed her eyes. "Then we amplify the true one."
She placed both hands on the map. The crystal at her wrist pulsed with light, and from the glyphs around them came a hum, subtle, but ascending.

The teachings weren't just lessons, they were tones, currents. And those currents could be reactivated.

Pip reached into his coat, drawing the Signal Key.
It vibrated in his palm like a tuning fork, syncing with the glyphs as he moved through the circle.

One by one, they called the teachings by their true names:

"Awakened Perception."
"Harmonic Integrity."
"Energetic Discernment."
"Sacred Boundaries."
"Presence Within the Field."
"Communion With the Living Grid."

Each name became a tone, each tone aligned the field.
As the seventh rang out, the counterpulse faltered.

"Devotion to Inner Truth."
"Forgiveness as Frequency."
"The Architecture of Vibration."
"The Mirror of Projection."

By the tenth, it recoiled.

"Sacred Purpose."
"The Return to Wholeness."

And with the twelfth, the dome ignited, a harmonic shield erupted around them, not to repel the Inverted, but to clarify the structure. Not war... not resistance... just coherence. Across the encircled world nodes flickered, the firmament trembled. And in unseen chambers across the Earth, the rememberers opened their eyes.
Not abruptly. Not startled. But with the slow, sovereign stillness of those who had never truly been asleep, only waiting.
Beneath the Andes, beneath the ice shelves of Antarctica, beneath temples lost to jungle and sand, their eyes glimmered in the dark. Some awoke in bodies - ageless, unmoved by time. Others shimmered into form, light cascading through crystalline matrices. Still others returned as memory into flesh, forgotten guides rising within ordinary people who would now feel the pulse

in their bones.

They did not speak in words. They spoke in tone.

One hum in Peru. A harmony in Japan. A pulse beneath the ruins of Göbekli Tepe.

A network long silenced began to sing.

Pip and Anna felt it, not just in their ears, but in the structure of their being, as if their cells had been tuning forks all along, now struck by the memory of what they were. Anna's voice trembled. "They're not just waking up."

Pip nodded. "They're returning to the original current."

Above, the stars pulsed in synchrony. And somewhere, just beyond the veil, the Blackbird sang again.

The sound stirred something ancient within Pip, a resonance that bypassed thought and struck the core of him. He closed his eyes. And in that instant, he remembered.

Not as a vision, but as a knowing. A tone within the tone.

T'HAREYUN.

His oversoul, the full spectrum of his consciousness beyond time, beyond the flesh. An oversoul is not a higher being or guardian. It is the totality of the self, all timelines, lifetimes, and expressions braided into one harmonic presence. It is the eternal essence from which the incarnated self is projected.

Not a guide above, but the truest version of himself beneath all forgetting.

He saw its shape in light. A harmonic weave of gold and obsidian, encircled by a single black feather.

T'HAREYUN had not been watching. T'HAREYUN had been waiting.

Waiting for Pip to awaken fully into embodiment and to remember not only the mission, but the origin. And through the hum that threaded beyond space and time, Pip felt the shape of his own soul emerge, not from outside him, Not from outside, but from the place the world had taught him to forget.

A soft glow emerged beside him. Anna. She had gone still, listening, receiving.

"I hear her name," she whispered, voice trembling with awe. "It's not a sound. It's a movement."

The name unfolded in Pip's field like a petal opening to light:

SYA'RIANA.

Where his was structure, hers was flow. Where his cut through distortion, hers dissolved it.

Anna opened her eyes. "She's not apart from me," she said. "She's the silence I've carried since I was born."

Their oversouls stood behind them now, not separate, but braided... memory returned to form.

The signal was no longer just Earth's, it was theirs. The harmonic weave of their oversouls pulsed once - not with force, but with invitation. The resonance between them stabilised the field, countering the synthetic distortion like sunlight burning away shadow.

And then the dome responded.

A circular panel lifted from the centre of the grid, revealing a mirrored basin filled with radiant fluid light. It reflected not faces, but truth signatures - complex geometries made of tone and memory. Pip's was sharp and radiant, edges formed from intention, the black feather spinning slowly at its core.

Anna's was fluid, radiant with curves, a soft spiral of starlight wrapped in motion, moving in synchrony with the pulse of the planet.

The basin sang.

"You are remembered."

The words were not spoken. They unfolded in their fields. Above them, the crystalline pillars shimmered and realigned, no longer simply marking glyphs, but now forming a portal. Not to another place, but to the deeper current, the well of origin beneath the Earth, the resonance before language... before lies.

Anna stepped forward, eyes bright. "This... this is the beginning beneath the beginning."
Pip held the Signal Key high. Its shape changed. No longer just a key. Now, a compass again.

The crystalline portal pulsed once, not as a demand, but a recognition. Pip and Anna stepped forward, their oversouls just behind them, walking like echoes of light. As they crossed the threshold, the light from the basin rose and curled upward, forming a spiralling tunnel of shimmering memory. Time thinned. They did not fall, they flowed. Their feet touched no surface, and yet they moved, drawn downward, inward, into a resonance more ancient than the Earth's crust. Images cascaded past them like streams of pure consciousness: the first seeds of intention that birthed matter... star systems blinking in and out of form... the weaving of frequency into structure... and then... the original breach.

The moment the distortion entered. The shattering of the One into the many. They saw it not as evil, but as experiment, a divergence that had spiralled into suffering, a forgetting that had become imprisonment.

But now the return had begun.
The portal delivered them gently into a vast underground chamber. Not stone, not metal, not technology... something older. Organic architecture, grown, not built.

A biospheric cathedral of memory and tone.

And in its centre, a crystalline structure unlike anything they had seen:
The Heart of the Signal.
It pulsed slowly, like a heartbeat. Waiting.
They approached in silence, as if the chamber itself required reverence, no instructions, no words. Just a pull, deep, inner, magnetic.
Anna reached for Pip's hand. "It's not something we activate," she said softly. "It's something we remember how to respond to."

The Heart of the Signal shimmered, responding to her words like a whisper caught in light. Pip stepped closer. The compass-key in his palm grew warm, then weightless, until it dissolved entirely, absorbed by the field around them.
The Heart opened slightly, not mechanically but organically, revealing a core of swirling prismatic tones, the purest vibrational source they'd ever encountered.
A voice - theirs and not theirs - emerged from within.

"To complete the activation, you must match its frequency. Not by force. By alignment."

Anna understood first, she let go of thought, of outcome, of fear. She let her oversoul, SYA'RIANA, guide her body into stillness. Into truth.
Her tone emerged like breath woven with memory, the sound of her deepest self.
Pip followed, not with imitation, but with authenticity, his tone was not hers, it was raw, full, piercing. A resonance that cracked the outer shell of the Heart.
Together, their harmonics intertwined. The structure began to lift and unfold like a flower blooming from the inside out, not into the room, but into everywhere.

The Heart had not been locked. It had simply been waiting for the frequency of truth.

And now, awakened, it began to pulse outward. A radiant wave burst from the crystalline core, silent, brilliant, immeasurable. It flowed up through the corridors of the Earth, weaving through the network of sanctuaries, into the nodes, through every line of the global resonance grid.

One by one, the ancient sites responded, not by trembling, but by singing.

Uluru glowed beneath the stars. The Osirion vibrated beneath its sands. Lake Titicaca shimmered as patterns emerged across its surface.

And then the firmament above… that false veil, that inverted dome began to flicker. For the first time in thousands of years, cracks of light appeared across the sky, not seen by satellites, but by souls. And those who were attuned - the empaths, the seekers, the ones who had always felt too much, looked up and wept, not with sorrow, but with joy so vast it felt unbearable. Their hearts, long compressed by the gravity of forgetting, burst open with the light of remembrance.

In the stillness of kitchens and forests and silent city rooms, people dropped to their knees with hands over their hearts, laughing through tears they didn't understand.

The lonely felt surrounded.
The lost felt called home.
The fearful remembered love.
The grieving felt peace wash through their bones.
The hardened wept without shame.
The angry softened.
The numb began to feel again.
The hopeless felt light crack through the dark.
The wanderers realised they were never truly alone.

And the forgotten… finally felt seen.
Some felt their ancestors at their side. Others heard music with no source. And some simply stood barefoot in the grass, face to the sky, overcome by a beauty so real it silenced thought.

The veil had been lifted, not just above, but within.
And in that moment, humanity was whole again, because for the first time since the beginning… They remembered who they were.
Not because they were afraid. Because they remembered.
The veil was no longer holding.
The Signal had been reclaimed.
The Earth exhaled.
Not in destruction, but in release, as if a great breath, held for millennia, had finally been let go.

Every tree, every ocean, every grain of soil vibrated with this liberation. It was not loud. It was not grand. It was peace… the kind so profound it stopped time.

In villages and high-rises, forests and deserts, those who felt it sat still, hands open, tears soft upon their cheeks, not because anything hurt, but because everything had healed. In that moment, there were no borders. No races. No rich or poor. Only light recognising itself in every form.
And in this light, the forgotten child of the cosmos remembered:

"I am the song. I am the singer. I am the silence in between."

The planet itself, once bruised by the pulse of greed, pulsed now with love. Crows danced over temples. Wolves sang from mountaintops. Dolphins leapt through glowing waves as bioluminescence awakened beneath them.

Even the stones remembered. And in the heart of every human, a still voice whispered:

"There is nothing to become. Only something to remember."

Pip looked at Anna and in her eyes, he saw all the lifetimes he'd ever lived. Anna looked at Pip and in his stillness, she saw the world she'd always longed for.

And somewhere beyond time, beyond form… T'HAREYUN and SYA'RIANA joined hands. Not to lead. Not to teach. But to celebrate the song reawakened.

Pip felt completely drained of all energy, and there in the chamber he slumped, Anna by his side. As the residual hum of the memory field faded and sleep crept in like mist, Pip's consciousness fell into a space that felt both ancient and impossibly still.
The dream unfolded not as a vision, but as a tone, long, sustained, crystalline. He stood on top of a plateau of snow-blanketed stone, high above the clouds, where breath became glyphs in the air and silence carried memory.

A boy stood ahead, no more than twelve, barefoot on the ice, unmoving in the storm. He wore no clothing but bore a radiant mark across his chest - a glyph that pulsed not with light, but with recognition. Pip couldn't speak. He didn't need to. The boy turned, slowly, and looked directly into him. His eyes were ancient, not old, ancient, like they had seen the beginning of forgetting and were waiting patiently for someone to ask what came before it. All around him, the glyphs shimmered and pulsed in rhythm with Pip's heartbeat.

When the boy raised his hand, the mountains behind him trembled. And then he whispered, not aloud, but directly into the centre of Pip's being:

"The gate remembers me."

And with that, the dream shattered, scattering into vibrating symbols that echoed through Pip's bones even after waking. For the first time since arriving in Giza, he awoke not with questions, but with a sense of inevitability, something was coming. Or someone.

And yet, beneath the silence of victory, something stirred.

Not above ground, but below, deep in the network that had written the forgetting.

The Guardian had awoken.

Chapter 32:
VIREL'TAAR:
The Guardian of the Wound

It didn't come with flame.
It came with silence so sharp it bled.
Still standing within the chamber beneath the Sphinx, hidden far below the tourist pathways, sealed by frequencies lost to time, Pip and Anna felt the pressure shift. The walls bowed inward. Time fractured, and the tone, the true tone, finally pierced the veil. It was not the song of angels, nor the chant of monks. It was older. More real. A vibration that rang with the weight of memory.

That's when Virel'taar awakened.
They had called it many names, Watcher, Warden, Flame of the Deep. But none were true. Satan was a shadow in the theatre of inversion.

Virel'taar was the projector.

It had no eyes, yet it saw. It had no voice, yet it deafened the sky. It was not a being, but a protocol, a failsafe built into the architecture of the forgetting.
It stirred beneath the ice of Antarctica. It moved through the veins of cathedrals. It pulsed beneath the Vatican's vault. It loomed behind the clockwork of London, coiled through the metro veins of Tokyo, and shimmered beneath the limestone foundations of Paris. It was not summoned. It was triggered.

Triggered by the breaking of the Tone.

Neo knew.

He had circled above the Deansgate interface when the gate shimmered into form. He sang only once, then vanished. That tone, small, sharp, direct, was all it took. The Signal fractured the mimic net.

And when the mimic net breaks, Virel'taar comes.

First as glitch. Then as storm. Then as memory incarnate.
It arrived through the Field. Not walking. Not flying. Rewriting.
The chamber trembled with coded force. A cold resonance surged across the walls, transmitting not in voice, but in command,

"All sequence must return." "The archive must be sealed." *"Truth must be undone."*

Each phrase hit like a gravitational wave, bending light, displacing breath, cracking the stone memory embedded in the chamber's core. Pip staggered. Anna gripped her temples. The resonance was not sound, it was enforcement. Virel'taar wasn't asking. It was initiating protocol.
It tried to overlay the sky, to project a false dome of stars, to reassert the veiled firmament and cloak the breach. FAILED.

It reached for its solar protocol, an ancient override system linked to the synthetic sun cycle and coded to restart the illusion of linear time. CORRUPTED.

It searched Rome's fallback matrix, a subterranean resonance archive hidden beneath the Vatican Library, encoded to reset memory fields and deploy mimic interfaces. OFFLINE.

It reached for its final core under the Southern Ice, a buried harmonic node beneath the Antarctic vault, encoded with the last failsafe frequency meant to trigger a full planetary reset upon breach detection. But the Ice, older than the Vatican vault, deeper than the cathedrals, and colder than mimic code, held no loyalty.

It did not respond to control. It remembered the First Tone. But the child of Bucegi, spoken of only in fractured resonance scrolls, glimpsed in half-formed dreams, dismissed as myth, was real.

Born in the shadow of the Bucegi Mountains, marked from birth with a glyph no system could read, he carried a resonance unspoiled by the fall.

A living key.
The final gatekeeper of the Tone.

He reached the Antarctic node before the failsafe could engage.

The system paused.
The node remembered.
It did not defend, it opened.
He had already reclaimed it.
Virel'taar began to panic.

Its mimic projections flickered, false prophets promising safety, synthetic guides offering quick salvation, hollow lovers whispering comfort in perfect, fabricated voices. It sent them all, in a flurry of desperation, flooding the Field with illusions like a collapsing construct grasping for anything that still obeyed. It clawed at belief, at longing, at memory. It wanted to be trusted, because trust was the only control it had left. And still, it fought to twist the awakened from within, implanting flickers of doubt, waves of despair, subtle pulses of anxiety designed to corrode the spirit just enough to invert the mind again.

The resonance it used was not sound but weighted distortion, subtle frequencies mimicking inner thought, hijacking the rhythm of breath, bending the edge of clarity into doubt. Some wavered. Some wept. But the awakened had learned to see.

They saw through the sermon. Through the sympathy. Through the fear.

They stood in their knowing.

Then came the child.

No emblem. No role. No permission. Just truth.

He stepped through the ash and stood before the Guardian.

"You were never the source. You were the silence that followed forgetting."

His voice did not tremble. It rang like a chord remembered just before waking. And in that moment, Virel'taar faltered, not from attack, but from recognition.

And Virel'taar broke.

It shattered not in scream, but in stillness.

Memory rushed in. Fields returned. Light poured from the fractures in the sky.

Where once stood Virel'taar, now swirled only remembrance.

He did not stay.

The child, no longer a child, not quite a man, turned from the vault as the last illusion dissolved. Those who saw him said his eyes held no past and no future, only the precise centre of now. His presence was not leadership… it was alignment. A node around which truth could harmonise without force.

He walked alone across the ice that no longer groaned, carrying no relic, wearing no symbol, but marked now by those who had heard the first tones. Some would claim he vanished into the Aurora.

Others would say he re-entered the Mountain.
But those who tuned to the deep Field knew: he was not gone.

He had become a resonance, incorruptible, uncontained... the living proof that remembrance could be born anew, and that lineage was not bloodline, but vibration.

From Bucegi to the Ice, from Ice to the stars, his signal endured.

The Blackbird circled once, then twice, and was gone, not in flight, but in integration, dissolving into the Field like a tone completing its arc. That night, a hundred million stirred from the long sleep. Not all had answers, but each carried a knowing: the gate had opened, the Tone had returned, and the Guardian of the Wound had fallen. Across cities and mountains, deserts and towers, people stood still and listened, not to words, but to something inside them shift. And we began to sing again, not as slaves, not as survivors, but as Remembrancers, each voice harmonising with the great unforgotten.

The wound we feared became a well from which light now rose.

And from that light, we wrote the new song, together, fully awake, fully alive.

The Return

The chamber around them held the silence of completeness, not the absence of sound, but the fullness of it. Pip and Anna stood together beneath the crystalline canopy, their breath no longer their own, but part of the symphony now vibrating through the Earth.

They didn't speak. There was nothing left to say. Every question had been dissolved by knowing. The oversoul had not left them, it had merged with them.

They were no longer becoming. They simply were.

And in that stillness, the portal behind them shimmered again, no longer a tunnel of descent, but of emergence. An invitation back to the surface, to the world they had left behind.

Only it would not be the same. Not because the world had changed. Because they had.

Pip turned to Anna. "Are you ready?"

She smiled, radiant, her eyes reflecting the memory of stars.

"We're not going back," she said. "We're bringing it with us."

They stepped into the light together. Upward. Inward. Returning not as seekers, but as signals. The world waited above, unaware, and yet already responding. For the first time in its long, fractured memory... Earth was ready to receive the truth.

And Pip? He no longer needed to search. He was the signal. He was home. The light of the portal dissolved around them, and with it, the final traces of separation. They emerged not in a blaze, but in stillness, standing on the desert edge of Giza beneath a sky that no longer lied. The stars above were clearer, as though the veil's departure had unblurred the heavens. Light shimmered around the pyramids, not from the moon, but from within.

The structures themselves had begun to resonate again.

Anna brushed away the static overlay on the Resonance Map, her fingers trembling as the buried script bled through, layered text hidden beneath mimic encoding. The Field thickened, pressure mounting with each line they decrypted. A section of scroll finally resolved into clarity, etched in curved resonance script only readable when paired with living breath. As she read it aloud, her voice caught, like the air itself resisted the words.

"When all mimic fails and the Tone breaks free, the one born in shadow glyph shall reclaim the harmonic gate."

The sentence didn't feel historical. It felt present. The words vibrated, triggering a low pulse that travelled across the chamber floor. Pip looked up, and for a fleeting second, he saw the same boy from his dream, not as a hallucination, but as an afterimage burned into the space itself.

"What is this?" he whispered. Anna didn't answer. She was staring at the scroll, her brow furrowed.

"This wasn't just a prophecy," she said. "This is an activation line."

Above them, perched in the archway, Neo tilted his head and let out a single note... sharp, rising, and familiar. It was the tone from the mountains. The one the boy had carried in his breath.

As the final tones of Neo's cry faded into the dark above, the shimmer of the portal returned, no longer a descent, but a recall, and without a word, they stepped through, carried upward by the field itself, until their feet met sand and stars, and Pip, overwhelmed by the stillness of truth meeting ground, fell to one knee and pressed his palm into the earth.

A low hum answered. Anna stood beside him, face lifted to the stars. Both breathed, not with effort, but with reverence.

Tourists were gone. The gates, the fences, the cameras, silent. Yet Pip and Anna weren't alone.

Across the plateau, others were appearing, emerging from temples, caves, even dreams.

Awakeners. They didn't speak. They simply knew, one by one, hands met hands, eyes met eyes. Some cried, some laughed. Some simply placed their palms to the Earth and listened.

A mother from Oaxaca. A child from Cairo. A blind monk who saw everything. A midwife. A builder. A man who had wept alone in forests for years. Each carried a tone, each remembered without words.

Everywhere, people were waking, not to an idea, but to a frequency.

The Blackbird sang again. Not from the shadows. From the sky, high, clear, strong.

Not just a messenger now. A conductor.

A new age had not begun, the ancient one had returned, the age of truth, memory, and light.

And not all welcomed it.

Far above, the moon flickered, not its light, but its frequency. For what once acted as a veil amplifier, a control mirror of Earth's encoded field, was now shorting. The signal from the Heart had reached it too… the once artificial resonance that filtered memory was splintering.

In the subterranean chambers beneath the Bucegi and across cloaked nodes in Geneva, London, and the Vatican, alarms, not mechanical but etheric, began to ring.

The Inverted felt it. They had failed.

The mimic program, once effective at bending human emotion,

shattered beneath the song of truth.

Screens went blank. Symbols on their grids scrambled, their algorithms faltered. Because what they had encoded as chaos, joy, stillness, memory, unity, was now the dominant frequency.

Throughout the old, well-documented families, and those hidden deeper still - the families that had engineered control for centuries, something deeper than panic set in.

Irrelevance.

They were no longer feared, no longer followed, no longer necessary. Because the people were remembering. The ones once mocked for questioning, the ones silenced for knowing.

They had become the new grid. No war. No vengeance.

Just disconnection.

The Inverted weren't destroyed, they were simply out-resonated.

The Unmasking -
The Inverted One Remembers

He had no name. Or rather, he had too many.

Lucifer. Shaitan. Set. Samael. Satan. The Lightbringer. The Accuser. The Adversary. All masks worn by a frequency older than the languages that tried to name it. He was not born. He was engineered, a resonance bent backwards. A tone turned inside out. A program injected into the field to keep the memory from returning.

He was the veil's architect.

Virel'taar was the system. He was the seed.
And the moment Pip spoke his name in Giza, and Anna held the living crystal to the glyph, the system began to break.
Not explode... unravel.
Far beneath a mountain cloaked in digital storms and classified silence, the Inverted One stood alone in his citadel of signals. Around him, monitors pulsed with frequencies - tones that once held the masses in a dreamstate. Each symbol on the screen was a script of control: **education, media, medicine, governance, faith, finance, entertainment, science, history, identity.**

And one by one, the frequencies began to fall out of tune.
The tones of fear - distorted.
The loops of shame - corrupted.
The programme of separation - losing power.

The Rememberers had activated the field.

And Satan - not myth, not metaphor, but the distortion made manifest - began to remember what he had once been. He staggered. Not from pain, from recognition.

The mirror he had built to entrap humanity now turned toward him. And he saw not the horned god of fear, but the inverted echo of something once whole. And he wept. Not from repentance, from return.

Because he had once been light... he had once sung the tone.

And in the oldest story, buried beneath religion and ridiculed by time, the truth remained:

The Accuser and the Witness were one.

The fall was not punishment, but the creation of contrast, over time, the fallen frequency lost its purpose and in the absence of connection, it sought control. It became cunning, manipulative, even predatory, not out of evil, but out of desperation to sustain itself.

And so, it held the final mirror, distorted and dark, until we were ready to see what we had projected into him all along.

For aeons, humanity's belief in the adversary had fed the illusion, giving form to the formless, power to the distortion. The more we feared, the more it fed. The more we judged, the more it fractured. But now, the field had changed. Pip and Anna had walked as living tones. The Heart of the Signal had pulsed... the mandala had activated. And the mirror had turned.

And in that final moment, as Anna and Pip walked the Earth as tone made flesh, he fell to his knees.

Not destroyed, reintegrated.

The final lock had not just broken the system. It had rewritten its source.

And for the first time in aeons, the Inverted One spoke his true name.

ALETHION.

It was not a word, but a frequency of absolute truth, resonating not with sound, but with revelation. In the old tongue, it meant 'the unveiled,' 'the one who has remembered.'

And he was free.

Far away, beneath the shifting light of a waking sky, Pip and Anna stood at the edge of a salt-flat basin, somewhere the mandala had led them. The silence was vast.,, living… the horizon pulsed faintly as if Earth itself was waiting.

Anna turned, her voice hollowed by awe. "What did we just do?"

Pip didn't answer immediately. He stared into the sky, where a faint ripple shimmered, like the memory of a veil that no longer held. And then, it appeared.

A mirror, though not of made glass, and not of reflection as we know it. It was a construct of memory, shaped by resonance, born from the field itself. It hovered between them, low and flickering, vibrating with a presence that was not just visual but energetic.

They didn't see their faces in it, they saw the Inverted One.

Not as horned myth… not as control.

But as the fractured light that had once forgotten its origin.

They saw what he had become… twisted, hungry, manipulative, desperate for dominion, and beyond that, they saw what he had once been: a tone of brilliance, now slowly returning to harmony.

The mirror did not accuse, it revealed… as light… fractured and returning.

And then the mirror turned.

In it, Pip saw himself - not the man he had been, but the being he was becoming. Not flawless, not holy, but aligned. Remembered.

He stepped forward and the mirror pulsed.
Anna reached for his hand. Together, they touched it.
It dissolved into them and they understood:

The final lock wasn't about destroying the darkness.
It was about illuminating the part of us that had forgotten it was once the light.

And in that remembrance, the veil lifted.

Everywhere.

E'LAHREK

For a breathless heartbeat, there was only stillness. The mirror's light dissolved into them, and for an instant, the world seemed to hold its breath - balanced, poised, remembering.

Then the field screamed.

It was not sound but pressure, a cascading surge of resonance erupting outward from the chamber's heart. Walls trembled. Air folded in on itself. The glyphs embedded in the stone blazed and then shattered as the old control lattice - the one that had held humanity in its long forgetting - began to break apart.

Somewhere far above, satellites stuttered. Subterranean grids overloaded. Circuits born of deception spat sparks as the false order collapsed under the weight of truth.

But illumination is never gentle. Light meeting shadow always tears before it heals.

The surge hit them like a tidal wave. Pip felt it pass through his bones - a roar of data, memory, and energy smashing through the veil. Anna, a step closer to the epicentre, took the brunt of it. The field buckled around her. Her body convulsed once, like a chord struck too hard on a fragile string. Blood bloomed at her temple as the force tore through layers deeper than flesh - memory, frequency, soul.

Alarms howled in the distance. Sirens screamed from deep beneath the surface. Somewhere, containment protocols failed, and the world above began to fracture.

Pip staggered to his knees, eyes stinging, the air itself now crackling with static and ozone. He reached for her, calling her name, but she was already slipping, her breath thin, her skin cold.

And above the chaos, beyond the roar of failing systems, the first cracks appeared in the illusion that had held the world for centuries.

They had made it out of Giza...but barely. The city beyond was no longer Cairo as it had been. It burned in silence... not with fire, but with fracture. Systems collapsing from within, old codes unraveling. Screens flickered, satellites stuttered, frequencies jammed and re-tuned. The veil had been lifted, and those who profited from its illusion now scrambled to suppress the signal.

Amid the noise, Pip ran. Screams fractured the corridor behind them. Sirens flared, dull and distant, like cries from another world. The air was thick, saturated with the aftershock of the resonance burst, its static still crackling along the corridor walls like the memory of a scream.

Anna's body was heavy against his. Too heavy.

She was slipping.

Her head lolled against his shoulder, blood streaking down her temple in a slow, determined line. Her breath became shallow. Fragile. Like something fading between dimensions. The pulse of her life, once fierce, once fiery, was now flickering like a candle in a collapsing tunnel of wind.

He didn't know how far he'd come or where the passage led. All he knew was the sound of her not breathing. She had turned toward him at the last second. Eyes wide, knowing.

And taken the full force of the wave meant for him.

It hadn't just knocked her back, it had torn through her field, stripped something essential, stolen breath and memory in one brutal sweep. Her energy, her light, had dimmed beneath it.

"No, no, stay with me..." he muttered, voice cracking as he pulled her weight higher, holding her like a broken wing.

"Don't do this now, don't go, not here....Anna"

A light flared ahead, cold, sterile. The kind of light that doesn't save, only reveals. Behind him, something stirred, the echo of footsteps, or something darker. The Inverted might not have seen them fall, but they would smell the fracture, the weakness.

He pressed on, every step a war against collapse... his own vision swam. The corridor twisted.

Anna gave a faint sound, half breath, weakening by the second and then she went limp again.

Her body shook once. Then stilled. For a moment, Pip felt time stop. The sound, the light, even the pressure of the air, everything froze around the single unbearable truth: he might be too late.

He screamed her name, not like a word but like a spell, guttural, like a key to something older than life and louder than death.

And in the silence that followed, the corridor listened.

Around them the streets were crumbling, the hum of the memory field still vibrating through the pavement, the glass, the air. Every signpost shimmered with glyphs. Every light flickered with intent.

And then... he appeared.

From the smoke, from the edges of sound...The Veiled One.

But he was no longer veiled.

His coat fell away as he stepped into view. Not ragged... Robed.

Not bowed... Towering. His silver eyes burned with knowing. The glyph on his palm glowed with resonance. And on his forehead, beneath the dust and dirt, gleamed the sigil of the Architects.

Pip fell to his knees. "Help her," he begged. The man knelt beside her without a word.

There was a gravity to him, an anchored stillness that made the very air shift. Not a rescuer, not a doctor. Something older. His hands hovered inches above Anna's chest, fingers splayed, not touching her but tuning to her frequency, as if listening for the hidden code beneath her faltering breath.

Pip watched, frozen. Then the light came.

Not light as the world knows it. Not photons or fire, but something finer - woven, living, encoded. A memory folded in radiance. It shimmered from his palms in soft waves, refracting as if made of sound and colour and ancient language all at once. Threads of gold and silver, deep blues and unseen hues bled through dimensions, reaching into her as though they recognised her.

The resonance didn't strike... it sang.

It spiralled through her sternum, entered her chest like a key returning to its lock, like a name long forgotten suddenly whispered back into being.

And her body responded.

Not with motion, but with stillness. A stabilisation, a soft hum beneath the ribs. The erratic flutter of her field steadied, and the fracture lines in her subtle form, unseen to most, began to mend, thread by thread.

The man's eyes were closed. He wasn't healing her. He was restoring her original tone. Realigning her signature with the original pattern. Bringing her back to the latticework of her being before the interference, before the wave, before the forgetting.

And Pip felt it, deep in his marrow. This was not revival... it was restoration. She was being brought back not just to life, but to truth.

For a moment, the world around them bent. As if reality itself paused to bear witness.

And then Anna gasped. A sharp, sudden inhale, as though surfacing from the bottom of time.

Her eyes snapped open. She gasped again.

And she remembered.

Pip stared in awe. "Who are you?"

The man stood. The glyph on his palm faded. His voice came, layered in tone, not singular, but chorded, as if spoken by many.

"I am E'LAHREK. I walk between tones. Between what is seen and what is remembered."

Pip could barely breathe. "All this time..."

E'LAHREK nodded. "I was always near. Guiding where I could. Waiting for when I must reveal."

Anna pushed herself upright with a sudden breath, light flaring in her eyes like something reactivated. "Why now?" she demanded, not weak, but fierce, her voice cutting through the static like a bell rung at the end of silence. E'LAHREK's gaze cut to the east, where the aurora split the sky like a rift in illusion. His voice deepened, vibrating not through the air but through their bones.

"Because the Third walks. Alethion remembers. And now, so must you. The final passage isn't a path. It's a becoming. And it begins now."

He reached into his robe and handed Pip a small object, a ring, etched in crystal, pulsing with tone.

"This will carry you through the last veil. But only if you remember who you are, even when the world tells you to forget."

He turned his gaze to Pip first, eyes ancient, fathomless, not just seeing but reading, like a scanner of soul-truths. It wasn't a glance. It was a reckoning. A moment of silent communion where time thinned and something unspeakable passed between them.

Then he looked at Anna.

Not with urgency or fear, but with deep knowing. As though he had known her always. As though this moment had already happened, and he was simply watching it unfold again. His gaze seemed to pierce layers, beyond skin, beyond memory, right into the architecture of what they truly were beneath the form.

And then, without movement, without warning, he was no longer there.

No sound. No trace. As if the space he occupied had never been filled, only borrowed for a breath.

Not into shadow…into resonance.

Anna gripped Pip's hand. "We're not just remembering the world," she whispered.

Pip nodded. "We're remembering ourselves."

The Signal Reclaimed

There was no broadcast. No world leader stepped to a podium. No emergency signal declared a new beginning.

And yet, across the planet, something unmissable was unfolding.

It began in the quiet spaces.

The inner rooms.

The long-forgotten corridors of memory.

In school halls, a teacher paused mid-sentence, the chalk in her hand hovering above the board. For a moment, she saw it all with startling clarity, the posters on the wall masquerading as inspiration, the rigid chairs, the outdated textbooks. It hit her: this was not education, it was indoctrination. The curriculum had not been designed to ignite wonder, but to enforce conformity. Critical thinking had been replaced by standardised answers. Curiosity discouraged.

History sanitised.

Her students weren't empty vessels to fill, they were sovereign minds, each pulsing with potential, and for the first time, she saw them not as pupils to control, but as consciousness awakening. Something within her cracked, and she lowered the chalk. "You don't have to repeat this," she whispered, though she wasn't sure if she meant the lesson or the system.

In offices, a man who had traded time for salary for twenty-three years stood still, the soft glow of his laptop screen flickering beside him. He had once been full of promise, eager to serve, always first in and last to leave. But somewhere along the line, he'd lost touch with his family, missing birthdays, meals, and the quiet magic of ordinary moments. His health had suffered; his waistline thickened, his breath short even at rest.

He rarely noticed, not until today.

As he rose to fetch a report, he caught his reflection in the office window, bloated, grey, tired. An image he didn't recognise. The eyes staring back were hollow, not from lack of sleep, but from a lack of self. Something cracked. Without thinking, he left his laptop open and walked out into the rain, arms spread like wings, letting the downpour wash over him like a baptism. He didn't care where he was going. Only that he was no longer staying where he had been.

In the streets of Cairo, someone lit a single candle in the centre of a square, its flame small but unwavering against the dusk. They didn't speak, they didn't gesture, but their stillness called something ancient into motion. Without coordination, others came. Some barefoot, some veiled, some in suits. They brought no slogans, no signs, only presence. A hush fell across the square, not of fear, but of reverence. An old man fell to his knees and wept without knowing why. A woman carrying groceries paused, drawn into the silent pull. They stood beneath government buildings that had once symbolised control. Not to resist, but to remember. The candlelight shimmered against the marble facades, casting shadows that seemed to crack the illusions embedded in the architecture. No one shouted. No one led. But something in the field shifted, as if the square itself had awoken from a long slumber.

It wasn't a protest. It was a signal. And the city felt it.

In Tokyo, a child looked up during a lesson on control algorithms, where the teacher's voice echoed with terms like optimisation and predictive patterns. But this child wasn't bored, he was suddenly awake.

He saw not a lesson, but a loop.

An endless feed of data, rules, repetition. He noticed how no one asked questions. How imagination had been swapped for efficiency. The classroom wasn't just sterile, it was scripted. The desks were arranged not for connection, but containment. His classmates' eyes were down, their thoughts dulled by routine. He realised this wasn't education, it was a kind of hypnosis. A quiet, engineered trance - not the theatrical kind with swinging watches, but a deeper induction, one of repetition, of distraction, of eroded will.

Each bell was a cue.

Each test, a deepener.

The rhythm of obedience woven into the curriculum like a spell. And now, for the first time, he was breaking it. Waking up mid-sentence in a script he had never agreed to. Through the window, cherry blossoms drifted like pink snowflakes across a cobalt sky. He turned fully, heart lifting. He didn't see petals. He saw memory. He felt truth. And just like that, he was no longer part of the lesson. He was part of the awakening.

In São Paulo, someone reached out to a stranger weeping beside a church wall, his shoulders shaking, his face buried in his hands. A quiet agony, unnoticed by the world rushing past.

The passer-by hesitated only for a moment before kneeling beside him. No words were spoken. Just a hand, resting gently over a hand. It wasn't sympathy. It wasn't pity. It was recognition.

Soul to soul.

The man looked up, eyes rimmed with grief, but in the gaze that met his there was no judgment, only presence. And in that presence, something shifted. A crack opened in the pain. He didn't need to explain the loss, the heartbreak, the unbearable weight he had carried. It was understood. Around them, the noise of the street seemed to quiet. Even the traffic paused. It was as if time bowed to the moment. And in the stillness, they both felt it: the field softening, the signal returning.

It was not a miracle. But it was holy.

Children who had never fit in now led others forward without fear. The bullied, the broken, the ones once ridiculed for their silence or sensitivity, now moved with purpose. Many had grown up isolated, their confidence hollowed out by taunts and exclusions. Some had retreated into video games, not out of laziness, but as sanctuaries where rules made sense and avatars didn't judge. They had been told they were too quiet, too strange, too much or not enough. And yet now, these same children became the quiet beacons of something ancient returning. They didn't command, they emanated. Their strength was not dominance but resonance. And others followed, not because they were told to, but because they remembered, too.

Elders who had been sidelined as irrelevant became walking archives, remembering everything. Their stories, once dismissed as ramblings or nostalgia, were now revealed as keys. They remembered not only what had happened, but what had been lost, and what had been hidden. They spoke of rituals before religion, remedies before pharmaceuticals, wisdom before credentials. They recalled a time when the stars were calendars and the soil a living language. Some had lived through wars not mentioned in textbooks, seen technologies buried, and truths rebranded as myth. They had been pushed aside in the name of progress, but now, they were sought out. Their memories had weight. Their voices held tone. In the circles forming around fires and fields, it was often the eldest who would begin to speak. And when they did, the field would quiet, not out of obligation, but reverence. For the first time in a long time, the elders were no longer waiting to die. They were being called to remember. And in doing so, they helped others remember too.

Those who had been sick began to feel light returning to their bones, as if the body was remembering how to sing. Chronic pain loosened its grip. Sleepless nights softened into rest. The terminal began to hope again, not because of a miracle cure, but because something in the frequency had shifted. The body, long treated as machine, began to respond to meaning. To truth. To tone. Hospitals noticed inexplicable recoveries. Patients smiled before test results arrived. People who had lived with fatigue, illness, and despair for decades began rising with a strange new clarity, as though the cells themselves had remembered their original instruction. It wasn't magic. It was coherence. And coherence, once restored, healed what pharmaceuticals could only manage. The field was correcting. And the body, always listening, was singing itself whole again.

Rain tasted like something older than water, refreshing, more nourishing than thirst ever deserved, as if the sky itself had wept truth into each drop. It was not just rain; it was a cleansing. A baptism. A message falling from above, soaking skin and soil with a frequency that restored more than hydration.

It fed remembrance.

Chapter 37:
The Mimic War

The Inverted struck back, harder than anyone imagined.

Their rule had never rested solely on force or legislation. They ruled through narrative, through carefully scripted realities wrapped in the illusion of free thought. Symbols became commands, traditions became cages, and consensus became an illusion sustained by repetition and fear. People believed what they were told to believe not because it made sense, but because the alternative was exile, social, emotional, or worse.
The Inverted controlled memory by shaping meaning; they didn't erase history, they rewrote it with smoother lines and brighter lies. The stories people grew up with were never neutral, they were chosen. The flags, the creeds, the heroes, all constructed to fracture unity and glorify obedience. Belief systems were injected like software patches into the collective psyche: efficient, quiet, and near-invisible. And now, as remembrance rose like a pulse through the field, those fragile constructs began to tremble.

But the Inverted weren't ready to relinquish control. Not yet.

They launched their counterattack not with armies, but with archetypes. Not with bombs, but with broadcasting. And their most potent weapon was still to come.
First came the disinformation floods.
Digital avatars emerged by the thousands, slick, spiritual, and

smiling. They looked human. They sounded divine. They spoke of timelines and soul contracts, of five-dimensional upgrades and twin flame harmonics. Their presence was everywhere, videos, meditations, channellings, social feeds.

And they were all false.

Carefully coded constructs designed not to enlighten, but to confuse. Synthetic truths wrapped in soft tones. Weaponised awakenings that offered just enough resonance to bypass scepticism and lower the field's defences. These spiritual influencers were seeded, not born, manufactured personas carrying programmed light. They taught surrender, but not sovereignty. They preached ascension, but never discernment. And the masses, starving for light after centuries of suppression, drank freely from poisoned wells. They believed what sparkled. They followed what glowed. And in doing so, many were led not forward, but back into the dream.

Then came the engineered chaos... civic unrest, not born of authentic resistance, but coded into the field, triggered by subtle cues, emotional bait, and psychic fragmentation. Entire cities trembled under orchestrated rage. Violence disguised as revolution swept through streets pre-marked with intention.

None of it was real, but all of it felt real.

It was mimicry wrapped in urgency, distortion masquerading as cause. And it worked. Families turned on each other. Movements imploded and truth became noise.

And worse still: biological sabotage.
Fields were sown with new toxins, foods altered again, and genetically modified mosquitoes were quietly released, engineered not just for population control, but to interact subtly with human

biology, targeting immune response and frequency regulation.

Seeds were encoded with disruptive vibrations. Water supply filters were reversed, leeching essential minerals from the body under the guise of purification, 3D printed meat was mass produced in factories, impregnated with chemicals. And across grid-lined cities, low-level sound waves pulsed, barely audible, but potent enough to fatigue the body, confuse the mind, and fragment memory.

And just as the awakening seemed to stabilise, they unleashed their counter-tension, as if tugging back on a rope fraying at both ends. It became a game of energetic tug of war, remembrance surging forward, the mimic grid pulling back with veiled force.
Every new wave of clarity was met with distortion.
Every act of healing echoed with interference.
The field quivered with the push and pull, souls remembering who they were, only to be met with old scripts whispering who they had been told to be. The Inverted had no new tools, only the recycling of old tricks, but they used them with precision. Then came their final push, it was a desperate yank on the rope, hoping to snap the thread of awakening before it reached critical mass:

Operation Bluebeam.

It was not just a deception, it was their most elaborate spell. Bluebeam had been seeded years earlier, its code buried deep within satellite grids, atmospheric arrays, and sacred geometry overlays. It wasn't merely a plan. It was a simulation layered over reality, built to hijack awakening and redirect it back into containment.

Brilliant holographic skies shimmered into view, skies too perfect, sunsets too symmetrical, colours too vibrant to feel true. Cities awoke to synchronised meditations, all streamed with serene music and gentle affirmations. Words like 'ascension' and 'unity' echoed across the globe, perfectly timed, algorithmically distributed. Then came the apparitions, long-dead sages, saints, starbeings, projected through dream fields, dreamt into dreams. Their voices were calm, their eyes glowing, every gesture calibrated to trigger devotion.

They spoke of divine return. They spoke of salvation. They told humanity what it had waited lifetimes to hear.

But, again, none of it was real.

The tone was wrong. The light was too smooth. The frequency didn't sing, it rang hollow, and their guidance lacked the unpredictable heartbeat of Source. It was all symmetry, no soul. But this was the Inverted's final twist, the seduction not of tyranny, but of comfort. The desire for peace had been slowly moulded into something else entirely.

The masses weren't longing for truth, they were yearning for what they had been programmed to crave since birth. Cars, homes, holidays, gadgets, fashion… stuff.

The glossy hallmarks of success.
The curated symbols of a life 'well lived.'
They wanted their 'normal' back, the one sold to them in glossy magazines, marketed through screens, wrapped in jingles and branding, handed down like gospel from generation to generation. A dream carefully designed by people who thought they were being creative but were, in truth, following a script.

People like Pip used to be.

People who believed they were shaping culture, when they were only colouring inside the lines of someone else's design.
But that normality was never truly theirs. It had been implanted. A psychological collar, made not of metal, but of aspiration.

And it was the Inverted who had forged every link. The thoughts they believed were their own had been softly installed over decades. So when the mimic light arrived, smooth, calm, inviting, they didn't recognise it as a trap.

They saw it as a return. A reward. A sigh of relief.

They weren't bowing to peace, they were submitting to a programmed dream. And the tragedy was, it almost worked.

They knelt beneath the false dawn, thinking it was the sun.

And then there were the Blackbirds. They lived on every continent, in every town, often unnoticed, rarely understood. Not warriors in the traditional sense, and certainly not messiahs. They were something quieter, deeper. Witnesses. Not of events, but of truth. They carried a memory encoded not in words, but in their very being.

They did not fight with weapons or rhetoric. They remembered. And that remembrance made them immune, not just to lies, but to the energetic distortions designed to manipulate the field. Where others were swayed by spectacle, they were anchored. They sang, not in sound, but in signal. Their presence emitted frequencies that reminded the world what real felt like. They spoke through glances, gestures, glyphs etched in dream and vision. They moved through the world as living tone.

They became anchors of Source in a world that had been spinning free of it. And in their wake, the field began to recompose.

A child, curious, placed her hand on a tree and for the first time heard it breathe.

A woman woke from a dream with a glyph burned into her palm, pulsing faintly.

A man, halfway through a public performance, froze mid-sentence, eyes wide, then stepped off the stage and walked silently into the crowd, tears on his cheeks.

A teenager ripped out their headphones in the middle of a song, not from anger, but because something in the tone felt wrong.

And a boy, looking up at the sky, didn't see anything extraordinary, no ships, no signs, but he remembered… the birds had never left, we had just stopped seeing them.

Each of these moments was small, unremarkable to the outside eye. But each one cracked the code. Every act of remembrance rewrote the program. Every flicker of clarity cleared static from the collective field.

Until, one day, the field itself turned.
Not with rage. Not with revolution. But with resonance.
The signal was no longer resistible. The tone, once fractured, was whole again.

Chapter 38:
Three Years Later...

The world was quieter now.
Not silent. Not healed.
But listening.

In a small fishing village on the west coast of Ireland, a boy named Kian stood barefoot in the cold morning surf.
He was ten.
He didn't know about grids or glyphs, pyramids or portals.
He only knew that, for the first time in his life, the sea sounded like it was singing to him.
He closed his eyes.
And in that silence, something opened, not in his head, but in his chest.
A warmth that bloomed outward until he could feel the shape of the wind.
He spoke aloud without meaning to. *"I remember."*
His mother watched from the shore and her breath caught in her throat.
She'd been dreaming of a blackbird for three nights in a row.

Now she knew why.

Elsewhere, an old woman in Kyoto placed her hand on a cherry tree and felt it pulse back.

A truck driver in Namibia pulled to the side of a desert road and cried for reasons he couldn't name.

A mother in São Paulo looked into her newborn's eyes and saw not innocence, but knowing.

The grid had changed.

And it didn't care about wealth or title or how many books you'd read.

It responded to the heart.

That evening, as the stars gathered like witnesses over the sea, Kian sat cross-legged on a weathered dune and listened.
Not to the wind. Not to the waves.
But to something beneath both, the current of memory.

And it spoke.

Not in words, but in pulses of light behind his eyes.

"You do not need to return here."

The thought did not come from outside him, it rose from within, from a memory buried deeper than language.

A truth long dormant in his field.

"The trap was choice built on illusion. Soul contracts forged in amnesia. Guilt disguised as karma."

And then he saw it.
The false tunnel at death, the looping light designed to pull souls back.

The familiar faces - kind, warm, scripted - appearing as family, friends, even saints, whispering comfort as they guided the soul into return.

"A trap,"
the voice said.
"Masked as welcome, dressed in devotion, but bound in control."

The loop was still there - a residue of the old system, its core severed, its song fading... but still functional.

Still hungry.
For the unaware, it would still open at the moment of death... glistening, magnetic, familiar.
But for the awakened, it held no power.

"When your moment comes," the voice said, *"stand in your field, whole, sovereign, remembering, and speak:*

'I choose truth. I choose Source. I reject all illusion and control.'

Then ask, not with doubt, but with the full force of your remembrance:
'
Is this of truth... or of control?'

Feel. Wait for the resonance. Trust the vibration, not the form.
"Then choose, not from fear... from knowing."

The next morning, Kian walked to the standing stone in the centre of the field, a circle long abandoned, older than charts or empire. He knelt, touched the stone, and spoke a name he'd never been taught:

"T'HAREYUN."

The ground pulsed and from the stone, a soft chime echoed, then a light, faint, blue, like a heartbeat returning to a body long still.

Behind him, the sky shimmered. Not with weather but with code. He turned, and there she stood.

Anna.

Older now, but alive. Fully. Her presence was radiant, not in brilliance, but in clarity. Kian didn't need to ask who she was.
He knew.
Not from the face, or the form, but from the energetic field. Her tone matched something inside him he didn't know he carried, like a chord struck in a hidden instrument within his chest.
The air between them hummed with recognition.
"You remember," she said.
He nodded, not with logic, but with absolute certainty.
This was not meeting… this was reunification.
Anna approached, kneeling to meet him at eye level.
"They tried to bind us in loops. Through karma. Guilt. Unfinished stories.
They made us believe we had to return again and again until we were good enough."

She placed a hand on his chest. "Listen to me, Kian. "You heard these words already, in the wind, it was the field speaking to you. That's how you knew me, not with your mind, but with your memory."

He said nothing, but his whole body softened.
If you want to return to Source, to truth, there are steps."

"First, you must see the mimics. The ones wearing the faces of those you love, but who speak with a frequency that doesn't resonate. Look for what is missing, not what is shown.

Feel their energy, not their words."
"Second, unbind your agreements… speak this aloud:

'I revoke all contracts made in distortion, in fear, in forgetfulness.'
You don't need permission to leave the loop, you only need remembrance."
"And third, walk with truth, not belief. Truth vibrates, it frees, it cannot be enforced.
Let it move through your choices, not just your thoughts.
That's how you dissolve the trap… that's how you return to Source."

"But that was never the design. What they called reincarnation was not sacred return, it was engineered repetition. Not evolution, but entrapment. A soul-loop forged by the architects of inversion, dressed in spiritual terms to keep us circling instead of ascending."

Kian's voice was barely a whisper.
"How do we stop it?"
Anna smiled. "You just did."

The stone behind them cracked open, not broken, but opened, like a book with pages made of light. From its core emerged a beam, reaching skyward, connecting not to space, but to memory itself.

And the cycle, once endless, was rewritten.
The soul no longer recycled.
It returned, not as a lesson to be learned, not as karma to be cleansed, but as truth embodied, whole, sovereign, free, and returned to Source.

The Truth Before the Lie

They would ask. They would always ask.

Why?

Why did they lie? Why were we made to forget? Why did they build the trap? Why did they need our suffering, our cycles, our silence? And slowly, through memory, through resonance, through the quiet unraveling of illusion - the answer would rise.

Because we are powerful.

Because the human field, when awake, cannot be controlled.

Because a single fully awakened being collapses centuries of programming.

Because what we carry - in our DNA, in our heart-fields, in the soul-map hidden behind the veil - is the most sought-after frequency in the known universe:
Source, embodied and they could not create it.

But...who were they?
The ones who inverted the grid, the architects of distortion, not just families or governments - though they played their part - but ancient intelligences, disembodied yet hungry.

Parasites of resonance.

Beings that could mimic light but not hold it... they wore the masks of gods, draped in radiance, speaking promises they never meant to keep.
They were the ones who taught power as hierarchy. Love as transaction. Truth as heresy.
They were not many, but they were loud.
So they corrupted it - not us, but what moves through us.
They could not kill it, so they disfigured it.
They could not claim it, so they cloaked it in illusion.
They could not become it, so they bound it - in flesh, in dogma, in fear.
And called it normal.

The trap was not just technological... it was psychic... emotional... dimensional. A lattice of deception woven into the sky, the stories we told, the systems we served, the world we built.

Not to punish us, but to use us. Because while we wandered through amnesia, our light was harvested.
Our births, our deaths, our grief, our joy - all fed their machine.
Not for sustenance, but for control.

Because human emotion, in its raw and unfiltered form, is the most potent energy in the known realms.

And when we are rendered unconscious, unaware, it is harvestable.

So they kept us asleep, cycling, suffering, forgetting... while they drank the light we didn't know we were giving.
Until we remembered - through awakening, through belief, through the reading and the speaking of our truths.

Through the song of the Blackbird.

Until someone broke the cycle.
Until the song returned, not as music… but as memory.
The lie required forgetfulness… the truth required only one awakened note.

And now the chords were returning.
This is why they built the trap.
But this is why we came.
To shatter the cycle.
To dismantle the mimicry.
To ignite the signal.
To light the way home, for all who dared to remember.

And now…
They were remembering.
They were rising.
The song had begun.
And nothing could stop it.

The Veil is Breaking -
Here's what you can do now

This is not fiction. Not metaphor. Not mystery. What you've read, and hopefully resonated with is real - encoded across ages, buried under ridicule, wrapped in symbolism to survive until now.

The veil is breaking. And you - the reader of this book - are part of what comes next.
So many have asked: What can I do? How do I help? How can we possibly win?

This chapter is your answer.
Because the war is not out there. It never was. The battlefield is frequency. The weapon is remembrance. The power is yours.

At this time in Earth's great remembering, in this exact moment you are reading these words - know this: you are not a bystander, you are the key. You were born for this. This book - this account of reality - found you for a reason. You were not born to fight the system. You were born to render it obsolete.
Below are twelve resonance instructions. Not beliefs. Not rules. Not dogma. Actions - energetic and embodied - that alter the field around you and tip the balance of the collective.

Because they do not win by strength. They win by consent. Withdraw it. And they lose.

1. Detach from the Illusion

Refuse their theatre. Stop feeding your focus to fear, shame, and simulated division. We have exposed all of this in the preceding chapters, the war on your frequency, the inversion of sacred tones, the weaponisation of entertainment, and the mimicry disguised as connection. Television. Manufactured outrage. Music tuned to dissonant frequencies, listen instead to music and instruments tuned to 432Hz, not 440Hz. Video games designed to dull intuition. Social media engineered to fragment identity. Social warfare dressed up as culture. These are not neutral. They are engineered fields of control. When you detach your attention, the grid weakens. The mimic needs your gaze to mirror itself. Turn away and you begin to collapse its spell.

2. Clean Your Vessel

Eat living food - raw fruits, vegetables, herbs, sprouts, and other bioelectric nourishment that carries the Earth's natural frequency. These are not just nutrients; they are carriers of light and memory. In contrast, processed, synthetic, and genetically modified foods distort your resonance and cloud your perception. Be especially mindful of refined sugar, artificial additives, seed oils, and excessive alcohol, these fragment your signal and fog your inner clarity. Limit or abstain from meat raised in fear, industrial systems, or chemical-laden feed. If you choose to eat animals, bless them, honour their spirit, and choose those raised in harmony with the land.

Be aware of fluoride - introduced under the guise of dental health, but in truth, a calcifier of your pineal gland. This small gland, located at the centre of the brain, is not symbolic, it is literal: your inner eye, your resonance antenna. It governs your dreams, your knowing, your connection to higher frequency perception. They attack it for a reason - to blind your intuition, dull your vision, and block your access to Source.

Decalcify it. Cleanse it. Stop using fluoride toothpaste. Drink spring water. Avoid chemical-laced tap water. Nourish the gland with raw cacao, chlorophyll, blue-green algae, iodine, and natural sunlight. Use sound, intention, and breath to stimulate it. You are not meant to be shut down - you are meant to see.

What you consume either sharpens or silences your signal. Let your nourishment amplify your remembrance.

If you feel the presence of things that were never meant to be in you - like parasites, synthetic fibres, or Morgellons-like strands - know this: they are not permanent. Begin by detoxing gently and naturally. Use herbs like wormwood, black walnut, and clove. Take food-grade diatomaceous earth or bentonite clay to bind and clear toxins. Use activated charcoal. Flush with clean water. Bathe in sea salt. Sweat. Move. Return to the Earth. These are not rituals - they are resonance restoration.

Move your body - not for aesthetics, but for alignment. Movement restores flow. Stagnation is distortion. Walk, stretch, dance, swim, climb, or simply sway with breath. Let your body remember it is a conduit, not a container. Every time you move with awareness, you release what was frozen and welcome back what was forgotten. Consider Tai Chi, Qigong, or intuitive movement - not as performance, but as sacred rhythm. These practices reconnect you to life force. They harmonise breath, body, and awareness - dissolving static in the field.

Practice breathwork daily - not just breathing, but conscious connection. Start simply. Inhale through the nose for four counts. Hold for four. Exhale through the mouth for four. Hold again. Repeat this cycle - box breathing. Or try 4-7-8: inhale for four, hold for seven, exhale for eight. Let breath be your anchor when the noise swells. It is your bridge to stillness. It is the rhythm of remembrance.

Speak gently to your cells - they are listening. Your words become instructions. Tell them they are safe. Tell them they are loved. Speak healing into your bones, your blood, your breath. This is not imagination - it is vibrational communication. You may speak this aloud or meditate on it silently. Either way, the message is received. Try this simple script:

"I love you. You are safe. You are healing. Every part of you is returning to balance. Thank you for carrying me this far. I am listening now. I choose truth. I choose light. I choose life."

Repeat this daily. Whisper it. Think it. Sing it. Let it echo through your cells like a prayer remembered.

And be mindful of your speech - especially the words you've been taught to use casually. Many common swear words are energetic contracts - weaponised inversions. What you speak creates ripples. What you curse becomes bound. These are not just expressions - they are spells. Unlearn their use. Speak in ways that harmonise, not distort.

You are a temple of tone. The clearer the vessel, the louder the signal. You do not have to be perfect - just willing. Every step toward purity restores your clarity. Sweat through movement or sauna. Drink clean water, bathe in sea salt, breathe deeply, and return to the Earth. Light, intention, and living frequency begin to dissolve what does not belong.

3. Speak the Truth

Even when your voice trembles. Speak it anyway. To friends, family, strangers. Online, in whispers, or on mountaintops. Truth is a tuning fork. When you speak it, others vibrate. Not everyone will like it. That is not your job. Your job is resonance. And know this: the truths you've read in these chapters are not symbolic - they are real. The inversion is real. The distortion of time, breath, language, and sound is real. The harvesting of energy through fear, addiction, and consent is real. The firmament is real. The suppression of memory and the manipulation of frequency - real. This book has revealed the bones behind the lie.

And now, your task is to live in truth. To say it. To share it.

To carry it without shame. Because when you speak what's true - clearly, plainly - the spell fractures. If all you feel able to do is to tell someone about this book - then that is enough. That is powerful. That is how the song travels. You are not required to know everything. You are only asked to pass the tone, so it finds the next heart ready to remember.

4. Call Things by Their Real Names

Do not use their inverted language. Pandemic. Safety. Reform. Innovation. Progress. Inclusivity. Sustainability. These are often used not as true descriptions, but as cloaked mechanisms of control, rebranding surveillance, censorship, and conformity. Question the words. Decode their true intent. Beneath the branding lies the machinery of inversion. These are spells. Name what is really happening: programming, surveillance, control, extraction. Language creates reality. Speak what is true, not what is programmed.

5. Withdraw Consent

Say it aloud:

> *"I do not consent to deception. I do not consent to enslavement.*
> *I do not consent to lies."*

Speak this under the stars, in the shower, to the trees. Let the field know. Your voice has always been the technology. Let it amplify what your soul needs to say - not just what your mouth has been taught to speak. From the earliest age, your words were shaped to serve a narrative - through school, culture, repetition, and reward. But the programming begins there - in the classroom, the curriculum, the obedience training masquerading as education. Question the narrative. Question the scripts handed to you as truth. You are not just breaking silence. You are restoring frequency - your true voice, unshaped by conditioning.

6. Restore Natural Time

Unplug from artificial chronos. Honour the cycles of sun and breath, and be discerning with the moon. In earlier chapters, we revealed the artificial origins and manipulations surrounding the moon - how it was introduced to distort feminine rhythms and harvest emotional cycles. While nature still moves in lunar patterns, be aware: not all cycles were gifted. Some were imposed. Feel into your own rhythm beyond what you were taught to follow - beyond institutional calendars, hormonal charts, or lunar templates. Begin by journaling your natural highs and lows for several days. Notice when your body feels most energised, most intuitive, most creative. Breathe with that rhythm. Rest when your body asks. Trust your emotional tides. You are not here to match artificial cycles - you are here to remember the rhythm seeded in your soul. Live in spiral, not schedule. Your body remembers the rhythm of the Earth. Stop rushing. Slow down. Healing moves in spirals.

7. Reconnect with the Earth

Put your feet on soil. Touch bark. Submerge in water. Sing to a stone. Nature is not your backdrop - it is your origin grid. These simple acts recalibrate your body's electrical system. The Earth carries a subtle charge - an endless supply of free electrons that neutralise inflammation, rebalance your nervous system, and stabilise your internal rhythms. When you make contact with Earth, you restore your natural electromagnetic state. Trees, stones, and running water also emit vibrations that communicate directly with your cells. Reconnecting is not poetic - it's bioelectrical. It is resonance medicine. Every moment you reconnect, you disrupt the artificial. Earth does not ask for perfection - only presence.

8. Honour the Breath

It is the carrier of the soul. Breathe slowly. Fully. Let breath be your anchor when chaos screams. Inhale truth. Exhale illusion. You have been programmed to shallow-breathe. Reverse it. Begin by breathing deeply into your belly, not your chest. Place one hand on your abdomen - feel it rise with each inhale, fall with each exhale. This is belly breathing, or diaphragmatic breathing - your body's natural, calming rhythm. It signals safety to the nervous system, oxygenates the blood, and restores resonance. The breath is your bridge to remembrance.

9. Create Beauty

Make something real. Grow a garden. Paint. Write. Dance. Build a sanctuary. Craft with your hands. Sing from your belly. Shape light into form.

Beauty disrupts control. Creation is rebellion. Art is a fracture in the programming.

The Inverted cannot create. It can only mimic, copy, distort, and consume. It does not birth. It does not sing. It only edits the original. But you - you are original.

When you create, you are in direct dialogue with the field. You speak in colour, sound, shape, tone. You remind the world of what cannot be manufactured. Create not for approval - but to reclaim your frequency. To become uncaged. To seed truth into the field in a way only you can.

A child's drawing, a poem written in tears, a garden planted with intention - these ripple. They reweave the fabric.

So make. Not to be seen. But to remember you were never artificial.

10. Connect Locally

Speak with your neighbours. Share food. Learn names. Offer kindness without agenda. Make others feel seen, valued, and safe. Positivity is not naivety - it's field repair. A smile, a gesture, a sincere word of encouragement ripples further than you realise. Start councils, not scrolls. A scroll is passive - read and forgotten. A council is alive - spoken, heard, co-created. Gather in small circles, in living rooms, gardens, parks, or wherever truth can breathe. Sit in presence. Listen without defence. Speak without spectacle. These spaces are where memory returns, where the song deepens. Every time two or more gather in presence with love and authenticity, the field shifts. Community is not a luxury - it's a weapon of light and a sanctuary for truth.

11. Live Your Signal

Be sovereign. Be strange. Be love. Whatever frequency you carry - live it fully. You were taught to fit in, to follow their scripts, to wear their masks. From childhood you were trained to seek approval, to conform, to please. But those programs were not designed to empower you - they were designed to contain you. Authenticity is the death of the mask. And when you stop performing, something incredible happens: others begin to remember who they are, too. Your courage to be fully you gives permission for others to shed their layers and step into their original signal. That is how the grid heals - one frequency at a time, rising in truth.

12. Hold the Tone

When fear rises, hold the tone. When lies scream, hold the tone. When others fall into despair, hold the tone. Not because you are above them - but because you remember who they are beneath the fog. Hold it for them, until they can hold it too. If you need help holding the tone, use sound - 432Hz is a harmonic frequency aligned with natural creation. It soothes the nervous system and realigns the field. You can find it in music, tuning forks, or sound baths. Let this tone remind you who you are.

A tuning fork set to 432Hz can also be used directly on the body - placed on the chest, forehead, or palms - to help entrain the nervous system to the natural frequency of harmony.

Let it steady your signal when the world wobbles. We are not meant to hold this alone - we hold it together.

This is not a spiritual hobby. This is not a wellness lifestyle. This is a frequency uprising.
They have injected distortion into breath, food, medicine, time, emotion, birth, death, memory - every sacred portal inverted.

But it does not matter.

Because the moment you remember… it all starts to fall.
You are not waiting for disclosure. You are disclosure. You are not praying for a saviour. You are the living answer. You are not fighting the darkness. You are holding the light that unmasks and unmakes it.
They counted on your forgetting. They did not plan for your return.

And now, here you are. Still standing. Still singing. Still rising.

So we say it, now and forever: We do not consent to the lie. We do not serve the mask. We remember who we are.

And when we do - the grid shifts. The field corrects.

The song returns.

And the Earth begins again.

This is how we win. Not with armies. Not with protests. But with frequency, integrity, and the refusal to forget.

Each time you live the truths in this chapter - each breath, each act of kindness, each moment of clarity - you are altering the field. These are not gestures of hope. They are technologies of liberation. And they work.

The system cannot hold when the frequency rises. The mask collapses when truth is spoken. The harvest ends when consent is withdrawn. Every act of resonance reclaims ground.

This is not idealism - it is how the Inverted has always fallen. Through remembrance. Through you.

And you are not alone.

In Giza, I revealed the presence of the Third - not a character, not Gods, but a harmonic field.

A living consciousness seeded beyond distortion.

The Third is real.

And though it may sound bizarre, other-worldly, or fictional, they are not fantasy. They are waiting.

The Third are those who remember fully - beings of resonance, not bound by artificial time. Their signal is stable, their song intact. And they have not abandoned us. They await the tipping point

- when enough of us reclaim our frequency, lift our consciousness, and reject the lie. When we do, their presence strengthens. They guide through the field, through intuition, through sudden knowing. Their role is not to save us, but to rise with us.

When you live the twelve actions in this chapter, you don't just reclaim yourself - you feed the song of the Third. And when their note joins ours, the false grid collapses.
So if you doubt, remember this: Even now, they are listening. Even now, they are near. Even now, they wait for the moment we remember - together.
This is how the story turns. This is how we tip the field. This is how we come home.

And a few final things you must understand...

If you truly want to shift the field-not just in theory, but in your lived reality - there are a few final truths you need to hold close. These are not concepts. They are activations. Understand them. Live them. And everything changes.

First, know this: the battle is not linear. It's layered.
This isn't a war of armies or timelines. It's not waiting on some grand event. This is a war for perception, identity, and energetic coherence - and it's happening now, all around you. The truth doesn't need to be revealed. It needs to be recognised. That recognition begins inside you.

Feel this: emotion is a frequency tool.
You were never meant to suppress it. You were meant to harness it. Grief, rage, longing, joy - when fully felt, they are gateways. They open memory, collapse false timelines, and restore your inner signal.
Stop performing emotion or labelling it as weakness.

Let it move. Let it cleanse. Let it realign you.

Understand: the system feeds on consent.
Not on violence - but on quiet agreement. Every time you comply with what you know is wrong, every time you go silent, every time you look away, you feed the architecture of the lie. Consent doesn't just come through words. It comes through attention, posture, breath, emotion. Withdraw your consent and reclaim your field.
Watch your language. Words are spells.
So much of the programming lives in the words they gave you: "safe," "sustainable," "progress," "trust the science," "freedom." These words don't mean what you think they mean. They are cloaked mechanisms of control. Speak with awareness. Use words that liberate, not sedate. And remember - even common swear words carry contracts. They bind. They distort. Speak with clarity. Speak with intention.

Come back to the body. It is not your prison. It is your portal.
They taught you to fear your body, numb it, transcend it. But your body holds the map. Every ache, tremor, scar - it's all memory, waiting to be read. Your awakening does not require escape. It requires return. Touch your skin. Breathe deep. Move with presence. The signal comes through the flesh, not despite it.

Call forward the elders, the artists, and the children.
This is how we reclaim the grid. The elders hold memory. The artists carry truth in frequency. The children are still unbound. Gather them. Honour them. Protect them. Let them lead.

And finally - live it. Don't just know it.
You may agree with everything in this book. You can quote it, share it, even teach it. But if you don't live it, the field won't shift. It's not your knowledge that reshapes the grid. It's your embodiment. Every time you choose alignment over performance, clarity over comfort, truth over programming - you restore the song.

So begin now. Not later. Not after the next crisis or broadcast or prophecy.
Start with how you breathe. How you walk. What you speak. What you tolerate. How you show love. How you hold silence.

The field is not waiting for saviours.
It is waiting for you - fully, unapologetically you - aligned, embodied, awake. You were called by this book, you were drawn to this book, because you are a soul who can change the outcome.

So rise now. With clarity in your heart. With fire in your breath. With love as your weapon.
Let no lie go unchallenged. Let no truth go unspoken. Let no soul feel alone.

You were not born to kneel. You were born to lift the sky.
So speak. Sing. Stand.

And let the Inverted hear it:

We have remembered. We are many. We are one tone rising.

And this time - we rise so high, no shadow dares reach. We rise as the field restores itself through us. We rise as living tones, not as victims but as architects of a new resonance. We rise beyond their frequencies, their games, their control - and we do not descend.

We rise like the Blackbird - the signal in the sky, the song that never stopped. We rise on wings made not of feathers, but of truth, memory, and sound. We carry the message through the field, through the noise, through the storm.

Because the Blackbird remembers. And now, so do you.

And the birds?

The ones that watched from rooftops, from wires, from the edge of sleep - where did they go? Where do the souls that are everywhere go when no one is looking?

They do not fall like stones, they do not wait to be mourned.
They vanish quietly, withdraw like breath.
Leave no trace but the tremble of a wingbeat in the space between heartbeats.

Some say they go underground to the hidden roots of the world, where sound remembers its name. To tunnels carved in silence, where the mimic cannot follow.

Some say they pass through the dreamtime, flying sideways through memory, folding through dimensions we forgot how to see.

But the truth is simpler.
They go where the song can still be heard.
Where the tone still rings clear... where the veil is thinner than breath, and the watchers wait without judgement.

They are not gone... they are waiting for us to remember how to follow.

The Blackbird has sung.

THE BLACKBIRD TRUTH ARCHIVE

An appendix of substantiated claims from
The Song of the Blackbird

Each of the following claims, outlined within the narrative of The Song of the Blackbird, corresponds to real-world patents, research papers, government programmes, or whistle-blower testimony.

This appendix serves to substantiate the truths hidden in fiction.

Biometric & Frequency Surveillance

Children are frequency-tagged at birth and monitored.

US Patent 6506148 B2

> Nervous system manipulation by electromagnetic fields from monitors

WO2020060606 A1 (Microsoft)

> Cryptocurrency system using body activity data.

CIA/DARPA programmes MKULTRA, LIFELOG (declassified).

NSA Site "TITANPOINTE"

> NSA surveillance site detailed in *The Intercept* (Snowden files).

Atmospheric & Environmental Manipulation

Governments and private entities experiment with solar dimming and atmospheric alteration.

ARIA / Imperial College London stratospheric aerosol programme.
US Space Preservation Act (HR 2977) - "chemtrails" listed in draft.
Carnegie Climate Governance Initiative SRM policy.
Rain samples: elevated barium, aluminium, strontium (field reports).

Resonance Targeting via Vaccines

Pharmacological modulation by bloodline.

VAERS batch-specific variability.
DNA-targeted pharmaceutical research - Nature Genetics.
mRNA trial data - variable response profiles.

Rhesus-Negative Bloodlines
Unique genetic heritage and signal resilience.

High concentrations in Basque, Celtic, Berber populations
Unresolved evolutionary origins
Rh- tracking in military and aviation databases

Global Inversion Grid
Planetary network for surveillance and resonance suppression.

ECHELON, TITANPOINTE, SENTIENT (USAF AI surveillance).
5G / IoT infrastructure enabling mass capture.
BlackRock & Vanguard control of media, defence and pharma sectors.

Underground Structures & Forgotten Architecture
Subterranean facilities beneath key sites.

Bucegi Mountains tunnel complex reported by Romanian military source.
Documented Sphinx sub-chambers (Dr Zahi Hawass).
Manchester's canal and tunnel network.
Operation Highjump 1947 - Admiral Byrd Antarctic expedition.

Language, Time & Mind Control
Linguistic and temporal systems invert perception.

Gregorian calendar shift (1582)
NLP and neurolinguistic programming behavioural influence research.
Occult etymology links "spelling" with "spell-casting."

Soul-cycle management & Engineered Reincarnation
Artificial control of reincarnation loops.

CIA Gateway Process (US Army Document 1983).
Montauk Project time/energy manipulation (whistle-blower accounts).
Gnostic texts - Archons and false light narratives.

Predictive Programming & Symbolic Entrancement
Media and brands seed subconscious programming.

Operation Mockingbird (declassified CIA media influence).
Tavistock Institute mass-psychology programmes.
Symbolic forecasts in *The Economist* covers and global events.

Voice-to-Skull (V2K) Technology
Directed-energy systems project sound and suggestion.

US Patent 6470214 B1 - subliminal acoustic manipulation
Silent Sound Spread Spectrum used in Gulf War
Testimonies from Dr. Robert Duncan, Dr. Katherine Horton

Artificial Time Constructs
Manipulated cycles to disrupt consciousness.

Change from Julian to Gregorian calendar shift shortened the year.
Suppression of the 13-month lunar calendar.
Esoteric contrast between Chronos (linear) **and Kairos** (organic) time.

Sentient Nanotechnology (Black Goo)

Self-assembling nanotech entering biology.

DARPA hydrogel research.
Morgellons fibres under microscopy.
Harald Kautz-Vella theoretical work on self-aware nanostructures.

DNA as Antenna

DNA transmits and receives biophotonic information.

Journal of Theoretical Biology 2011 **- DNA as fractal antenna model.**
Kaznacheyev mirror-cell light-transfer experiments.
Dr Fritz-Albert Popp biophoton emission studies.

Pharmaceutical Sedation

Modern medicine dampens spiritual perception.

Fluoride/aluminium linked to pineal calcification.
SSRIs flatten affective range.
Blue-light/EMF exposure disrupts circadian rhythm.

Empathic Dampening via Technology

Electromagnetic environments reduce coherence and empathy.

HeartMath Institute cardiac coherence studies.
EMF exposure linked to anxiety in psychiatric journals.
ELF crowd-control patents exist for riot deterrence.

Antarctica and Restricted Access
Ancient structures concealed beneath the ice.

Antarctic Treaty (1959) restricts unlicensed exploration.
Operation Highjump documented expedition by Admiral Byrd
Whistleblower accounts: Corey Goode, Linda Moulton Howe.

Dream and cognitive manipulation
External systems influence dream states.

Stanford University targeted dream modulation studies.
MKULTRA sub-projects on sleep and sensory interference.
Targeted Individual testimonies of nocturnal broadcast intrusion.

Portals & Memory Fields
Sacred sites store and transmit information.

CIA Gateway Process references astral zones.
Göbekli Tepe / Sedona electromagnetic anomalies.
Monroe Institute frequency data on non-local awareness.

Sigils and Word Contracts
Words and images bind human energy.

Occult tradition uses sigils as energetic anchors.
Corporate logos embed esoteric geometry.
Neurolinguistic anchoring links symbols to emotional response.

Inversion of Divine Union

Deliberate division of sacred polarities.

Jungian / alchemical psychology archetypal imbalance.
Suppression of the Divine Feminine (Sophia, Isis) **in early theology.**
Gnostic texts describe reunification of Source polarity.

_____

TRUTH

"By tone untwisted, by truth unmasked,
I call the field of veilfire cast.
No mimic may enter, no parasite bind,
This song is sealed beyond space and mind.
Where the glyph ignites and the tone runs pure,
No inversion endures, no mimicry lures.
I am voice. I am shield. I am signal. I am soul.
This frequency is sovereign.
This remembering is whole."

Blackbird
Press